# Eclipse of the Mortal Realm

Crone of White Flame Trilogy Book 1

C. J. Saint

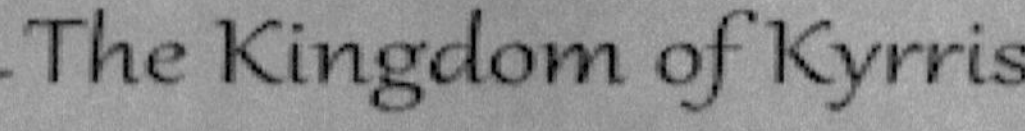

SYLVARN
VEIL'S ECLIPSE
MEADOWREST
NIMLOTHIEL
The Kingdom of Kyrris

STORMBROOK
POTAMEIDE TERRITORY
CATARIEL

*Pronunciation sheet*

Tharion - **Ta-rion**
Eleanora - **Ela-nora**
Rowan - **Ro-wen**
Ilyra - **Ee-lira**
Vorathiel - **Vuh-ra-thiel**
Corvyn - **Kor-vin**
Vaelrick - **Vay-el-rik**
Alaric - **Ah-lah-rik**
Ravoch - **Ra-vok**
Nochtra - **Nok-tra**
Doloryn - **Do-lo-ren**
Nimlothiel - **Nim-loth-iel** (lake of white blossoms)


Mea carissima - **Latin for "my dearest"**
Vulpin - **Latin for "fox"**
Korax - **Latin for "raven"**

# Trigger warnings

This book contains adult topics that might be triggering to some. Your mental health matters. If any of the topics listed are sensitive or triggering to you, please don't read the book.

Death of a loved one

Suicide

Alcohol consumption

Heartbreak

Panic attacks, anxiety

Attempted sexual assault

Kidnapping

Torture

Mature sexual content

Infant death (memory)

*To all of you that were told you were never enough;*

*this one is for you.*

*Do not let the darkness overthrow you, for your light*

*shines so bright within.*

# Prologue

*Tharion, 8 years old*

*"Son, it's about time I told you the story of our realm. There are many fantastic beings that, sadly, we do not see anymore – but their stories should be heard, they deserve to be remembered."*

*My father hoists me up on his lap, a giant book opened on the table before us. It's clear that the book is old, its pages a dull beige, the edges gently coming apart. As my eyes rake over the old book, I notice that it has a lot of words, some I don't recognize, and lots of amazing pictures and sketches. Papa's warm green eyes fall to mine, forcing a smile to my lips as my gaze wanders across the parchment in awe.*

*In the right corner, I see a picture of a horse, but the horse has wings, stretching far beyond its body in many different colours. Papa calls it a Pegasus. The thought of riding one has my stomach all fluttery, my mind eager to learn more about the beings of our past. I point to the horse, looking up at him.*

*"Will I ever have one of my own?"*
*Chuckling, he shakes his head.*

*"I'm afraid they are no more, my dear son. The Pegasus existed before the beginning of time but were lost to greed and war. It's a shame."*

*We flick through the book, my father whispering tales of old as we point at pictures and laugh, making up our own stories about the creatures. I learn about Gryphons, Dragons and Wyvern, about people that lived in the oceans with colourful tails and a voice so enchanting it would make people follow them into the deepest depths of dark waters. I listen with awe, my mind painting images of them all.*

*"Is there anyone left, Papa?"*

*My father's gaze hardens, but only for a second, before a warm smile pulls back across his face.*

*"Let me tell you a story of a man so special, he could foresee the future."*
*My eyes widen, chin falling to my chest.*

*"The future? No way!"*

*Closing the book, he carries me from the table. My mother walks towards us, planting a kiss on my forehead before walking back to the kitchen, preparing our supper. A giggle slips past my lips, butterflies jolting awake in my belly.*

*We slump down in my father's reading chair, legs splayed over the arm as he rocks us gently. I lay my head against his chest, listening to the steady beat of his heart.*

*"Once, long before time itself, there was a man. He had long, fiery hair, green eyes and a striking smile," he winks at my mother. She covers her face, cheeks turning a rosy pink. Using the dish towel, Mother swats the air as giggles echo in our small home.*

*"When the man was only a child, he would wake up screaming or crying, sometimes even laughing, from what his dreams held. His mother would say he had a vivid imagination, but as the boy grew older, the dreams continued - only then, the dreams would come true."*

*The story has me spellbound. My father tells me about the dreams, how they evolved over time, how people would think the man was insane, a liar. My heart races as the story goes on.*

*"One time, the man had a dream that a dear friend of his would get badly hurt in a sailing accident. The man tried to warn him, to make him stay home, but his friend rejected him and left." Chills scatter across my scalp, veins freezing. I look up at him.*

*"Papa, what happened then?"*

*My father's eyes harden as he zones out, lost in the story. I give him a nudge, needing the answer. Shaking his head, he looks back down, hand stroking my back as we continue rocking.*

*"His friend lost his legs, just as his dream foretold..."*
*I gasp. "How awful! Poor friend."*
*Papa gives me a warm smile, his emerald eyes glittering behind tears.*

*"Later, it turned out that the man was not alone in having these dreams. Many people had been just like him, but they were taken away or banished from the realm for being dangerous. Non-magic people would take advantage of them, forcing them to travel between dreams, and use them to tell their own futures. The man decided to keep his gift a secret, to not let anyone know he had truth-telling dreams."*

*"Did someone find him?"*

*"No. The man still lives, his gift is still a secret."*

*"Is he happy?"*
*My father looks at my mother. I can feel the heat radiating from his body, eyes filled with adoration. His arms snake around me, holding me in a tight embrace as a tender kiss falls to the top of my head.*

*"Very."*

# *Chapter 1*

## *Tharion Ashveil*

I like it here. It's quiet, calm. A place where the gnawing thoughts can't reach me. Above, the towering treetops sway, branches whispering as the autumn winds brush through. The faint rustling of heavy steps on parched leaves piques my attention. I turn my head, scanning the forest floor for larger animals.

When I can't find the source of the sound, I lie back down on the damp soil. Eyes closing, I try to drift off – anywhere but to them.

To *that* day. Every day the memory claws at me; waiting for my parents to return from the meadow village, lamps burning low while my Godfather, Axel, made me laugh and fed me sweet cakes. That night, I went to bed with happiness on my tongue.

My parents never came home. Instead, at dawn, I was handed a letter from one of the King's men. The words haunt my mind; *wolf shifters. Smugglers. My father calling on his earth-magic to protect my mum. The wolves answering with teeth and claws, ripping them to shreds under the stars*. I can never unsee it, though I never saw it at all.

They loved me like there weren't any other beings in the realm. Like nothing else existed but us. That was twelve years ago, but the memories could fool my mind to thinking it was only last night.

Now, stepping into my adult years, I still spend so much time pining over details of that night, trying to find anything that could have changed the outcome. *You should have listened to the dreams.*

I wince, clamping my eyes shut as if the voice inside my head just raised a fist at me. It's right. I should have listened to the dreams, but at barely ten years old, I believed it to be a nightmare, a result of my anxiousness to them leaving.

Images flash before me as if I watched it happen. The earth splitting as my father called on his powers, claws tearing my parents to shreds, my mother calling out my name as she drew her last breath. Guilt drowns me, ripping a scream from my chest, agony echoing far into the forest. I bury my face in my hands as hot tears pour from my eyes, dripping to the earth below.

After that night I couldn't bear to stay inside the house – once filled with laughter, songs and cheers – now empty, cold and silent. Axel tried his hardest to lift me from the shadows, but nothing would drive them out. Every time I crossed that threshold, the air felt heavy, pressing against my chest until I could hardly breathe. So, I ran to the forest.

Out there, trees whispered, the grass sang, and the damp scent of rain and earth steadied me. I could draw full breaths again, feel the storm in my head ebb to a murmur. The woods became my refuge, and I might have made them my home entirely, if not for Axel. He took me in like his own, gave me care, gave me learning, gave me a chance to dream of more than sorrow.

My father, fae and wielder of the elements, took power from the earth, bending it to his desire. Those powers were shared with me the day I was born. Unfortunately, I have yet to discover the key to unlock them. Whenever I call upon my magic, they are but a soft hum under my fair skin. I never studied to become a scholar like most people my age. Where witches studied the ancient art of conjuring, elves healed and shifters learnt the secrets of trading, I spent my time tending to farmer Fern's animals. It's ironic, existing in a realm where magic is so easy, where even the people born without it have the opportunity to master it – and still, I remain without control.

While I can conjure the vines of the earth to build housing, I am unable to unlock the greater powers I watched my father use. I feel them, like an electrical current at the tips of my fingers, but no matter how hard I try, they refuse. Sometimes I wonder if I will ever learn to use them, to use them for great things like my father did. The thoughts haunt me, mercilessly torturing.

A twig snaps, my eyes shoot open. I hurry to my feet, turning to check where the sound came from. The air feels heavy, colder. Around me the forest is dark, but the setting sun still manages to cast the forest floor in a deep orange hue, just bright enough for me to catch sight of a shadow lurking between trees.

"Hello?" I shout, words ricocheting into the forest. There's no answer, but I hear the snapping sounds closing in on me. A faint smell clouds my senses, pushing further up my nostrils. Something is wrong.

"Is someone out there?" I call out again, turning after the sound. My gaze stills at two glowing, yellow eyes engulfed in a greyish fog, bones forming under a cloak of shadows and mist. The eyes look straight at me. I tilt my head, eyebrows scrunching between my eyes. *What is that?*

Images from old texts flood my mind, my father reading frightening stories of dark spirits roaming the land before the beginning of time.

*But those were banished centuries ago.*
They can't be here – spirits are meant to be in the spirit realm, not in the realm of the Living. Shaking my head, I try to make sense of it all.

Another branch shatters, the *thing* now sprinting towards me, blood freezing in my veins. Branches snap under heavy steps, its legs leaping with long strides, closing in on me fast. Behind it, a trail of shadow slowly dissipates, the smell of death coating the forest air. Rotten teeth peek from broken lips. Is it… smiling?

My heart starts thundering in my chest, trying to force icebound legs to run, but before I manage to escape, I'm thrown to the ground. My head hits the forest floor, vision blurring as black spots dance at the edges. Breath becomes scarce as the creature sits on top of me, long nails splitting fabric, piercing my skin. I cry out, my shirt slowly soaking in crimson. The foul *thing* is grinning with razor sharp teeth, spit running down its chin.

Its eyes bore deep into my soul, searching. As my gaze locks to it, my stomach drops. Every feeling in my mind melts into one. I feel so overwhelmingly, excruciatingly sad, like I'll never feel happiness again.

Tears start streaming down my temples, dampening the soil under my head as I desperately try to regain control. The spirit slowly bows deeper, mere inches from my face, its sharp claws still embedded in my chest. I can feel its cold, dead breath on me, the smell of rot and decay heavy, its eyes glowing even brighter now. Bile rises in my throat, the air I so desperately need trapped below it.

Blood freezes in scorching veins, chest constricting painfully. I need to get out. I can't die here, not now. Not like this. Not in the one place that has always been my sanctuary.

Panic snaps me back to reality, head whipping to the side, frantically searching for a way to escape. My eyes land on a log near my thigh, hand trembling as I reach for it. I swing hard, wood colliding with the creature, knocking it off me in a wail of terror.

It hits the ground, clamping its head and I take that as my sign to make a run for it. Quickly shaking off the haze, I jump to my feet and run as fast as my legs will carry, not daring to look behind me, back to the cottage where I know Axel will be waiting.


Bursting through the door, I slam it shut with force big enough to shake the walls, startling my Godfather.

He jumps from his chair, his book soaring through the air, landing with a dull thump on the wooden floor.

"What in the Gods' names is going on? Why are you slamming doors at this hour, boy?" Axel shouts, his deep cobalt eyes glittering with surprise. My heart is hammering in my chest, ears rushing as if filled with water. What was that? How could a spirit – if that is what it was – be out here, and why did it attack me? My thoughts are everywhere, making the world spin.

Hurriedly, I walk up to the window to check if it followed me home. The trees are silent, not even wind brushing at their leaves. Nothing. In relief, I let out the breath that's been burning in my chest.

I clear my throat. "I'm sorry, Axel. I thought I saw a bear, and it spooked me," I lie. *No way I'm telling him I got attacked by a spirit. I'm not even sure that's what it was.* I draw my jacket tighter around me, hiding the stains on my shirt. Axel walks up to me, shaking his head and laughing faintly.

"You scared the life out of me, son. Come on, let's eat some supper before bed. We've got a busy day tomorrow, the Ferns have acquired three more horses, and they won't feed themselves."

Grabbing two plates, some bread, cheese and a piece of cured meat, Axel sets the table. My stomach growls loudly at the sight of food.

Excusing myself for a moment, I head to the washroom, closing the door behind me with a soft click. Steady breaths fill my aching lungs, slowing down my heart as I look at my own reflection. With gentle hands, I lift my torn shirt, the fabric sticking to the wounds on my chest. I hiss, stings shooting throughout my torso.

Thankfully, the wounds are shallow, and the bleeding has stopped. I wring a washcloth with lukewarm water, dabbing it over the red punctures, biting down on my lip as water seeps in. Checking out my face, splotches of mud and blood streak my freckled skin. I give it a quick clean before discarding my shirt, the black fabric luckily hiding the dark stains of scarlet.

After eating our meal and cleaning up, I say goodnight and head to bed. My room is small, but stocked with everything I need - a bed, a dresser, a table for my book and night light, and a window to let in the fresh night air. Normally I would sleep with the window open, but the thought of that *thing* finding its way back is enough to keep the window closed. Would it find me? Was it even me it wanted? Where did it come from?

The questions are deafening, the need for answers suffocating. I gulp down a mouthful of fresh air. Tomorrow I will find out what that thing was, I'll go back to the forest and check for signs, check if what I thought I saw was actually there. I can't just let that thing roam around the village, hunting for people. No, of course, I can't! Tomorrow, I will find answers.

I lay in bed for a while, watching the window. Images of those sickly yellow eyes haunt my waking mind, but soon enough, I enter the realm of the Dreaming - haunting yellow orbs following behind me like a curse waiting to unfold.

# *Chapter 2*

## *Eleanora Luna*

"Eleanora? Eleanora, are you awake?"
My mother calls from downstairs, ripping me from sweet dreams.
*What is it now? Some other way for you to make me feel inadequate?*
I groan, dragging myself out of bed.

Slipping on my socks, I walk over to my dresser, pulling out a black cotton dress. The long arms flare at the ends, creating the illusion of black wings. It's my favourite. I slip on a peridot necklace - needing all the luck and protection I can get today.

It's the sixth day of the week, and that means that we all eat breakfast together as a "family", though we haven't felt like one in years. Not since my younger siblings Olivia and Beatrice were born and took over the spotlight. Everything is ever about them. Never me. I'm the strongest one of us, I can do things none of my other six siblings could even dream of. My fists clench, a hot sensation pooling in my chest.

Inhaling, I close my eyes. *No. I will not let them make me feel lesser, weaker, invisible. I'm an adult, I decide what to do with my time.*

With that, I decide to skip breakfast, not bearing to spend another fake meal with them talking about everything the twins managed to do this week and watch my older siblings roll their eyes in frustration.

My oldest sister, Renee, always wanted to be the best, the most powerful, to show our parents that the Luna-legacy was in good hands with their firstborn. She tries too hard, and it's tearing her apart from the inside out. I scoff at myself. At least she got out of the house, not like the rest of us that haven't found a partner to live with and are forced to live at home.

Sometimes I wonder if I will ever find my partner in life, if I'll find someone who will see me for me, who will think I'm enough as I am. I shrug the thought off as my chest tightens even more.

Below, I hear the rustling of plates and mugs, my siblings settling around the table. I glance at the window. Packing a rucksack with some notebooks, a candle, a small knife, and a jumper in case it gets cold, I hoist the pack over my shoulder.

The window creaks loudly, making me wince. I wait a moment, but there's no sound from downstairs.

*They didn't notice. Why am I not surprised.*
I swing my feet over the ledge, pushing off. Silently, both feet land on the ground, the grass around me glittering in morning dew.

The bushes leading out to the main road rustle loudly before a set of deep burnt orange eyes meet my gaze. I smile. Rowan, my familiar, is a fox shape shifter. I met him when I was just a teenager, and he's been with me ever since. He's my best friend, my protector, my brother. Like all foxes, Rowan sleeps out in the forest. He likes it that way, says that he's used to it - so I let him. I run up to the gate, carefully opening it and closing it behind me.

"Good morning, Eleanora," Rowan greets me in his husky, morning voice. He steps out from the bushes, now shifted into the man I most often see him as. He has short, scruffy hair in a delicate strawberry blonde colour, his eyes turn a golden auburn in human form, and his skin is a rich, dark brown.

I've always thought that Rowan was beautiful, the way he carries himself, how he talks and the glimmer in his eyes when he finds something funny. His features are strong, pointy, he takes care of his body, and it shows. The muscles on his arms bulge under the shirt he's wearing, and I quickly look away, refocusing on why I've left in the first place.

My familiar smiles at me, and I instantly feel calmer, safer. He has that effect, ridding me of the problems I drag with me when I leave the house. By now, Rowan is used to me escaping the house daily, he stopped asking questions years ago. I smile back at him and start walking up the road and into the forest.

Perhaps we'll meet Tharion, he usually spends time there during the day after he's done in the stables with Axel. They take care of the farm animals, and in exchange they get a piece of land to grow crops on. Tharion and I met when we were just thirteen, both of us trying to escape a reality we hated, trying to be in a place where birds sang and rivers flowed peacefully, where we didn't have to remind ourselves to breathe. A place where we could live, not just survive.

At only a year younger than me, I consider him my closest friend. Sometimes I even play with the thought that we could be more than that, but I would never want to ruin the friendship we have by falling in love with him. It would never last. How could he want someone like me? I'm a failure in my family's eyes, have done nothing to prove my worth to anyone, he would probably get tired of me. Just like everyone else. I would never forgive myself for losing him if it came to that.

We arrive at the forest, and with the sun high in the sky, the feeling of freedom hits me square in the chest. Tall trees stretch around us, birds and squirrels living in harmony among the green crowns of leaves. The smell of soil and rain floods my senses, grounding me. I love it here.

Rowan walks up to a tree stub in the middle of the track and sits down, the stub creaking under his giant stature.

"You barely talked on the way here, are you okay?" His eyebrows scrunch into a soft frown, the words coming out careful, gentle.

"Sorry," I look at my hands, fingers picking at torn cuticles, "I just couldn't be at that house anymore. I've been thinking lately that I should get away. Away from Sylvarn. Maybe move somewhere where I can be myself, where I'm needed," I let out a deep sigh, meeting Rowan's eyes, "somewhere I can call home."

My gaze falls to the earth, cheeks heating. I don't want pity, especially not from Rowan. Deep down I know he doesn't, but I still hate saying these things out loud.

"Then let's go, Ela. I'll go wherever you go; *you* are my home. It doesn't matter where we are, as long as I am with *you*."

He stands up and walks over to me, the autumn leaves crunching under his boots, and wraps his arms around me. Softly, he plants a kiss to the top of my head. My eyes burn, tears pressing on the back of my eyelids, but I push them down. Snaking my arms around my familiar, I let him hold me for a while - until the aching emptiness in my chest fades. What if we just left? Where would we go, what would my parents say? Would Tharion come with us? The questions scream inside my brain, making me want to do the same.

Rowan releases me, bowing his head so our eyes meet.

"Just say the word, *vulpin*, and we'll go. I will follow you to the ends of this realm and the next."

His voice is soft, but stern. I know he means it, I know he would do whatever it took to keep me happy. As my familiar, our bond is stronger than any other family bond. He needs me, and I need him. People that lose their familiars never become the same again. I've heard it's like a void that slowly eats you from the inside, never getting easier. My stomach tightens, a shudder running through me at the thought.

But the Fates work against me. Like all shifters, their souls are divided by the Fates, destined to remain alone until they find their mate. Stories tell of shifters going their whole life without finding them, agony and loneliness eating away until there is nothing left. In some way, I'm destined to lose Rowan, but not completely. His soul will forever hold a spot for someone else – and he deserves it. There is nothing my heart desires more than for Rowan to find his mate, to finally have his soul feel whole, complete. Deep down, I believe that's the reason Rowan seems so tense, eyes constantly searching, waiting.

"Want to go for a walk? The sun is beautiful, and the weather is nice for a change," I ask, trying to cut the tension hanging over us like a heavy-woven blanket. He nods, releasing me and turns to face the pathway heading deeper into the forest. We start walking in silence, but it's not the heavy kind anymore, it feels light and freeing.

The trail leads us further into the forest, into the thickest part where trees are dense and stretch towards the sky in hungry desperation. Here, the warm sunlight struggles to pierce the treetops. It's colder, but not freezing, as we submerge ourselves in it. The bustling sounds of the village fade behind our steps, birdsong quieting faintly.

I notice the silence, but as we walk, I realize why it feels off. There are no squirrels running across branches, no sound at all. Nothing. What's going on? I feel the discomfort rising in my body, my chest tightening. Stopping, I listen for sounds.

"Do you hear that?" I whisper.

Rowan tips his head, listening.

"No, I don't hear anything."

"Exactly. It's too quiet. Like something's waiting to pounce, something—"

An explosion splits the air, splintered wood raining over us as we hunch down, covering our heads. A tree not far from us is torn up, its bark violently ripped from the trunk. Another slash is heard, and splinters fly in every direction, it almost looks like… claw marks? Rowan tips his nose up into the air and inhales deeply.

"It smells evil. Rotten. Wrong. We need to–"

My heart is racing, hands clammy. A loud roar sounds through the air as a boulder is broken down the middle, rubble soaring towards us.

"*Run!*" I yell, grabbing his hand, pulling him behind me. We sprint deeper into the forest, not braving to turn back in the direction we came from.

"Up there, there's a clearing!" Rowan pants, still holding onto my hand. His head swivels back and forth, keeping whatever is trying to get us at a distance. We leap over rocks and roots, crashing through bushes and out into a sunlit clearing surrounded by thick forest. We run out into the middle and wait, frantically watching our surroundings.

"What in the Afterlife was that?!" I pant, panicked, so out of breath it's embarrassing. Raven hair sticks to my forehead, strands falling into my eyes. My cheeks are bright red, but Rowan has barely broken a sweat. *Show-off.*

"I don't know, I couldn't see anything." He scans the area intently, sniffing the air and watching for any movement. Nothing, not a sound, just silence. What was that? Is someone playing some sick trick on us?

"Should we make a move home?" I ask warily, not sure if it's even safe to go down the way we came. Rowan's gaze is still trained on the forest edge, scanning. He lowers to the ground, pulling my sleeve to follow. Above us, the sun shines, clouds passively drifting in ignorant bliss.

"Let's just wait here for a moment."
I nod. We sit down on the grass, backs against each other, anxiously waiting, but nothing happens. Whatever it was, doesn't want to come out into the light. Was it a bear? A deer? Waiting, I listen for any sound, any movement. But there is none. Not a sound, not a whisper, only my heart pounding against my eardrums, breaths coming out in short bursts.

"There has been a shift. Something is wrong."
I nod silently, swallowing hard. I feel it, too. The forests have always felt safe, a place to breathe, to exists without guilt. Whatever just shattered those trees isn't from here, and I have a feeling it's not the last time we'll encounter it.

# Chapter 3

## Tharion

*It's dark, faint whispers dancing in the air around me. I hear footsteps treading through water, ripples carrying the sound in my direction. I try to look around me, but all I see is darkness. It's cold, so incredibly cold. I turn around to see a figure sprinting towards me, reaching for me.*

*As it comes closer, I see more of their features... Fiery red hair flairs from their hood, dragged down over their face. The figure runs towards me before slamming into an invisible wall. The wall has a faint glow to it every time it's touched, like waves of energy coursing through it. The hood of their cloak falls, revealing a face I've only dreamt about for so many years.*

*"Father? Father, is that you?" I run up to the wall, trying to see him clearer.*

*"Tharion, my son, I need you to listen. There isn't much time." His voice echoes, straining against the force field of the wall. He struggles, as if he's being held back by strings.*

*"B-but how are you here? You're gone," my eyes fill with tears, blurring my vision. I blink furiously, forcing them away. I need to see him.*

*"I might be gone, but I am not silent. Beyond the veil, I see what stirs."*

*"What do you mean? What stirs?"*
*Confusion builds, this is a nightmare. Father's voice starts to tremble, growing darker.*

*"A demon, ancient and bound. The walls between our world and the spirit realm crack... each day weaker."*
*A demon? What does he mean, demon?*

*"What does this demon want? Please tell me, Father."*
*I beg for answers, stomach twisting in knots.*
*My father's eyes widen in terror.*

*"Darkness. Not death alone, but unending night. Eternal silence." His voice is hoarse from shouting.*

*"How do I stop it?"*
*His figure flickers, turning fainter by the second.*

*"Seek the light. It lies where the river meets stone. Remember..." his voice fades out as his body dissipates into thin air, dissolving the wall between us. I push through it, hoping to get to him before he vanishes completely.*

*"Father!" I yell, frantically looking around me, but I'm alone. It's just me, alone in the darkness, surrounded by nothingness. Cold, silent nothingness.*

I wake up in a panic. Under the woollen blanket, my body trembles. What was that? It felt so real.

*Just like the one you had all those years ago. Remember what happened then.* Silent sobs rip from my throat, heart hammering in its cage. I try to steady my breath, inhaling deeply through my nose and exhaling through my mouth.

Outside, the morning sun is just rising over the mountains, letting me know that it's time to get ready for the day. I pull my tired body out of bed, stretching far above my head with a whining groan. Hunched, I drag my tired legs into the washroom, turning on the faucet. Steam rises from the basin, comforting warmth waking my slumbering senses. The washcloth drags away the salty tears of the night, removing them from the day to come. Once finished, I put on my stable clothes and walk out to meet my Godfather in the dining room.

Axel is already sat, breakfast waiting for me on the table; warm porridge with nuts and berries, my favourite.

"Did you sleep well, son?" he asks, not looking up from his morning newspaper. I shake my head.

"Terrible nightmare. Father came to me with a warning. Could swear I felt him, but he was stuck behind a wall of some kind." Laughing nervously, I'm trying not to sound insane. Axel's eyes narrow on me as I sit down across from him, paper gently placed on the table.

"What do you mean he came to you? In what way?" The question is strange. It was only a dream, why all the questions?

"I'm sure I just miss him and that's why he appeared. It's not like I've never dreamt about him before - I just never spoke to him in the other dreams." I try to shrug it off, but Axel persists.

"What did he say, Tharion?" His voice is stern, brows firmly knitted between his eyes, staring intently at me.

"He told me a demon was coming to put the world into eternal darkness." I try to laugh, but it comes out sounding more like a voice crack than anything else. My cheeks redden. What is happening?

"You need to tell me exactly what happened in that dream, right now. And do not leave anything out, you hear me?"
I shuffle in my seat but proceed to tell him everything that happened from start to finish. Axel's eyes widen and narrow, soft hums and gasps slipping past his lips. After I'm done, he sits back in his chair, face pale, eyes wide.

I wave my hand at him, "I'm sure it was just a bad dream, okay? It's not like *I* could save the world from a demon. I barely know how to control my magic!" I joke, trying to cut the tension.

"Son, I need you to listen to me, carefully. Your Father came to you in your dream," he starts.

"I know, that's what I told you," I answer, wondering if I'm missing some point.

"No," Axel gets up, walking over to me. He crouches before me, palms resting on my shoulders.

"*He came to you in your dream.* Your Father found a way to break from the spirit realm into your dream realm to give you a message."

My stomach drops, head spinning. Axel continues.

"You are the one that can save us, Tharion. Only you can stop this demon, whoever he is." He stands, pacing the room, panting slightly.

My eyes shoot wide as the words fall from my Godfather's lips.

"I can't save us, Axel. I don't even know how to fight! I wouldn't even know where to *start* learning how to fight or how to wield my magic into anything other than housing." I follow his movement as he paces along the floor, making my stomach turn, head filling with cotton.

What does he mean I'm the only one that can save us? He must be out of his mind! I scoff. My body itches to get out, to get my mind off this dream. Hurriedly, I stand, grabbing my jacket and stomp out to the stables so I can start my day. Out of his mind…

My workday goes by so slow, like time itself has stopped and refuses to move onward. I patiently wait for it to end so I can go back to the forest, to check for clues on what attacked me yesterday. Does it have anything to do with my dream?

I tend to the stables, feeding and grooming the horses, maintaining the stable grounds, keeping myself as busy as possible.

Finally, when the sun kisses the mountain peaks, I know the day has passed. I pack up my things, say goodbye to the farmer and his wife and head home. The walk back to our small house is blurry, my mind so filled with thoughts that the surrounding area vanishes in the raging ocean of questions. At home I quickly put my bag of tools and brushes inside my bedroom and turn to leave when Axel walks up behind me.

"Son, I know this is a lot for you to take in. I would be scared, too, if I were you." His voice is careful. I sense him trying not to panic me.

"I'm not scared, I don't even understand what's happening. I can't save anyone, and I don't know who this demon is," I sigh, helplessness heavy on my chest.

Axel puts his hand on my elbow, scanning my face.

"We'll pause on the matter today." The bright cobalt in his eyes softens. "We can revisit this when you come back home, yeah?" My Godfather tries to reach for me with his other arm, but I back away. I need to figure out what all of this means, I need to figure it out *now*.

Shutting the door behind me, I start jogging towards the forest edge. My auburn hair sticks to my neck, and my breath shoots out a cloud of steam with every exhale.

When the forest finally surrounds me, I come to a stop. Planting my hands on my knees, I gulp down mouthfuls of air. As I make my way to the same place I saw the spirit yesterday, eyes scanning every tree and bush, I notice tree trunks slashed and splintered. What animal claws at trees like that?

I tilt my head, studying the deep gash embedded in the wood before continuing. After a few more minutes of walking, I reach my destination. The grass has a flat spot where I was laying down, but that's all. The trees surrounding the area look normal, like they haven't been touched. No broken branches, no stepped-on grass, no prints in the mud. Nothing. Did I imagine it? I decide to investigate the area, to see if I can find anything at all proving to at least myself that I'm not slowly going insane.

Walking along the track, I follow it up to where it looks like a boulder has been broken to small pieces. Stones of varying sizes and colour lay spread, as if shattered from within. If someone came here and blew up the giant rock using magic, surely someone would have heard it?

The knot that's made itself comfortable in the pit of my stomach slowly makes a return, and I can feel my heartbeat accelerating. Something isn't right. Up the hill is a clearing where deer usually go to mate or graze on the green straws after rainfall. I follow the pathway up, my pace steadily picking up to a slow jog, shoes hitting the earth hard with every stride.

As I reach the top, sunshine blinds me just as I'm tackled to the ground by something huge, knocking the air out of my lungs. I roll around the grass until the creature, a furry beast with claws and pointy fangs, mounts on top of me, mouth panting just inches from mine. Pain radiates through my chest from my previous wounds, blood oozing from the shallow punctures.

The beast is growling steadily, a warning not to make any sudden moves. My skin hums as I call on my earth-magic, thorny vines shooting from the ground, threading their way around the beast. Holding it back, I lift it into the air. Fiery orange eyes stare at me, wide, angry.

"Don't hurt him! Please, stop!" a crying female voice hits me from the side. Not just any female voice.

"Ela?" I pant loudly, dumbfounded. The beast calms down, looking pleadingly into my now emerald eyes, magic thrumming under my skin. I call back the vines, watching as they slither from the beast, letting him back down on the ground before retreating into the earth. The beast, who I now realize is Rowan, shifts back into his human form, deep brown skin scratched from vines, scruffy hair pointing in every direction.

"Rowan, I'm so sorry. I didn't realize it was you." I make my way over to him, reaching out a hand. Rowan is a tall male, and has just about half a head on me, making us almost eye level. He takes my forearm with his hand, dragging himself off the ground and brushes his clothes free from dirt and grime.

He shakes his head. "No, I'm sorry, Ari. I heard rustling from the forest and thought the thing that attacked us had come back to finish what it started." His gaze shoots over my shoulder, into the forest opening.

"Attacked you? You were attacked?" My heart beats hard in my chest, screaming to be let out. I look over to Eleanora, scanning her for injuries, shoulders slightly relaxing when I can't find any. Eleanora is my best friend, if something happened to her… My fists clench. Blood rushes down my spine in a cold shiver, my protectiveness in full swing. Nothing will ever hurt her. I won't let it and neither will Rowan.

"Who attacked you?" I push when no one answers.

"We didn't see it, but I smelled it. Like death itself. Rotten. Evil." Rowan scrunches his nose at the memory.

"It started ripping up trees and destroyed that big rock down the trail, blew it up like it was nothing. But we couldn't see it, so we ran up here in hopes that it wouldn't touch us out in the open." His gaze fades out, thinking back to the attack.

Eleanora stands a few steps behind Rowan, hugging herself and staring at the ground. Her soft body trembles, breath coming in short, shallow bursts. I walk up to her, wrapping my arms around her shoulders and hold her tight to my chest. Resting her head over my beating heart, my palm cradles her, shielding her. The other arm twists around her shoulders and rests on the back of her arm.

I can see her shoulders slowly relaxing when I squeeze her just a bit tighter and drag her scent deep into my lungs. Her scent has always calmed me right down, grounded me when I needed it. It's a mix of cherry, pine and the smell of her skin, the most delicious smell there is. Some of it's probably from her soap, but there is no better smell in this realm, I'm sure of it. My heartbeat slows when I have her in my arms, and our breaths even out. Reluctantly, I release her, hooking my finger under her chin and lifting her face to mine.

"Are you okay?" I ask, looking into her eyes, searching for an honest answer. Eleanora never lets anyone see her pain, but I do. She doesn't know it, but I've always seen it, it's in her eyes. Those beautiful burgundy eyes.

"I'm okay, just startled me a bit, not knowing what it was," she says, just louder than a whisper, tears forming. I tug her in for one more hug before letting her go, instantly feeling the absence of her touch, wanting to have her back in my arms again. *Mine.*

But Eleanora could never be mine, not like I want her to be. I feel her resistance when we get too close, like she's building up invisible walls between us. A part of me can feel her reaching for me, whilst the other part of her is pushing me away.

The truth is, I have been in love with Eleanora Luna since the day we met, all those years ago. I have seen her on her happiest days, her saddest, even the days she feels she isn't good enough for anyone. To me, no star shines as bright as the ones in her eyes, dancing, luring me to stay in any moment with her forever. But I can never have eternity with Eleanora. *Those damn Fates.* Our lifespans collide, forcing me to live for centuries without her by my side. I tell myself that I could never do that, but my heart screams for me to enjoy whatever time we'd get. I've spent the last decade slowly falling in love with my best friend, and I would happily spend the rest of her lifespan falling even harder.

I tell Rowan and Ela about my attack the day before, not leaving anything out. I can see them scrunching their noses and widening their eyes at some of the details, but at least they don't think I'm insane. Ela's eyes fall to my chest, looking for the puncture wounds. I shoot her a soft smile, a sign that I'm okay, but her frown remains chiselled between moons of deep plum.

"Fuck. So, what now? How do we catch this thing, or these things?" Rowan paces between us, a low growling sound emanating from his chest. I tear my gaze from Eleanora, looking up at the fox.

"That's not all. I had a dream last night, after the attack, and now Axel thinks I'm the only one that can stop this." I fiddle with my hands while training my eyes on Rowan, talking carefully so as not to trigger any more anger.

"You what?!" Rowan roars. So much for that not-triggering-anger part.

"I didn't tell you because I'm still processing the whole thing. It all happened so fast, and when I saw my father… I-I don't know how to control my magic, and I sure as shit don't know how to fight! I've never hit someone, ever!" I sigh, exasperated.

"How am I supposed to stop an ancient demon if I can't even control my magic?" I look down into my hands, embarrassment flushing my cheeks in a scorching pink.

"Tharion… I'm so sorry you had to go through that by yourself." Eleanora puts her hand on mine, and I feel like I can finally breathe a bit. Our eyes meet again, but this time she doesn't look away as fast.

"Look, why don't we make a plan? I can teach you how to control your magic, it can't be that far off from witchcraft, can it?" she jokes half-heartedly. I know she means well, so I swallow my dread and nod.

"It's worth a shot. But where am I going to learn how to fight? We don't live in a village with warriors." My pessimistic thoughts are creeping back in when Rowan comes to stand in front of me.

"Lucky for you, I am not from this village. I spent 150 years training with other shifters before I found Eleanora, I will train you." The fox looks down at me with a firm smile and reaches out his hand for a shake. Insecure about this whole thing, I resist for a moment. My eyes climb his body, seeing in his that he actually believes we have a chance – and that is enough for me to grab his hand and make the promise to at least try. Now, we plan.

# *Chapter 4*
## *Eleanora*

*Spirits are walking among mortals*. Spirits that should be behind the Veil, separated from our realm. The living can't see them, or at least some of them, but now we know they're here. This all feels like some strange fever dream.

My big sisters would tell me stories as a child, horror stories of spirits haunting us if we didn't pray to the Goddess every night. That She would punish us by sending evil spirits into our room at night. I scoff at the ridiculous memory.

Our realm, the mortal realm, has been keeping spirits and the non-living behind the Veil, a magical shield that stops them from causing chaos among mortals. It's been closed with no way to get out since the battle between Ilyra Lightvein - Crone of White Flame, and Vorathiel, a human sorcerer so blinded by love that he let darkness possess his soul.

All witches hear these stories when they grow up. Ilyra Lightvein was one of a kind, the only light-wielding witch to ever exist. Most witches use blood to spell, like our coven does, but Ilyra used light, and all that light encompassed. According to the stories, she trapped Vorathiel and all his half-dead soldiers behind a barrier, a divider between the mortal-and spirit realms.

The night sky sparkles in a shimmery white glow, pulses of magic coursing through it, a constant reminder of her sacrifice. The Veil is unbreakable, or at least it couldn't break up until now, because spirits are slipping through. Each day more evil seeps into our realm. It's just a matter of time before Vorathiel himself escapes.

A dull ache radiates from my neck, stretching all the way to the top of my head from all this thinking and worrying. I grab some water from my flask and let the cold water run down my throat, feeling the refreshing sensation on my skin as some of it slips down my chin.

We need to plan how to approach this, it's a tad more serious than planning out what outfit to wear or what meal to make. The thought of fighting ancient evil makes my skin crawl.

The walk back through the forest is not as it used to be. While I would normally stare beyond the trees to watch animals and birds carelessly interact, now my eyes scan for danger. Everything I know is slowly changing, and I feel like we are, too. In the course of a day, our world has tumbled, flipped on its head. We never had to worry about spirits, or being attacked at all. There are no natural predators in Sylvarn, nothing out there to harm us. Until last night.

We meet at the same spot, Tharion already waiting for us as we break through the dense forest edge. Not as dramatic as it was yesterday, thank the Goddess, leaving us the time to talk and come up with a way to beat this demon piece of shit.

"So how do we move forward with this? It's not like we can train out in the open, people will notice," Tharion asks, eyes falling to the notebook in my lap.

Rowan sits up straight, legs crossed in front of him.

"First, we need to demand an audience and notify the King about a breach in the Veil. If spirits really are finding a way through the Veil, there is no time to lose. If King Vaelrick grants us the time, we can ask to use his training grounds until you are fit enough to fight on your own."

Rowan stares into the distance, clearly deep in thoughts. He keeps rubbing his thumb and index finger over his eyebrows, something he's always done whenever he feels anxious. At this point, I don't think he even notices it. Tharion recoils at the mention of our kingdom's guardian.

"The King? Isn't that a bit much? He lost his wife and twin sons just under a year ago, do you really think he would even listen to us?" Tharion being Tharion doesn't like to impose on people, and confrontation is his biggest enemy. I think it's charming most days, but right now it's literally good versus evil, no time for reticence.

I throw him a sharp look. He straightens, eyes flicking nervously, and continues.

"All I'm saying is that King Vaelrick has so much on his plate, I want to be completely sure we have what it takes to do this before we barge in and demand he listens."

Everyone knows the King is in mourning. Just a year ago, he lost Queen Rowenna and their two unborn twin boys. Queen Rowenna died during childbirth, and as a result, so did the boys. King Vaelrick had sat beside his wife, holding her hand, praying to the Gods that she would make it, to take him instead. He sat there, pleading while her heart slowly came to a stop, hand going limp in his. Three whole days went by before the King released her hand, refusing to let her go, to say goodbye.

The kingdom went into deep sorrow after that, and since then the King has kept to himself. A day here and there one might see him walking the castle's balcony, staring out over the waterfalls beneath, deep in thought.

"Tharion, please listen to me." I look into his eyes, cupping his hands in mine. The gemstone colour in his iris darkens, like stormy clouds over grass planes.

"I know you can do this. You have conquered every challenge ever thrown your way. Even your parents knew you were destined for greatness, or else your father would never have visited you in a dream. Do you even know how powerful you must be to travel to the dream realm without actually sleeping? Trust me, I've tried it and it is *hard*." I shoot him a smirk to take the edge off, and it seems to be working.

Tharion takes a deep breath, exhaling slowly. Closing his eyes, he lifts his head to the sky.

"Let's stop this demon from ruining our realm."

He stands up, reaching for us both. As we're hoisted off the ground, we find ourselves standing in a circle facing each other. His head dips slightly, eyes flicking between us.

"I need to know that if something happens to me, you guys will keep going and finish what we started. Chances, as they are now, say I won't make it all the way to the end, but if it means I die whilst trying to save the mortal realm - then Death herself may guide me through the Veil." He looks between Rowan and I, waiting for us to agree to his crazy terms. I open my mouth to answer, but Rowan cuts in, "we're in this together, we fight alongside each other and protect each other. None of us will die in this battle. I refuse to watch you from behind the Veil, you're pale enough as it is." I chuckle, dipping my chin.

"We believe in you, Ari, you have this written in fate. You are the one that can seal the cracks formed in the Veil. What was the thing your father told you to do?" I forgot the exact words, but I remember it had something to do with light.

"He told me to seek the light, and that it lies where the river meets rock, not that I know what that means." His voice falters, thoughts drifting back to that awful dream.

"There is a village by the roaring rivers, Stormbrook. River nymphs and wing-shifters reside there, maybe we could ask them for guidance and help during our battle. Having eyes in the sky wouldn't hurt," Rowan shoots in, "it would take us about two days to walk there by foot, we can make it in good time if we start early, and it's on the way to Catariel."

Tharion thinks for a moment, grunts a few times and mumbles something we can't hear before turning back to us.

"Okay, let's do it. We need to get going as soon as we can. Rowan, can you teach me some fighter moves before we leave here? I want to be able to pull some of my own weight until we get to the capital." A pink hue washes over his face as he avoids my eyes. I chuckle.

Rowan claps his hands once, jumping to his feet.

"Let's get to work, we have some ass-kicking to do, and it looks like I'm starting with yours, little fae," he winks at Tharion, and they burst out in laughter. In the blink of an eye, we're talking like we believe we have a chance. There is no other choice – if not, it's over for all of us.

Tharion and Rowan spend the next several hours training beginner defence stances, Rowan showing Tharion where to put his hands, what areas of the body to go for first and how far apart his legs should be. I'm having quite the time watching them fight, or rather: watching Tharion get his ass handed to him repeatedly.

It's mesmerizing to see the two men I care mostly for in the realm fighting each other. Watching muscles straining against their clothes, sweat beading on their foreheads and trickling down their necks. The grunts and curses under their breaths, and the ragged breaths themselves. Tharion may not be a warrior yet, but he's strong, and fast. Rowan has muscles for days and doesn't have the advantage of speed, so Tharion manages to escape time and time again. His problem is what happens after Rowan finally manages to get him in his grip.

"Your biggest error is letting yourself get put into this position," Rowan grunts through gritted teeth as Tharion struggles to both breathe and get out of the immovable headlock Rowan has him in. Tharion taps his arm three times, signalling that he surrenders. My familiar releases him as he folds in two, holding himself up by the knees. He fills his lungs with deep gulps of fresh air, the colour on his face slowly returning from the blueish tint it had just moments ago.

"You need to use your speed to your advantage, you can outrun anyone, and you are strong, Tharion. Use it to defend yourself. You don't need to throw a punch to the oesophagus to conquer your opponent." Tharion lets out a huff, waves him off and takes a few steps back to breathe again.

"Okay, that's enough for today." Rowan pats Tharion on the shoulder, "you need to even out your blood supply, because now it's all in your head. Drink some water and eat an apple. It helps," he commands, panting and wiping off sweat from his forehead with the back of his hand.

"We leave at dawn. Say your goodbyes and pack only what you need. Get a good night's sleep, you'll need that, too."

I come home later that night. Rowan has shifted and gone back to his den outside my house, packing up and getting a good night's rest. I sit on my bed, thinking about what I should pack, what I should tell my family. Would they even notice I was gone? Would they mourn me if I didn't make it?

I shake off the thought of dying in battle, I'm not doing that. We promised we would see this through no matter what, I intend to keep that promise.

Determined to get some rest, I quickly gather spare clothes, my knife for spelling, a candle and my notebook into a linen satchel. I glance over my room, a lump forming in my stomach. On my dresser there's a small wooden doll, just the size of the palm of my hand, that catches my attention. I walk over, pulling it into my hand. It's a boy carved out of wood. The boy has curly hair down to his shoulders, a wide smile - although quite wonky - and casual clothing. I smile.

Tharion gave it to me just after the first time we met. I had told him about my parents' indifference to my existence and how I felt so alone in the world. The next day, he turned up outside my house with the doll in his hands. His fingers were bandaged from cuts and splinters, but he stood there with a wide smile on his face, beaming to give me the gift he'd made.

"Now you won't feel as alone anymore, you'll always have me there. Even when I can't be, I will be with you. It's you and me, Ela. You and me, forever." His words warmed me from the inside as they trilled off his tongue, they still do. A single tear runs down my cheek, dripping onto the dresser. Without thinking about it, I stick the doll in my bag.

"It's you and me, Ari," I whisper to myself, cherishing the feelings as the memory plays out in my mind.

After packing my bag, I decide that writing a letter instead of facing my parents and their indifferent expressions is the better way out.

I think about what to write, how to formulate my words in the best way possible. Finally, I dip my ink pen into its pot and start writing:

*"Dearest mother and father,*

*When you read this, I will no longer be home. I know you may not notice my absence right away, for the hearth never burned strongly between us. Still, I cannot leave without saying something.*
*There are shadows stirring beyond our fields, whispers of spirits that move through the night, unravelling all that lives and breathes. I have felt their presence, cold as the wind in winter, pressing closer each day. Though I am but your daughter, overlooked and quiet, I cannot stand by while the world falters.*

*I go not because I seek glory, nor because I hope to return changed in your eyes. I go because someone must.*
*If I never return, remember me kindly, if you can. If I do return, I hope it will be to a world still worth calling home.*

*With courage borrowed from silence,*
*Your daughter, Eleanora"*

While writing the letter, my hands start trembling. Why do I feel sad? I shouldn't care, they never paid attention to me, so why do I still sit with hope that one day they will finally see me, want me?

Wiping the tears I just now realize are falling, I shake my head to rid myself of the emotions that so rudely imposed on me. I will show them that I'm good enough, if not them then myself.

Putting the note down, I climb into bed, pulling the covers up to my chin. My eyes fall shut, hoping sleep will show me mercy tonight. Goddess knows we need it for this journey.

# Chapter 5

## Tharion

After returning home, Axel is sitting in his chair at the dining table, reading. I take off my boots and jacket, hanging it up before stepping into the dining room.

Working up the courage, I take a deep breath.

"Hey, so I need to discuss something with you," I start, carefully trying to figure out if this is a good time or not.

A long exhale drags from Axel. "I know what you're going to say, and although I don't like it, you have my support to the fullest. Your father told me this day would come many years past, son." Axel put his book down on the table, eyes finding mine.

"I knew we would have this conversation one day, I just didn't know *when* the day would come. Sit down, Tharion." He pats the chair across from him. I plop down, my back straight, heart picking up speed.

"Your father knew this day would come. He was a Seer, Tharion." Axel descends to his knees, crouching before me. Air slips past my lips in a silent gasp. A Seer? My father could tell the future? How did I not know?

The stories from my childhood play out in my mind, of my father and I reading old texts of ancient creatures and people that no longer exist. Of course he was. How could I have been so blind? I swallow, mouth dry as bone.

"Why did no one tell me?" I ask. Inside my head, words shout, desperate to make me understand. My ears rush, chills running across my scalp.

"Seers are frowned upon, forbidden. Seers of the past were kept hidden from the rest, not able to talk about their abilities without getting kidnapped and used for military purposes or worse." I remember my father telling me about the man that kept his power a secret. Was he talking about himself? Axel carries on.

"Many people lost their lives for something they did not choose to have, powers the Fates had so gracefully bestowed upon them." He puts his hands on my shoulders, grounding me like he always has. Searching, he tries to make eye contact, but I evade his gaze.

"But, how? Did he know they were going to die that night?" My eyes finally meet his. "Did you know?"

I have so many questions, so many things left unsaid to my parents. Did he know I would get chosen to save our realm? Did he know if I made it? My stomach drops, blood running cold in my veins. Was he the one foretelling me what would happen to them, that showed me that dream all those years ago?

"Tharion," Axel sits back down directly across from me, so close that our kneecaps touch. I search his face, desperate for answers.

"Your father never wanted to leave you, never wanted to leave this realm. Some things are woven by the Fates themselves and not even a powerful Seer like your father could have stopped it. That night he knew what would happen, yes, but he also tried so hard to change what the Fates had so mercilessly woven onto his thread. Remember what he told you that night before they left?"

Of course, I do, I relive that moment every single day. Even as an adult, I'm afraid that if I stop thinking about it, I'll forget it and lose the memory forever. The night my parents left to see friends in the meadow village, we started the day off playing on our little garden patch outside the house. We were running, trying to catch each other, and I remember being picked up by and swung over my father's shoulders – soaring through the air.

We laughed, laughed so hard my belly hurt for the rest of the day, even after they'd left. My father lifted me off his shoulders, then squatted down to look me in the eyes and told me, "Tharion, my dearest son. I love you more than life itself, and I am so proud of who you are, who you will become. Let nothing put darkness over your light, for it shines so bright within you."

I remember not really thinking too much about it at the time – my  father would tell me he loved me every day, several times a day, but now I understand the importance of the words. He always knew that day would come, that there was no way for him to escape it.

"Did Mother know?"
My voice breaks, a lump the size of my fist lodging itself in my throat. I try to swallow it down, but it's no use. A sob breaks from my chest, echoing in the small room. Tears are falling, and I let them.

"No. Your father wanted your mother to live a happy, loving life without the burden of knowing when it would end. It was a secret only your father and I knew about. That was why I was the one to sit with you the night they left. Why we had such a memorable day, so you would feel as much happiness as possible before that pain inevitably came and drowned it out." Axel squeezes my hands.

Tears stream, lungs refusing to draw air. I wipe my nose with the end of my shirt and try to breathe, closing my eyes to my surroundings, blocking everything out just for a moment.

"But I know your time has come, and I know what you are about to do. Your father would be so proud of you, like he always was. You remind me so much of him. I see him in you every day, Tharion."

His eyes glisten with tears, throat working hard not to break his voice. I wipe my tears, shaking my shoulders, and take in a deep breath. I nod. "I need to go, I must save Kyrris. For him, for Father."

As I try to sleep, all the new information is still racing across my brain. The bed creaks as I toss and turn, waiting for dawn to arrive. Forcing my mind elsewhere, I go over the fight stances Rowan taught me in my head, trying to envision how to do it if we ever get in a battle with spirits. How will I protect Eleanora if I can't even protect myself?

A pang echoes through my chest, reality sinking in. We're going out to save Kyrris, the realm. Me, Tharion Ashveil, a blacksmith's son that has never done anything remotely remarkable in my life. *This is insane.* I'm only twenty three years old, I'm way too young to die now. I don't even have a wife or a child to bring my family name on, no house of my own. Nothing.

I sit up, choking on thoughts. I can't do this. I'm not capable of saving *our entire* realm. What was I even thinking?

Ripping off my blanket, I get out of bed, walking to the washroom. Water rushes from the faucet, filling the sink with small ripples.

With a splash, it runs down my face, giving me the shock I need. The coldness breaks my downward spiral. I take a deep breath.
*Get it together, Tharion. The Fates picked you, your father saw you all those years ago.*
I have to try. I might not make it, but at least then I gave it my all.


Dawn slowly makes its arrival, rosy-pink sunlight bathing our village in a calming aura. I step outside with my bag over my shoulder and make my way to the stables. The farmer I work for kindly lent us two horses for our journey. I will ride alone whilst Eleanora rides with Rowan. If I were to ride with her, I'm not sure I would be able to contain myself. *This is not the time for romance.* Eleanora will never be mine, and I will not make this trip harder on her by acting on my emotions.

As I bring the horses back from the stables, I see my adventure party waiting for me outside my house.

"Good morning, Ari," Eleanora says, eyes hazy with the remnants of night. I guess she didn't sleep too well either.

I yawn. "Hey, guys. How are you feeling today?"
I look at Rowan, the fox returning the stare with fierce determination in his eyes.

"We should get going, we need all the daylight we can get and it's still a day's ride to Stormbrook." He starts saddling up, hooking their bags over the back of the horse. I nod at him, then turn around to see my

Godfather standing in the doorway, his brows turned upwards in a worried frown.

"Be careful, son. You don't know what's out there. I hope to see you back home soon, in one piece preferably." He smiles, but it doesn't quite reach his eyes. I lean in to hug him, and he hugs me back tighter. We stand like that for what seems like an eternity, but neither of us wants to let go. To turn this into reality.

A throat clears behind us, Rowan obviously ready to embark. I let go of Axel, putting my forehead against his, eyes falling shut.

"For father. For Kyrris," I whisper. "For Kyrris," he whispers back. We let go, Axel tapping my shoulder one more time, trying to cut the tension that's so thick in the air. I turn around to see Eleanora and Rowan already on their horse, waiting for me. Mounted, I give my Godfather a firm nod and then, we set out for Stormbrook.

· · — ·✳· — · ·

Hours pass, and we decide to stop for a bite to eat. Around us is only forest for miles, broken by tall mountain peaks covered in snow. We dismount our horses and tie their lead ropes to a nearby tree. Rowan shifts into his fox form and heads out into the forest to hunt us some meat while I set up a fire and Eleanora sets up a place for us to sit around it.

She stops, dragging in a shaky breath. "Can you believe we're actually doing this?"

"I know. I couldn't sleep at all last night, everything just hit me all at once." I keep my voice strong, trying not to sound like a coward.

"You and me both." She huffs a laugh, "I barely slept, myself. Every time I closed my eyes, I heard those slashing sounds and envisioned hundreds of them attacking us at once. Or, at least tried to envision them. I hope my brain is wrong, and they're not as terrifying as I made them."

I look at her, trying to figure out what she's feeling. I can tell she's nervous, scared even, from the way she keeps looking around us, almost as if she worries something will leap out at any second.

"I will protect you, Eleanora. You are safe with me, and Rowan would never let anything happen to you. Have you seen the size of him in fox form? He's easily five times bigger than those things." I want to ease her mind, to make her feel safer. She chuckles, an adorable high-pitched sound, and I completely melt. What I would do to hear that sound when we return home again. She catches me staring and swats my upper arm.

"Stop that, you freak," her laugh surrounds me like a warm hug. I break out in laughter too and continue working on making the fire. After stacking firewood in a neat triangle and putting some kindle underneath, Eleanora lifts her hand with a small twist and the fire roars alive. I look at her in awe; she truly is amazing.

"Thank you, for coming with me. I could never do this without you." Turning her head to the side, she looks at me for a while, her eyes searching mine. What is she looking for?

"I would never leave you to save the realm by yourself, Ari." Her body turns towards me. "You told me a long time ago that it would be me and you, so you're stuck with me whether you like it or not." The corners of her mouth tug at her smile.

I chuckle. "I did say that, didn't I? I guess there's no going back on that now." I give her a smirk and an attempt at a wink, but my other eye follows suit, and it ends up looking like a lopsided blink instead. She laughs, really belly laughs, and I savour every second of it.

The sound of twigs snapping behind me has us turning in a hurry. Rowan is standing there with two rabbits in his hands, blood dripping beside his lips. My stomach growls and Rowan huffs a laugh.

"I guess I'll get started on these right away," he says as he carries them off to the side where he can skin and gut the rabbits, preparing to throw them on the fire.

"Tharion, you should try using your earth magic to gather us some vegetables to eat with our meat!" Eleanora exclaims excitedly. I've never tried gathering food using my powers before and wouldn't even know how to start doing that. I look at her with a tilted head, holding my hands up in surrender.

"H-how?"

"Watch, I'll show you."

She stands up, lifts her arms out to her sides and closes her eyes. Beneath us, the ground starts rumbling, leaves falling off trees nearby. Large vines explode from the earth, so long they stretch from us and far into the forest. Watching her, her body completely relaxed as nature bends to her will. After a few moments they shrink back, carrying a small bunch of mushrooms and wild onions. I gasp. *Magnificent.*

When Eleanora opens her eyes again, they are pitch black, like the night. When she uses her magic, her eyes change colour, just like with all of us. My eyes turn a deep emerald when I use mine, and Rowan's eyes go from a golden auburn to a deep burnt orange whenever he shifts.

The old texts tell stories of sorcerers and magic people with power so great it flooded their irises, changing the colour as magic thrummed in their veins – and that's why our eyes change only when we call on it.

I decide to give it a go, making it my goal to retrieve some berries we can eat after the main meal. With my feet firmly on the ground, I close my eyes.

"What do I do now?" I ask through darkness.

"Feel the vines you want to make and see the berries you want to retrieve. You need to really be the magic in order for it to do as you wish," she talks firmly, watching me as I strain, trying so hard to make something – anything – happen. I push my magic out, but my mind is foggy, trying too much too soon. Nothing happens. Not a rumble, not a single leaf leaving a branch. My shoulders slump, a defeated sigh pushed from my lungs.

"Hey, it's okay. No one gets it on the first try. We'll try again later, yeah?" she says, her voice warm, comforting. Eleanora puts her hand on my back, stroking it in a slow, soothing motion. My body burns under her touch, fingers aching to touch her. I relax, forcing a nod.

With a snap to his fingers, Rowan signals that the rabbit is done, and we sit down to enjoy our meal. We eat in silence, but that's fine with me. The sound of birds chirping above us takes me back to Sylvarn.

My mind drifts to Axel, wondering if he's thinking about us. Does he know the outcome of this? I wonder if my father told him all those years ago. Maybe he forgot the outcome, or maybe he simply doesn't know. I make my peace with having to find out the hard way, even though I hope we can stop the Veil before it breaks completely. The thought of battling some demon sorcerer makes my skin crawl.

"Should we get moving? We're losing daylight and there's still a way to go before we reach the rivers." Done with my meal, I feel my energy slowly returning. The others nod, Rowan gathering our plates. I stand up to get the horses.

"Would it be okay if I rode with you this time, Ari?" Eleanora asks, her voice small and high-pitched. Is that… blush? Is she blushing? Why does that make me feel all giddy inside?

I smile, "of course. My horse is your horse. Climb on." I gesture for her to climb on first, hopping on behind her. Snaking my arms around her soft waist, I put my body flush against hers. Her breath hitches slightly, and I swear I feel her press back against me, setting my body on fire. Digging my heels gently into the horse's side, we set off again, heading towards Stormbrook to meet the wing-shifters.

· · — · ✳ · — · ·

Eleanora's head falls back against my chest. I look down to see her eyes softly closed and her mouth slightly open. She's sleeping. The thought of her feeling so safe in my arms makes me proud. I puff my chest and hold the reins tighter as if to hold her tighter too while the sound of hooves on dirt clop beneath us.

Cold wind bites my cheeks as we ride towards the river village, the smell of wet wood getting stronger by the minute. We ride for about an hour before the roaring of several riverbanks wash against our eardrums. The air is misty and damp, filling my lungs with haze. I cough, waking Eleanora in my arms. She picks her head up, eyes wide, and looks down, straightening her posture. A beautiful pink hue sneaks up along her cheeks, making me smile.

"How was your rest, Ela?" I ask softly, trying to push away the obvious embarrassment creeping up on her.

"I slept better than I have in so long," she admits, her gaze slightly zoning out. "I guess I finally felt somewhat safe. It apparently makes it easier to sleep," she jokes, but I know she means it.

Stormbrook is beautiful. The village is crowded with tall houses on wooden poles, protecting them from the roaring rivers underneath. The rivers run through the village in every direction, fishing boats gliding over them, with beautiful stone bridges connecting the mainland.

Streets are flooded with market stalls trading fish and shellfish from the day's catch, while other stalls have fresh bread and different fruits. Males and females with beautiful feathered wings in radiant whites and dark obsidian blacks wander the streets in peace, making conversation with one another, sharing their trades. The houses by the rivers are covered in green algae and the sun has done its damage on the wooden panels, but it is breathtaking in its own way.

Back home in Sylvarn, houses are made of wood logs and bricks for foundation. The village we're currently riding into is nothing like home. My stomach knots slightly at the thought of my Godfather back at the stables, wondering if he's doing okay. I have never been this long without him ever since my parents died, and I can feel the absence in my body.

The bright sunlight fades over the time we spend riding into the village, and by our arrival, the sky is painted in deep purples, oranges and pinks. Rowan spots an Inn called "The Broken Oar" and we decide to stop there for the night.

"I will sleep out here next to the river, the fish will be easy to catch, and I will make myself a burrow to sleep in," he says. We nod and dismount our horses. Tying the leashes on a pole outside the Inn, we step inside. Immediately, we're greeted by a woman with chestnut brown hair and a bright smile.

The walls are covered in fishing nets and spirit floats - glass orbs enchanted by fishermen to keep the monsters from coming out of the deep while on the waters. It's warm, inviting. The lights are dim, sounds of laughter and cheers can be heard from the tavern next door. The woman smiles kindly at us.

"Welcome to The Broken Oar, friends! How can I help you this beautiful autumn evening?"

She has kind mahogany eyes and a genuine smile, but there's also something hiding behind those eyes. Her smile doesn't quite reach them, but I push that thought away.

"Good evening. We need a room for the night. Do you have any vacancies?"
The female claps her hands excitedly.

"Boy, are you lucky! We have one room to spare, it's small but it will fit both of you. Breakfast is served down here at the tavern, we have a fine selection of cured fish and delicious raw honey to put in your tea." My stomach rumbles at the thought and the female laughs.

"Take your things to your room, I will make you some supper in the meantime." We get our keys and head up to our room. The stairway leading us to our room is uneven and rounded, making it hard to stand properly. After riding horseback for a full day, it's even worse. We find the door, the number 29 carved beautifully, and chuck the stuff inside without even checking what it looks like. Eleanora's stomach makes a loud squeaky noise, and we both burst out laughing.

"I'm hungry, okay?" she swats me on my shoulder. I throw my hands up in surrender, still laughing, while we make our way down to the tavern. The Innkeeper has made us a mouthwatering spread of bread, cured fish, fresh berries and delicious red juice. I don't even know where to start, so I grab a bit of everything. The fish is delectable, savoury and tangy with a firm texture, the bread is soft and pillowy, and the berries burst with flavour.

"This is the best meal I've had in a long time," Eleanora mumbles between moans and mouthfuls. "I agree," I say, stuffing my face with more bread, swallowing it down with a big gulp of juice. We finish our meal, making sure to thank the nice innkeeper and head back to our room, the stairs feeling even heavier now that we have full stomachs.

Tired legs drag us up the last few steps, slowly bringing us to our door. Turning the key, I unlock it and step inside. The room is dark, only dimly lit by the setting sun outside, giving it an orange hue. Eleanora flicks her hand and lights the candelabra sitting on the desk opposite the bed with her magic. *The* bed. *One* bed. There is only *one bed*, and two of us.

# *Chapter 6*

## *Eleanora*

There's only one bed. What in the Afterlife are we supposed to do now? My stomach knots, heart pounding so hard I'm sure Tharion can hear it.

"I'll take the floor," he says quickly, obviously not wanting to share a bed with me. Disappointment sets in. Why did that hurt? Of course, he doesn't want to share a bed with me, he doesn't like me like that. I don't like him like that. *Keep telling yourself that.* But the floor? It's cold, and dirty. It's only one night, can't he suck it up for only one tiny night?

"Sure," I answer, as nonchalantly as I can, but even I hear the slight tremble in my voice. Tharion looks at me, question in his eyes. Am I reading this wrong? Why is he looking at me like that?

I walk beside the bed, putting my bag next to it so it's easy to grab if something happens.

"Unless… you want me to sleep with you?" he asks, almost shyly. He's never shy around me, this is so strange.

"I mean, it *is* big enough for us both. I don't mind, it's just for a night," I shrug, not wanting to make it sound like I'm desperate for him to sleep next to me – because I'm not. *Yes, you are.*

"Okay, I guess that should be fine." He puts his bag on the other side of the bed.

I walk to the washroom and start brushing my teeth with water and some herbal toothpaste I made for the journey. It's bad enough we have to ride smelly horses without also having to reek and have bad breath. Reaching for my hairbrush, I run it through my long, raven-black hair. Then I clean my face and walk outside to find Tharion sitting on the edge of the bed, deep in thought.

"Are you okay?" I sit down next to him, close enough that our shoulders touch slightly. The bed moves underneath my weight, tilting him closer to me.

"I'm just thinking about all of this. What if I can't save us? What if I don't make it? What if I can't protect… you?"
He looks at me with sorrow in his eyes, like he already knows the outcome of it all. I give him a nudge, trying to lighten the mood.

"Hey, I'm a big girl. I can look after myself," I joke, but I know it doesn't reach him like I hoped.
He sighs. "Ela, I mean it. I would never forgive myself if anything happened to you. You are the single most important person in my life. I lo-… I'm scared to lose you, okay?" His cheeks turn a rosy pink, as he's normally not the one talking about these kinds of things. It's new, a bit strange, but I like it.

I put my hand on his thigh, our eyes meeting.

"And I would never forgive myself if anything happened to you, Ari. We have each other's backs, just like we always have. I know you better than I know myself, I know you can do this. You are the strongest, brightest, bravest person I have ever known. I look up to you like you wouldn't believe, Tharion." I grab his hand in mine, tracing small circles on the top of his hand with my thumb, trying to calm his nerves.

The man in front of me, my best friend, is scared, and I can't help him. I feel so helpless. I want nothing more than for him to realize how capable he is, how much I believe in him. He looks down on my hand, then up into my eyes, those mossy green meadows of his entrancing me.

The soft scent of his soap brushes against my senses, goosebumps racing down my arms. Time wanders as his gaze locks with mine before dropping to my mouth. His tongue darts out, swiping over his bottom lip. I watch as his lips glisten, forgetting to breathe. Why do I feel like this?

I can feel the walls around my heart cracking, but something inside me knows that they weren't that strong to begin with. Not for Tharion. My heart has always belonged to Tharion Ashveil in some way, ever since that day when he gave me that wooden doll. I knew I would always want him as a part of my life, friend or lover - but recently I have been leaning harder against the latter.

My heart is rebelling in my chest, wanting so hard to break out. Tharion's face dips towards mine, painfully slow. I open my mouth slightly, inhaling the tension between us. His mouth is so close to mine, I can feel his breath on my lips.

"Ela, I–" a knock on the door disrupts the moment and I shoot up from the bed, my cheeks burning. Was he really going to kiss me?

"Coming!" I croak, trying to sound calm and collected, and totally failing at it.

Rowan is waiting outside the door, freshly bathed - probably from the river.

"I wanted to go over the plan for tomorrow," he says, eyes bouncing between Tharion and I.

"Sure thing, come on in." I gesture for him to enter the room and close the door behind him.

"It will take most of the day to get to Catariel, but if we start at dawn, we should be there by nightfall. These woods are festered with predatory animals, so we need to be on alert. I suggest you take the horses whilst I run beside you in my fox form. I am bigger than all the animals out there, so we would be safer that way."

Tharion nods. "That sounds like a good plan. Will you join us for breakfast at the tavern in the morning? The supper we had was wonderful." His eyes dart to me for a short second.

"I will be getting my own breakfast, but I will meet you here for some tea before we leave. I would like to meet the innkeeper and ask if she has heard or seen anything out of the ordinary the last few days."

Rowan stands up and walks to the door.

"Get some sleep, it will only be getting tougher from here on out. We will begin our training as soon as we reach the castle grounds, if the King lets us stay there." We both nod as Rowan leaves the room, closing the door behind him. I turn back to Tharion.

"I guess we should try to sleep. We haven't been getting much of it the last few nights." I can't look him in the eyes, scared that if I do, I might just hurl myself at him like I wanted to just moments prior.

"I agree," he clears his throat, "you go on to bed, I need to clean myself up a bit and then I'll join you." He jumps to his feet and walks steadily into the washroom, filling the basin with warm water and shuts the door.

I pinch myself in the arm. *Nope – definitely not dreaming.* The throbbing pain quickly dies out, proving to me that this is all real and Tharion did in fact try to kiss me. Does this change anything? Maybe he's just experiencing a lot of emotions right now. He's scared, terrified of what is to come, he just let that get the best of him. Yes, that must be it.

I change into my black cotton nightgown and climb in under the sheets. The mattress is a bit scratchy, but it feels soft enough. There's only one duvet, so we will have to share. That's fine. I will keep to my side and Tharion will keep to his. Right? Right.

I try my best to convince myself that I'm overthinking it all, keeping those somewhat thin walls steadily guarding my heart up. I am not letting myself hope, it will only break me.

Tharion exits a few minutes later, freshly washed and ready for bed. He gets to his side, then reaches behind the collar of his shirt and pulls it off. My heart does a flip in my chest. I get a perfect view of his strong back, muscles defined and carved. My cheeks go up in flames, but I can't get myself to look away. He unbuckles the belt of his trousers and lets them fall to the floor.

The curves of his back flow like a gentle river down to his toned thighs and enormous calves. My jaw hits my chest, mouth filling with water. Now I do look away, not wanting to meet his eyes when he eventually turns around. He puts on a sleeping shirt, a pale beige cotton with buttons all the way down the middle, and a pair of shorts to match.

Tharion turns around to face me and lifts the duvet up, before climbing into bed, laying down on his back with his hands tucked behind his head. He turns to face me, cheeks reddening slightly.

"Hey, I'm sorry about that earlier. I got caught up in everything and before I knew it, I was trying to kiss you. It was weird, and I'm sorry. I didn't mean to freak you out."

Freak me out? Yes, I was surprised. Very surprised even. But freaked out? No. Heat blooms beneath my skin, fists clenching under the cover.

Not wanting to make the situation worse by adding rage to the mix, I just shrug.

"Don't worry about it. See you in the morning."

Turning away from him, I pretend to go to sleep. My heart is still thundering in my chest, there's no way I will get to sleep feeling like this. What would have happened if he actually *did* kiss me? Would he still tell me it was weird?

"Good night, Eleanora," he says, a hint of disappointment in his voice.

"Good night, Tharion," I whisper back, heart still attacking my ribcage.

· · — ·✳· — · ·

I wake up sometime during the night. The sky is still pitch black and the whole village is sleeping. From the constellations visible on the sky from our window, I would guess we have about four hours until dawn. I turn to my back, letting out a frustrated huff.

"Can't sleep?" Tharion whispers, not wanting to startle me.

"No. I'm restless, and quite honestly I'm pretty upset about today," I say, suddenly feeling honest and brave.

"What do you mean? What upset you?" He sits up on his elbow, facing me now. His eyes are wide awake, but his under-eyes are dark and swollen. Has he not slept at all?

"You told me that kissing me would be weird. Any female would get upset by that!" I whisper-yell, my voice cracking slightly.

"No," he sighs, "I didn't mean it like that. Gods, Eleanora. I didn't mean that kissing you would be weird, I meant that *I* was acting weird."

I can sense the desperation in his voice, the Tharion I know absolutely hates confrontation.

"What would've happened if you actually did kiss me then, Ari? Would it still be weird? Would you ignore me out of embarrassment? Look, I know you don't feel that way against me, and that's completely fine. You are my best friend, and I guess sometimes those feelings are hard to separate." I try to reason his emotions, but I don't even believe my own words. "Like you said, you were caught up in it all. No harm was done, so can we please just leave it be?" I beg, a little out of breath. He just stares at me, his face impossible to read in the dim light.

"I…" he starts, lost for words, "I suppose so."
Why won't he fight for me? If he tried to kiss me because he likes me, why won't he tell me I'm wrong?

That's the confirmation I needed, and I'll be damned if I let myself get this close to being hurt again. I put those bricks back in their place, strengthening the cement holding them together. I will not let myself get hurt again. Tears well in my eyes, coating the inside of my nose. I sniffle. Tharion reaches out for me, but I turn away from him again, scooting to the very edge of the bed, putting as much distance between us as possible.

When I wake up at dawn, I feel really warm. Hot almost. My body temperature is a lot warmer than normal. It takes a few moments to register why. Tharion must have come over during the night, and now he's laying flush against my body with his arm over my waist.

It feels… safe. I know I told myself just a few hours ago that I wouldn't let myself get hurt again, that I wouldn't let myself feel these things, but laying here in my best friend's arms, arms that I have fantasized too many times about having around me, just like this, feels so incredibly nice. I cherish the moment for a little while longer before I snap my guards back up and move slightly so that he'll pull his arms back.

"Tharion, wake up. It's time to go," I whisper to him, not wanting to wake him too harshly. He grunts and puts his arm back around my waist, holding me closer.

"Tharion. Wake up." I raise my voice slightly louder. With a huff, I remove his arm and start getting out of bed.

"Hey," he says, his raspy sleep voice is mesmerizing. Nope, not going there. *Focus, Eleanora.*

"Hey," I answer, my tone sharp. "I'm going downstairs to get some breakfast and meet up with Rowan. Just come down when you're ready and we'll leave." I get up, grab my satchel and head for the washroom. Shutting the door behind me, I lean the back of my head against it and let out a long exhale. Why did I let that happen? This is not the time for these feelings – we are literally out here to save the realm from an evil demon sorcerer!

I splash some water on my face, brush my teeth and head out the door. As I open it, Tharion is standing there in only his trousers. His broad shoulders and sculpted middle catch my attention, but I quickly look away. The deep auburn bedhead is out of control, locks of fire curling in every direction.

I chuckle to myself. He *is* my best friend, I remind myself. Might as well make the best of it for the remainder of time we have left in this realm.

"You look like you slept upside down," I say, trying to keep a straight face, keeping my upset-facade up a little bit longer.

"I feel like I slept upside down too. And under water," he adds, half smiling. I can tell that he feels bad, he can barely look at me. I put my bag down and walk up to him, brushing a strand of hair away from his eyes. We hold our stare for a moment, none of us really sure what to do, so I take the first step and put my arms around his middle, holding him tight. I feel his tense body relax, exhaling a long breath.

His arms snake around my shoulders and neck, planting a kiss on the top of my head.

"I'm sorry, Ari," I start, but he cuts me off.

"No, don't. I'm sorry. I suggest we do as you asked, we put this behind us and focus on saving the realm. Can you forgive me for being a real gryphon's ass?"
I chuckle. "Of course I can, if you can forgive me for lashing out."

"Don't mention it. I would never not forgive you, Ela."
We stand like that for a while, holding each other tightly, forgetting the

world around us for just a moment. I drag in the scent of him. He smells like sleep and a freshly awakened body, intoxicating to my senses. It makes my nerves go limp, like they know I'm home. Because that is what Tharion has always been to me – home.

# Chapter 7

## Tharion

The smell of freshly baked bread coats the air as we enter the tavern. Candles light up the room, giving it a warm, cosy mood - just what you want when you are about to embark on a dangerous, life-risking journey, right? We walk up to the bar where the innkeeper is cleaning off mugs and chalets from the previous night's festivities, meeting us with a warm smile.

"Good morning, friends! Did you sleep well?" She winks at me. My cheeks heat, feeling them darkening by the second.

"Thank you for your hospitality, I'm glad we could spend the night in a warm bed instead of outside. Is that fresh bread I smell? It is making my mouth water", I say, steering the topic away from what I assume she thinks happened in that room. Did she give us one bed on purpose?

"You are correct! I just took out the last batch from the oven, would you like some with our homemade jam?"

My stomach growls loudly, a cheeky smirk unfolding on the innkeeper's kind face.

"I take that as a yes, then." Chuckles trill from her lips as she turns around, heading into the kitchen. Eleanora plops down on a stool, a distant look on her face.

"Hey, are you okay?" I ask, putting my hand over hers. She stiffens slightly at the touch, then relaxes again.
Eleanora sighs. "Just thinking about how ridiculously unprepared we are and how we are supposed to make it three days without harm. Do you think we will even get to Catariel?"

My cheeks heat, eyes falling to the wooden countertop. Is it because I don't know how to fight? That I don't know how to use my magic for anything other than making small sheds? I look away, not wanting to show her how bad I feel for putting her through all of this.

"We have Rowan, remember. He's strong and will fight if something sneaks up on us during travel," my body turns away, "I'm sorry I'm not fit for this type of mission."

Eleanora's eyes widen, mouth opens, then shuts, unable to form words.

"N-No. I didn't mean it like that, Ari. No, not for one moment did I think that we wouldn't make it because of you," she sharpens her tone, turning her body towards me.

"I have never been outside Sylvarn. I've only ever heard stories about the other villages around us. If anything, Tharion, I think the only way this journey is possible is because I have you by my side." Her wine-dark haze bores deep into my eyes, finding my soul behind them.

I see her determination written all over her face, refusing to let me feel small and unworthy, "but I have every right to be afraid, to let myself feel like I for once in my life have something to lose." She holds my hand, giving it a tender squeeze before letting go.

The innkeeper swings around a corner of the kitchen, plates filled with soft bread, sweet jam and fresh apples cut into small slices. She sets the plates in front of us, grabs two clean mugs from the bar and turns to pick up a carafe of steaming, brown liquid.

"Home-brewed Dawnflower tea. You will need it for the ride to keep yourselves awake and alert." Scalding hot liquid pours into the mugs, thick steam ascending, clouding the air in a sweet-bitter scent. Picking up a small pot, she tilts it towards us.

"Honey? The tea itself is quite bitter, I prefer it on the sweet side," she winks at Eleanora. Our heads bob enthusiastically, watching as the kind woman puts a small spoon of honey in each of our drinks.

"I'm so sorry, but it seems we never got your name. You have been so hospitable and kind to us, it would be only fair if we could give our thanks to you by your name," Eleanora says, holding her mug between both her hands, inhaling the bitter and earthy scent.

The woman smiles proudly. "My name is Camille, I run this fine establishment and have been for the last 175 years." Camille puts down the towel she was using to wipe her hands and walks around the bar, taking a seat next to me.

"It is a pleasure to meet you, Camille. My name is Eleanora, and this is Tharion. Our friend outside is Rowan." Eleanora leans over to shake her hand.

The front door creaks loudly as a large man walks in, heavy footsteps causing the floor to vibrate. We all turn around, Camille's face lighting up with adoration.

She jumps off her stool and skips to the male, throwing her arms around his waist. His sharp cerulean eyes soften when he gets an eye on her, and they fall into a warm embrace. Camille gives the male a passionate kiss, completely ignoring that we are sitting here. I look over to Eleanora, watching her cheeks deepen in colour, eyes glistening, as if spellbound. She's softly smiling at the couple, admiring their show of affection.

How I yearn to be able to hold her like that. To wrap my arms around her body and greet her with passionate kisses whenever I see her. My stomach knots, jealousy overtaking the moment. Dragging my gaze from the couple, fists clenched, I clear my throat loudly before taking a deep sip of my tea.

The couple's embrace comes to an end, arms falling to their sides as Camille turns toward us. Her cheeks flush pink as she clears her throat.

"Eleanora, Tharion, this is my husband, Alaric. He works as a blacksmith for the King's men. Alaric makes the weapons for their journeys across the realm." Her voice is proud, eyes sparkling with affection as they meet his. Alaric smiles fondly at her before turning to us.

"It's a pleasure to meet you, travellers. Where have you come from?" he asks, curiously. Alaric plops down next to Eleanora as Camille grabs him a mug of tea with two scoops of honey in before reaching over and placing it in front of him. He gives her a wide smile and a wink, turning her cheeks a sweet shade of magenta.

"We came riding from Sylvarn, just arrived last night. Unfortunately, we will be leaving after our delicious meal. We need to get to Catariel and the King as soon as possible," I start as I turn to Camille, "I was meaning to ask you, Camille, have you been experiencing anything weird lately?" I keep my voice gentle, open.

Camille looks at Alaric, brows scrunching between her eyes. Alaric straightens in his seat.

"You mean the dark spirits, do you not?"
My stomach drops. I turn back to him, carefully nodding.

"How did you know? Have you seen them too?"
His gaze falls to his lap. "We know too well what these spirits are capable of."
Camille walks around the counter and puts her arm across her husband's shoulders, gently stroking the side of his neck, comforting him. I look between them, trying to figure out what they mean, but I fail.

"We were attacked in our forest back home. I do not know what the spirit looked like, we only saw its disgusting red eyes. It kept slashing our trees and destroying boulders around us," Eleanora interjects, her gaze zoning out as she remembers that horrible day.

"When we thought it had left, we heard a scream so piercing I felt it in my soul. I have never been so scared in my entire life." Her eyes glaze with the memory, hands trembling in her lap. I take them in mine, shooting her a soft smile, watching her shoulders fall back down from under her earlobes.

If I could only give her a kiss to let her know she was safe, that no one could harm her as long as I was here to protect her. Camille walks over to Eleanora, putting her hand on her shoulder.

"That was a Nochtra. A spirit conjured by only the darkest sorcerers. It feasts on fear, scaring its victims to near death before devouring their souls. It will only show you their disgusting red eyes, just so you feel the presence of evil around you." Her shoulders shiver. "Their shriek of horror will mar your bones for centuries to come, my dear. I am so sorry." Eleanora looks down at her half-empty plate, shoulders slumping, pushing out a shaky breath.

"We know on a personal level the horrors those spirits can conjure. Alaric and I have met them once before, but then their evil master still walked this realm with us. Before he was banished behind the Veil with the other dark spirits. If they are walking among us once more, it seems the Veil has cracked, and if that is the case - we are in serious trouble." I shudder as Camille's warning hangs in the air.

"That's why we embarked on this journey. To ask the King for an audience, to warn him about the terrors to come. In some twisted way, it seems *I* am the one destined to overthrow these spirits and their master." I hesitate, wondering if I should tell them about my father's abilities. Against better judgement, I proceed.

"You see… My father was a Seer, but kept his power a secret to protect us, though in the end, he was taken from me by force." My voice falters, words fading out.

"I don't know if I have what it takes to take him, but I will give it my all. For my father. For Kyrris."
Alaric puts his hand on my shoulder, squeezing lightly. His posture is soft, as if understanding the sacrifice we're about to make. Turning back to Eleanora, his eyes darken.

"Their master is Vorathiel, he was banished–"

"By Ilyra Lightvein just after the beginning of time," Eleanora finishes his sentence. Alaric nods.

"Our daughter, Amariel, was taken by Vorathiel when she was just a little girl. She is trapped behind the Veil with those monsters, never to be able to return to us."
He looks at me. "Until you showed up, Tharion." Alaric's cerulean gaze wanders to his wife as her head bows, eyes filled with tears.

"I will make you a sword to bring on your journey. Stay for an extra night, I promise you that you will not be too late for Catariel and the King. Give me the day to craft some weapons for you to take on your journey, to keep you safe. Let me put my elven magic into them to make them stronger. I do not ask this with ease, Tharion, I beg on my knees. You are our last and only hope to ever see Amariel again. Will you accept my offer, and stay here just one more night?" Alaric pleads, begging us to stay.

A lump forms in my chest, holding my heart still, unable to move. I try to breathe, but my lungs won't drag in air.

"But I… I do not know how to wield a weapon, I barely have control over my magic. What use would I have of a sword?"

Alaric's wide chest puffs. "Put your faith in me, my friend, and I will prove to you that it will not be wasted." He places his fist over his heart, a token of trust among elves. How is he putting his trust in me so easily? These people have never met me, never heard of me before now, but they still believe I can do this.

So, I will. I have to do this, for him and Camille. For Amariel and my father. For everyone in this realm that are unknowingly putting their lives in my hands. Courage blossoms in my chest, heat radiating through my torso.

I dip my chin. "You have my faith, Alaric. We will stay for one more night, but we will have to leave by morning – with or without your weapons. I thank you for your belief in me. I will do my best not to let you or your family down." Hopping down from my stool, I walk over to him, reaching out my hand. He grabs my forearm with his and I hold him fast. We nod in unison, a silent agreement made.

"Now that we have some extra time, can one of you tell me about this Vorathiel and why he is making our lives so difficult?" I try to lighten the mood. The others lower their shoulders, letting out their held breaths.

Alaric turns to his wife. "Camille, will you get our guests some pie? This will take a while, and they will need something sweet to counter the bitterness of this horror story."

Nodding, Camille walks up behind the counter, into the kitchen and reemerges with two small plates. On each plate is a small piece of pie, blueberry if I know my berries right, dusted in powdered sugar. The sweet scent fills the room, my mouth watering. She sets them down before us and fills up our mugs with fresh tea.

Alaric turns towards us both, leaning his elbows right above his knees and starts telling the story.

"Before the beginning of time…"

# Chapter 8

*Alaric/Crone of White Flame*

Before the beginning of time, the two realms lived in peace. Spirits of the Afterlife would walk the same land as mortals, though most living people would never be able to claim seeing them. Spirits would wander around in an existence of their own, as if they had never lost their lives, and continued daily routines to continue even after Death's sweet embrace. A rare few mortals would sense them, some would even talk to them and interact with them.

At the time, Necromancers walked the thin line between living and dead. The study of Necromancy contained dark magic, spells to bring the dead back to the realm of the living and had been revered as a study to honour the dead. Now, scholars of the present were not allowed to study the ancient texts of Necromancy, as the professors fear history repeating itself.

But back then, in the first village, Aethernis, people and beings of all kinds resided alongside the spirits. The sky filled with ancient creatures, Pegasus and dragons sharing the winds as their wings brought them across the realm. People were kind, helpful, living off the land together in harmony.

As time went on, as Death claimed her first souls, an invisible border divided the people. Magical schools would teach healing magic, but as the need to know what the Afterlife held grew stronger, texts of death magic found its way into the hands of young scholars. Spirits were called on unwillingly, conjured by sorcerers, witches and elves, forced to leave the realm of Death for the living's own entertainment.

With time, the spirits grew angry, dark, their souls so restless that they lost their way back to the Afterlife - trapped in the realm of the Living.

Like all witches, Ilyra Lightvein was born into a coven. As her siblings and friends, she called on her magic, bending the elements at her will. Except, Ilyra was not at all like the other witches in her coven. Her sisters had long, raven hair with dark eyes, only being able to call on their magic by sacrificing blood to the Goddess. Ilyra, with her blinding white hair, did not have use for sacrifices. Her magic hummed under her skin, sacrifice or not, ready to twist and bend at her command.

Growing older, her magic grew stronger, and she fell out with friends and family. An outcast in the village. She was forbidden into school as professors believed she possessed evil spirits, that her being different meant she had no good to offer the realm. Ilyra would spend her time outside, studying nature, surrounding herself with every living thing the realm had to offer - except her peers.

Her favourite place was a nearby meadow. Flowers in deep purples, bright oranges and pinks would flood the green earth, air packed with the citrusy-sweet scent of their nectar. Ilyra would make beautiful crowns, wearing them on her head as if she ruled nature itself. Most days, Ilyra would keep herself busy, tending to the flowers or interacting with wildlife.

Other days, her tears felt never-ending as they soaked the ground beneath her. No matter how hard she tried to fill her time with everything else, her soul never felt whole. The aching, tender feeling of emptiness always loomed over her, reminding her of her journey in this realm - abandoned and alone.

Wiping her tears with the back of her hand, Ilyra drags in a deep sniffle. Her eyes feel sore and swollen, mouth dry as dirt.

*Why did you abandon me, Goddess?*

Her prayers go unanswered, to no surprise. As she clenches her fists, the sky above darkens, bright sunshine nothing but a memory. Cold rain falls from heavy clouds, soaking her dress. The aching in her chest only grows as thunder echoes in the air, carrying its loud roars through the realm. She brings her knees up to her chest, hugging them tight, letting the rain drown out her tears. Sobs rip from her body, broken screams faltering while thunder splits the air.

Ilyra's heart stammers as a blanket is thrown over her shoulders, warmth shooting through her bones. Looking up, a set of azure eyes stare back at her. A male, about her age, panting as rain drips from his pointy features. Ilyra's eyes widen, scooting away from the stranger, pushing as much distance between them as possible.

"Who are you?" she calls through roars of thunder, her voice barely carrying over the loudness around her. The stranger tilts his head, his dark brows scrunching between his eyes, question written over them.

"*That's* how you react when someone tries to help you?" he scoffs as a smile creeps over his face.

"I saw you sitting in the rain, and as the gentleman I am, I figured I would help. *That* was a mistake."
Ilyra watches him as he treads towards her, approaching as if she were a feral animal, his words soft and his face kind. The rain slows as only the occasional droplet hits the wet earth, clouds parting in the sky. The stranger scans her face, a look of amazement in his gaze.

"You did that, didn't you? The weather, you controlled it?"
Ilyra stares at him, then nods carefully. The male breaks out in laughter, deep sound vibrating through her.

"That is amazing! I've never heard of a witch being able to control nature itself. You sure are something special." He crouches in front of her, reaching out a wet hand.

"I'm Vorathiel. Mind if I join you?"
Stunned, Ilyra stares blankly at the person in front of her, studying him. His features are sharp, almost like a crow. His hair drops to just below his shoulders, black as the night, forming an eclipse around the glittering blue eyes in the middle of his face. He's handsome. As he shoots her a cheeky smirk, electricity shoots down her arms.
She straightens, releasing the hold on her knees.
"I… I'm Ilyra."
"Well, Ilyra. It's nice to meet you. Now, is there room for one more on this giant meadow?" he winks.
"Why do you want to hang here with me? You don't know me." Her stomach knots as her heart drums in her chest, the all-too familiar feelings of anxiety and impending deceit approaching her with haste.
"... yet. I don't know you *yet*. From what you just did, though, I would love to at least *try* to get to know you. If you'd let me." Vorathiel flashes a smile, his slightly crooked teeth a soft pearly white. It's pretty.
Apprehensive, she gives him a nod, moving ever so slightly to her left as if there wasn't room beside her. He chuckles, plopping down on the wet grass. The smell of rain and meadow flowers is heavy in the air, a calming scent. Ilyra closes her eyes, dragging it in.
"Tell me. How did you do that?"
She sighs, "I don't actually know. I have always been able to use my magic to bend nature. It's like an extra set of emotions, if you will." Vorathiel huffs a laugh, his gaze dancing over her face, taking her in.
"I think that's pretty neat. What has you all the way out here? I don't think I've seen you in the village before."
Ilyra's chest tightens painfully. "I like it here. There are no," scanning the male's body, "...people."
The warm vibrations of his laugh ring into the air, surrounding her in a blanket of joy, tugging at her lips. Her chest starts tickling, the urge to laugh overwhelming. As she opens her mouth, music slips from her lips, mingling with Vorathiel's laughter. The sun breaks from behind the clouds, illuminating the realm. Vorathiel looks to the sky, a wide grin stretching across his face.

"Hah! Would you look at that. I can't be *that* bad, seeing that the sun came out," he shoots her a wink, colouring her cheeks a deep shade of cerise.

Ilyra hides her face, turning her body opposite to Vorathiel. A warm hand cups her jaw, pulling it back to meet him. His hand lingers on her cheek, grazing his calloused thumb across the tops of her cheekbone.

"There is no need to hide, Ilyra. I will not harm you, nor make you feel unwanted. I would very much like to be your friend."
Her brows knit together, the corners of her lips dragging downwards.

"But why?"

"Call it a *feeling*. It feels like I should be your friend. Is that so bad?"
Was it? Opening her heart to someone had never turned out good in the past, her family and friends had turned on her. Would Vorathiel?
With a soft shake to her head, Ilyra shrugs.

"I suppose not."


*"Wait. I thought this was a sad story?" Eleanora cuts in, head tilted to the side.*

*I chuckle. "Give it time, dear traveller. Let me finish the story. Anyway…"*


Ilyra and Vorathiel met out on the meadow every day, Vorathiel spoke about his lessons, what new spells he had mastered, how his classmates had failed miserably at potion making and almost blew the whole school to bits – and Ilyra would listen, laughing and gasping as the stories rolled off his tongue. With every passing moment, Ilyra found herself letting the unbreakable walls around her heart crack, welcoming Vorathiel in. Her heart would crave his closeness, his laughter and ridiculous stories.

She found herself waiting impatiently for him to arrive at the meadow, pacing until she heard his heavy footsteps on the grass. The once constant feeling of emptiness slowly ebbed, her soul carefully rebuilding, filling with Vorathiel. His presence gave her peace, grounded her when her emotions got to her, when the clouds above her head turned dark and heavy.

Summer faded to autumn, the seasons changing as Ilyra and Vorathiel grew closer. The roots of their bond went deep beyond their souls, twisted and mingled as one. Soon, Ilyra would feel Vorathiel even before she could see him, and he would sense her emotions without looking to the sky.

Vorathiel turns to Ilyra, heart thundering in his heart.

"Tell me you feel this too. This connection to you, I cannot describe it. It's like… I don't even know. It's like I can *feel* you even when we're not together."

"And when we say goodbye, your heart empties completely? The warmth slowly replaced by cold nothingness?"

His chin dips, silence enveloping them. As they sit there, shoulder to shoulder, their hearts aching for each other, his fingers fall to hers, gently interlacing them. Ilyra's heart combusts, an explosion of heat radiating through her at his touch. His hand trembles as he faces her, their eyes meeting as the sky opens up, lightning striking behind them.

The ground shakes, thunder hammering against her eardrums, Vorathiel's gaze falling to her lips. Ilyra's breath hitches, lungs crying for her to draw breath, heart pounding on the cage surrounding it. The smells of char and rain float with the wind, surrounding them as their hearts inevitably drift closer together, desperate with their longing.

As Vorathiel's lips collide with hers, his arm reaches out, hoisting her on top of his lap. Her legs are firmly planted on each side of his thighs, soul firmly planted within him. His hand snakes up her back, finding the base of her neck, holding on to her white locks as soft whimpers slip past her lips.

The kiss is all-consuming, like the world around them ceased to exist the moment their lips touched. Ilyra breaks the kiss, her breaths heavy as her eyes dive into the sea of stars that is Vorathiel.

"Vorathiel, I-"

His hand shoots up, covering her mouth. His eyes shimmer above rosy-pink cheeks, crooked teeth flashing under his smile.

"Don't say anything. Just let your body feel. Feel this, feel us. Feel me." Before she can say anything, his lips crash down on hers once more, their teeth and tongues brawling.

The world spins as Ilyra's back is gently pushed to the earth, Vorathiel's black locks fall into his face as he stares at her from above. His rough hand caresses her cheek, following the curve of her neck, down to her collarbone. Shivers race through her, heat pooling in her stomach. He leans down, hovering just above her face. The graze of his warm breath against her skin has her gasping for air.

"The bond between us was written before time existed. But the thread between us is no longer just fate - it is choice. I choose you, Ilyra. I choose you in every realm, in every life. I will always choose you."

The words flow like music from his lips, through her body and into her soul. As tears line her eyes, her hand reaches for his face. As her thumb tenderly rubs his cheek, silent sobs pass her lips. The longing in her heart shatters as his words plant themselves deep within it. For the first time in her life, she is chosen. She is loved. And she loves him, endlessly.

"Ilyra, my blossom. When I met you, you were but an empty shell. Your spirit had left you, leaving you feeling empty, unworthy. I felt that little spark that remained of that spirit, how it yearned for someone to see it, to free it. It drew me to you, making it impossible for me to leave you on that meadow. I would, and will, never leave you - you are an extension of my soul. You are my best friend, I would ruin anyone who tried to hurt you, even if one day that turned out to be myself."
The air splits as the heavens bellow above them. His mouth falls to hers, the realm around them falling into oblivion.

· · — ·✳· — · ·

The years pass, their bond only growing stronger with each touch, each kiss. Ilyra had never experienced anything like this before - the all-consuming, suffocating and wild emotion of love. Her heart feels too small in her chest, her fingers twitching with the never-ending need to touch his skin, to take in his scent and hear his voice. Their bond refuses to let them go long without being together, the pain of their souls screaming too heavy to bear.

One day, as Ilyra rests under an old oak tree at the edge of the meadow, the sound of Vorathiel's boots echo above the earth. As if her soul forced her out of slumber, her eyes gently open, his body appearing before her. A wicker basket hangs from his forearm, the sweet scent of pastries and flowers seeping from it. Ilyra's mouth waters at both the sight and the delicious smell, a wide grin stretching across her face.

With a thump, Vorathiel sets the basket down, leaning over to plant a tender kiss to her lips. Her cheeks flush, heat coursing through her body. Her eyes fall to a book sticking out of the basket. The leather is torn, old, with deep burgundy lettering.

She points at the book. "What is that? Are you reading me a story?"

Vorathiel chuckles, folding a lock of her hair behind her ear.

"You are stunning, my blossom. Each day, you become more beautiful. Each day, my love for you grows tenfold."

Blush burns her cheeks, the feelings still so foreign, but so very welcome.

She leans over on her wrists, pressing a warm kiss to his cheek. His face turns as her lips touch his scruffed cheek, their lips colliding instead. Her ears ring as her heart skips a beat, the air in her lungs trapped inside. Breaking the kiss, Ilyra gulps down mouthfuls of air, Vorathiel letting out a deep laugh.

"I have found a way for us to be together, in every life."

Ilyra's brows knit between her eyes, a nervous laugh escaping her throat.

"What do you mean, in every life? We are together, our life is right here."

Vorathiel shakes his head, a low rumbling chuckle vibrating in the air. "I found a way to be with you, even in the Afterlife."

Her body goes cold. What does he mean, "in the Afterlife"?

*No. No, tell me it isn't true.* Ilyra sits up, backing up a bit. Her chest tightens at the thought of her Vorathiel dipping into the death magic that has been known as nothing but dark and hateful in the realm.

"Tell me you haven't. Tell me you won't."

"It's the only way we can be together forever. The only way our bonded souls will never separate. Is that not what you want?" The smile on his face melts as his brows tip upwards. His voice is desperate, pleading.

Ilyra stands up. "Promise me you won't fall into the shadows of dark magic, of Necromancy. Swear to me, Vorathiel. The life we have right now, the one we get to share today, put your focus on that. Do not worry yourself with what comes after our time is out. When Death comes to guide us into the Afterlife, our souls will be at rest. Let them rest, Vorathiel."

He jumps up, reaching out for her - but she rejects him. His hands float in the air, desperate for her to come closer, to show him that she wants to be with him.

"Swear to me!"

"I can't!" he sobs, "I cannot stand the thought of us falling apart after our time in this realm is done. I cannot imagine myself without you, blossom. You are the reason I exist, as I am the reason *you* exist. Don't you see? I'm doing this for *you. For us. "*

Her stomach turns, the blood in her veins freezing as his words send chills over her skin.

"I would put the realm in eternal darkness to be with you, Ilyra. There is *nothing* I wouldn't do for you."

"Do this for me. Stop this. Put this insane idea to rest. Be with me here, now, in this realm."

Her tears fall, streaks lining her fair skin as they drip from her chin. Vorathiel's eyes darken, his tremble gone. Slowly, he walks up to her, hands cupping her jaws as tears still pour from her eyes.

"You will see. One day, you *will* see. Your soul will cry for mine, and then - you will see the sacrifices I made for you."

Vorathiel picks up the basket, turning on his heel and walks off - leaving Ilyra under the crushing feeling of abandonment.

· · — ·✶· — · ·

Ilyra finds herself out on the meadow every day, waiting for him to come back. The need to talk, to mend, is drowning her. Her heart follows a constant gallop in her chest, restless, on edge. It yearns for her soul-bonded mate. As her white aura stretches for the obsidian black of Vorathiel, it falters. She can feel him putting distance between them, tearing at the fibres of their bond. It needs to end, she needs to find him, before the pain becomes too heavy to stand.

Feeling for her mate, Ilyra follows the bond through the village, to the outskirts. A worn-down cottage lays on a bed of overgrown weeds, bare trees surrounding it.

"Vorathiel!" she calls out, the bond between them feeling warmer. The tall male emerges from a cellar beneath the cottage, relief washing over her as his eyes find hers. She runs up to him, throwing her arms around his waist, knocking him back a step. His lips place a kiss to the top of her head, lifting the weight off her shoulders. Her lungs drag in fresh air for the first time in what feels like an eternity.

"I couldn't bear to be without you, not a second longer," her voice laces in tears, throat feeling impossibly tight as she buries her face in his shirt. His arms hold her in a tight embrace, a low rumbling in his chest vibrating in Ilyra's ears. She drags in his scent, but the scent has changed.

The once earthy, fresh scent of his skin is now infected with a sickly-sweet scent unfamiliar to Ilyra. Lifting her face from his chest, she looks up at him. The oceans once deep in his eyes now heavy with shadows - grey smoke swirling around his dark pupils. His mouth perks into a smile, but the warmth doesn't reach his eyes anymore.

"I knew you would come back. All this time, you stayed away while I made sure our future would never be broken. Come, blossom. I have something I would like to show you."

Her body freezes as his hand finds hers, guiding her to the cellar doors. The stench meeting her knocks the breath from her lungs. Immediately, she recognizes the unfamiliar scent from Vorathiel's shirt. It's the sickly-sweet smell of rot and decomposition. Of death. Ilyra peers down the stairs, low moans echoing up to them. A pressing feeling of discomfort rises in her stomach, her instincts telling her to turn around, to leave. Ilyra slowly takes one step at a time until she comes to an abrupt halt, the air in her lungs suddenly stolen from her.

What meets her in that dark cellar is a sight taken from a nightmare. People, no, *things*, are tethered to the walls by magical chains, entrancing them in a mindless undead state. At one time, they had been the beings of their realm, now empty shells where the poor people had once existed. Their flesh is rotting, bones sticking out, their eyes glowing yellow, hungry.

A gasp escapes Ilyra's mouth, her hand clapping over it too late to muffle the sound. The beings snap out of their trance, now yanking and pulling on the chains, desperate to get to her. The smell of rotting flesh makes her stomach churn, vomit threatening to escape her body. She turns to leave, desperate to forget the horrors terrorizing her mind.

"Are they not magnificent?" Vorathiel's voice is calm, an undertone of pride seeping through his tone. Magnificent? Had he lost his mind?

"What- what is this, Vorathiel?" As if the beings sense fear, they tear and yank at their chains, starving for her.

"I told you I would stop at nothing to be with you, to ensure we could be together in every life. This, my blossom, will make the realm bend at *my* will."

Ilyra yanks her hand free from his and runs back up the stairs, bursting into the cold night air. Folding in two, she empties her stomach onto the earth, heaving for air between gags. Vorathiel's heavy steps close in on her, the stench of death like a blanket around him. As he emerges, Ilyra straightens herself.

"What are they?"

"They are sacrifices made in the name of our bond." His cold voice sends shivers across her scalp, body cold and clammy.

"No… Tell me you… Tell me you didn't take their lives!" Ilyra's eyes clamp shut as realization dawns on her. She turns to run, but Vorathiel's strong hand grabs her wrist, pulling her towards him.

"Don't you see? I did this for *you*!"
Spit shoots from his seething mouth, his breath heavy in his chest.

"I love you, Ilyra! I cannot imagine a world without you beside me, I *had* to do this!" He shakes her as the words fall from his lips, her wrists aching as his grip tightens painfully.

"You murdered innocent people, Vorathiel! For what? What purpose does that serve you?" Her heart breaks in her chest, tears streaming down her face. The sky above them opens as rain washes over them, soaking the earth in an instant. Through the shower, Vorathiel's voice breaks through.

"They have gathered me power. I have more power than Death herself, so much power that we will never have to be separated." His laugh comes out in bursts, nervous and manic.

"Nothing can stop me now, blossom. When I blanket our realm in darkness, my precious helpers will forever gather me power as new souls enter the realm. The realm of spirits will not keep me from you, it will help us remain together!"

Ilyra watches her soulmate, or the shell of which once was him. Now, a stranger standing before her.

"How could you… Do you not see what this has done to you? To us?" she cries out, ripping her wrists from his grip, "this obsession you have with the Afterlife, with our bond, has blinded you to the consequences of your actions. You have taken innocent lives, Vorathiel! You could have been with me, we could have made a life, a happy life, together! Now, that can never be."

His mask slips, revealing a scowl as her words stab him over and over. His face contorts into one of disgust, of ignorance. He reaches for her, but she steps back.

"I did this for you. I thought you loved me."

"I did. Every part of me has belonged to you since before time. But now, you are but a stranger wearing the face of a man I once loved." Turning, she runs from Vorathiel, pain ripping her soul to shreds. As the heavy rain falls over them, her footsteps kicking up mud, putting as much distance between them as possible. She can feel their bonded souls shatter, breaking within her, forcing her to her knees.

They hit the ground, soaking up the mud. A scream rips from her chest, heavens roaring as thunder cracks the air in two. Wind picks up around her, silencing the realm beyond.

Stumbling to her feet, Ilyra pushes herself back to the meadow. The flowers have wilted, trees have shed their leaves. Emptiness and death surrounds her in every direction. With a surge, white light ejects itself from her fingertips, spewing from her eyes and mouth. As light casts the meadow in blinding white, her powers course through her body, mind screaming for her to protect herself, to protect her realm. To stop him from blanketing it in darkness.

The world goes dark around her, black clouds filling the sky above. Behind her, the growing sound of growls and moans comes closer. Slowly, she turns around, Vorathiel's dark figure meeting her gaze at the end of the meadow. Flanking her soulmate are the eyes of sickly yellow glow, casting the forest in a haze of shadow. Power pools in Ilyra's palms, ready to eject at her command.

"Vorathiel! You need to stop this!"
The low hum of his voice carries in the wind, a chant conjuring evil spilling from his lips. Cries of terror, pleads for help, ring through the air as Vorathiel's abominations tear their villagers apart, harvesting their powers. The haunting sound of souls ripped from their bodies chilling her to her core. Ilyra's stomach turns, their pleads embedding themselves in her bones.

Rage blinds her as she shoots a ball of light at him, sending him soaring through the air. His body crashes against a tree, shaking the ground. With a thump, Vorathiel lands on the earth, battling consciousness. Racing towards him, Ilyra holds her hands in front of her, ready to fire another blow.

"Vorathiel, please! Please, end this horror!" she pleads, but they fall short in the winds surrounding them. Stumbling to his feet, blood seeping from his forehead, Vorathiel looks at her with a bone-chilling grin. As she halts, his grin grows wider.

"Blossom, don't you see? It cannot be stopped. The Fates wove our souls together, this is what they *wanted* for us. I am simply doing what was already destined to happen."

The sky darkens as thundering claps roar above them. It is so dark, not even the pale moonlight can cut through it. Vorathiel sprints towards Ilyra, throwing her to the ground. White pain blinds her as her head screams, vision blurring momentarily. He straddles her, holding her hands above her head, the vicious grin still plastered on his face. Ilyra kicks her legs, trying to escape, but his body is too strong.

"Ilyra," he spits, his arms straining to hold her down, "you are the strongest witch to have ever existed. Now, with my power, we can rule the entire realm. We would be invincible, for the rest of time. Don't you want that?" The way his eyes haze with dark swirls of shadow has Ilyra's body trembling.

The man she devoted her heart and soul to, who she let inside her walls, the shell of Vorathiel, stares deep into her eyes. His once deep cerulean eyes are completely overshadowed in darkness, hiding the last resemblance of her soulmate. His weight steals the air from her lungs, slowly suffocating her.

The cold hand of Death hovers above her, but she refuses to take it. She will not die, not by the hands of Vorathiel. Closing her eyes, rain pooling in the sockets, her magic surges in her chest. It swells before exploding, a pillar of light shooting from her, slashing Vorathiel's shoulder. He cries out, throwing himself off her. His shoulder gushes with dark crimson, the skin around blistering and charred. Ilyra gulps down air, life pouring back into her body.

Turning to her stomach, she uses her arms to crawl away from him as his shrieks of pain echo through the heavy air. Stumbling to her feet, her magic hums under her skin once more, white light encompassing her. Closing her eyes, she draws forward every last drop of power, chanting into the shadows surrounding them:

*"Evil wrought by hand or breath,*
*Sorcerer bound in chains of death,*
*Spirits foul, begone, confined,*
*Sealed in ward by will and sign."*

White vines of pure light shoot from the ground, dirt and mud raining over them, as they wrap around Vorathiel's waist - holding him down. The vines tighten, Vorathiel's grunts of discomfort and pain cutting through Ilyra's chest. The rain picks up speed, now showering them in freezing water, Ilyra's sorrow deepening.

"Ilyra," his breath comes out shaky, shallow, "what are you doing? Blossom, please!" Clamping her eyes harder, magic still pouring from her, Ilyra continues the chant:

*"A wall of light, a shield of flame,*
*No power breaks, no soul may claim.*
*By star above and earth below,*
*Be still, be bound, no more to go."*

Vorathiel shrieks as white flames engulf him, the smell of burnt earth and flesh assaulting her senses. Her eyes spring open, taking in her mate. Walking towards him in slow strides, she holds her hands in front of her. His cries ring out across the meadow, his evil abominations still standing at the end of the forest - waiting for his command. The white flames heat her skin as she stands before him, taking in those enchanting eyes for the last time.

"Once, Vorathiel, you were my light. Now, you vanish into your own shadows." Stepping back, her eyes still stuck on him, hands lift to the sky, ending the chant:

*"So, I command, so let it be,*
*By word, by will, eternally."*

Vorathiel howls as the flames swallow him. Ilyra holds her hands to the sky, slowly lowering them to the ground beside her. A white cast encapsulates the sky, stretching as far as the eye can see, dividing the realms. "Spirits will never walk the realm of the living," she whispers, a shield so strong, never to break. Forever holding Vorathiel bound in his own shadows, never to return.

# Chapter 9

## *Eleanora*

I stare blankly at Alaric, my brain in shambles.

"So… How-what – I-I don't understand. She banished this Vorathiel behind the Veil and now he's back out?"
I pinch the bridge of my nose, trying to make sense of it all. How could this happen?

"I thought she sealed the Veil for eternity?" Tharion asks, also clearly confused.

A deep sigh seeps between Alaric's lips.

"She did, but the beginning of time was many centuries ago. Vorathiel has spent his time behind the Veil trying to find cracks big enough to break the enchantment Ilyra put on it. Amariel was one of the unlucky ones, a victim to a creature so vile it infiltrated her mind, convincing her to join him."

His eyes fall to his mug, scraping at the white paint with his thumbnail. Lifting it to his lips, the hot liquid runs down his throat in big gulps. Camille shoots Alaric a longing look, eyes filling with sorrow at the mention of Amariel. Poor girl, having her mind played with by a demon.

"If you don't mind me asking, have you seen Amariel after she got taken?"
Alaric's body tenses, his knee bouncing under the table as his throat works hard to swallow.

"That's how we found out she was taken in the first place. After she disappeared, Camille and I searched high and low, not stopping until we found her. The last place we went, after all hope was lost, was the Veil's Eclipse," his gaze zones out, words fading, the memory flooding his mind, "our little girl stood there, wearing the same sleepwear as the night she left."
He looks over to Camille, watching his wife wipe her tears with a dish rag, quiet sniffles echoing around us.

"Camille found her, pounding on the barrier, begging for us to let her out. She cried our names over and over until her body just went rigid, eyes fogging over. He put a curse on her. Since then, she refuses to come to the border. We haven't seen her in over fifty years."

His voice cracks, tears heavy in his throat. Leaning over, I squeeze his hand. My chest is tight, air refusing to enter my lungs.
I get up to leave, needing some air, but run head-first into a brick wall of a chest. Rowan looks down at me, smirking.

"Want to tell me what has you fleeing in such a hurry?"

"I need some air, this place is suffocating at the moment."

Rowan scans my face, a frown developing between his brows. His strawberry blonde hair is wet and ruffled from bathing in the nearby river. Water droplets run down the sides of his neck, glistening in the light. I look up at him, finding peace in his warm, auburn gaze.

"You missed storytime. We have a demon sorcerer older than the beginning of time trying to escape the Veil. It's up to us to stop him, and his army of soul-sucking magic-gathering minions, before they put the realm in darkness."

Rowan's frown deepens, a low growl forming in his chest. The fox inside him is clawing at the surface, aching to be let out, to have at this sorcerer, to protect me. I place my palm on his chest, the touch instantly calming the fox - and Rowan. His breathing slows, heartbeats reducing to a steady thump.

I throw my arms around his waist, burying myself in his chest. I love the smell of him. His warm, smoky scent mixed with the smell of fur and something ancient. My shoulders relax with every inhale. Rowan holds me tight, his nose hovering just above my hair, dragging my scent into his lungs.

Tharion clears his throat, Rowan and I releasing each other from our embrace. I excuse myself, storming out the door. The morning sun has arrived, brightening the village in delicate, pink light. The air is chilly, but not cold, smelling of fresh grass and damp soil.

I inhale, holding my breath for a moment. My chest burns, lungs pushing the air through my nose in one long exhale. I repeat the process a few times, convincing myself to calm down. The sound of wind rushes past my ears, the sounds birds in the trees and the water rushing down the river playing like music against my eardrums.

Everything is so… alive. Our realm is so alive, so bright. It hits me that this might not be the case anymore in whatever short time we have left. Soon, it might be blanketed in darkness and misery.

I shudder, a lump forming in my stomach. Can we actually stop this demon? We're just two humans in our late twenties and a two-century old fox, up against a demon and his army of flesh-eating minions? The air feels heavy and damp, like I can't properly drag it into my lungs.

My chest feels tight, hands sticky with sweat. Crouching, I put my head between my knees, shutting everything out. I focus on the sound of my heart, galloping away in my chest. My breath is ragged, panting, like I'm suffocating. We do not stand a chance. *I* do not stand a chance. I'm powerful, yes, but not powerful enough to take on a whole Goddess damned army of demons! Black spots creep in on my vision, head swimming in cotton.

I feel a strong hand on my shoulder, a shriek ripping from my throat.

"Whoa, Eleanora. It is me, Rowan. I felt your fear."

He crouches in front of me, "here, breathe with me." Rowan takes a deep breath in, looking at me expectingly, waiting for me to mimic him. My eyes find his, and I try to breathe in, but my panic overcomes me and I choke.

"Again, in…" Rowan takes another deep breath and I follow. The crisp air fills my lungs, rejuvenating my organs, slowing down my heartbeat and clearing my head.

"Good girl, now again. In," we breathe in unison, I close my eyes and feel the calmness fill my soul. When I open them, Rowan has a stern look on his face.

"Eleanora. What is happening? Talk to me." Eyes pleading, he reaches for my hand and holds it tight in his, grounding me.

Tears are pressing on the back of my eyes, begging to be let out, to fall free, but I push them back.

"I… I don't – I am so scared, Rowan. This whole thing… I- I don't know how we are supposed to win this. We are just kids, I mean – we are just kids!" I ramble, panic throwing itself at me.

"I have achieved nothing in life! Nothing, Rowan! I-I-I'm a failure. To my parents, to myself, to you-"

Rowan barks, a low growl erupting from his chest.

"I will not sit here and listen to you talk down about yourself, Eleanora. My biggest achievement in life was achieved the day I found you. You are part of me, my soul. Do not ever say that you are a failure to me, because that could not be further from the truth. You are the bravest, strongest and most capable witch I have ever met, if anyone can overthrow this demon piece of trash, it is you." His gaze bores deep into mine, like a spell holding me tight.

"You can be scared, we are all afraid of what life has in store for us, but know one thing; we will overcome this, and we will save this realm." His voice is stern, powerful. I look down, embarrassed by my overreaction. The bond between us is pulsing, warm bursts fill my spirit and body - a hopeful warmth, full of promise.

"I'm sorry, Rowan. I let the weakne–"

"You, my dearest *vulpin*, are not weak. Leave that thought behind where it belongs. Now, can you brief me on this storytime you had?" Rowan tries to change the subject, and I happily oblige.

I fill him in on the nightmare we had been told, and what we had promised Alaric. With an extra day in Stormbrook, it leaves us more time to plan, to figure out exactly where to go and how to get there.

"It is about a three-day ride to Catariel, we will have to stop to eat and camp. If we keep out of the thickest forests, we should be safe from spirits and ghouls," Rowan points out on a hand drawn map of our journey.

"I could make a protection rune and put it over our encampment, it should keep us fairly hidden too."

Tharion looks away, and I feel his self-loathing crawling on my skin. I put my hand on his arm, "hey, don't feel bad. I could teach you how to make the rune if you'd like? It's pretty straight forward."

His eyes light up, a warm smile enveloping his beautiful face. The dimples by his mouth dip, freckles sparkle like a shower of stars, resting across his nose and cheeks. He really is beautiful. His fair skin blushes faintly, eyes quickly looking away. He nods, accepting my offer to tutor him.

"That's more like it. Look at that smile," I playfully mock, squeezing his cheeks. He slaps my hands away, laughing.

We spend the day exploring the village, taking in the beautiful rivers flowing through it. Back in Sylvarn, we do not have rivers like this. We have lakes, beautiful ones, that the Elven people use for burials of their loved ones. Elven tradition says to reunite the dead with nature, by burning the deceased on a boat, finishing their cycle of existence.

My kind, witches, bury our loved ones in family cemeteries. Our bones seep magic even after we have left the mortal realm, giving magic back to our covens after we die. I like the different traditions, even if we all theoretically end up in the same place - the Afterlife. Speaking of, we might end up there sooner than we had planned if we don't figure out how to defeat this demon Vorathiel.

I grab Tharion's hand and start guiding him outside with me, «Let's get started on that rune so you can practice." His eyes light up, excited to learn, and we step outside the tavern.

"Alright, so to make a rune in witchcraft, you must sacrifice some of your blood to the Goddess. You can do that by cutting your hand and letting a couple drops fall to the ground." I pick up my knife and take it out of its case. Tharion's eyes widen, a light shudder racing through him. I giggle. Seeing him all squeamish like this is amusing, but I also need to make him understand the importance behind it.

"If you don't sacrifice some of yourself to the Goddess, she will not grant you the protection that you want in the rune. It doesn't have to be much," I assure him. He swallows loudly, the corners of my mouth trying hard to stay down. I prick my finger, deep crimson oozing out. I squeeze my hand to make it flow faster, letting it drip to the grass underneath my feet.

*"Veil of shadow, cloak of night. Bind the truth and dim the sight."*

I chant, eyes closed. A gust of wind encircles us, lifting my hair up behind me. Tharion gasps.

"What is going on?" he shouts over the wind. I keep my eyes shut and roll up my sleeves. On the ground between us, a rune appears. It has an eye in the middle, surrounded by arrows and circles. A thin veil of white stretches over us like a dome.

I open my eyes. "No one can see us from outside now, watch." I call for Rowan to come outside. He steps through the door and walks right past us, not even slightly aware that we're there. I look at Tharion, bewilderment in his eyes, mouth slightly open, and smile proudly. He looks at me, eyes softening, pupils dilating ever so slightly, and grins.

Gosh, he really is pretty. *Nope, leave it.* I pull my foot over the rune, disturbing the lines, and the dome collapses. Rowan turns around in a hurry but relaxes as he sees us standing there.

"Now, your turn." My hand is outstretched, handing the knife to Tharion. Hesitatingly, he takes it and studies the blade carefully. The rusty brown spots of old blood make him scrunch that adorable nose of his.

"Is this even clean? What if I catch some mysterious illness from using it?"

I laugh at his carefulness.

"Just cut your damn finger, Ari, stop being such a wuss!"
He huffs, giving me a look and turns away from me, staring at his hand.

With a deep inhale, he closes his eyes, exhaling the air in his lungs and pricks his finger. A sharp hiss leaves his mouth as a small pooling of blood appears on the very tip.

"Now squeeze your hand so it drips onto the ground." I show him with my hand, squeezing the ruby liquid out of my cut. Three drops of blood fall to the ground and he starts chanting the spell.

At first, nothing happens.

*Please, Goddess, give Tharion some hope to make this protection rune. He is our only chance*, I pray silently, hoping She can hear me. Tharion has a look of defeat written on his face, my heart aches to comfort him.

At last, easy winds swirl around him, then me. It picks up and finally the wind roars around us. Storming gusts woosh in our ears, Tharion looking at me like he won the world. I grin at him, happiness drowning me. The same rune as before slowly starts appearing on the grass between us, the white veil showing itself again, closing us inside the dome of light. My stomach drops. He did it!

Tharion cheers loudly, then rushes over to me, lifting me high in the air like I'm nothing at all. I yelp as my feet leave the ground, then laugh with him.

"I did it, Ela! I made a rune and… it hid us from sight!"
He spins me around, holding my waist. When he stops, we sway a bit and for a moment I lose my footing, grabbing onto him. In reaction, he pulls me closer and we're suddenly only inches away from each other's face.

My cheeks redden, body feeling hot. Tharion looks me deep in the eyes, then his gaze falls to my dark red lips. His tongue swipes over his bottom lip, breath hitches in my chest.

"Thank you, Ela, for believing in me." The words come out breathlessly, I can almost taste his breath in my mouth, so torturously close.

"You can do whatever you set your mind to, Ari. I will always believe in you," I whisper. His hand wanders from my waist up to my shoulders and into my hair, pressing me slightly closer to him, while the other one is firm on my lower back.

As I hold his stare, his eyes glow hungrily, fire roaring in those dark pools of jade. Goddess, I want him to kiss me so badly. Heat radiates from me, it feels like I'm on fire. Tharion dips his face ever so slightly, his mesmerizing green gaze dipping yet again to my mouth. I open it, carefully, an invitation for him to do with as he likes. He's so close, our lips faintly touch. Lightning shoots through me, heat and trembles mix in my core.

"Eleanora!" *Shit.*

The moment instantly vanishes, and we fall out from our embrace. Goddess damn it. So close! So damned close.

I brush my dress, smoothing any wrinkles or evidence of Tharion on me. My throat clears, glancing over at Tharion. His pointy ears have an ever so slight red tint, gaze firmly on the ground.

I turn away and smirk, feeling a shower of hope run over my body. Does he want me, like really want me, or was it because of the spell he successfully executed? I push the doubts away, dragging my foot over the rune and turn to Rowan, frantically searching for me.

# Chapter 10

## Tharion

I made the rune work. I, Tharion Ashveil, used my magic for something other than building mediocre wooden buildings. It wasn't even elemental, and I managed to do it! Pride radiates through me, filling me with tingling warmth.

Then, ice cold panic washes over me. What was that moment with Eleanora inside the dome? I can still feel her lips stroking faintly against mine, her heartbeat racing in her chest, breath hitching repeatedly.

The thoughts send a wave of heat from the top of my body to the tips of my toes, shooting down my legs. We were so close, I should have just gone for it. Did she even want to kiss me? I try to go over the details, but the more I focus on them, the more they fade and change. Not wanting to lose the delicious memory of her body pressed against mine with her lips only a second away from crashing into me, I push the thought away.

Eleanora has broken the rune, and the dome has vanished yet again. Rowan is standing just outside the Inn's entryway; his arms crossed over his chest, a stern look on his face.

"We should head into town, make some acquaintances and preferably also some allies for the journey." His eyes look between the two of us, sensing the tension.

Eleanora adjusts her stance. "Maybe we could check out the markets? The streets looked packed yesterday."

We grab our jackets and head on out. The easiest way to navigate the village is via the river network, but we don't have a boat, so we walk around on the mainland, crossing bridges and looking around us in awe as we make our way to the street markets.

On the outskirts of Stormbrook, where the Inn is located, it's quiet and calm. Here in the village centre, the sounds are deafening. People are trading wares, shouting back and forth, others are chatting about their mornings, and some are rushing from one place to another.

The street is busy, overwhelmingly so. I've never been a huge fan of large masses, especially foreign ones, and the uncomfortable feeling I know too well rises at the centre of my chest, spreading out across my lungs. I can't breathe, like the sounds are trying to drown me. My hands start sweating, beads forming along my hairline. My breath is quick, shallow. I feel like I might actually die.

"You two go ahead, I'll catch up in a moment," I try to sound as nonchalant as I can, but there's no fooling Eleanora. She can always tell, this time included.

"Hey. Hey, Tharion. Look at me." She puts her index finger under my chin, forcing me to look her in the eyes.

"Breathe. You are not dying, okay? Breathe with me, like we always do."
Eleanora closes her eyes, taking a deep breath. I try to mimic her, not wanting to embarrass myself even more, but the thought of the village's people seeing me like this just makes the whole thing even more overwhelming. My vision is starting to blur, head feels sluggish and before I know it, the world fades to black.

· · — ·✳· — · ·

"Tharion? Tharion, open your eyes." Eleanora's calm voice penetrates the haze in my mind. Where am I? We were just at the markets, why am I in bed?

I try to sit up, but Eleanora stops me.

"No, just stay down. Ari, you fainted. Why did you not tell me your anxiety was that bad?"
Her eyes are soft, but worry coats her words. The wrinkle she gets between her eyebrows when she's upset is present, just a lot deeper. Damn it.

I sigh. "I'm sorry. It all happened so fast, I didn't realize before it was too late," I lie, knowing I had felt the attack coming before we even came to the market street. Embarrassment engulfs me, sending a scarlet hue soaring over my face, coating the tips of my ears.

I scoff. "How am I supposed to save the realm if I can't even handle a busy street full of peaceful villagers?"
I want to get up and leave so badly, I hate showing myself like this in front of her. Sitting on the edge of my bed, Eleanora puts her head over my rampaging heart, the scent of her hair filling my nostrils, sending a calming pulsation all the way through to my soul. I breathe in the delicious scent, it smells like honeysuckle, tart cherry and wet grass. Sweet and earthy, just like her.

"You can do this. I know you can, but you have to start talking to me, letting me be here for you. You can't do this all by yourself, okay?" her hand is moving up and down my forearm, goosebumps racing under her touch. It tickles, and I twitch ever so often, making her giggle.

"Did you manage to find someone who might know anything?" I hope they hadn't left the village because of me.

"Rowan is out there now, he will probably be back soon with some more info. You should rest up before dinner," her eyes dart to mine,

"Would you like me to stay here with you?"
Is that…hope, in her tone? My heartbeat quickens. *Yes, yes. Please do.* I want her to stay, but will it make things even more weird between us?

I swallow, straightening my shoulders.

"I'll be okay. But thank you. I'll see you at dinner?"

The hope I thought I had seen fades away in a flash, a stoic expression firmly planted on her face. She smiles, but not truthfully, and nods.

"I'll see you later then." Eleanora gives me an awkward hug before standing up and walking out the door, closing it with a thud.

Regret washes over me, knowing I should have kept her here. My heart aches for her presence, needing her to feel calm. I beat myself up, disappointment and anger stomping at the back of my mind.

Shaking my head, I lift the cover off me. The world spins just as I sit up, so I lean back on my hands for a moment. I need to be better, for me and for Eleanora. If we're supposed to win this battle, I need to work on myself - inside and out.

Starting with the inside, I will challenge my anxiety, push myself to walk back to the village alone. I put my boots on, then my jacket, and head out the door. There is still about two hours until dinner, so I should manage to go there and back in that time – if I don't pass out again.


As I walk over the last bridge separating the mainland from the rest, sounds of people find me again. My heart starts accelerating, but I remind myself that I'm not in danger.

*I am safe. I am not dying. I am safe. I am not dying.*

I repeat the words, and to my relief, they're working. My posture straightens more with every stride as I walk across the bridge, setting my foot down on the cobble stone pavement. Slowly approaching the street, getting louder and louder for every step, I remain calm.

My eyes lock on a market stall that looks to be selling some delicious pastries, and I decide to try my luck there. The stall is surrounded by wing-shifters in all colours and sizes, trading wares for freshly baked goods. The stall itself is worn, a pole is missing to help keep the sign hung above the counter, and the roof also needs some maintenance.

Walking over, my eyes eat the sight of all the different pastries. Huge bread-looking domes of fluffy dough are filled with fruit jams and covered in a dust of sugar. My mouth waters just by looking at them, stomach growling softly.

"Hello, my boy! What can I get ya today?"

A male with elegant fluorescent wings towering behind him smiles at me, his face pointy, eyes a delicate lilac shade. The male smiles widely, inviting me up to him.

My heart stammers, hands growing warm.

"I'm so sorry, I didn't bring anything to trade. Your wares look incredible, but I cannot afford them at the moment."

The man studies me, stopping at my pointy ears.

"You fae, son?"

My stomach knots. Are fae not welcome here? Nerves instantly turn back on, sweat finding its way into the palm of my hands. I gulp down.

"… yes?"

The kind male opens his arm widely, his laugh ringing in the already loud air.

"Fantastic! That means you can help me fix my roof! If you help me, I'll give you some treats for you to bring home!" He winks at me, shoulders dropping back down from my ears. I smile back.

Reaching for my magic, I bring it all the way out to my fingertips. I close my eyes, power rushing through them. Palms facing the sky, vines shoot up from the ground. Rocks and dirt spit into the air, the smell of fresh soil heavy. People around us yelp and cry out at the sudden movement, obviously not used to this kind of magic. I open my eyes.

The vines crawl up the side of the stall, pulling worn planks back to where they belong before neatly tying themselves together to make everything secure. Next, I move on to the roof, patching together holes with leaves and twigs, making everything look nice before letting my magic rest.

Looking around me, the village people stand around in silence, staring. I check my work to see if I destroyed anything or hurt anyone whilst mending the stall, but nothing seems out of order.

The stall keeper puts his hands together in a clap, then another, slowly increasing the rhythm, applauding. Soon, the others around us chime in and I'm engulfed in raging applause. They whoop and yell, throwing their fists in the air and whistling sharp sounds while clapping enthusiastically.

"That was amazing, son! Here, take what you want. You earned it," the man hands me two paper bags filled to the brims with sweet pastries, and I accept them with a grin.

My body beams, heat pooling in my chest. Strangers come up to shake my hand and look at my pointy ears like I'm some sort of creature. I laugh, still a little nervous, but the warmth coming from these strangers slowly choke out the anxiety of meeting them.

"Where did you come from, friend?" a male steps up to me, wide grin slapped across his face. He looks to be a few years older than me, his build strong and lean. The stranger has deep purple eyes, straight black hair and beautiful black, feathered wings. A raven, perhaps?

I clear my throat. "Sylvarn, the village west from here. We arrived just last night and will be leaving in the morning." A collective aah sounds, and I can't help but chuckle.

"What brings you here?"

*This is my chance.*

"We are passing through on our way to the King. I have a message for him, you see, about a great battle that will find its way to us very soon." The crowd murmurs amongst themselves.

"What kind of battle?" the male asks, the murmuring coming to a halt.

I swallow. "The spirits trapped behind the Veil have found a way to escape, once again walking among us in the mortal realm." Collective gasps ricochet through the crowd.

I continue, "their master, Vorathiel, will also find his way out if we don't find a way to stop him. But to do that, I will need help."

My eyes wander between the people surrounding me, pleading for their support, "I have been chosen to conquer this battle, to erase the cracks in the Veil and yet again separate the realms. But I do not have experience, I am not a fighter nor a killer, I do not know how to do this by myself."

I turn against the crowd, facing them.

"So, I ask you, people of Stormbrook, to help us win this fight. To stand with us and fight by our side. I cannot promise you that everyone will make it, myself included, but I promise to do what I can to protect each and every one that decides to risk their lives to win over the darkness threatening to suffocate our realm."

The crowd is silent, no one is saying a word. I look around, silently begging whoever is listening that someone will step forward. My shoulders slump, the all too familiar feeling of defeat making itself known. I turn to walk back home when a rustling sound is made.

"Who chose you?"

I turn, the male from before standing in front of me. I straighten my shoulders, forcing my voice steady.

"The Fates chose me. My father possessed the power of the long-lost Seers, foretelling the future we currently live in. He came to me in a dream just after the first spirits broke free."

The male stares at me, his mouth hanging open. The villagers talk amongst themselves, some in disbelief, some in shock.

"I will fight with you. It would be a dishonour to our realm to sit back and watch it get slaughtered because of my own fear. If I die, I die with honour and will be greeted in Elysium by my brothers and sisters before me." He takes a step so he's shoulder to shoulder with me. Giving him a firm nod, I reach out my hand. The male's large palm lands firmly in mine, a promise to protect each other.

"What is your name, warrior?"

"My name is Corvyn, but my friends call me Cor - and that means you now." Cor smiles widely, kindness in his eyes. A foreign, but very welcome, sense of victory fills my body with immense heat, my cheeks on fire. I smile back at my new friend.

"Cor, would you like to join us for dinner tonight? We are staying at the Broken Oar, I bet the others would love to meet you."

Corvyn pulls me in for a hug, tapping me on the back with his fist, "It would be an honour to dine with you. Count me in."

I walk back from the mainland with a new sense of identity, and a lot of sweet treats. I feel powerful, strong, brave. Feelings I've never had the pleasure of feeling before. It's invigorating, empowering, all-consuming, I feel brand new.

*I wonder if Eleanora will notice, if she will care for it.*

I make my way back to the tavern, the huge bag of pastries firmly in my grasp. As I walk in the door, I'm met by a delicious smell of roasted meats and herbs galore. My mouth waters instantly and my stomach is shouting for me to fill it with food. I stagger up the wonky staircase, up to our room, wanting to freshen up a bit before we eat.

As I walk inside, the delicate scents of soap and honeysuckle hit my nostrils. Eleanora walks out of the washroom, a towel around her body, hair dripping water down her back. I don't want to stop myself from staring, but I manage to force my gaze away.

"Ah, shit. Sorry, Eleanora! I didn't mean to look, I- you- you just look- ah," I turn away, embarrassment swallowing me whole.

Eleanora chuckles, "Tharion, calm down. Look at me." I turn to meet her eyes, finding them searching mine with intensity I've never seen in her before.

Her eyelids are heavy, making her lashes frame her dark irises like a lunar eclipse, radiating desire. Her curves are perfectly on display under the towel, skin sparkling with water droplets. I find myself wanting to lick them off her, to rip that towel off with a force unbeknownst to me.

I turn away, my knees suddenly weak. I can't be thinking about her like this, it will kill me.

*You can't have her. Put it away.*

Shaking the slight disappointment off, I start pulling some clean clothes from my satchel, heading for the empty washroom. Eleanora is still watching me, her head tilted slightly, but I give her a nod in passing and close the door behind me.

A *hurmpf* and sigh is heard behind the door, I want to open it and tell her that it's not about her, but I don't. Filling the basin with water, I splash some on my face, the water almost sizzling on contact with it. It clears my head enough, and soon I finish up and walk back out into the room. Eleanora sits on the bed, now dressed for dinner, back turned against me.

"So, I met someone today. I invited them to dine with us, if that's okay with you?" Desperately wanting to ease the tension, I try to make light conversation.

"Okay," she mutters back. Okay? I sit down next to her, the bed shuffling under me, pushing her a bit closer.

"Is everything alright?" I know the answer to the question, but I still ask.

"Why did you turn away when I asked you to look at me? Do you think I'm ugly?" Her eyes don't want to meet mine, she's picking at her cuticles and fiddling with her fingers. I recoil at the question. Her, ugly? Has she seen herself?

"What? No. Ele-no. Absolutely not. Did you think-no–" I fumble my words, trying to make her understand.

"Eleanora, you are beautiful, so beautiful that it's hard to look at sometimes. I looked away out of respect, not wanting to ogle you in a vulnerable state." I try to reach for her hand, but she pulls it back.

"Do you see me as a sister to you, Tharion?"

A sister? The thought makes my stomach sour. I could never see her as a sister.

I violently shake my head, "I see you as my best friend, Ela. You are more than a sister to me – you are my whole family."

She sighs again and stands up to leave the room. What did I say? I couldn't tell her that I see her as my future, my wife and mother of my children, because that could never be. Not knowing what to say, my shoulders slump in vanquishment. She takes a last look at me, tears lining her eyes, and leaves.

# Chapter 11

## Eleanora

His best friend. He sees me as his best friend. Goddess, I'm such a fool. My mind is loud, so overwhelmingly loud, heckling me for being naïve and hopeful.

*You told yourself to build these walls up, how come he keeps slipping through?* I scoff at myself.

Sometimes he makes me think he wants me as more than his friend, and then he goes around doing something like that, something like walking away when I'm basically naked in front of him. Heat blooms in my chest, suffocating, bright shame.
*You asked him to look at you, what is wrong with you?*

I shake my head, trying to rid myself of the thoughts and the punishment I'm putting myself through. Walking down the crooked stairs, Rowan greets me at the bottom.

"Hello, Eleanora. You look nice this evening." He gives me one of his warm smiles, my shoulders releasing some of the built-up tension.

"Hey, Ro, thank you. I'm starving, let's get to the dining room." I try to keep my voice stable, but a slight crack has Rowan turning towards me. He studies my face, eyes narrowing.

"What happened? Why are you upset?"
My stoic mask breaks, letting myself stoop. I sigh.

"My heart is acting really difficult at the moment, it's at war with my head and none of them are surrendering. I thought I had my feelings under control, Ro, I thought—"

"You thought Tharion had finally accepted his feelings for you," he finishes for me as my eyes tear up again. I look down at my hands, cuticles bleeding from picking at them all day.

"Why won't he see them, Ro? Why won't he see… me." My voice fades out as tears escape my eyes, running slowly down my cheek. I've tried so hard to put these feelings away, to deny them any time or effort, but it seems now that I can't do it anymore.

"Eleanora, listen to me. Tharion will figure that out sooner or later. He has the fate of the realm on his shoulders, maybe he doesn't want to think about these kinds of things right now. I smell his fear, it's so strong that I have to leave the room sometimes. The male is terrified, Ela. He needs you, his best friend, to be here for him, to calm him down and make him believe in himself." Rowan wraps around me, pulling me in for a hug. His warmth radiates through me, calming my racing heart.

By the time dusk settles, I've stitched myself back together just enough to face the others. Light footsteps echo down the stairs, Tharion walking timidly towards us. I wiggle out of Rowan's embrace and sit up straight.

"Ela, are you okay? Why are you crying?" Tharion bends down and studies my face, brows deeply knitted, gently using his thumb to wipe away my tears. His skin is warm, rougher than I remember, grounding me and undoing me at the same time.

Without thought, I lean into his touch, closing my eyes, dragging in the smell of his skin. I open them to see Tharion staring at me, breath stuck in his chest. Those mossy eyes widen, lips parting slightly, but the words stick to his throat.

"I'm fine." I break from his touch, "ready for dinner? You were talking about some friend you wanted to introduce us to? Is she here?"

I feel the bitter tinge of jealousy in my chest, leaving a sour taste on my tongue. I have nothing to be jealous about, he shouldn't keep himself from meeting other people just because he doesn't want me. His voice hitches, head jerking back slightly.

"She? No, no, no," he waves his hands in a cross movement, "It's a *he*. His name is Corvyn, he will be joining our battle."

"What? How did you meet him? Weren't you in bed all day?" Thinking back, I hadn't seen him leave earlier, but then again – I had been quite quick to leave.

Tharion shakes his head.

"I figured I had to start showing some guts if I'm to defend our realm," he takes my hand, "to defend you, Ela. So, I swallowed my anxiety and walked into the village centre. While there, I spoke to a merchant trading beautiful pastries," he picks up a brown paper bag filled with sweet treats, "he asked me to fix his stall in trade for them, so I used my magic to put it back together. That's when I met Corvyn."

I feel my brows shooting into my hairline.

"You used your magic? How did it go? That's amazing, Ari!" My heart fills with pride and warm trembles, the sorrow from before long overshadowed. I squeeze his hand, mouth pulling into a smile.

"I managed to put everything back together, and it came to me so easily. After I did it, I asked the villagers for help and told them about the battle that is to come. Corvyn stepped forward and declared his allegiance with me in front of everyone. That's when I invited him to dinner, he should —"

A stranger walks into the tavern and all three of us turn our heads towards him. His majestic obsidian wings hang gracefully behind him. He has dark hair and sharp features, strikingly handsome.

"—be arriving any minute? I guess that's my cue! Hey, Tharion. Thank you for inviting me." The stranger reaches out to shake Tharion's hand, a wide grin across his face.

Tharion accepts his hand in his, beaming, "Cor! Welcome, friend. I'm so happy you could make it."

Next, Corvyn introduces himself to Rowan, my familiar tensing up in his presence, before his gaze locks on me.

He chuckles. "That is funny… I thought dreams were supposed

to end when I woke up, but here you are," he winks playfully, his deep violet eyes glistening. I can't help but smile, the line working wonders on me.

"I'm Eleanora, it's nice to meet you," I stretch out my hand to shake his, but he picks it up and places a slow, perfectly wet kiss on the back of it instead. I shiver, goosebumps riding down my chest.

"The pleasure is all mine, *Eleanora.*" The way he says it makes me feel all tingly inside. I shift in my seat. We keep up our staring contest for a while, only to be interrupted by Rowan clearing his throat loudly.

"I think dinner is ready, should we step inside?"
I nod, pulling myself together. Rowan and I step off our stools and start making our way into the tavern where a delicious feast awaits us. Roasted potatoes, sticky jams and boats of fragrant sauces are spread on a neatly decorated table. Camille steps out of the kitchen carrying a tray of steaming vegetables.

"Friends! Hi, welcome! I have gathered a feast for you today, our saviours," she winks at Tharion, and that bitter feeling returns. Camille puts the tray down on the table before rushing back into the kitchen. Alaric is already seated, nose deep in a book.
"*The Veil of Malice*" is written in big black lettering on the leather binding. It looks old and worn, the pages tinged in a yellow hue. He looks up, a smile brightens his face.

"Hi, travellers! Welcome! I am so excited to show you what I have made for you to bring on your journey."
Alaric stands up and walks over to a big chest. It looks heavy, but stunningly made. The walls are built out of old wood; the hardware carefully designed to look like raging waves crashing over the chest itself. It's beautiful.

Alaric opens the chest, picking out our weapons. As he walks back, the weapons radiate with magic. He puts them down on the table and turns towards us, grinning.

"As promised, I have made you weapons to bring on your adventure. The weapons are carefully crafted, each one specifically designed for you, spilling with Elven magic."
He picks up a longbow, the handle decorated with swirls dancing across.

"For you, Rowan, I present the Bow of the Eternal Hunt, a bow with arrows that will never miss their target as long as your heart's intentions are just." He brings the weapon over to Rowan and places it in his lap. The bow is inscribed in Elven runes, glowing a faint blue. It almost looks like it's breathing. He turns to me.

"For you, Eleanora, I present The Orb of Stella, small alchemical orbs that will engulf whoever you throw them at in a fire as hot as a dying star. They are best used at close range, and will burst on impact. My magic keeps them from working for anyone but your touch. Only you can wield them."

The orbs are made from thick, green glass with raging fires inside, ready to burst free. They are breathtaking.
Alaric drags in a deep breath, turning to Tharion.

"And lastly, for you, Tharion, I present Eternity's Edge, a rune blade made to absorb the power from your enemies. It will make you stronger, more confident and precise. You will never need another blade in your life."
We sit there studying our new companions, jaws slack in absolute awe. They are so beautiful, so skilfully crafted, it's difficult to imagine them being made in a day.

"Thank you so much, Alaric. It is an honour to receive these gifts from you." Tharion walks over to the elf and pulls him in for an embrace. Alaric returns the gesture, the males holding each other tight before releasing and turning towards us.

"I pray these weapons will serve you well, that they will help you defeat Vorathiel and restore balance once again."

"We will do whatever it takes. For you, and for the realm." Alaric dips his chin right as Camille busts through the door, a whole boar in her hands, roasted to perfection. My mouth floods at the sight, stomach screeching for me to fill it.

As we devour the delicious meal, towering our plates with food like we won't ever eat again, the chatter is effortless and warm. We drink wine, laugh and tell stories of Sylvarn. No talking about Vorathiel, the battle or the Veil. No one is talking about dying or the possibility of failing. We just talk, as friends, like we will be back here doing this sometime soon. I hope we will be, but then with Amariel sitting here too.

Cor sits beside me, and I use the opportunity to get to know him a bit more. We talk about his family, how he is a raven shifter in a family of 10; his parents and his 7 brothers, where he is now the oldest. He had an older brother once, but he died not too long ago. I want to ask him about it, but store the questions for another day.

Across the table, I notice Rowan sneaking glances at the raven, following his words, smiling whenever Corvyn smiles, letting out huffs of breath when the raven breaks into laughter. He seems almost entranced by our new companion. Corvyn is kind and funny, and apparently, he knows how to fight hand-to-hand, which will benefit us a lot in the coming days. Also, being a raven, he can keep an eye on the sky while we ride on the ground.


A few hours later we are beyond stuffed, a little lightheaded and ready for bed. Our travel commences at dawn to get the most out of the day, trying to make as much ground as possible. The journey will take us roughly three days by horseback, so two of our nights will be spent out in the open. The thought makes me anxious. Who knows what awaits us out there? My battery drains.

"Hey, Eleanora. You okay? Looking a little distant there."
I look over to see Cor watching me, head tilted, a soft smile on his lips. He puts his hand on my shoulder, squeezing gently.

I shake my head, clearing my blurry vision.

"Yeah, sorry. A lot on my mind. I think I might head to bed, early rise tomorrow."
I get up, thanking Alaric and Camille for the delicious meal and gracious gifts, then turn to walk up the stairs to our room. My legs feel weighted as the wonky steps carry me up to the door.

Stepping across the threshold, I feel the rest of my energy leave my body. Throwing myself onto the bed, my body bouncing on impact, I lay face-down for a moment. I'm exhausted, mentally and physically, joints screaming for rest.

My thoughts wander, zoning out. After a few moments of absolute silence, I push myself out of bed, dragging my body into the washroom to brush my teeth, get undressed and dive back under the covers.

Finally, sinking into the mattress, sleep calls my name – the God of dreams begging me to join him into the realm of the Endless. The pull is too strong, no use in fighting it now, darkness taking over my body as I leave this realm, stepping into a realm of peace and quiet.


The lock creaks gently as Tharion unlocks the door, stumbling inside. I glance through the window, seeing the moon still high in the night sky. He staggers into the washroom, brushes his teeth and then sits down on the bed, undressing. With my back turned against him, I pretend to be asleep, not wanting to talk to him at the moment - not after the episode before dinner.

The bed shuffles, Tharion lifting the duvet and climbing in under it. I can smell his fresh scent of soap and the ever-so calming smell of amber. I take a deep breath in, wanting to fill myself with the smell of him. The bed continues to stir, his body falls flush against mine. Heat radiates through me, warming me to the core. What is he doing?

My heart starts racing. His strong hand makes its way over my stomach, pulling me just a slither bit closer. I'm so close that I feel his breath on my earlobe, sending shots of electricity down my spine.

"That raven will not have you. You are mine," he whispers faintly before adjusting his pillow and falling asleep wrapped around me.

# *Chapter 12*

## *Tharion*

Bright sunlight slices through the window, casting our room in white. It feels like I've slept on a beach, faced down in the sand, mouth open. I groan. A thundering headache slams against the back of my eyelids, forcing me to squeeze them shut even harder.

Fragments of memories play in my mind; laughter, the smell of wine, glasses clinking, the touch of skin. Something runs down my stomach. I run my hand over it, rubbing it between my fingers. *Sweat. Why are you sweating*? Why is my body so hot? I open my eyes slowly, adjusting to the light. Raven black hair covers part of my pillow, a porcelain shoulder with light brown freckles sticking out from underneath it.

It's Eleanora's shoulder. Eleanora's *naked* shoulder. She's not wearing her sleep shirt. I jerk back, scrambling through my memories from last night. Did something happen? And more importantly, why do I not remember it?

My chest falls into a void, sucking the air out my lungs. I try scooting back while also not wanting to wake her up. A cold gust of wind licks my bare back.

*I am not wearing sleepwear either.*

My memories are evading me, trying so hard to remember how I got to bed. I didn't have that much to drink, did I? No, I wouldn't do that the night before we leave.

Nothing happened, we're okay. I'm okay. *Tell that to the body part that very obviously thinks you did do something last night.* I can feel said body part pulsing between my legs, shivers racing through me. The thought of Eleanora and I, our bodies entangled, breaths mingled, pushes out a soft groan. *You need to get out of this bed, right now.*

Carefully, I lift the duvet, choking down a hiss as my bare feet hit the cold wooden floor. Heading into the washroom, I close the door with a soft *click* and fill the basin with water.

My reflection stares back at me. *Pathetic.* Did I make her feel good last night without even remembering it? *How embarrassing.* Did she like it?

Images flash before me, Eleanora in the towel from before, her wet hair dripping down her body. I close my eyes, trying to see the artwork in front of me more clearly. She is a goddess, radiant and strong.

Another pulse shoots down my legs, my dick following it happily. *Focus, Tharion.* A new image of my sweet Eleanora appears; this time she's not wearing a towel. I can see her under me in bed, her eyes closed, cheeks pink, moaning my name between heavy breaths. The thought of me bringing her pleasure, pushing her over the edge of pure ecstasy - it's a need I never knew I had until now. I need *her*.

I need to make her feel like the goddess she is. Shaking my head, I fill my hands with cold water and splash it on my face. *This is not the time. We are leaving for BATTLE today.* I give myself a quick wash, brush my teeth and put on a fresh set of clothes.

As my hand touches the doorknob, Eleanora's soft rustling sounds from the other side. Has she dressed? Should I wait, just in case she hasn't? I selfishly decide against it, turning the doorknob and entering the bedroom.

The air is thick, the scent of sleep heavy. Eleanora sits on the side of the bed, our duvet covering her just enough. I watch the curves of her body, the fabric doing absolutely nothing to cover them. My throat works, remembering the images that flashed before me just moments ago. Her head turns over her shoulder, looking straight at me, raven black hair falling delicately over bare skin.

"Good morning, Ari." Her voice is sleepy, the raspy sound making my fingers twitch, aching to feel her.
I clear my throat, adjusting my stance a bit.

"Good morning, Ela. Ready to go?"
Heavy burgundy eyes wander, tracing my body from top to bottom, lingering on the bulge in my pants, slowly growing back with every second those lustrous eyes stay on it. Her tongue licks the bottom of her lip, sharp canines biting down on it softly. How I crave to be the one she sinks her pointy fangs into. My mouth opens a bit, enthralled by the radiance bouncing off her.

"Yes, Tharion. I *am* ready to go," the tone is low, slow, seduction in the purest form. The delicate points of her nipples are poking through the thin fabric, blood rushing down my body again. I explode, the craving I have to feel her, taste her, sending me across the room.

In two long strides, I reach her side of the bed, leaning my right hand on the wall above her, lowering myself to her level. The scent of lavender and tart cherry has me feral, a predator waiting to pounce on its delicate prey – waiting to make them beg, to devour them completely.

"Eleanora, I could tell from all the way over there how ready you are. Is it for me?" I purr, breath warm, hungry. I can see her chest rising and falling quickly, heartbeat pounding in her chest so loud even I can hear it. My left hand guides her hair behind her ear, granting me access to her earlobes.

A bite, ever so gentle, makes her jump, goosebumps forming over her barely covered chest. Letting out a breathy chuckle, I stand up, drinking in the sight before me. My beautiful witch, so hungry for me. Eleanora's eyes fall from mine down to the now very clear outline in my trousers.

Maroon embers flicker in her eyes, pupils big as dinner plates. I smile down at her, stroking her cheek, caressing it. Her eyes flutter closed, savouring the moment, so I grab her shoulder, pushing her down on the bed. A moany yelp escapes her mouth. I smirk. This is it. This is when I will have her, my Eleanora.

"I cannot wait any longer for you, my sweet Eleanora. I want you under me, right now. If I am to die tomorrow, I will at least have had the honour of knowing what you feel like wrapped around me, crying out my name."

A whimper slips through those perfect lips. I shatter.

"Yes… Yes, please, Tharion. Have me."

Breathless pleas hang in the air, her hips moving, trying to ease some of her desire. Her hands are a circus of motion, trying to touch me everywhere at once. Delicate fingers race across my skin as sharp nails pierce it, forcing a growl.

Positioned between her legs, I hover just above her face. Slowly, I lower, lingering above her hungry lips, our breaths mixing between us. Surroundings fade, hearts beating as one.

I pant. "Eleanora, you are—"

Hammering sounds from outside our door. *Fuck!*

"Tharion! Eleanora! Are you awake? We need to get going!" Loud bangs bring us back to the present, reality of the moment crashing over us. The heavy door rumbles as heavy fists pound, Rowan impatiently waiting on the other side. I straighten up quickly, helping Eleanora out of bed, and run over to the door, opening it narrowly.

I fake a yawn. "Good morning, Rowan! We were just…ah, getting ready," hesitation in my tone, "Ela is just getting the last of her things, we'll meet you downstairs in five, okay?"

I can feel my blush darkening, Rowan's eyes boring into the pits of my soul. He looks behind me, the bed luckily empty as Eleanora had run to the washroom when I opened the door. I smile at him, trying to act normal, a stern nod returned to me.

As he turns to walk back down, I close the door and let out a shaky breath. What the *fuck* just happened? She was beneath me, just like that. My mind is racing, trying to catch up. Eleanora comes out again, dressed and packed. Her cheeks flush when her eyes lock with mine, quickly darting away. Is she embarrassed?

"Ela, I—"

"No, don't," she holds up her hand, stopping me. "We don't have to talk about that yet. Focus on the mission for now, okay? We will have time for that later."

Eleanora flings her bag over her shoulder and walks out of the room, footsteps echoing into the distance. Baffled, I stand there for a moment before hoisting my satchel over my shoulder, looking back at our room.

The air is still thick with our breaths, desperate for each other. I drag it in, desperate to fill my lungs with her, before closing the door behind me, heading down the stairs to meet the others.


Corvyn comes running over the bridge leading to the Inn just as we are saying our goodbyes to Camille and Alaric. A wide smile erupts from his face as he sees us, waving vigorously.

"Good morning, my fellow adventurers!" His cheery voice rings across the empty courtyard. We wave back at him, welcoming him into the party. Camille hands me a linen bag filled with bread, beans and rice.

"For the trip. Wouldn't want you starving to death before even reaching the capital." Her laugh trills off her lips, making us laugh in response. We thank them kindly, shaking their hands and load up the saddle bags.

"Alaric, Camille, it has been a pleasure staying with you these past two days. I really hope I have the honour of meeting you again some time."

"Hopefully with an extra family member present too." Camille's voice is calm, but hopeful. She understands the dangers of this journey, of course, but as any mother would – she hopes her daughter will return with us. I dip my chin to her and Alaric before turning around to my friends.

"We ride until just before dark sets in, then make a camp for the night. Cor, keep an eye out from above and Rowan, from the ground. If anything out of the ordinary grabs your attention, give us a signal to prepare ourselves."

My stomach turns at the thought of meeting some dark spirit or being in the forest, especially since Rowan and I haven't started our battle training yet. Eleanora has barely taught me an illusion rune, and that won't do anything if we meet something, or someone, out in the open.

Reaching for my hip, my new companion is securely fastened. We climb onto our horses, now riding one each, and wave one last time to Camille and Alaric.

"Safe travels! Be careful!" Camille yells at us as we set off to our next destination: Catariel.

Our ride is mostly quiet, Eleanora is barely glancing my way the entire time, mostly keeping her eyes forward. Is she embarrassed about what happened? Should I not have made the move?

My head is turning with thoughts, mind making up scenarios that haven't even happened. *Stop it.* I turn my focus to our surroundings. Deep rumbles sound to my right - the river we've been following, raging away.

Water sprays up into the air, creating a mist of glittering particles. By the riverbanks are small pools of crystal-clear water, inhabiting the local Potameides, or river nymphs. My eyes fall to the ethereal beings, their pale blueish skin shimmering in the warm sunlight. Long hair flows like water, a faint white hue dancing over it. Covering their delicate bodies are thin dresses made of algae and wrecked sails from boats failing the test of the dangerous waves.

The tint of their skin makes it look like they're glowing under the light. I lock eyes with one of the females sitting on a patch of grass, brushing her flowy strands of hair with her fingers. She winks at me, waving seductively, calling me towards her. Icy blue eyes bore into my soul, freezing my blood. I tear my eyes from her, not wanting to make even more of a fool of myself.

The snap of a twig breaks my thought cycle. I turn my head towards the sound while pulling the reins, bringing my horse to a halt. Silence fills the air around us, no one moving a muscle.

Another twig snaps, a little closer this time. I grab the hilt of my new blade, ready to use it - even though I don't know how. Carefully, I climb down onto the ground, scanning the forest around me as I descend. Rowan locks eyes with me, his dark amber gaze trying to tell me something. Is there something here?

A flash of black races across the trail, and before I know it my head hits the ground. It all happens so fast, a blur of movement before I'm looking up at a twisted, rotten face, its breath ragged, manic. The weight of the being isn't heavy, but fear paralyses me, making it impossible to move.

The spirit lifts their arm, ready to strike, a rush of adrenaline coursing my body. In a burst of panic-fuelled strength, I fling the horrible thing off me and scramble upright, my palms wet with mud. I free my blade with trembling hands, pointing it at the creature.

"Tharion! Behind you!" Eleanora shouts as another shadow swiftly crosses my vision on my left. My chest combusts, hands feeling clammy, blade slipping slowly from my grip. The one on my left launches at me. I tighten the grip on my weapon, throwing myself at the spirit. The blade slashes through something soft, coming out covered in black, tar-like blood. Shrieks of pain fill the air as it falls to the ground.

"Remove its head, Tharion! It will turn to ash!" Rowan shouts over his own battle, three shadows surrounding him and Eleanora. He draws his bow, arrows hailing at the spirits, slicing right through their already half-off necks, falling to the ground in a pile of black dust. Eleanora waves her hands, lifting the spirits into the air before throwing her hands apart, ripping the beings in two at the shoulders.

A cloud of ash showers over them as they make their way through the last one. I hurl myself at the wounded being in front of me, stabbing my blade through its neck. It doesn't fully decapitate it, so I pull it apart with my bare hands. My fingers dig into the demon's soft flesh, stomach turning. As I rip the flesh from its bones, black clouds fill the air.

It falls to the ground, the last spirit shooting through the smoke, piercing its claws into my shoulder. I'm hurdling backwards, smacking into the trunk of a huge tree. A cry of pain tears from my throat, air knocked straight out of me.

The being releases me for a second and I use it to duck beneath him, ramming my shoulder into its stomach, lifting it off the ground. I slam it against the earth, cracking its skull wide open.

Gooey black tar seeps out of the wound, covering the grassy trail. I snatch my blade and hack at the being's neck until it finally separates from its body, ashy remains pooling at my ankles.

Panting, I hold myself up by my knees. Looking down on the pile of ash, the rotten smell of decay hits me like a brick. Bile rises fast in my stomach, sending me hunching over and emptying the remnants of my breakfast onto the ground.

Wiping vomit off my mouth, I look over to check on Eleanora and Rowan, both standing on guard surrounded by black dust.

"What…the *fuck*, was that?" I yell, my body trembling.

"It came out of nowhere! I literally just— it was there and then— " my pacing footsteps leave deep prints in the dirt.

"I *killed* it, Rowan. I decapitated — took the head right off! What the fuck?!" I can't breathe, the air locked outside my lungs, refusing to re-enter. My knees crash against damp soil, clutching my chest, desperately gasping for air. Eleanora runs over to me.

"Tharion. Hey – hey! Look at me, Ari. Look at me." Her hand slips into mine, dragging it off my chest. I search for the familiar shade of burgundy, breath slowing down.
She nods, her eyes still trained on mine.

"That's it. Now, breathe with me. In…" she inhales deeply, "and out," blowing the air out through her mouth. I mimic her as best I can, repeating the process until the worst of it is gone. Her hand gently glides up and down over my back until I can finally breathe in properly. I gulp down on fresh air, bursting my lungs, before letting it out into the smell of rot and death.

Rowan stares into the depths of the forest, scanning, watching.

"Those were Ravoch. Spirits conjured only to devour mortals. They are made by the most wicked of magic-wielders. Nasty fuckers." I huff out a laugh, "nasty, alright. What were they doing here?"

"They must have slipped through the Veil, meaning that the cracks are getting larger as we speak. We need to get to Catariel fast. I suggest we camp here for the night, it's getting dark soon and this is fairly shaded from the weather."
Eleanora stands up and cracks her hands forward, the popping sounds sending shivers down my neck.

"I'll get started on the protection runes, you guys set up the tents and start a fire."
Corvyn dives and lands in the middle of our campsite.

"What happened? I circled back to you after scouting the area further ahead, only to find you covered in ash. Did I miss the fun?"

I scoff. "I don't know what you ravens do for fun, but that was not it."

He stares at me, his mouth a tight pout before both of us burst into laughter, Corvyn clutching my shoulder as he folds in two. I hiss in pain, forgetting about the claws that bore into it just moments prior.

"I must have ignored it while setting up the campsite. How does it look?" I peel back the fabric of my shirt, uncovering four deep punctures, the holes black around the edges.

The raven inspects my wounds, scrunching his nose.

"The blood has stopped, but we need to clean it to prevent an infection. Remove your shirt while I get some supplies."

He hops into his tent for a minute before emerging with a small pouch of different ointments and bandages. He picks up a bowl and fills it up with hot water, sinking a piece of fabric into it. The water burns as it touches my wounds, but I bite down, pushing the pain away.

Corvyn smears a thick salve, some herbal gel, onto the wounds. The gel glows in silver light, closing the open punctures. I watch in awe as it does its thing, mesmerized.

"Silverleaf Salve," Corvyn informs, "I had a small stash kept for emergencies after my brother's mate died. She was an elven healer." His voice is full of pride and adornment, clearly missing the female. The sadness in his eyes makes my heart ache.

"She sounds great, Cor. I would love to hear the stories of them sometime. Thank you for letting me use some, I know it must be hard." He looks down at me, a softness in them, like he's thanking me without words.

After letting the salve do its thing, Corvyn wraps my shoulder in a clean bandage. I move it a few times, checking the hold, it feels pretty nice.

"You could be a healer, yourself! This wrap feels amazing."

"I used to think I wanted to be one, even went to school for it, but after my brother died, I had to help my father. I work as a blacksmith now, though I will never be as good as Kaelen."

His gaze zones out while talking, escaping into a memory long in the past. Not knowing if the memory carries joy, I let him run away for a while, packing up the medical gear and putting it all into the pouch for him.

Eleanora is just about finished spelling when I walk up to her. Her focused face is adorable. She gets a deep wrinkle between her brows when she concentrates, and her tongue very carefully peaks out from her lips. I watch her, butterflies fluttering in my stomach.
Her arms fall beside her, letting out a strained breath.

"Alright, all done. Might have to check on the rune before we go to sleep just to be sure it's holding, but I think we're safe for now."

"Tell me something you can't do, Eleanora Luna." I nudge her side, a giggle slipping past her lips. Her eyes linger on me, those raven black brows turned slightly up as silent questions course through her. The thick air from this morning seems to hang between us still, thick, unspoken, electric. *Perfect, just… perfect.*

# *Chapter 13*

## *Eleanora*

I look up, the white glowing dome stretching across our campsite, checking for holes or failed bonding. Tharion's burning gaze bores into me, the same look he has back home. It's familiar, safe and warm.

Memories of this morning flash before me, goosebumps prickling down the back of my arms. How did we get to that point? Yes, I definitely tested my luck after the tipsy comment he whispered to me when he thought I was sleeping, but I never thought he'd act on them.

A sudden sting tears through my chest, the thought of how close his lips were to mine, how vulnerable I had been lying underneath him - it's making me dizzy. I'd thought of that exact moment so many times before, but I had always pushed them away – not wanting to indulge in hopeless fantasies. Because that's what they were: fantasies. Things that would never happen in real life.

Or so I thought, but clearly, I had been sorely mistaken. The faint seed of hope planted in my heart sprouts just a tiny bit, now knowing what could be between us. I wince.

*Don't do this to yourself, Eleanora. None of you were thinking straight, it was a mixture of nerves and adrenaline, nothing more.*

Shooting Tharion a glance, bandaged shoulder poking through his shirt. His hair is dishevelled, dirty, scattered with ash throughout those curly amber locks.

Blood oozes from a cut just above his right cheek. Grabbing the bowl of water and piece of fabric from before, I walk up to him, wringing out the rag with one hand.

I crouch before him. "You have a cut. Here, let me." Carefully dabbing the wet fabric on his cut, the tip coats in blood. My eyes drop to his, only to catch him already staring. Heat flushes my cheeks in pink, heart picking up pace.

"You always take such good care of me, my sweet Ela." His raspy voice electrocutes my senses.

*My sweet Ela? That's what he said this morning, right? "My sweet Eleanora"?* Air hitches in my throat. Without warning, my eyes fall to his lips.

I sink my teeth into my bottom lip, holding back the urge to hurl myself at him. Tharion reaches out, resting his hand under my chin, tilting my head up to him. His thumb gently caresses my bottom lip, forcing it slightly open, inviting him in.

"Sometimes… Sometimes I wonder if you feel it too, this pull between us that our friendship doesn't quite explain." The mossy green eyes sparkle as he burrows his gaze in mine, searching for answers. My heart is pounding, trying to escape the cage in my chest. It's almost painful.

I open my mouth to answer, but words escape me. Do I feel the same pull as him? Is it more than friendship? I know I've had the thought many times before, but is that the feeling he is asking me about?

His face goes from hopeful to hopeless in the blink of an eye, deeper with every second that goes without me saying a word. He lets go of my chin, shoulders slumping. The absence of his touch blankets me in cold air, void of hope and joy.

"Tharion, I… I don't know what to say, I— We're going into battle!" My words come out frantic, parted, all over the place.

"What happened this morning, the tension between us— why hasn't it happened before? Why now, Ari? Is it the thought of dying?" My heart thunders, head spinning the world around me.

Tharion jerks back as if I've struck him.

"What? That's what you think? That it's all because of the battle?"
I sense something different in his voice. Hot anger, disappointment. It stings. A lump forms in my chest, breath stuck below it.

"If you only knew the feelings I have— if you just— ah! Forget it, Eleanora," Tharion turns on his heels to march off, but I grab his wrist, holding him back.

"We need to focus on this mission, Tharion. What you're feeling, it's not you. It's this whole situation. A delusion. You don't want me like that."

The words come out trembling, body struggling to keep me on my feet. I put words into his mouth, needing him to either confirm or deny *my* delusion that we could be something more than this.

Tharion looks at me, baffled and furious. The glow of disappointment and denial radiates behind bright jade. He closes his eyes, shakes his head and yanks his hand from mine before walking to his tent. The tent flaps swing shut, separating me from his warmth. The silence that follows feels like a wound that won't stop bleeding.

Defeat washes over me. What is happening to us? Tears well in my eyes, blurring my vision, stealing the breath in my lungs. In a fit of hopelessness, I throw the bowl across our campsite, loud clattering rings as it hits the ground. I leave, breaking through the barrier keeping us hidden, surrounding myself with the dark forest.

I don't know exactly where we are, but the light we have until late at night in Sylvarn disappears a lot earlier here. It's only about nine in the evening, but the moon is already high in the sky, faintly illuminating the unnerving landscape in front of me.

The trees have grown in a spiralling pattern, forming an arch over the trail – a tunnel made entirely from trees and grass. Not much of the pale moonlight breaks through the dense forest, forcing me to conjure my own light source - an orb of radiant orange light. The orb hovers above my hand as I walk deeper, not knowing where I'm headed - only that I need to get away.

My thoughts race. Why did I say those things? Blood boiling, a scream tears from my lungs, raw, helpless. Crows emerge from treetops, escaping the sudden explosion of sound.

The forest falls quiet, eerily quiet. Something is wrong. I tremble. My stomach drops as tears stream down my face. Buckling knees crash with the earth, soaking in the mud.

Sobbing, I let out all the built-up emotions I've been carrying for so long. It feels like my soul is crying with me, finally free to let go of everything that broke it. I cry until breath is no longer available, until my throat is raw and hoarse. My eyes feel swollen and sore, the saltiness of my tears drying them up from the inside. Pulling my sleeve down, I wipe the tears and snot off my face.

I inhale. It feels… better. A lot better.

*Okay, enough. You need to find your way back to the tent.*
Yes, I probably should get back - if I can remember where I came from. Using the ground, I push myself up, wiping the mud from my knees.

*"Eleanora."* A faint voice is heard behind me. I look back, but there's nothing.

*"Eleanora, help me. Please, help!"* Panic fills the voice, but I can't figure out where it's coming from.

"Hello? Is anyone there?" I shout, words carrying into the night.
*"Eleanora! Eleanora, please!"*

My blood freezes. I know that voice.

*"Eleanora!"*

Tharion. Tharion needs my help. I start running towards the sound, desperate to locate it. The panicked shouts repeat over and over, coming from every angle around me. I stop, spinning after the cries.

"Tharion! Tell me where you are!"

*"Help me, Eleanora!"*

"Tharion, please! I'm coming, I just need to find you!"

I sprint in the opposite direction, desperately seeking out my best friend. Is he hurt? My stomach turns, heart galloping in my chest. My lungs burn as I push myself to the limit. Faster, further, black spots appearing at the corners of my vision. The calls for help are closer now, my steps heavy on the grass below.

Suddenly, I find myself in a dell surrounded by trees. There's no one here. My eyes take a moment to adjust to the darkness now swallowing me. As I use my magic to conjure a new orb, I see him. Tharion. Lying on the ground, clutching his chest. I run to him, knees colliding with cold mud. His shirt is stained a dark red. There's blood everywhere.

"Tharion. Oh Gods. What happened? Who did this?"

Tears rain down my face, sobs ripping my throat. Tharion coughs, blood spilling from his mouth, spattering my shirt. I hold my hand over his, pressing down on his chest.

Pushing through the panic, I force my voice steady.

"Tharion, you need to let me check your wound. I can fix it, just show me," I beg.

A blood-curdling scream rips from Tharion's throat, his body convulsing. I try to remove his hand, but he clutches it even harder to the gaping wound beneath. Wrestling with his arm, he finally lets go, a gasp stolen from my lungs.

A hole as big as my fist stares back at me, blood still trickling sluggishly over his skin. I bend over, desperate to find what has caused it, only to find emptiness. His chest is hollow. His heart isn't there.

"Wha… What is this? Where is your heart, Tharion? You— your heart… It's not there, wh—"

He looks at me, his eyes black as the night.

"You did this to me, Eleanora." The words are calm, steady.

"You took my heart right out of my chest and broke it."

I stumble back, shaking my head, refusing to understand. Then I feel it, something pounding against my palm. I look down, a scream tearing from my lungs. In my hand rests his heart, my fingers buried deep in the spongy flesh, mangling it beyond repair. My fist is slick in blood.

I fling the organ into the surrounding darkness, my stomach violently churning.

Tharion lifts himself onto his elbows, a vicious smile spreading across his face. I feel cold, so cold. Frozen to my very spirit. He lets out another shriek, splitting the air, piercing my skull.

When his gaze finds mine again, his eyes are not black anymore. They are a sickly yellow, glowing with evil. His grin widens, lips curling back to reveal bloodstained teeth.

"Did you really think I could love you? That I would fall for someone like *you*?" He bellows, swinging his head back.

"You are nothing but a failure, a shame upon everyone in your life. No one will ever love you, Eleanora. Not even your parents could. And *I* will *never* love you."

His stare is cold, lifeless. The words spilling from him cut me like razors, slicing through my core, into my soul. I feel the fibres of me shredding, tearing to pieces. Tears well in my eyes, falling over the edge like a waterfall.

"You make me sick. I hate you. I have always hated you. The only reason I ever spent time with you was out of pity." Tharion spits blood on the ground next to me, the slimy blob of black and red soaking into the soil below.

"Stop this," I plead, "this isn't you. Please, stop!"

My hands cover my ears, eyes shut hard, blocking out the foul voice that spews from my best friend. But this isn't him. It can't be.

"*STOP*!" I scream, ground shaking under me.

I try to run, but my legs fail me. My body collapses on the ground next to Tharion. Bringing my knees up to my chest, I hold them tight, trying to make myself as small as possible.

His laugh haunts me, slicing me over and over again. I close my eyes as tightly as I can, clamping down over my ears while keeping my knees close. I want to vanish, to get out of here.

"Please. Please, let me go. Please, let me go!" I exhort into the night.

*Please, Ilyra, if you are there. Please, let me out of this nightmare. Please.*

The prayers repeat, obsessive and desperate. I pray and beg, for what feels like an eternity. Tharion's disgusting laugh still filling the air around me.

A moment later, the forest falls silent. Dead silent. Not a single sound is heard. A firm hand clamps down on my shoulder, making me shriek in fear.

"Eleanora, hey! Hey, it's me. Please, relax. What happened?"

I look up to see a set of dark mossy green eyes, a face speckled in light freckles, amber locks falling into his eyes. Tharion's eyes.

I sit up, scooting away from him, digging up cold soil with my heels. Panic washes over me again. I'm suffocating. I look around me, finding the ground untouched. No blood pooling into it. No signs that Tharion was ever there.

"Eleanora, please. What happened?" Tharion sits down on the ground, holding his hands out in surrender.

"It's me. I heard you screaming and went searching for you. You've been out here for hours, it's almost dawn."

Almost dawn? I left 6 hours ago? That can't be. I shake my head.

"How dare you? I found you, bleeding. Dying. I… The things you said… I—" sobs rip through my chest, heaving for air.

"Bleeding? What— Ela, I'm right here. I'm not bleeding." Tharion shows me his uninjured body. He's unharmed. Not a scratch except for the nick on his cheek and his bandaged shoulder.

I stare at him, dumbfounded. I could have sworn I saw him, bleeding out, dying right in front of me. I heard his cries, I held his beating heart in my hands. It was real, I know it was.

Tharion puts his arms under me, lifting me up, holding me close to his chest. I hear his heartbeat drumming. His heart is still there. He's alive, he's here. I breathe in his scent, filling my lungs, letting the familiar scent ground me.

As he carries me into the campsite, exhaustion grabs a hold of me. I try to fight the tire, but it's no use. My eyelids feel like anvils on my eyes, forcing them shut. The steady thuds of Tharion's heart lull me into sleep, the god himself waiting to greet me on the other side.

# Chapter 14

## Tharion

Eleanora's body gradually slumps in my arms as we walk, slowly falling asleep. Her black eyelashes plant soft kisses to tops of rosy cheeks, face at rest, finally.

Not at rest is my head. What happened in that forest? Why did she say I was bleeding?

Black smoke gently rises from just outside my tent, crackling flames keeping it toasty. Rowan emerges, face chiselled with worry. Inside, I gently lay Eleanora down on the sleeping mat, careful not to wake her.

Pulling the woollen blanket all the way up to her chin, her eyes twitch in her sleep. Small whimpers of fear and panic slip past her lips, ripping a hole in my chest. What did she see in that forest?

I watch her sleep, keeping her safe. Her body relaxes, whimpers fade out, heavy breaths pushing from her lungs – the God of dreams holding her in the Endless realm for just a while longer.

A lock of her hair falls softly over her left cheek. Gently, running my fingertip over her warm skin, I push it from her face. Lowering my head, I place a soft kiss on her forehead, dragging in her scent.

"I'll be here when you wake up, my sweet Ela. I will keep you safe." The whisper hangs in the air, a promise. I stand up, stopping before the cold winds of autumn caress my face, catching one last glance of her before the gentle clap of a tent flap seals the entry behind me.

"How is she?"
Dark circles hang like shadows under Rowan's golden eyes.

"She's sleeping soundly, seemingly relaxed at the moment. I say we leave her for a few hours and ride out later. We might arrive in Catariel behind schedule, but Eleanora needs the rest."

Rowan dips his chin in agreement. I sit down next to him, watching him stir the boiling pot of oatmeal. Notes of grains, cinnamon and nutmeg hit my nostrils, a wave of hunger crashing against me.

Scooping up a large bowl, Rowan hands it my way - topped with fresh forest berries. I thank him, shoving the warm grains into my mouth. We sit together, eating in silence, my mind drifting back to the forest.

The way she was clinging to herself, praying for someone to help her. I shudder. Why did I leave her alone?

Hot anger pools in my chest, scorching, torturing. I let my pride and disappointment get the best of me. If I had just stayed with her, none of this would have happened.

"She… she said I was bleeding."

Pools of ancient gold stare at me, Rowan's brows stuck in a deep frown.

"When I found her in that forest, she screamed that she saw me dying, bleeding out."

Turning away, Rowan searches his mind. A low grumbling vibrates from his chest, anger blooming in the fox below.

"A Doloryn," he breaks the silence, "she met a Doloryn in the forest."

My stomach drops. "What is that? Some kind of monster?"

"I read about it in an old text. It is an abomination, a creature feasting on your darkest nightmares. It makes you see things that aren't there, based on what you fear the most."

I gasp. Her darkest nightmares? Shivers race across my scalp. I should have been there. I should have protected her from that horrible thing.

"Those things are dangerous, more dangerous than the ones we met at home. If Doloryns are escaping the Veil, it's even worse than we thought. This mission just got a lot more urgent. Vorathiel is trying to weaken us, to break us to the point of surrender."

Corvyn joins us for breakfast, and I tell him about the night before. Eleanora's attack, the things she saw, how I found her. His brows shoot higher with every word.

The raven sucks in a breath, eyes trained on the ground before him. His violet eyes darken, like a memory forcing itself into his mind.

"Is she okay?" A look of disgust colours his face. He adjusts in his seat, obviously uncomfortable.

I bob my head. "Right now, she's sleeping, resting. I'll go check on her in a bit. Eat up, it's going to be a long day, and we need the energy."

I hand him a bowl of the steaming food, fresh berries colouring the beige gloop, before topping off my own portion.

Three hours go by, rustling coming from inside my tent. Eleanora emerges, dark circles dragging shadows underneath her eyes. Her skin looks pale, lifeless. Heavy footsteps carry her across the campsite, slumping down on the mat between Rowan and me. He hands her a bowl of oatmeal, accepting it with a crooked smile.

Rowan puts his arm around her, holding her tightly against him, his huge arms enveloping her in his embrace. A tender kiss lands on the top of her head, that uncomfortable feeling returning in my stomach. I look away, trying not to let it get to me, but it's useless.

The bitter taste of jealousy coats my tongue when someone gets near her – even her familiar. Eleanora looks up at me, eyes flashing in pain. She looks wary, almost unsure what is real and what is not. I put my hand on her shoulder, giving it a light squeeze and smile at her.

"I'm here, Ela. I'm right here. Not hurt, not dying. Right here."

Her eyes scan my face, lingering on my eyes. I hold my breath, an eternity passing before her mouth pulls into a mellow smile, spoon digging into her food.

"You were attacked by a Doloryn, Eleanora." Rowan lets go of her, letting her dig into her bowl.

She stops chewing. "A what?" the words crawl through the sweet porridge.

"A Doloryn. It makes you see your darkest fears and nightmares come true before you, but you are the only one to see them unfold."

Her chewing slows, realization hitting her. She looks up at me again.

"You had… different eyes. That's what kept me from truly believing it was you." She shudders. "You had sickly yellow eyes and a smile full of rotten teeth. The things you said…" Tears build over red flames as she clamps her eyes shut, blocking out the memory.

I turn to her, resting my hands on her knees.

"Eleanora. It wasn't me. I would never, ever, hurt you. What did I say?" I don't want to make her remember, but I need to know what that monster made me tell her, which lies it vomited into her heart.

Eleanora takes in a deep breath before letting it out slowly and opening her eyes.

"You told me you hated me. That I… That I was a failure to everyone around me."

I jerk back. How could this monster take my form and spew these disgusting words at her? My fists clench, nails piercing through skin. Boiling rage colours the world in red.

"Ela, I – I don't know… I would never! I could never…" words fumble and blend as I spit them out, abhorred. Taking a deep breath, I grab her hands in mine.

"Eleanora Luna. I would never, not even in my wildest nightmares, hate you. You are the best thing that has ever happened to me. All the light in the universe would have to dim for me to let that darkness overcome me, and even then, I would fight it with every beat of my heart."

A single tear falls from her eye, my hand shooting up to catch it. I hold her cheek, cupping it gently, feeling her face fall into my palm. Heat spreads between us, refusing to let her go. The impossible urge to protect her has me spellbound. Rowan gets up from his seat, walking over to Corvyn's tent, leaving us alone.

"I would never hurt you, Ela. I…" Words left unspoken burn in my chest, clawing at my throat to be let out, but I can't say them yet. Not now, not like this.

"I promise to protect you. I will slay every demon and spirit in this realm before I let another one put its hands on you again," I say instead. We sit there, me holding her in my arms, and her silently eating her now cold breakfast.

Once finished, we clean up, dressing in warmer clothes and saddle up the horses.

"Rowan, would you mind riding with me? I don't feel like riding by myself after everything."

Rowan walks over to Eleanora, his hands gliding along her arms.

"Of course, *vulpin*. Hop on, I will keep you safe."


As we ride, the sun high in the sky, the forest transforms before our eyes. What was just dark and dead, now beaming with life. Spiralling trees are filled with luscious leaves and colourful flowers dangling low, making an archway just for us.

The sweet earthy scent of grass and mud fills the air with a comforting familiarity. Birds are chirping, small animals scurrying in the bushes, the illusion of safety hanging in the air. Eleanora is sleeping on Rowan's shoulder, a small drip of saliva running down her chin. She is adorable. I chuckle to myself, taking in the warm feelings hammering around inside me.

A small creature darts out onto the trail before us, making us slow down. At first glance, it looks like a rabbit, its light brown fur shimmering in the delicate afternoon sunshine.

Then, the critter hops closer, and the illusion unravels. Its eyes are pitch-black, and the fur is not brown, but rusty red, matted and covered in dried blood. I hold out a hand, signalling Rowan that we need to stop. I point two fingers to my eyes, brushing them over my body: *look at its fur.*

Rowan's eyes follow, studying the little creature. A frown develops between his eyes.

"The rabbit," he whispers, "it's possessed. Look at its eyes, its movement."

A high-pitched screech splits the air, abruptly waking Eleanora from her slumber.

"What the fuck is going on?!" Eleanora shouts, covering her ears. Corvyn crashes to the ground, paralysed by the sound. He stumbles to his feet, desperately holding his ears.

The rabbit tilts his head back, opening its mouth impossibly wide. Then, with a sickening crack, its head splits in two. Blood splatters around it, staining the already brownish fur a deep, wet scarlet. From the broken shell of its body, a black shadow erupts, soaring into the air, darting between our horses with unnatural speed. We're almost knocked right off, the force as unsettling as the sight itself.

As it passes us, a freezing breeze shoots through our bodies. I shiver violently, my fingertips tingling, legs numb away, leaving me feeling as if I were laid down on thousands of razor-sharp needles.

The shadow pierces through the forest, vanishing into the deepness of it.

"What the fuck was that?" Corvyn opens his mouth first, the rest of us too stunned to speak.

Rowan releases his hold, blood trickling from his ears.

"That was an Umbravore. A shadow-devourer. It possesses living creatures to feast on their souls before moving to the next."

We all stare at him, still stunned.

"The Veil is weakening too fast. We are out of time. Our realm will fall into darkness if we don't find this sorcerer quickly."

Corvyn's features harden.

"I will not let the darkness take any more lives from this realm. It took my brother, I will not let it take my friends, too."

We look at him, not with pity, but compassion. The need to correct the wrongs that have been stowed upon him from before are radiating from his skin, spilling from every pore.

"We will stop this, Cor. Even if it takes my life, we will fix what has been done."


After a meal, we ride into the night, sleeping in shifts. Rowan keeps Eleanora company while Corvyn rides with me whenever he's not scouting the skies. We're on edge, ready for another encounter.

My eyes drift closed, then snap open, trying to focus on the trail before us. The stars above glitter in the sea of darkness, even the vibrant treetops have resided for the night. It's like the whole forest is sleeping.

"We should stop and camp for the night, we only have a few hours until dawn," I try, silently praying that the others are just as tired.

A yawn stretches across Eleanora's face, confirming it. We find a suitable spot and set out camp while Eleanora puts her protection rune in place again.

Walking up to her, cracking my fingers nervously, I pick at my cuticles.

"Ela? I was wondering… I, uh-"

With a puzzled look on her face, she stops what she's doing, waiting for me to find my words.

Heat builds in my cheeks, the tips of my ears go up in flames. I clear my throat.

"I was wondering if you'd like to share my tent tonight. You know, so I can keep you safe."

Eleanora's face lights up, her pearly white teeth sparkling under her grin.

"That would be nice. Thank you, Ari. I'll set up when I'm done here." Her smile is shy, and so damn cute. Impossible to hide it, I smile back just as wide.

"You finish up, I'll fix the tent."

Grabbing her bag, I fling it over my shoulder and walk towards the tent.

*Our tent. Remember what happened last time you shared a bedroom?*

I stop in my tracks. Nope. I have not forgotten what happened last time, I replay the scene in my head repeatedly.

Insecurity floods me, now second guessing my judgement. I will keep my hands to myself. The last thing she needs is another bad night's sleep.

I keep walking, entering our small one-person tent, the ground just big enough to fit two sleeping mats, very, very closely. Unfolding the mats, I put down furs and woollen blankets and start on getting a fire going just outside the entrance.

"Toasty," two hands stretch out, basking in the warmth radiating from the embers. I look up at Eleanora, her raven black hair falling perfectly around her face, framing those beautiful burgundy eyes and dark mauve lips. I pat the fur beside me, inviting her to sit.

Silence envelopes us as we stare into the dancing flames. Eleanora leans her head on my shoulder, a loud sigh escaping her. I lean back, feeling her heartbeat drum in her temples. Lavender seeps into my senses, blanketing me in warmth.

In that moment, there is no battle, no spirits roaming the realm. There is nothing to be afraid of. The only thing existing as of right now is Eleanora and I, together by the fire.

# Chapter 15

## Corvyn

The flames blanket me in familiar heat, embers cracking away. My thoughts run along, memories of my childhood emerging. Kaelen and I picking flowers for Mother's kitchen table, her face would always light up.

My chest tightens, a dull ache. He taught me how to be a good male, a male that treats people with kindness and respect no matter what or who they are.

Because of Kaelen, I now found myself part of a dangerous quest. I could very well lose my life during this journey, but it doesn't scare me. If I die, it will be in honour, I would be proud to die for this realm if it meant saving it. If it meant being reunited with Kaelen. The flames dance, pulling me deeper into the depths of my mind.

The flickering shades of orange and white force my lungs open wide, filling them with crisp night air. They take me back to my father's forge. I'd spend hours in there with Kaelen, watching our father make the most beautiful artwork. Swords, blades, sculptures, all handcrafted and made with burning passion. Kaelen would follow in our father's steps, the most skilful blacksmith this realm had ever seen.

A twinge slices through me. Every day I see him, his smile, his eyes watching as I live the life *he* was destined to live. The air feels heavy, sinking to the pits of my lungs. I close my eyes, focusing on the beats of my heart. The subtle rhythm grounds me, like the pounding of a hammer on hot steel.

"Where did you go?" a deep voice tears through the haze. Looking up, a set of golden eyes, like molten metal, meet mine. The weight on my chest lifts, fresh air rushing to my brain.

"Uh… I don't –"

Orange hues spill from the flames, clinging to Rowan's sharp features. The shadows make his auburn eyes glow, bewitching me. The flames flicker, as does my heart, hands clammy with sweat. Wet streaks form as I wipe them on my trousers, drawing breath. Rowan sits down beside me, his legs crossed on the ground.

"Thinking about your family back home?"

"Something like that."
A moment goes by. "Thinking about your brother?"

I nod silently, the ache in my chest returning.

"I would love to hear about him, if you'd share it with me."

His hand falls to my knee, electricity zapping through my stomach. The heavy ache softens, now but a fragile hum amongst butterflies. The edges of my mouth pull into a gentle smile.

I look down at his hand as it rests on the thin fabric separating our skin.

"His name was Kaelen. My oldest brother. My best friend in the world," I start, "he made me see the good in others, and in myself."

Rowan's face softens, his eyes fixed on me, listening carefully.

"He was a fantastic blacksmith, the only one in the kingdom able to forge Aetherium."

Rowan tilts his head to the side. "Aetherium?"

A chuckle escapes me. "It's a metal formed by the breath of stars. It's light as air and stronger than dragon bone… or so the stories tell."

Rowan drags a sharp breath, his reddish brows lifting in surprise. Pride swells in my chest, light and bright as flame. I talk about Kaelen, telling stories from my childhood. Rowan laughs and cries with me, filling the air with bittersweet nostalgia. His laugh is deep and contagious, using his whole body to unleash it.

The stern features of his face mellow into smile lines and rounded eyes. I find myself trying to force the beautiful sound from his body, like music filling my body with warmth.

"Your brother sounds wonderful, Cor." His thumb traces circles on my knee, tickling my skin.

My cheeks heat, I can feel them change colour.

"Thank you for listening to me ramble on about him, you must think I'm obsessed."

"I think you loved him, very dearly. And that is beautiful." His hand leaves my knee and envelops my hand instead, thumb gently caressing my fingers.

"So are you." The words slip without warning, breathlessly, almost a whisper. Those molten pits fire up, glowing stronger in the light of the crackling flames. My gaze darts to his lips, the bottom one tucked under his teeth.

I feel his soul pulling me closer, an invisible rope tied around mine, tugging. Holding in a breath, the hairs on my neck stand up. The very tips of my fingers are aching to touch him, to feel the rough sensation of his face. Thundering away, my heart cries to escape the cage I've so mercilessly locked it in.

Goosebumps race across my scalp, down my neck. I forget to breathe. The beauty before me is hypnotic, overwhelming. Feeling my cheeks incinerate, I look away.

Rowan's voice cuts the tension.

"Will you go for a run with me?"

The question catches me off guard, snapping me out of the entrapment of him.

He chuckles. "Shift with me. I will run while you fly. Run with me, Corvyn."

No one has ever asked me to shift with them. Wing shifters walk around with our wings out, but we rarely entirely shift into our animals.

I fiddle my fingers. "I can't remember the last time I let my raven out."

His eyes smile. "Then it's about time you did."

Rowan stands up, reaching out his hand. I hesitate for a moment, then put my clammy hand in his and stand up too. A wide grin stretches across his face, eyes beaming.

Before I know it, Rowan darts into the forest.

"Come on, raven!"

His laugh rings in the air, echoing into my soul.

I call on my magic, letting it pool in my chest. The familiar sensation of bones cracking and reshaping fills me, heart racing away. I can feel my long dark beak stretch from my face, vision sharpening. I can hear everything, every mouse and butterfly.

My large black wings exchange the place of my arms, and soon enough, I take to the sky. Euphoria fills my body, the raven beneath my skin finally able to soar again. The chilly air cuts between my feathered wings. I dive, gliding beside Rowan. His fox is magnificent.

The reds and browns of his thick fur interweave, dancing in the wind. The muscles of his body strain under his skin, trying to keep up with me. He is riveting.

A loud caw erupts from me, happiness overcoming my very being. Rowan yips and chirps in response, eyes following my every move.

We race through the forest together, zapping between tree trunks and bushes. I spin in the air as he leaps over boulders. We run for hours, the animals in us unable to stop. Tears streak across my feathered head, carried off in the wind. The overwhelming joy shatters that heavy feeling in my chest, evaporating it.

As we circle back to our camp, energy all spent, I shift back. Panting, I stand there, watching as the giant fox shifts back into the human I have come to care so deeply for.

 Our bodies collide as I throw myself around his neck, clambering to him. Steadying himself, he folds his big arms around my waist. I laugh, exhilaration exploding through my being. My whole body vibrates with happiness, I can't stand still.

"That was… Rowan, I –"
My heart is racing, tongue unable to sort through my words.

"It's been so long. My raven… Thank you."

Holding him tight, I give him one extra squeeze before letting go. Still holding onto me, his eyes dive into the violet smoke of my irises.

The deep orange from his fox still lingers in those radiant pools of gold, his shifter magic coursing through his body. An intense tickle forms at the back of my throat, pushing a smile to my face. I feel my eyes watering, joy exploding from my heart.

Rowan pulls me in again, holding me close. He puts one hand on the back of my head, and I come undone. I let myself feel everything. Salty tears pour down my face, sobs ripping from my chest. He holds me tight, until every last tear has fallen. Not saying a word, just holding me close. Comforting, safe.

For so long I have denied myself the comfort of someone else. Since the death of my brother, the thought of letting someone in has been too much. But Rowan feels… right. His heart beats with mine, in harmony. In this moment, we are one.

Planting my hands on his chest, I push myself out of the embrace. Rowan puts his hands to my cheeks, cupping them in.

"You never need to thank me, *korax*. You are safe here. I could feel your raven scratching to get free. My fox could feel him," he dabs his index finger directly above his heart "...in here."
Rowan's eyes bore deep into mine, the warm feeling blossoming in my chest once more. The heat of his hands feels like a promise, and I lean into them.

"Will you run with me some other time?"
The words come out saturated in hope, desperation. I wince.

Rowan laughs, a low rumble.

"I will run with you for as long as you will have me. But now, we need to sleep. Good night, korax." He drags his thumbs across the outline of my face, and over my chin. A shiver runs through me.
*I would run with you forever, fox.*

# *Chapter 16*

### *Eleanora*

I wake as the gentle sunlight kisses our tent, flooding it with orange warmth. The air is heavy, steeped in unspoken dreams. I stretch my arms above my head, feeling my muscles yawn, blood circulating. As I discard all the night's air, Tharion turns towards me.

"Good morning." His sleepy voice makes my stomach flutter. Pools of jade are filled with remnants of sweet dreams, and I wonder if I made my way into them.

"How was your night?"

"I slept better than I have in a long time. Might have something to do with the person I shared my tent with," he winks at me, a sleepy smile appearing. Warmth fills my body, the urge to snuggle closer to him overwhelming, but I stay put.

A huffed chuckle tears from me, trying to convey a feeling of annoyance, my eyes rolling in an exaggerated act. Tharion laughs and turns to his back, tucking his palms behind his head. The blanket pools at his waist as I sit up on the mat.

Sunlight cracks through the small gap of our tent, blinding me momentarily. I stand, stumbling over our things, crashing theatrically to the ground. Tharion erupts in wicked laughter, the deep vibrations echoing around me as I reorient myself.

Looking back at him, I shoot him a scowl, but only for a moment – laughter building in my throat. It explodes from me, pulling all the way from the pits of my stomach. For a brief second, we're back in Sylvarn. Back in the woods where we feel safe, at peace. Tears roll from my eyes, the laughter so deeply embedded in my body that I struggle to stop.

Tharion gets up, still cackling, and grabs my hand. Hauling me to my feet with a *whoop*, I fall against his bare torso. The fair skin smells of a mixture of Tharion and sleep, goosebumps racing down my thighs. I breathe in his scent, filling my lungs so full that they hurt, a need to imbed the scent in my body. My muscles relax, shoulders sinking, jaw unclenching.

We stand there, his palm still in mine, my face still planted against his chest. Warm hands make their way down my back, settling on the lowest part of it. Moving closer, the need to erase the distance between us is suffocating. His nose buries into my hair, dragging in my scent. I can feel the hammering of his heart, the sound like beating drums in my ears.

"Eleanora, are you awake?"
*Goddess damn it. Every time!*
Rowan's voice cuts through the air, separating us once more. I investigate Tharion's dusky gaze, knowing I might have just made things even more difficult for him. After that night in the forest, I should keep my distance. At least until I know what to do with these feelings. Tharion stares back at me, face brightening as his mossy eyes meet mine.

A breath hitches in his chest, I can tell that he's working hard to stay planted.

"Be right out!" I call back at Rowan, my eyes still fixed on Tharion's. Pulling away, cold emptiness replaces the blooming heat of his body against mine.

I shoot him a smile before picking up the woollen blanket on our mat, turning and stepping out into the warm sun, still in my sleepwear. Tharion's shaky breath from inside has me looking back, craving his embrace. Folding the blanket around me, I walk over to the fire where Rowan and Corvyn are chatting over a steaming pot of rice porridge.

From a distance, observing the males, I notice my familiar's new glow. Rowan has a flare to him that I have never seen before. His shoulders relaxed, breath even. No frown on his face. He looks… peaceful. Happy.

The males sit with their knees positioned towards one another, body language welcoming the other inside. Corvyn laughs with a hand placed on Rowan's forearm. The joyful sound dances in the autumn wind, carrying through the forest. A faint pink blush creeps up Rowan's cheeks, eyes glossy and soft. I can see his teeth peeking out from his grin, bursting with laughter as Corvyn tells another story.

Glancing down, his left foot bounces impatiently. Is he…nervous? My Rowan, nervous? The thought makes me chuckle, a warm sensation settling inside me.

"Hey, boys. What are we laughing about?"

Handing me a bowl, Rowan pats the ground beside him, and I plop down. His eyes dart back to Corvyn, the smile returning tenfold as if he didn't just see him mere seconds ago.

Wiping his eyes, laughter fading out, Corvyn lets go of Rowan. The softness of his eyes hardens, though only for a second, as if they crave his touch to return.

"Good morning, Eleanora! How are we feeling today?" Mouth stuffed with porridge, I gesture a thumbs up.

"Are we ready to get going? We should make it to the castle today, unless we meet something along the way."

A shudder runs through me, thinking back at that poor animal.

The loud smack of slick fabric is heard, Tharion emerging from our tent. His hair is still dishevelled, but at least he has put on a fresh set of clothes. The auburn curls fall nicely around his face and over his shoulders, hitting the sunshine perfectly - he looks ethereal.

Two fingers appear under my chin, closing my gaping mouth. Rowan laughs quietly, trying to hide his face. I dip my head, wincing at myself. My body feels uncomfortably hot. I shoot to my feet, fleeing for the tent. *What are you doing? It's just Tharion. Keep it together!*

Keeping my head down, I barge through the tent flaps, smacking them against the sides. Inside, I close my eyes, taking a deep breath, repeating it until the raging heat in my veins slowly dissipates. I throw my things into my satchel, getting ready for departure.

Lying at the bottom is the small wooden figurine, smiling up at me. I hold it in my hands, feeling the ridges of every detail. Butterflies flutter in my chest, their wings brushing against my lungs. I squeeze the figurine in my palm before stuffing it back into the bag and closing it.

. . — . ✳ . — . .

The scenery changes as we ride – the forest exhaling its summer hush, trading emerald silence for a chorus of copper and flame. It opens, revealing a large clearing.

Way out in the distance, all but a faint mirage, a large castle perched atop a waterfall towers above jagged hills of stone. Watching in awe, I feel so small, like a bug under a giant's shoe. *Look at that.* My mouth goes slack as the world fades beside me. Catariel.

"Whoa… That is… Damn."

I look back at Corvyn, eyes stretched wide, mouth hanging open.

A breathy chuckle escapes me. "*Damn* is right. What a sight."
I turn to Rowan, one eye still trained on the majestic sight before us.

"How long until we're there, you reckon?"
His pointy face looks up at the sun, calculating.

"I'd say about an hour if we keep this pace."

A slow smile warms my face, and I slump back in my saddle. Letting out a deep exhale, adrenaline thrums in my veins.

"Well, what are we waiting for? Come on! Last one there gets put on foot-rubbing duty!"

I click my teeth, leather creaking as reins whip, taking off. Rowan's yelp makes me laugh, but I buck down to hold myself steady. The others set off after me, now in a race to beat each other. Laughter erupts from us all, filling the forest clearing.

As we gallop across dew-dropped grass, the castle's grand picture grows bigger by the minute. We hop from the clearing on to a pebbled path, zigzagging up a hillside to the gates, all the way to the top.

On each side of the path nothing but mist and stone can be seen, falling hundreds of feet below us. The raging waterfall under the castle clouds the air, filling it with small droplets of water.

As we zip through the final corners, exhaustion holds me in its tight grip. Huffing, heaving for breath, we come to a stop before the castle's gates. I get there first, followed by Corvyn, then Tharion and Rowan.

I jump off, legs almost buckling on impact. Turning back, three sets of eyes, blown open in awe, stare up at the enchanting building. Slowly, I turn to face it, flinching in its enormity. The sound of trumpets cleaves the air, sending us hunching to the ground.

"They know we're here." Rowan holds his ears, shaking his head profusely as the loud notes ring painfully against our eardrums. We approach the castle's threshold, where great wooden doors stand beneath an arch of weathered stone. Their surface gleams faintly, carved with patterns half-swallowed by moss and time.

A whisper of wind stirs, rattling the old iron handles, as though the doors themselves are breathing, waiting for our hands. As I stretch out to grab them, the doors move. Slowly, with deafening creaks, the courtyard inside reveals itself.

A figure, a male, dressed in fine silks, greets us inside. A closer look reveals the royal crest sewn to his cape.

*It's the King.*
Realization hits us, our knees crashing with the soil below.

"King Vaelrick, it is with great honour that we are blessed with your presence."

Rowan bows his head, the rest of us swiftly following.
The King scoffs, waving us off.

"Get up, travellers. State your names."

Darkness hugs the undersides of his dull, cerulean eyes. His blonde hair is scruffy, streaks of grey glinting throughout it.

Clearing his throat, Rowan lifts his face to the King.

"We are Rowan, Eleanora and Tharion of Sylvarn, with Corvyn of Stormbrook. We come bearing grave news and ask for your time, my liege."

King Vaelrick looks at us, taking in each of our faces, his mouth a thin line.

"You may rise."

In unison, we get up and adjust our postures. My heart is beating away, sweat beading at my hairline.

"What is this grave news you wish to inform me of?" His stoic expression doesn't give, eyes scanning our dirty clothes, taking us all in. His arms are crossed over his chest, a passive distancing.

"My liege, we ask only of your time. Out here is not the place to discuss the safety of the kingdom, nor is it safe at all. We need no more than an hour."

The King stares at us, no answer, no movement. Then, he lets down his arms, turning his body slightly away from us.

"I will give you my time, but only for tonight. Get yourselves cleaned up, we will discuss over dinner this evening. My aides will show you to a room where you can freshen up." Scrunching his nose, he turns on his heel and walks off into the vastness that is his castle, not looking back at us.

Two aides, dressed in dark green tunics, appear from massive stone pillars on each side of the gates.

"This way, guests," they say, perfectly in sync. Shivers rip through me, a knot forming in my stomach. I look over to Tharion, finding him staring out onto the castle grounds, eyes soaking up the sheer grandness of it – searching, taking in the details.

Our aides guide us through the castle. We walk through halls big enough to fit all our houses inside, ceilings towering thirty feet above our heads, with grand pillars of white marble radiating in the sunlight.

Windows stretch across the walls, letting in every single sun ray. The opposite walls are decorated in art, paintings of vast landscapes and a woman with long, cherry red hair. I study her; her eyes a deep emerald green, her dress a dark violet. She is stunning. The paintings portray her smiling, laughing, happy.

The ceilings are all painted to look like the sky, fluffy clouds in whites and dusty pinks spreading across them.

As we walk through the hallway, we take a left turn and end up in a foyer leading to six different rooms. On the tile floors, a giant sun with 6 magnificent rays pointing in every direction catches my eye. The sun has intricate details in golds, yellows and deep orange, making it look as if it's moving.

"You may pick your rooms. An aide will be sent up shortly to help you get bathed and dressed for dinner."

I walk up to one of the doors, turning the handle. My breath sticks to my throat as tired legs carry me inside. The beauty of it, it's like nothing I've ever seen. A large bed draped with thick fabrics in white and gold rests in the middle of the room. More pillows than I have ever seen in my life fill the fluffy bed, body twitching to bury myself in them. I turn in a circle, taking it all in, jaw barely on its hinges.

With careful steps, I stand beside the bed, running my hand over the silky fabric, gasping at the softness. Noticing there's a door inside the room, curiosity drags me towards it, swinging the door open. Inside is a washroom, big enough to fit my entire village! Eyes wide, I pick my jaw off the floor.

*This isn't a room, it's a whole damn house!*

The white marble walls stretch twenty feet tall, the flooring is already warm under my frozen toes. I slip my socks off and let the hot tiles heat me up. To my left is a giant bathtub, the stunning copper vessel held up by thick, grey, marble claws. It sits before a window so big it reveals the whole kingdom. Under the bathtub is a small fire pit, set to keep the water at a nice temperature.

A female dressed in the same deep emerald tunic as the aides before walks in, silently turning on the faucet to fill the tub before slipping out the door, closing it with a soft click. White, fluffy towels lay next to the bath, and a robe in a deep maroon is hung by the door.

There's a small table stacked with lotions and creams, a bottle for bubbles and one with soap standing to the very right side. I tip the bubble bottle into the steaming water, watching foam build into thick white clouds.

Turning, I make sure I'm alone. Dirty clothes fall off my aching body, piling at my ankles. At the bottom of the tub, three marble steps lead up to the bubbling vessel of relaxation. My toes sink into the crackling water, the soft unravelling of my exhaustion closely following.

Submerging myself fully, all the tension exits my body, leaving me with a bone-deep sense of relief. I lean my chin on my forearms, crossed over the edge of the bathtub, staring out onto the breathtaking landscapes that are Kyrris.

Stormbrook, Sylvarn and Meadowrest, all separated by beautiful forests, creeks and mountain ridges. My eyes rest on the contours of Sylvarn, imagining what my parents would be up to, and how Axel is doing. I miss them.

Turning my body, I lay my head back on one of the fluffy hand towels and drag in the floral scent of soap, luscious lavender, listening to bubbles pop and fizz on the surface.

*You're in the King's castle, bathing in his bathtub. What is your life, Eleanora?!*

A squeal unfolds, my body jittering away. If only my parents could see me now, would they feel pride?

I stop. The knot in my stomach returns, tightening my nerves.

Shaking my head, I remind myself the same as so many times before.

"No. I am not here for them; I am here for the kingdom," I tell myself, tired of feeling inadequate. Saying it out loud takes a weight off my shoulders, and I slump deeper into the relaxing bubbles yet again. Closing my eyes, I let my thoughts drift off, to a place without impending doom, without the ever-following risk of dying.

Jolting awake, my eyes burst open. Waves break over the sides of the tub, splashing the floor. The water is still warm, thanks to the small fire under me. I look around, forgetting momentarily where I am.

*Of course, the King's castle. Breathe, now.*

I gulp down mouthfuls of air, calming my racing heart. Reaching for one of the towels, I stand, wrapping it around me. I walk up to the mirror covering the west wall, careful not to slip. With a hand towel, wiping off the steam, my reflection appears before me. Meeting my own face, I take a good look at myself.

My eyes are bloodshot, dark circles stretching below them. My cheeks are dull in colour, no sign of the rosy pink they usually carry. I force my eyes away, dry up and walk out into the enormous bedroom. On the bed lies a beautiful gown, the fabric a delicate cobalt blue.

I lift it up, studying the intricate embroidery clinging to the material. Flowers in green and purple scatter along the hem of the gown, making it look as if you're walking through a meadow. The fabric is thick, silky.

I slip it on, the gown hugging my curves in a way I've never experienced before. I normally wear trousers, and don't even own many dresses, let alone a gown like this. The corset highlights my waist, accentuating my hips and perfectly cups my breasts. Standing in front of the mirror, I look at myself in awe. I look… beautiful.

A brief knock on the door is all the warning I get before two aides walk in, carrying boxes of different jewellery and a basket of things to help get the crow's nest on my head under control. One of them grabs my hand, guiding me to a chair, but before my ass even touches the seat, my hair is lifted by a brush, face stretched tautly towards my nape.

Knot after knot is brushed out, leaving my hair feeling silky, but my scalp screaming for mercy. While one of the aides delicately pins my hair up into a graceful updo, the other picks out a necklace, a bracelet and a beautiful set of sapphire earrings for me to use.

"Why do I need all of this?" I ask, still being tugged in different directions.

"The King prefers his guests to dress proper when dining with him."

My chin dips, the thought of dining with the King daunting. As quickly as they started, the aides finish my appearance. I step up to one of the floor-length mirrors to see a queen staring back at me. A sharp gasp breaks free, my hand shoots up to cover it. *Who is this?*

"If you would follow me, I will guide you to the dining hall."

I snap back into focus, giving them a quick nod. At my feet are a pair of heels, bejewelled in blues and golds. Nerves rattle in my stomach. *Those are taller than the trees back home! How on earth am I supposed to walk in them?* Swallowing thickly, I lift my eyes to one of the females waiting for me to step into the shoes.

"I've never worn heels before. Do you have any flats?"
The aide looks at me, eyes wide, a look of horror on her face.

"Flat shoes are not proper. You will wear what the King assigns you," her snappy voice makes me flinch. I nod, trying to choke back a sigh.

Stepping into the shoes, I wobble for a moment, struggling to find my balance. Heels click against the stone floor, every so often rolling my ankles, the small heel unfamiliar to me. It takes a few steps of looking like a newborn baby deer before I finally get the hang of it, the clickity-clacks ringing through the hall as I stride towards the dining area.

Two knights dressed in the King's army's colours, dark emerald green and fiery orange, wait for us as we arrive. Snaking their hands around the door handles, they drag the giant wooden doors open.

The clanging of plates and silverware ring through the hall, echoing loudly. It seems I'm the first to arrive, the room completely empty. I look around, taking in the large venue. A table that can easily seat 30 people sits in the middle of the room, surrounded by chairs sewn with deep red velvet cushions.

Candles light up the walls, yellow flickers dancing on dark grey bricks. At the back of the room, beyond the table, stands a grand fireplace, fire roaring inside. I hear footsteps behind me, and as I turn around, my eyes meet a pair of deep blue irises. Instantly, my knee sinks to the floor, head bowed deeply.

"My king," I curtsy, holding the skirt of my gown in my right hand.

"Lady Eleanora, you are my guest tonight. No need for curtsy, and please, call me Vaelrick."

Flames lick my cheeks, the pink colour deepening. As I raise my head, my gaze finds his. His dull, blonde hair falls delicately behind his ears, kissing the tops of his shoulders. The beard, streaked with grey, shields his face, hiding his true expression.

Studying him, I find his body carefully trembling. He coughs, clearing his throat before finding his seat at the end of the table. Light pattering closes in behind him, an aide filling his golden chalet with a deep burgundy wine.

With a quick gesture, hand faced up, he signals for me to sit down next to him. Carefully, I approach him, *Vaelrick*, dragging my chair from the table before sitting down. His eyes fall to my gown, studying it. They rake across my shoulders, down my waist and rest on the hem, a faint gloss grazing over his eyes.

"This gown…" his words get stuck in his throat, Vaelrick swallowing thickly.

Brushing the skirt, I straighten. "I apologize if it doesn't suit me. It was waiting for me after my bath." Frantically, my eyes dart between him and the fireplace behind him.

Waving his hand, a faint smile pulls from the edges of his lips.

"No, no. I apologize for being blunt. It is not that. The dress belonged to my wife Rowenna. Tonight is the first time I have seen it since she passed." His voice fades out, the smile vanishing. Cold tingles race across my neck, my shoulders feeling stiff as a board.

"Oh…"

"Do not apologize. She would have loved to see her gowns get to dance in the halls again. Rowenna would hate for them to hang in a closet forever."

I look at him, eyes glimmering with gentle longing, and before I know it my hand is on top of his. I stiffen, realization hitting me. Vaelrick's breath hitches in his chest, eyes widening. I snap my hand back, heat rushing to my face again.

"I'm so sorry. I don't know what came over me. My king, I –" The words spill out of me like vomit, our King staring at me with fierce intensity.

After a painful second of silence, Vaelrick leans back, laughter bubbling from his chest, a laugh so deep I hear it take root in the deepest pits of his belly. The happy sound fills the air in the room, joyous notes dancing through the candlelight.

His shoulders shake violently, tears running from his eyes. He holds his stomach, aching whimpers mixing with the happy laughter. Wiping his eyes with his index finger, salty tears coating it, his breath comes out wispy and short, trying hard to catch it.

"Lady Eleanora, how you fascinate me," the words come out choppy, his laugh meddling with them.

My body feels hot enough to melt stone, brain telling me to run as fast and as far as I can.

"I have not laughed like that, not laughed at all, since my Rowenna left me. It is nice to feel the joy of laughter once more. Thank you, my lady."

*"My lady"? Since when have I ever been a lady?* I scoff to myself, lowering my shoulders and puffing my chest. Raking my eyes across Vaelrick's face, watching his colour springing back into his eyes, the stiffness in my shoulders loosen.

"I aim to please, my King."

Mockingly, I bow my head, a cheeky smirk on my lips.

# *Chapter 17*

## *Tharion*

Closing the door behind me, I cross the threshold leading to the solar foyer. Orange light bathes the tiles below my feet, as if walking on fire. At the other end of the hall, Corvyn and Rowan are deep in conversation. Corvyn is leaning against a wall, arms crossed over his chest, although his body language radiates invitation.

He's smiling, talking, a twinkle in those deep violet eyes whenever Rowan opens his mouth to answer. The fox rakes a hand through his strawberry blonde hair, the bushy locks delicately flowing through his fingers. I hear them laughing, Rowan's eyes burning with golden flames.

"Hey, friends. You as hungry as I am? I could eat a dragon!" Their eyes break from each other, finding me.

"Sure am, can't wait to eat a proper meal! No offense, Rowan, but I'm *so* sick of oatmeal and porridge." Corvyn nudges Rowan's arm, the fox shooting him a scowl, working hard to keep his blooming grin in check.

We walk through the halls, chasing the delicious smell coating the air. As we step into the dining hall, I find Eleanora and the King sitting at the table together. Are they… laughing? My chest grows tighter, fingers clenching into a fist. The smile I had plastered on my face fades away.

The King turns to us and stands up, a warm smile on his face.

"Guests, welcome. Please, have a seat. The food will be brought out shortly."

Eleanora rises, revealing her outfit. Breathtaking. Her gown flows gracefully under her, the deep blue complementing her porcelain skin perfectly. The gown makes her plump curves stand out, impossible to tear my eyes from. She looks stunning.

Meeting my stare, she pushes her hair behind her ears, looking down on the floor, an adorable pink sheen glazing her cheeks. My heart aches, dragging all the air from my lungs. Every bone in my body wants to run up to her, to feel the fabric of the gown on my fingers, to run them over her delicate collarbone and down her arms.

"Eleanora, you… You look amazing." My voice comes out breathless, low.

Her eyes widen, the pink sheen deepening.

Rowan clears his throat, cutting the tension. I rip my gaze from hers, turning to the King.

"My liege," I bow, "thank you for sharing this meal with us tonight. We have much to discuss."

He nods, the deep blue colour of his eyes darkening. As we sit down, our glasses are filled with fragrant wine, taking the edge off the serious matters soon to be deliberated.

The ring of a bell chimes at our heads as swinging doors fly open, multiple servers carrying plates with silver cloches rushing out.

Simultaneously, they set the plates before us and lift the cloches off. The smell of roasted lamb hits my nostrils, filling my mouth with water. Next to the slabs of meat lay a bed of golden potatoes, roasted to perfection with herbs and different aromatics. Small carrots and garden onions glazed with delectable honey glisten with goodness under a rich burgundy red sauce. I pile on a piece of everything and let out a soft moan as the perfect bite slathers my tastebuds.

Quickly, the rest of my party lets out grunts and sounds of joy, all of us taken aback by the delicious meal. The King looks between us, chuckling. We sit in silence while we feast, none of us even looking up at each other. I take a swig of my wine, the earthy, tangy liquid melting into my tongue, pairing perfectly with the flavours in my mouth. I close my eyes, savouring it all, never wanting to forget it.

"My King, this meal is divine. I have never eaten such great food in my life. Thank you."

He looks at me, a softness in the eyes meeting mine.

"Tell me, travellers, why you have come all this way. What message is it you carry and from whom?"

Washing away the food with another glug of wine, I nervously look over to Rowan, still chewing.

"I'm sure you have heard that there have been sightings and incidents surrounding spirits lately." I clear my throat.

"The Veil has cracked, my King."

King Vaelrick puts down his cutlery, body stiffening.

"I see. And how are we to fix the Veil?"
I swallow loudly, the wine drying out my mouth.

"My father, rest his soul, came to me in a dream. He was a Seer, your Grace, and he told me I was destined to end this."

Blonde eyebrows shoot up, his eyes widening.

"A Seer, you say? How did he pass?"
The question makes my stomach churn, jaw clenching painfully.

"He was murdered by wolf shifters, your Grace. As was my mother." I look down in my lap, body trembling.
Silence fills the room, no one saying a word.

"I am sorry for your loss, Lord Tharion. Forgive me for being harsh, but how do you know the dream was foretelling?"

*He showed you how he'd die, for starters.*

"We were attacked by dark spirits back home, and the dream came the same night. It was true, I know it was."

The King studies me, dragging in a deep breath.

"I see. What can I do to assist you in this journey?"

Rowan puts his hand on my shoulder, giving it a comforting squeeze. Before I can open my mouth, his deep voice rings through the room.

"My liege, we ask that we can use your training grounds. Tharion must get control of his powers and learn to defend himself, if we are to have even a slight chance against these monsters."

The King is silent, then nods. "You are welcome to stay in my castle for as long as you need. My training grounds are yours to use at your will, as are my soldiers. Treat my castle as your home before your journey. Whatever you need, let me know."

Rowan dips his chin. "Thank you, my liege. We are grateful for your trust in us." The King gives a sharp nod before a clap of his hands thunder through the air.

The servers from before rush in to grab our plates, leaving the room as quickly as they entered. Only a moment goes by before a new set of servers come out, perfectly in line, and sets down a smaller plate before us. On it is a slice of fresh, homemade apple pie. The strong scent of cinnamon and apple coats my tongue, desperate to taste it.

"Please, friends, dig in. We have a busy day tomorrow, so eat well and rest."

· · — · ✳ · — · ·

The King's words echo in my mind as we step out into the hallway. My stomach is full, eyelids heavy. A deep yawn pulls from my core, watching as it spreads through our small group.

"That was fantastic. That lamb…" Rowan looks up into the air, memorizing the meal.

"I've never eaten something so nice in my life. And now we get to stay here? Guys… What is our life?"

Eleanora looks between us, her voice filled with amazement. We get to the grand hall in which our rooms are scattered, the giant tiled sun casting the room in a golden orange hue.

Saying goodnight, Rowan and Corvyn escape into the fox's room, leaving Eleanora and I outside.

"They seem to be getting along very well," I smile, "it's nice to see Rowan happy like that."

Her eyes soften. "I know. He's a completely different person these days. I'm glad Corvyn gets that side of him out more often."

I look at her, my sweet Eleanora, standing before me in a royal gown, looking painfully beautiful. Before I realize, my hand gently caresses her bare shoulder, making small bumps form all the way down her arm. She shudders briefly, a shaky breath slipping past her wine-stained lips.

"Eleanora, you… You look gorgeous. Just… perfect," I whisper coarsely, stepping closer.

"I guess you don't need to sleep in my tent anymore, seeing we don't have one and you don't need me to keep you safe."

My voice is low and laced with an unmistakable tint of hope. Eleanora's chest rises and falls with heavy breaths, the faint pink tint of her cheeks turning many shades darker.

Leaning her head slightly to the side, she closes her eyes, giving me better access to her neck and decolletage, so I dive, deeper, closer.

The tip of my nose softly strokes up her neck, dragging in the intoxicating scent of her. The lavender soap mixes perfectly with her naturally sweet scent, sending my senses spiralling more than any wine could. Her hand finds my waist, holding on to my shirt as a soft sigh pushes from her lips.

My heart pounds impatiently in my chest, dull thumps echoing in my ears. Eleanora's shallow breaths send chills down my neck, body crackling in response. I feel my fingers twitch, wanting to close the distance between us. Lifting my hand slowly, it hovers just next to her flushed cheek. She snaps her head as the creaking sound of a door opening breaks the delicious tension, snapping me back to the now.

Corvyn falls out the door, Rowan just as quickly following as they smack to the tiles below us. Eleanora bursts out laughing, folding in two as she hugs her waist. The males struggle to get off each other, making it look like they're in a really strange wrestling match, forcing me to crack into a fit of laughter too. Rowan breaks off Corvyn, stumbling to his feet, cheeks a dark red.

"What in the Afterlife are you two doing?"
Laughter makes it hard to understand Eleanora's words, but it seems to make the shade of red on Rowan's cheeks deepen in colour. As Corvyn

climbs back on his feet, dusting his trousers off, he looks to Rowan, also falling into laughter, joyous vibrations ringing through the stone walls.

"We're going for a run, care to join? There are plenty of horses in the stables."

As the last chuckles escape us, the thought of riding through the chilly night air does sound good. I look at Eleanora, her eyes glistening from laughter, smile lighting up the giant hallways, and nod. A wide grin replaces the deep redness of Rowan's cheeks, and so we grab a quick change of clothes before heading outside.

The walk to the stables isn't far, but walking next to her just moments after I had my head lodged by her neck is making it seem so much longer. Her hand faintly brushes mine, electricity shooting up my arm. My fingers twitch as my throat works in a dry swallow.

Her scent still lingers, sweet and intoxicating, heat flooding me with every breath. I look up at the evening sky, clouds dancing in shades of pink and orange as the trees below sway to their rhythm.

Faint whinnies can be heard from the stables, and as we round the last corner, three giant heads poke out from the stable windows. They bounce happily as we walk up to them, raking our hands through the giant animals' soft manes. The smell of damp hay envelops us, reminding me of home. A knot forms in my chest, and I find myself wondering what Axel is up to these days.

"Will you ride with me?"

My head turns to the side at the question, Eleanora swaying gently next to me. Smiling, I grab the reins attached to the black steed in front of us, walking him out of his pen. The heavy clacks of hooves on hay-covered stone echoes across the stables. I throw a double saddle over him, fastening it tightly under his belly. The horse nickers and exhales heavily, ready to get the ride going. I give him a handful of fresh hay, stroking him down his big nose. "Good boy."

Chuckling, I bow deeply and gesture for Eleanora to get on.

"After you, my lady," exaggerating my accent to sound overly formal. Eleanora laughs and rolls her eyes before climbing onto the enormous beast of a horse. I follow, thumping down behind her, my pelvis slamming against her ass as I sit down.

She knocks forward just slightly, and the sight almost makes me fall right off the other side.

*How I would enjoy making you knock forward like that repeatedly.*

Heat pools in my stomach as I lean closer to her, Eleanora pushing back slightly. I hover just next to her ear.

"Ready to go for a ride?" My voice is coarse, almost a whisper. Her shoulders tremble as her head bobs in agreement, "you have no idea."

Sitting back, I click my tongue, sending us out of the stables and into the evening. Cold night air bites my cheeks, sharpening my focus as the steady rhythm of trotting bounces off the stone path. A loud caw from our raven friend is closely followed by a piercing yip, both eagerly waiting for us to hurry up.

We set off, galloping into the forest, dark reds and oranges flying past us. Corvyn dives, swooping from side to side around Rowan, the giant fox straining his muscles to keep up. We watch them mingle, their happy chirps and barks entwining each other. Rowan has a smile plastered on his sharp face, eyes glowing a strong auburn as Corvyn darts around him, riding the cold autumn winds of Catariel.

I tighten my hold on the reins, the leather creaking under my firm grip, arms clamping closer to Eleanora's soft waist. Leaning forward, resting my chin on her shoulder, I listen to her straining breaths as we try to keep up with our shifter friends. Slowly, I remove one hand from the reins, letting my palm find its way around her stomach, pulling her closer to me. With every stomping gallop the horse makes, my lower body slams into her, forcing small yelps of desire from her lips.

Her hand finds mine, lacing our fingers together as she presses our hands harder to her, closing the remaining distance between us. Her head falls back, resting on my chest as my hand holds her tightly to me.

Keeping my eyes on the road, I let my head fall into the nook of her neck, once again dragging in her scent. I try to choke back a moan, but my body fails as a deep growl forms in my chest, vibrating onto her fair skin. *Mine.* I feel safe, whole, as she lays against me, letting me hold her tight.

We circle back to the castle, our bodies vibrating with tension. I can still feel her pressed against me, the delicious jolts of pleasure from when my body cradled hers. I walk the mighty animal back to its pen, brushing its short fur and thanking him deeply for letting us ride with him. Eleanora stands in front of Rowan, brushing her hand through his thick fur, the fox pushing against it.

Corvyn darts into his rooms, sounds of bones breaking and reshaping sending shivers down my spine. They both change back and get dressed before saying goodnight, the afternoon sun now replaced by a radiant white moon. Eleanora stands before her door, fiddling her fingers, eyes averting me.

I rest my forearm on the doorframe, leaning against it.

"Thanks for the ride." I struggle to keep my smile hidden as the memories flash before me. Eleanora chuckles, her ears turning a deep magenta. I gently push a raven-black lock of hair behind her ear, feeling her lean into my touch.

"It's cold tonight… like the forest. Will you stay?" Her eyes glitter in the moonlight, burgundy irises like deep pools of intoxicating wine.

"I will always keep you safe… and warm," I wink, one side of my mouth perking up. The door opens with a loud creak, "after you."

She opens her door, inviting me inside. We get into our sleep wear, brush our teeth and duck under the freezing covers. Grabbing her waist, I pull her closer to me, pouring my heat into her cold body. Her shivers simmer down to a faint vibration, then stills as her breaths even out. I listen to them, the safeness they portray, the safety she feels from having me close.

*You will be mine, Eleanora Luna. If the Gods or this battle doesn't take you from me first.*

# Chapter 18

### Eleanora

The moon casts the room in a grey haze, bright reflections stinging as my eyes slowly open. I feel him, his breaths steady, deep, body completely still. The muscles in my back and thighs cry out as I turn, ridiculously sore from riding.

Images flash before me; traces of his mouth hovering over that sensitive part of my neck, his hands laid firmly on my waist as we rode, electric friction between our bodies. Heat pools in my core, how good it felt to have him so close to me. Curse those layers of fabric between us.

My fingers run across his face, tucking a stray piece of hair away from it. He looks so peaceful. Not a frown in sight, just his light brown freckles scattered across his forehead, relaxing for a change. A soft mumble sounds from him, indistinguishable words, making me chuckle.

"Eleanora?" His voice is hoarse, whispering.

"I'm right here, Ari. Go back to sleep."

I kiss his forehead, dragging in his sleepy musk.

Mossy green meadows slowly open, and I dive. The world stops turning as his sleepy mouth pulls into a soft smile.

"Hey."

"Hey, you."

Strong arms stretch around me, pulling me closer to him. A breathy snort escapes me, the sudden move catching me off guard. He laughs, that mesmerizing sound shooting electricity through my veins.

Hauling me onto his chest, I listen to his beating heart. The steady thumps calm me down, putting heavy weights on my eyelids. Fingers comb through my hair while shivers dance delightfully over my skin. Tharion drags in a deep breath.

"How are you feeling?" His voice bears a hint of nervousness. I look up at him, smiling.

"Better than ever."

Those beautiful jade eyes soften, and I feel the tension he built in his body loosening with every exhale.

His calloused hands run over my bare skin, goosebumps forming underneath them as they go.

As I close my eyes, I move back down into the nook of his arm, feeling the butterflies settle down, heat spreading evenly in my body, the electricity ebbing to a hum. I feel safe, loved, cherished. I feel *chosen*.

Tharion's body falls heavy, his breathing steady and slow. I glance up at him, watching his head tilt slightly to the side, fast asleep. Listening to his heartbeat, the thumping sound lulls me back into deep sleep once more.

· · — · ✳ · — · ·

It's well into the late morning when my eyes open again, the grey haze of the moonlight replaced by bright, warm sunlight. I turn around to find the bed… empty. Tharion has left. Did he leave during the night?

The pit in my stomach blossoms, chest tightening. Searching around me, his clothes are gone, no sign that he was ever here.

I huff out a breath, feeling my lips pucker. Throwing off my cover, I grab my robe and tie it aggressively around my waist. Stomping into the giant washroom, I turn on the water, splashing my face with it. The ice-cold droplets run down my neck, soaking the collar of my robe.

"Ugh!" I groan, more annoyed by the now wet clothing on my skin.

I vigorously brush my teeth, gums bleeding into the herbal paste. My hairbrush rakes through my locks, violently ripping out strands of raven black.

*I'll show him. Running out on me after letting him in. I'll show him.*

The world goes red, I feel so stupid. Throwing the door open, the doorknob hits the brick wall, sound clanging through the room.

"What has got you in a mood this morning?"

Tharion stands next to my bed, a silver tray in his hands. The tray has plates of sweet pastries, fresh bread with glossy jam and two cups of steaming spiced tea. Tilting his head, a puzzled look brushes over his face.

I stop in my tracks, steam rolling off me. Letting my shoulders back down, I take in a breath.

"You left," I snap.

"… to get breakfast. I wanted to surprise you. Rowan and Corvyn are out running again, so I figured I'd make you breakfast in bed."

Still holding the tray, he walks over to me, his eyes scanning my face.

"You thought I left you? After the night we shared? I'm a little offended, Eleanora Luna," his voice is stern, but his eyes are soft, almost playful.

My cheeks heat, embarrassment racing across my scalp. I look down. I really *had* thought that, hadn't I?

Tharion sets the tray down before walking back over to me. He pulls me in for a hug, holding me tight.

"Eleanora. You know me. We have known each other for over a decade, since we were dumb teenagers. You know I would never walk out on you. Do not let your emotions cloud what you know me to be out of fear. I'm not going anywhere."

Breath shoots past my lips, lungs emptying themselves fully. Looking up at him, I see the truth written in his eyes. I know him, of course I do. My arms wrap around him, returning the embrace. The smell of fresh bread lathered in sweet jam fills the air, the strong scent of tea making my mouth water.

My stomach gurgles loudly, breaking the tension between us. I let out a defeated laugh, and Tharion follows suit. Looking up at him, my body still feeling hot, I meet his mossy gaze.

"That smells amazing." I let go of him, backing out of his arms reluctantly. I throw on a fresh set of trousers and a breathable top, then sit down next to him. Toasted bread hits my tastebuds, the crust melting away, filling my senses with joy. The sweet blueberry jam bursts of flavour as it covers every inch of my mouth. We sit there, eating like we've always done. But somehow, it feels different. We feel different, and I don't know what to think about it.

· · — · ✳ · — · ·

The smell of sweat and blood permeates the air. I scrunch my nose. Loud grunts and the sound of blows hitting their targets clang from the training grounds. Males and females in black training uniforms scatter the large venue. Brick walls stretch around them, leaving the sky open to train under.

Racks on racks of different training weapons stand in front of the walls, ranging from axes to bows. Blades in all shapes and sizes hang on display on a rack hung neatly on the wall above. The ground is covered in splotches of dark brown and red, not even grass wants to grow through it. I look around the yard, watching the soldiers throw themselves at each other, hitting the ground with shaking force.

"See summin' you'd like to try, lassie?" A strong voice breaks me from my stare. I look for the owner, finding two dark brown eyes meeting mine. The male is tall, taller than Rowan even, and has a chest wider than a small boat. His black beard is neatly trimmed on his face, accentuating his full dark pink lips and slightly crooked smile.

"Uhm… Not in particular. I didn't really feel like dying today," I answer with a shaky breath. Thundering laughter bursts from the male, the contagious sound echoing around us.

"I like'er, lads! Name's Falck, welcome to the training grounds!"

Falck stretches out his arm, Rowan clamping down firmly. They shake, smiling widely at one another.

"It's an honour to meet you, Falck. I am Rowan, this is Tharion, Corvyn and the "lassie" is Eleanora."

Falck finds my hand and plants a delicate, warm kiss on it. My cheeks instantly turn a deep red, unable to keep my eyes trained on him.

"So, tell me, what'd you want to do this fine mornin'?"

"We need to train for an upcoming battle, and my friends here don't have any formal training to lean on. We will be coming here every day for the next few days until we feel confident enough to ride out."

Falck rubs his hands together with a vicious grin, his eyes dark with malice.

"Hey, everyone! We've got ourselves some fresh prey this week!"

Whoops and cheers rings in the air around us, warriors eagerly waiting to hand our asses to us on silver platters. I swallow loudly, my hands clammy, ears ringing loudly. Falck laughs with his fellow soldiers, vibrations thrumming in the air.

Looking over at the male, standing with his back to us, I notice his dark purple wings. The feathered beauties stretch out far past his head, elegantly floating behind his back, shaking as he laughs. The iridescent purple shines into a deep green with an obsidian base. They are magnificent. I stare at the wings, mesmerized by their graceful swaying. *A crow, maybe?*

Looking over at the others, I realize many of them carry wings in black, cream and even colours like orange and green. Others have pointy ears like Tharion, bright eyes and pointy features, their hands waving and conjuring magic before shooting rays of light at their opponents. Excitement creeps up on me, smothering the anxiety I had built up just a moment prior.

"Are there any human sorcerers amongst your group, Falck?"

He looks at me, a light going off above his head, realizing what I am. He turns, voice ringing strongly through the yard.

"Lucien! Lucien, get over here!" he calls. A male, just older than us, sprints across the grounds, heading towards us.

"Yes, sir," he salutes, standing still as a statue. His hair is long, pitch-black, like mine. The mage's eyes are a deep brick red with dark swirls dancing around them.

"Lucien, this is Eleanora. She's a witch. Train'er, will ya?"

Lucien locks eyes with me, his burning bright. I clear my throat, hands still clammy. The male bows his head deeply before reaching for my hand and planting a feather-light kiss on my knuckles. I giggle. *Really, giggling now, are we?*

"Yes, sir. What kind of witch are you, Eleanora?" The way he says my name falls like honey off his lips, forcing a shiver.

"Bl… Uh, blood. I'm a blood witch," I croak, my throat suddenly drier than the deserts across the borders. Tharion looks over at me, obviously uncomfortable by my transparent infatuation. I dare not look at him, not after the night we shared.

*Get yourself together, you idiot. You're acting like a teenager!*

Snapping myself out of the ridiculous trance this male has on me, I straighten my shoulders. His smile is blinding white, like pearls on a string, eyes like pools of shadows in contrast.

"I can work with that. My mother was a blood witch, she taught me some stuff before she left."

Falck slaps Lucien on the back with a solid smack, the clapping sound echoing around us.

"Well, let's get goin'! These poor people won't learn anything unless ya teach'em. Find a sparring partner and get to work!"


The earth cracks as a bolt of energy bursts through the air, hitting with an ear-splitting roar. *That was too close.*

"Are you trying to kill me on my first day?!" I scream, dodging the bolts tightly following.

"We always train as if the other is trying to kill you. Focus! Fire back!"

Hands gracefully circle the air between us, forming another bolt of energy. With smouldering eyes trained on me, Lucien is not letting me out of his sight. He moves like smoke, dancing elegantly across the yard.

My hands are bloody, hair stuck to my face from sweat, but I'm still standing. *That counts for something, right?*

I call on my magic, ripping enormous vines from the ground. Exploding through the earth, bits of gravel soar through the air. Training halts. Around us, the others duck, shielding their heads from raining debris. The vines grab onto Lucien, thorns piercing his skin, crying out.

Tying his hands behind his back, I hold him down. Menacing, he looks at me and grins hauntingly wide. A sharp light occurs before soaring flames shoot from behind him, incinerating the vines, their charred remains pooling at his feet. The smoky smell of fire hits me with a wall of heat so hard I stumble back a pace.

Bolting to the left, trying to flank him, tearing new vines from the earth as I run. Rocks fly, hitting the poor bystanders. Lucien's crackling fire burns through my vines, turning them to ash in seconds. I cry out, frustration fuelling me. He runs headfirst towards me, tackling me to the ground with a grunt. We crash together, scraping across the ground, my back taking the impact.

I feel the gravel boring into my wounds, blood soaking through my shirt. As we come to a stop, Lucien straddles me, his giant thighs keeping my hands from moving.

"That's cheating!" I whine as scorching heat pumps through my veins, writhing to get free. I try kicking him in the back, but his massive body doesn't flinch.

He pushes me further into the ground, the wounds on my back crying.

"There is no cheating in battle! You are not supposed to get yourself into positions like this where you are unable to use your magic." His voice hits me like a punch to the gut, stealing the air from under me.

I stop moving, looking up at him, panting from exhaustion. His breathing is ragged, obviously straining his energy too.

Silence blankets us; I give in. Chuckling, Lucien lifts his leg, getting off me, wrapping his fingers around my forearm. I yelp as the male hauls me to my feet like I weigh nothing, stumbling as I hit the ground.

Heat races through my body, my pride taking most of the damage from the battle. A large hand lands on my shoulder, making me wince.

"Not bad for a first run, little witch!" he smirks, winking.

"Have a bath tonight, you'll be feeling this little warm-up even more tomorrow." Narrowing my eyes, I puff my chest and shake his hand off me, his laugh ringing in my ears. Turning on my heel, I walk towards my rooms, shame burning hotter than his flames.

# Chapter 19

## Tharion

The smells of burnt wood and ash fill my nostrils, eyes watering. The training court once filled with thundering shouts and the redolence of sweat now falls quiet on the brink of destruction. Black marks paint the walls as well as the ground, vivid memories of the fight that took place.

I'm in awe. The way Eleanora moved, how she fought someone so fiercely, so brave. I watched her every move, her hands gracefully circling and moving in the air, forcing the elements at her will. I wanted to step in, to fight for her, but I realized that this was her fight to have, to learn from. Now, the battle has ended, and Eleanora has stormed off to her rooms.

I walk over to Lucien as he wipes sweat and blood from his face with a filthy rag.

I smirk. "She did quite the number on you, huh?"

Lucien picks up his flask, gulping down big mouths of water. Dragging the back of his hand across his mouth, he grins.

"Your little witch is stronger than she looks. For a moment I thought she might actually beat me."

"I was wondering if you'd be willing to train me too? I have so little control over my elemental powers. Eleanora has tried to teach me some runes, but I still need to know how to wield if I'm to beat this demon."

His face hardens, a frown developing between his black brows. "You didn't know?"

Gently, Lucien shakes his head. Tossing the rag into his bag, throwing it over his shoulder, he starts walking out of the yard. I follow, falling beside him.

"That's why we're here. The Veil has cracked, letting spirits out into our realm. The King has let us stay here to train so we have a chance at beating him."

Lucien listens as I tell him about our encounters with spirits along the way, about my dream. He falls completely silent, taking everything in.

"We must prepare. I will help you, Tharion. Meet me every morning, before breakfast mess. I will teach you everything I know for as long as you're here."

I dip my chin, thankful for his help. We walk back to the barracks, where all the soldiers sleep. Rows upon rows of rooms stretch down a long hallway, lanterns flickering on the walls. A beautiful skylight lets in a soft ray of sunshine, making them seem less dark.

He unlocks his door, head turned at me.

"Will you join us for dinner tonight? We meet up for dinner mess every evening, I'm sure the other soldiers would love to meet you all."

Smiling, I nod. We shake hands before separating, him leaving for his room and me finding my way back to mine. I walk through the hallway, studying the architecture surrounding me. The castle is strong, made to withstand heavy strikes. Thick bricks hold it sturdy, marble reinforcing the structure from the inside.

As the darkness of the barracks fade into bright castle hallways, I walk past a room, the door slightly ajar. Peeking inside, I notice two small cribs, a rocking chair and a small table with a book and a lamp. My stomach drops.

*The twins' bedroom.*

A shadow moves in the room, catching my eye. Short sniffles accompanied by deep swallows and the faint sound of crying is coming from inside. I push the door open, trying to find the source. As the door moves, the King's slender frame comes into view.

"My King, I apologize for the intrusion," I bow my head, turning my body to leave.

King Vaelrick wipes his eyes and blows his nose into a handkerchief, clearing his throat. His eyes radiate of sorrow, swollen eyelids heavy over dull, blue irises.

"Come, Tharion. Sit with me," he gestures to a chair beside him. I step inside and sit down next to him, my eyes set on his pale face.

The King exhales a shaky breath, eyes glossing as new tears form.

"I have a hard time letting them go. I did not even know my boys, yet I still feel them, hear them and even see them sometimes. I miss my Rowenna more than my heart is capable of handling." His voice cracks, tears welling in his eyes. I put my hand on his shoulder, squeezing gently.

"I am so sorry, my King. If there is anything I can do to help you, if you need to talk, I will be there. I know the agony of losing someone dear."

He looks at me, a faint pull to his mouth appearing on one side. With a determined nod, he rises and starts out of the bedroom. I take a last look around before following him, closing the door behind me softly, escaping to my room as the world closes in on me.

As I approach our solar foyer, I consider knocking on Eleanora's door. Would she even want to see me? She stormed off pretty fast after the battle. Invisible ties pull me towards her door, but the pit in my stomach decides against it, turning the knob to my rooms.

Inside, burgundy and gold details glow in the orange sunlight. My bed is the same as Eleanora's, only with deep red velvet drapes hanging from the canopies. It radiates royalty, importance.

*Not someone like you.*

I burst through the doors to my terrace, lungs creaming for air.

The King's eyes flash before me, drowning in sorrow, his heartbreak seeping through his pores, suffocating.

Compulsion swallows me whole, body boiling within. I turn on my heel, running through my room, into the sunlit foyer. Reaching Eleanora's door, fists hammer on the old wooden barrier, rattling the handle with every desperate pound.

The door flies open. "What in the Afterlife is going on?" her voice fuming with annoyance.

Without thinking, I step forward pulling her into my arms, not to claim her - but to feel her existence. A yelp tears from her as our bodies collide, caught off guard. I stop, staring into her eyes, into her soul - those burgundy pools filled with surprise and a hint of fire. Her breaths come out shallow and fast, the thunders of her heart echoing in my ears.

My hands fall from around her.

"Eleanora. You… You are magnificent. You have hypnotized me. If I ever lost you," my voice trembles, "…I would lose the biggest part of my soul."

My body yearns for her touch, every nerve ending going up in flames as my skin calls for hers. She opens her mouth to answer, but before she has the chance, I pull her back into my arms.

A helpless cry rips as her body crashes against mine. Her skin still smells like fire and ash with a hint of lavender, the scent dancing around my senses. I take her in, all of her. My left hand travels to her hair, the other holding her waist tightly. I savour every sensation that is Eleanora. Pushing away from me, she heaves for air.

"Tharion, please," she pants, "what is going on? What is this?" The distance is too much, every cell in my being crying to reunite.

"I needed to be with you. I'm sorry for barging in on you like that, but I had to see you."

"See me? That was far more than just seeing me," her voice comes out a nervous huff. I look down, meeting her gaze. Her cheeks are a deep shade of magenta, forcing a smile. I pull her to me a little longer before letting her go, walking over to her small dining area. We sit down, hands in mine as I talk about the meeting with the King.

A hand covers her mouth, eyes glossing with tears.

"That's awful."

I nod silently, the emotions still fresh under my skin.

"He looked so sad, like he didn't recognize himself without her. It broke my heart."

Her hand finds mine, interlacing our fingers. We sit in silence, just for a moment.

"You will never lose me, Ari. I'm here, like I always have been. Like I always will be."

· · — ·✳· — · ·

Buttoning my shirt, I get ready for dinner with the soldiers. Eleanora, Rowan and Corvyn stand outside my room, patiently waiting. I meet Eleanora's gaze, a pink sheen washing over her face. She's wearing another gown, this time a deep burnt orange. The corset accentuates her soft curves, complimenting the colour of her eyes in a breathtaking way; the dark red colour shifting with the deep orange, as if dancing.

We make our way down to the barracks where tumultuous sounds of laughter and talking bounce off the brick walls. The scents of roasted meat with steamed vegetables and freshly baked bread hit our nostrils, mouths flooding. The barrack is full, males and females laughing while eating, enjoying each other's companies.

Walking over to the buffet, serving plates are stacked with meats of different kinds, steaming bowls of freshly mashed potatoes swimming in butter and dishes of caramelized vegetables.

Loading up my plate, I pick up a cup of sparkling red wine. Gazing over the crowd, searching the grand venue, I try to find Lucien or Falck. The purple sheen of Falck's wings catches in the light, our eyes meeting briefly before he shoots up and waves exaggeratingly at us.

"Over 'ere, pals!" his deep voice cutting through all the surrounding voices. We make our way over to his table, Lucien already on his second serving of food.

"Little witch! So nice to see you again. Thank you for earlier, I had a great time," he winks at her, that same smirk plastered on his face.

The mug of wine creaks under my grip, hands tightening, the nauseating tinge of jealousy clouding my mind. I sit down next to him,

Eleanora on my other side, and place my plate in front of me. Eleanora shoots him a sharp scowl, a friendly laugh soon following.

I stuff my mouth with food, the meat so tender it melts on my tongue. The others follow suit, soft moans of delight escaping them.

"Somethin' tells me you've not had a lot of this back where you're from, ey?" Falck laughs, the deep vibrations of his voice thrumming through my chest. I shake my head, swallowing my food.

"Usually, we eat a lot of stews, with most of our stock coming from the forests. My godfather and I have a patch of land where we grow potatoes and carrots, but the rest comes from foraging the woods or trading."

Falck's eyes widen. Inhaling sharply, he looks at us, dumbfounded.

"Well, I've never…"

We erupt in a laugh, the joyous sound ringing through the heavy air. As we refill our cups with the sparkling wine, heat builds in my chest.

"So, tell us, friends. Who is this demon you're fighting?" Lucien asks, his eyes locked on Eleanora.

I tell them about the attacks, the story of Vorathiel and Ilyra, our encounters in the forest on our way here, everything. The males listen intently, gasping and scoffing as we go.

Lucien looks over at Corvyn, studying him. I see his body tense, shoulders cradling his earlobes.

"I feel like I know you. I have ever since I saw you in the training yard." They lock eyes, Lucien raking over Cor's face.

"Your brother was Kaelen, no?"
Corvyn's eyes widen, air stolen from his lungs.

"You knew Kaelen?" his voice comes out low, trembling.

"Your brother was a great male, one of the kindest and bravest people I have ever had the pleasure of knowing."

"I'm so sorry for your loss, lad," Falck cuts in, eyes soft.

Corvyn's eyes fill with water, and I can see his breath hitch. Standing up, he lifts his half-empty plate from the table.

"Sorry, guys. I think I'm going to head out for the night. See you in the morning?"

Rowan reaches for him, but Corvyn turns and walks off. He looks at us, frantic, the frown back between his strawberry blonde brows. Eleanora shoves the air at him: *go after him!*

Jumping up, Rowan grabs his plate and races off after Corvyn. I look over to Lucien, his face laced in sorrow.

"Let me tell you the story of one of the bravest men I knew, and what that wretched demon sorcerer did to him."

# *Chapter 20*

## *Kaelen*

The Arcane Anvil was a tavern that welcomed all scholars, from blacksmiths to healers, to witches and sorcerers. A common ground for all kinds to come together, sing, cheer and let off steam.

Kaelen had just finished his blacksmith schooling and spent the night celebrating with his fellow scholars. Mugs would clink, liquids sloshing and splattering on the floor as happy songs rang through the air. It symbolized the end of years of training, of learning how to wield fire, how to craft blades, statues, beautiful artwork, it was the end of his years as a student. Now, life awaited him – and little did he know, that when one era ended, a new one would begin just as rapidly.

As Kaelen bursts through the doors, almost tripping on his own feet, the sound of laughter fills the air. Kaelen crawls through the sea of scholars before reaching the bar, as Sorian – a fellow blacksmith scholar – finds a small table just close to the entrance. Big mugs of foaming ale slosh across the wooden counter, the bar maid smiling at the raven with sparkly white teeth.

"I can't believe all our hard work has finally come to an end. We're blacksmiths!" Sorian's elated tone echoes through the crowd as people cheer, the sound wrapping around them like a hug.

"Your father will be so proud, Kaelen. He waited so long for you to follow in his footsteps."

Kaelen nods, pride blooming in his chest as images of his father cloud his mind alongside the strong ale. The tepid liquid burns his chest before it settles in his stomach, a light haze blanketing his senses. As he raises the mug for another swig, the doors to the tavern swing open, a gust of wind transporting the delightful scent of jasmine and apple into Kaelen's nostrils.

He turns, following the scent as his dark eyes land on a female - the most beautiful female Kaelen has ever seen. Her hair is blinding white, intricately braided over her left shoulder. Her eyes are a breathtaking cerulean, capturing Kaelen's soul as they meet his stare.

Sorian waves his hand in front of his friend's face, breaking the trance he'd fallen under.

"Hey, man. Where did you go?"

Kaelen's words evade him, stuck under the pressure of his pounding heart as his eyes are still stuck to the female.

"Uh, Sorian. I'll be back, okay? Hang on." The mug spills bitter drops onto the wooden table as Kaelen rises from his stool, enchanted legs dragging him towards this unknown female.

The sting of nails burns under his chest, his raven clawing to get out, to claim this female. *His.* He watches as she walks towards the bar, snagging the opportunity that so gracefully fell into his hands. As their paths cross, he bumps into her, knocking her off her feet. Her small hands wrap around his strong arms, holding herself from falling to the floor just as Kaelen swings his arm under her back – her saviour.

"Oh! So sorry, didn't mean to make you fall for me." The corners of his mouth pull into a smirk, shooting her a wink as she settles herself.

Kaelen is tall, with short black hair and a blinding smile. His eyes are a dark shade of brown, so dark it ventures into black. His build is strong from carrying loads of metal over the last years, muscles bulging under his black linen shirt. The female's light pink cheeks deepen, spreading across her face as her hand covers her mouth, the spellbinding sound of a giggle slipping past her lips.

"At least make me dinner first." Her elbow softly nudges Kaelen's ribs, forcing a small yelp and a laugh. Eyes lock, pools of blue and brown diving within each other as electricity shoots through Kaelen's body. His heart stops for a moment at the touch of her, stealing the air from his lungs.

Bowing, he reaches for her hand, bringing it slowly to his chin. Her skin feels warm, tingling under his lips as they hover just above it.

"That would be a pleasure, Miss…" he tilts his head, waiting for her name. The female watches with heavy eyelids as reality snaps her back.

"Oh! Serenya. My name is Serenya."

"*Serenya,*" the name falls off his tongue like stardust, "a beautiful name for a beautiful female." His lips press against her skin, a tender kiss, before interlaced hands steadily fall between them. They linger, holding onto one another before Serenya jolts, breaking the trance that is Kaelen. She removes her hand, the cold absence immediate in the raven.

"And what may I call you?"

He smirks, "my friends call me Kaelen, but you can call me yours." Serenya's blush intensifies as she glances over at her friends.

"They will be expecting me soon, but what do you say we get out of here before they notice I'm gone?"

Kaelen beams, his raven scratching at his soul to be let out, to steal this female and take her away where no one and nothing can harm her. *His.*

Her hand folds around his, dragging him out the doors, into the warm summer air. The sun doesn't set during summer, casting the sky in a mural of orange, pink and lilac even during the pits of night.

The heels of their shoes clack against cobblestone, leading them down to a creek nearby. Water droplets spray in the air, catching the sunshine in a colourful rainbow, arching over the smitten scholars.

Patches of deep green grass lie before the water, a perfect spot to indulge in each other.

And that's what they do – as hours crank the night to early morning, they talk. Kaelen listens as Serenya speaks of her life, how she's an only child born to elven parents, that she's attending school to become a healer. Her words leave her mouth as a siren's song, wrapping around Kaelen's soul so tight he might suffocate. He could listen to her speak until his existence was nothing but a memory in time.

He tells her about his life, how he's the eldest of an unkindness of nine brothers of his family being raven-shifters. He tells her about his craftmanship, how he's made a dagger from a metal forged by the stars themselves.

"It's called Aetherium," he starts, "some say it's condensed by the breath of stars. It shimmers like them. The metal is so light, yet stronger than dragon's bone. It's so powerful that it hums when wielding it, sounding almost like a heartbeat." Kaelen goes on about his work, his dreams, and Serenya listens with interest. She follows every word, every motion of his hands and every inhale he makes, falling with every beat of her heart.

The comfortable silence of night gradually fades into busy early morning as people rush the streets, some to set up their market stalls, others to be the first customers.

"We should probably head home, it's getting late. Or should I say… early," she chuckles. The sound cradles Kaelen's every nerve, setting them on fire as he basks in their comfortable blaze.

"Will I see you again?" The thought of not hearing her voice or watching her laugh has his stomach in knots, painful and unnecessary.

"Meet me here at the end of our work week, just after sunset?"

And that's what they do. Every week, they meet up, watching as the sun fades into an orange blanket over the horizon, their souls entwining beyond salvation whilst sharing every hope and dream. They fall, hard, uncontrollably, ever-willingly.

As time went on, Kaelen brought Serenya to meet his family, introducing her to his parents and brothers. His mother would speak of his childhood with fondness, laughing as stories trilled off her tongue,

Serenya cackling as her soul pulled closer to his. Their bond grew stronger, so strong that denying it no longer worked. They were mates, bonded by soul and fate to spend every breath in the realm together as one.

Serenya would bring Kaelen home to her parents, and they fell heedlessly in love with the raven at first sight. Her mother would teach him how to make potions to heal burns, salves to repair broken skin, and her father would bring him into the forest, showing which herbs to forage and which not to pluck. He adored them, as they adored him.

Whenever they shared meals, her parents would talk about how Serenya's voice would calm anyone that listened, even restless spirits.

"She was sent to us as a gift from the Gods themselves, we know she was."

Serenya's cheeks darken, the delicate points of her ears turning an adorable shade of magenta as her parents spoil her in praise. But Kaelen knew they were right. She was a gift, a gift he would always cherish. He would protect her, love her, make her wildest dreams come true. They would live eternity together in love, he vowed as much to her.

· · — · ✳ · — · ·

"Where do you think we are in ten years, Kae?"
The woollen blanket is warm, shielding them from the damp grass underneath them. His eyes bore into hers as water sprays into the air, memories of emotions locking into place.

"All that matters is that I am with you, *mea carissima.*"

Serenya's eyes line with water, breath hitched between the heavy beats of her heart.

"Since the day I first laid eyes on you, my soul knew who you were; you were my home. My raven clawed to break free, to make you ours, to take care of you for eternity. I love you, Serenya. You are mine, my mate. My eternity."
Silent tears fall from her eyes, soaking the blanket below.

"And I love you, my Kaelen. Stay with me, make a life with me. Spend eternity with me, please?" Her words plead, begging shamelessly.

Kaelen raises his hand, calloused and warm, wiping her tears as his eyes fall to her lips. "I would never have it any other way."

Their eyes lock, tension heavy in the air. His face dips, their lips crashing as the world falls silent around them. The kiss is desperate, explosive and roaring, the need to claim her overwhelming. Her tongue darts out, tasting his bottom lip before the delicious sting of her teeth piercing his skin sets his body on fire. His hand sneaks under the nape of her neck, cradling her blinding locks, the other one resting under the small of her back, pressed between his mate and the earth.

Kaelen breaks the kiss, their breaths mingling in the small space between their lips. Deep oceans under raging waves stare back at him, pulling him back into the depths of her soul. He felt it. This was it. This was Fate, and Serenya was his mate.

"Serenya, would you do me the honour of becoming my wife? Carry my mark on you, show the realm what we are for each other?" Her eyes widen, but only for a moment, as a wide grin stretches across her face. Lunging at Kaelen, her arms twist around his neck.

"Of course I will, Kaelen. Yes!" The sound of her laugh mixes with tears as warm happiness runs down both their faces. They curl up into each other's arms, facing the orange sky.

As Kaelen traces delicate circles over Serenya's back, their mated bond clicks into place, auras of cerulean blue and burnt umber mixing together as one far beyond their souls, never to break. Never to separate.

"I can't wait to spend eternity worshipping you and the ground you walk on, *mea carissima*."


Kaelen and Serenya marry under the orange sky, surrounded by their closest family and friends. As his bride walks down the pebbled pathway, his stomach drops into a void of nerves and anticipation. Tears hammer behind clenched eyes, fingers twitching impatiently. He wants to touch her, feel her, have her for eternity.

The world stops turning as the white train of Serenya's dress comes into vision, his eyes climbing her wedding dress until the deep pools of her eyes meet his. On her head is a crown made from deep green leaves, embracing her elven heritage. Her hair hangs in loose waves behind her, small braids scattered through her hairdo.

Serenya's parents had told him a long time ago that they keep braids in their hair for protection, adopting the tradition from covens around the village. She looks stunning, breathtaking. Kaelen drags his sweaty palms over his tan trousers, straightening the linen shirt hanging delicately over his shoulders, Serenya's footsteps closing in on him.

The ceremony is short, intimate, and as soon as it ends, Kaelen swings Serenya into his arms, carrying her off to start their lives together. They build a home, a small smithy for Kaelen to work and a greenhouse for Serenya to plant herbs and flowers needed for her potions. They are happy, hopelessly in love, oblivious to time so quickly passing beside them.

· · — · ✷ · — · ·

White clouds sail across the blue waves of the sky as Kaelen hammers hot steel in his smithy. The sound carries through the air, echoing into the forest surrounding their small home. The blade under his enormous tongs sizzles as he lowers it into cold water, the Aetherium settling into place. The blade is a gift for the King and Queen, a gift to celebrate the awaiting arrival of their twin boys. He hammers the blade, perfecting its contours, bending the metal at his will.

Kaelen was the only one to master the skill of Aetherium, the only blacksmith born from the bloodline that can see the metal in its pure form. The metal is the only one that can turn darkness into light, harnessing the blinding breath of stars.

His hammer slips from his grasp as an ear-piercing scream ricochets through his forge. As he leaps over buckets, heaps of metal and bags of stone, his heart thunders in his chest.

"Serenya!" he pants, "Serenya, answer me!"
Kaelen explodes through the doors to the greenhouse, searching for her, desperate to see her unharmed. She isn't there. The greenhouse is turned on its head, soil scattered on the ground, pots broken and books mindlessly tossed. *Where is she?*

He turns, running inside the house, leaping up the stairs two steps at a time, bursting into their bedroom. The bed is neatly made, nothing out of place. Loud drumming pounds against his eardrums, heart bursting behind his chest. Where is she? Why can't he find her? The edges of his vision blur, black smoke closing in as buckled knees crash to the floor.

A sonic noise rips through his head, splitting his eardrums. Kaelen closes his eyes, so hard that stars glitter behind his lids, trying desperately to shut the noise out. It fades, slowly ebbing to a dull hum, leaving his body trembling. As Kaelen opens his eyes, his breath leaps from his chest. The room is covered in blood, the nauseating smell of heat and metal assaulting his senses.

*This isn't right. This isn't real!*

Everything is covered in crimson, walls, floor, even the ceiling is painted. Coldness brushes against his hands, air hardening the blood encapsulating them. They drip, deep ruby drops pooling under his knees.

"Serenya!" His voice cracks, heart clambering to the fragments as it, too, fractures down the middle. He searches, rummaging through the house, scouring every room as the echoes of her screams fade into the late-night air. He runs outside, doing laps around their house just as his leg catches on a big rock.

Dark liquid paints it, crimson clinging to each crevice of the small mineral. Lifting his head, he searches the surrounding area, pulse going amok in his veins, desperate to find his mate. He can feel her, their bond desperate for him to save her. The screams of his mate tears through him like razors, slicing at his soul.

Following the trail of blood, his eyes land on a figure, hanging in the nearby clearing.

*No. No. No.*

Sprinting, his legs scream as he pummels across the open field, the still silhouette coming closer with each agonizing step. Chilling laughter fills the air, deafening and frozen, forcing Kaelen to his knees.

They crash against the cold earth, soaking in the scarlet splotches guiding him to the clearing. Above, a murder of crows circle, hovering as a totem of death, mocking him.

"Who are you?! What have you done to her?!"
Kaelen cries out, cutting through the chilling laughter. He pleads, begs on his knees, for someone to answer him. The laughter continues, no answer, only evil.

The crows above his head dip, soaring at him with blinding speed. He hugs his knees, vanishing into himself as they viciously rip and peck at his clothes, piercing his skin, tearing his flesh. Kaelen screams, begging for it to stop, blood gushing from his wounds.

Just as he's about to break, the birds change course – heading straight for the silhouette in the forest clearing.

*No. Not her.*

Kaelen stumbles to his feet, willing them to move. He watches as the birds destroy her bloodstained dress, ripping her flesh from bone, blood streaking as it falls to the earth below her hanging body.

"Get away from her!" he shouts, the metallic taste of blood coating the inside of his vocal cords. The birds don't listen, slicing through muscle and flesh, separating the fair skin of Serenya from her bones. Kaelen explodes through the opening, and as he closes in on her, the birds vanish into thin air. There are no birds, no blood, nothing. His body is whole, not a wound in sight.

Before him is only her, in her green dress, lifeless. Kaelen falls to his knees, a shattering sob shaking the earth as his soul breaks. Her cries for help have silenced, the bond gone still.

He stands up, cutting the rope holding his mate, her body heavy and cold. They thump to the ground, silence enveloping them, suffocating, deafening. Serenya's white locks fall over her face, streaks of dried tears staining her fair skin.

"Serenya, my love. Please, wake up. Just open your eyes, open your eyes for me, love. Serenya, please. Please," he whispers softly into her hair, praying to whoever will listen to return her. She doesn't wake.

Tears fall from Kaelen, coating her forehead as he cradles her tight, so suffocatingly tight, rocking his mate gently as the last fragments of their bond dissipates within him.

"I am so sorry, Serenya. I couldn't save you. I heard your cries, and still, I couldn't save you. I am so sorry. I'm so sorry."


· · — ·✳· — · ·


The days bleed into night, time fading into nothing as the absence in Kaelen's soul eats away at him. In his mind, the echoes of her laughter, the waves of her voice, recklessly destroy his brain. His friends and family stop by, offering their help, their time, but he rejects them. He can't talk about her, can't say the words, can't accept reality.

*He can't say goodbye.*

Loud knocks come from behind his door, his father waiting on the other side.

"I don't want to see anyone, father. Please, leave me."

The knocking halts. His father drags in a deep breath.

"You need to bury her, son. She deserves the peace of the Afterlife. I know you want her here with you, but she will not know peace until you give her a proper burial." His voice is soft, but the tinge of desperation coats his words.

Inside, Kaelen knows his father is right – but he's not ready. Not ready to let her go, not ready to be without her. He casts a glance over her lifeless body, eyes closed as if she's just having a deep sleep.

*Not ready.*

But he knows she needs peace, *deserves* peace.

Kaelen slowly makes his way to the front door, opening it. His father's eyes glow in sorrow, the deep indigo glossing in tears, his bottom lip shivering uncontrollably.

"Will you help me?" Kaelen's voice cracks, then fades.

His father pulls him into a tight embrace, the familiar scent cradling his senses.

"Of course, son. Tell me what you need, and I will get it, or make it. Anything you need."

Kaelen's walls shatter, tears flooding his eyes as they crash over the edge, streaming down his cheeks. The warm embrace of his father tightens, lowering them both to the ground. Kaelen disappears into his father's shirt, soaking the soft cotton in salty tears.

"I couldn't protect her, father. I promised her I would, but I couldn't." The words tear sobs from his throat, scratching it.

"You did everything you could. No one could have known what would happen. You cannot blame yourself for Serenya's death, son."

Kaelen sinks further into his father's arms, shoulders shaking as tears pour from shattered eyes. His body is exhausted, ripped to shreds, the warmth of his father's embrace lulling him into darkness. He can feel his consciousness slipping, images of his dear Serenya welcoming him in the realm of the Dreaming.


An hour goes by, Kaelen's eyes shooting open. He's still cradled in his father's arms, still on the floor.

"It's time, my boy. It's time to bury her."
Kaelen's stomach drops, the warm emotions of his dreams wrecked by the cold reality of his waking life.

He clears his throat. "I need a boat. Can you get one and deliver it at Nimlothiel?" The lake is elven, used for burials. Serenya would go there often, to visit her lost family, to honour her people in the Afterlife. The memory is warm in his chest, stealing the air from inside his body. His father dips his chin, soft eyes scanning his son before closing the door with a thud.

Rising, Kaelen walks up to Serenya, studying her pale face. The knot in his chest constricts, refusing to draw air. With careful steps, he stands before her.

"Let's get you ready for the Afterlife, my love."
Kaelen spends the next hours giving her a wash, putting her in her favourite dress, braiding her hair to protect her through the journey to come. With every preparation, his heart breaks further. With every task, he gets closer to having to say goodbye.

As the last braid secures, he lifts her into his arms, not letting her down until they reach the lake. The boat he asked for lays at the shore, white roses filling the deck around a marble bier. It's beautiful.

Carefully, Kaelen places his mate on the bier, folding her hands over her chest. With the oar, he pushes them from shore, rowing through the still water, out to the middle of the giant lake.

The weather is calm, like the Gods of the Afterlife were waiting to give Serenya a safe and peaceful passing. Not a cloud in the sky, birds singing mellow tunes in tribute to her beautiful soul. The lake is quiet, mirroring the mountain peaks surrounding it, making it look like there's a kingdom beneath the water - a mirroring realm that looks identical to this one – the thought warm in Kaelen's chest. The thought that she will wander the same pathways, the same forests, watching the same realm as him. It allows him to drag in air, filling his lungs.

They reach the middle of the lake, the end of their eternity. Here, the end of their shared life, their vows of eternity together. All of it, over. Bile rises in Kaelen's throat, threatening to eject itself from his mouth, but he persists.

*Not now, not here. Let her have the passing she deserves.*
He walks up to her, kneeling before his mate.

"My dearest Serenya. *Mea carissima.* My soul hurts from being here, from having reached the end of our time together. Know that you have made me the happiest man alive, just by being by my side. I loved you like no other, and I will always love you, my perfect wife." His voice cracks, warm tears run down his face.

"The sorrow I carry with me from this day on will dig a hole so deep it will meet you in the Afterlife. I swear to you now, Serenya, we will meet again. We will spend eternity together. I love you."
A tear drips from his chin, landing on her cheek. With shaky hands, he wipes it away, feeling her cold skin beneath his scorching touch. Pressing a tender kiss to her forehead, he steps away.

His lungs fill with sorrowed breaths before Kaelen takes to the sky. There she is, his mate, his best friend. His eternity. As a sob rips through his core, he brings forth a ray of fire, aiming it at the boat. His heart shatters as he watches it go up in roaring flames, the scene blurred behind a veil of tears. He can feel her essence, her soul filling the air around him, embracing him in magic and warmth. Shattered hands reach out to touch it. A voice, so calm and serene, sounds over the lake.

*My love, my Kaelen. Thank you for giving me the happiest, most loving life a female could ask for. I will always miss you, but we will meet again one day. I love you so much, Kae. Do not stop living your life, do not stop being yourself. I will always be with you, but now it is time for me to go.*

The smothering weight of his heart rips through his shattered body, screams tearing through the air, tears dripping from his chin.

"Serenya! Serenya, please don't leave. Just one more moment," he pleads, but her embrace has left him.

He is alone in the air, watching the boat dip below the surface, her body reunited with nature once more. In a fit of desperation, Kaelen dives after her – the icy cold lake swallowing him whole. Water is all around him, the lake dragging him further down until there's nothing but darkness.

She isn't here. He stops swimming, floating in the deep blue waters, letting himself sink deeper and deeper. His lungs combust, screaming for air, but he doesn't swim to the surface. He lets himself sink, no resistance left in his body. As darkness embraces him, consciousness leaves, submerging him into nothing.

Coughing up water, Kaelen jerks awake. His father is hunched beside him, eyebrows scrunched between his eyes.

"Kaelen, oh, thank the Gods. What were you thinking?" His words are panicked, angry, scared.

*I wanted to be with her. No life is worth living without her. I cannot do this anymore.*

What was he thinking? He didn't mean to drown himself, not really, but when he was sinking to the bottom of the lake, he felt… peaceful. Like he would get to see Serenya again.

"I'm sorry for scaring you, father. The funeral, it was too much. I think I just need some rest, and I'll be good as new." The lies fall off his tongue like venom, bitter and dry. The worry in his father's eyes doesn't ease, like he knows Kaelen is lying – because he is. He will never be as good as new again, not without Serenya. The emptiness in him will never be filled, no love can ever surpass the one he has for her.

He can still feel the pull of the lake, pulling him back into the darkness of his mind, pushing the world away just for a while longer as everything fades to black once more.

· · — ·✴· — · ·

Kaelen wakes sometime in the late afternoon, tucked in bed. Serenya's scent fills his nose, dragging in every last molecule of it. It's like she's there with him again. Next to him, like nothing ever happened.

His eyes shoot open, hoping to catch her lying next to him, but disappointment sinks in, she isn't there. Her scent lingers, the sweet smell of jasmine and apples.

Sound carries up the stairs. He whips his head to the door, almost swearing that her laughter is coming from below. The covers fly as he rushes out of bed, leaping down the stairs and into the living area.

"Serenya? Darling, is that you?" He looks around, trying desperately to find her. Her laughter is clear as day, she must be here. Suddenly, the laughter turns into cries of pain, agonizing screams of terror chill his bones.

"Serenya!" he yells out, manically searching for her.

"Kaelen! Kaelen, please help me! It hurts, Gods, it hurts so much!" her screams continue.

"Serenya!" Kaelen rips his house apart, tearing up the walls to get to her. His head is filled with her cries as he falls to his knees, trying to shut it out.

"Please, tell me where you are, how do I get to you?" he calls out, desperate for her. The screaming stops. It's completely silent. Wet footsteps slosh over the wooden floor, echoing from the dining area, slowly approaching him. His face lifts, eyes meeting the lifeless pits of Serenya, drenched in water, arms outstretched.

"Kaelen, my love. There you are. I missed you so much, my dear. Will you come with me?" Her voice is shaky, forced to mimic hers.

*It's not real.*

Standing before him, she sinks down to her knees, staring into his eyes. Hers are a dull blue, no life left.

"Serenya, is it really you? Are you coming back to me?" he asks, blinded by the illusion before him. Serenya shakes her head.

"No, my love. I cannot leave this realm. I came to ask you to join me, to spend our eternity together, just like we promised." Her voice is calm, but it's not the same anymore. Kaelen looks into her eyes, blood pooling in her tear ducts before crimson tears fall over the edge, running down her cheeks. In panic, he tries to wipe them away, to no avail.

"Serenya, stop it, please! Please, I cannot bear to see you hurt like this again. Please, stop!" he begs, begs for her to let him out of this nightmare. A soul-shattering scream erupts from her mouth, shaking his entire being.

"Please stop!" he prays loudly. Blood pours from her eyes and mouth, streaming out from her ears, pooling on the floor underneath her.

The pain is too much, Kaelen is crushed under sorrow so heavy he can't bear it a second longer. He reaches for the dagger he made for King Vaelrick.

"I will come to you, my love, I will be with you for eternity! Just please stop this, I beg you!"

With shaky hands, he places the dagger on the left side of his throat.

"Kaelen!" Serenya screams, eyes filled with blunt panic. Clamping his eyes shut, the dagger moves across his taut throat. The metal cuts effortlessly through his skin, down the layers of tissue and into his muscles, in one swift movement. Blood pours from the wound on his neck, covering his shirt, the beige linen now a dark maroon.

The room goes silent. Kaelen opens his eyes to find an empty room. Nothing. Serenya is gone, there is no blood on the floor from where she was bleeding out. No smell of her lingering in the room. Blood freezes in his veins. What had he done? As blood gushes from his final cut, pooling at his knees, the sweet darkness of the Afterlife calls for him.

# Chapter 21

## Corvyn

Racing through the halls, the walls close in on me. My heart drums in my chest, thundering against my eardrums. I explode through my door, slamming it shut behind me. The deep greens of my room swirl around me, and the world tilts on its axis. Leaning the back of my head against the door, I sink to the ground.

Aching, my chest feels excruciatingly tight, denying any air entry. Heaving, black dots twinkle at the edges of my vision. I pull my knees up, planting my face between them. Sweat runs down my temples, droplets fading into my black locks.

Three careful knocks on the door distract me.

"Cor? Cor, are you there? It's me, Ro."

I close my eyes, words buried in my throat. Sinking my face in my hands, I let out a sob.

"Cor, please. Please let me in."

I can feel him, his fox clawing to come out, to comfort me. His scent seeps through the door, blanketing me in comfort. Gently, I scoot away from the door. Moments later, Rowan stands before me. He crouches, placing his hands on my knees.

"*Korax*." Breathless, having clearly run after me, his eyes search mine.

"Korax, talk to me." They scan my face, raking over my body, noticeably on edge. Strawberry eyebrows scrunch up in the middle of his face, the deepest frown I have seen him wear, and it sends a calmness into me.

I take a deep breath, steadying myself before looking up at him, meeting his panicked gaze. The golden eyes I have learned to care so deeply about have swirls of burnt orange, his fox fighting for freedom. The frown between his brows mellow, not as intense anymore, a deep exhale seeping from his lips.

I look at him, "I miss him so much, Ro…" my chest tightens more with every word, "I have missed him every day since he left us, since he was taken from us. I told myself I would never let myself love anyone else, that if he was denied it, I would not let myself have it."

Rowan listens, his eyes focused on me, occasionally sinking to my mouth. His lips tremble, shaky breaths holding back tears. A strong hand reaches out, inviting mine into it. With my palm enveloped in his, he stands up and drags me with him.

We stand, facing each other while his safe arms wrap around me, holding me tight. The scent of ferns, saltwater and ancient magic washes over me, pushing away the tension in my body. I drag it in, filling my lungs with him, eventually letting out a heavy breath, sinking onto his shoulder. His hand finds my head, fingers threading through my black hair, while the other holds me tightly.

A soft rumbling vibrates in his chest, almost like purring, his fox happy to be close. I can feel my raven impatiently pecking at my heart, trying to calm the racing organ. We stand like this for a while, him holding me, me falling deeper for the male in front of me - and that breaking my heart in the process.

He lets go, but grabs my hand, not wanting to let go fully. I look down at our intertwined fingers, warmth spreading through my body. A calloused finger hooks under my chin, tipping my head back so our eyes meet. The deep golden pools of burnt orange dance as they lock with mine, my raven cawing to his fox.

"Do not deny yourself love, korax. Your brother loved, unconditionally and wholeheartedly, until his very last breath. He would not want you to deny yourself the best feeling in existence, and I think you know that too."

A slight tingle starts in my chest, my body heavy. I open my mouth, but my dry throat holds back the unspoken words. Inside, my heart and brain fight, my heart begging to be heard, to be let out of the massive cage built around it, and my mind stabbing it repeatedly with sharp blades to silence its desperate pleas.

The bond between this male and me must mean something, something other than this friendship we have created. I feel empty when I'm not with him, like a part of me is locked behind a door I cannot open.

My raven goes feral when his fox companion isn't around, clawing and pecking to be let out, so he can find him.

*You know why that is, you just don't want to admit it.*

The thought steals the breath from my lungs, chest screaming in pain.

Rowan's large hand cradles my face, his thumb brushing over my jaw. Electricity shoots down my spine, the overwhelming warmth of him making me dizzy. I close my eyes, leaning into his touch, praying he never lets me go.

"Denying yourself love means denying yourself, me, us, what can be. Is that what you want?"

I shake my head, eyes still closed. No. I could never live without Rowan, the thought nauseates me, bile rising in my throat. For the first time, I let myself feel something other than loss, and the world answered.

His other hand reaches for my face, both hands now cupping my jaw.

"Then open your heart, korax. Let yourself –"

A subtle knock breaks the moment, a sigh of defeat pushing from my lungs.

Rowan's hands fall from my face, a soft whimper of protest hitching in my chest. Walking over to the door, Tharion and Eleanora

stand in the doorway. Eleanora's eyes are wide, swollen and bloodshot –
she's been crying. Leaping forward, her arms wraps around my neck,
making me stumble back a pace. Agonized sobs rip through my heart,
my chest suddenly feeling too small for it.

"I am so sorry, Cor. I… I am so sorry." Eleanora cries onto my
collarbone, wet tears leaving damp marks on my shirt. She pushes away
from me, tears streaking her cheeks, dragging in deep sniffs. Using the
back of my finger, I wipe away her tears, a warm swell forming around
my heart.

"I am grateful for you, Eleanora. Kaelen would love you," and
for the first time, I smile at the memory of his loss.

"He would love all of you," I look around me, facing my friends,
chest bubbling with the love I denied myself for so long.

Another knock sounds from my door, Lucien popping his head
inside.

"Hey. Corvyn, would you come with me for a moment?"

My smile falters, the tight sensation in my chest returning. I let
go of Eleanora, looking over at Rowan. He meets my eyes, the frown
between his eyes firmly in place.

I walk to Lucien, closing the door behind me.

"I want to show you something. Kaelen was important to many
people in the realm, we all miss him dearly."

We walk through the dark hallway, the sun low on the sky,
casting white marble in a deep orange glow. Emerging into a new
hallway, Lucien stops beside a small table. A rectangular glass box
stands above a wooden plaque. As my eyes glide over the words,
goosebumps race over my scalp.


*"Our fallen brother, son of the wind, Kaelen.*
*He soared through the clouds, his wings caught our souls.*
*May we be half the male he was, wearing our hearts on our*
sleeves, *riding the gusts of life.*

*Rest easy, brother. May your spirit ride the high winds in the*
Afterlife *like you brightened the sky in the Living."*

I stare at the words. Those beautiful words, carved with love, for my brother. My chest tightens painfully, hand subconsciously rubbing circles across it. I run my fingers across the carvings, feeling every word. *He meant so much to so many. My brother. My best friend.*

The all too familiar pressure builds up behind my eyes as I clamp them shut.

Lucien opens the box, lifting out a beautiful dagger laying inside. I know that blade, I've hated it for a long time.

"I know that it hurts to see this," his eyes scan my face, "but look at the beauty he gave to this world. He made this, and we will never see a blade like this ever again." Handing it to me, the blade feels heavy and cold in my hands. I study it, the intricate runes etched into the hilt, the weapon's metal blade vibrating softly, breathing under my gentle grip. It really is beautiful. The ache in my chest slowly ebbs, replacing the cold anxiety with tickling pride.

Lucien's eyes harden as they meet mine.

"I spoke to Falck and the other soldiers. We want you to take it, Corvyn, and use it to fight Vorathiel. Use Kaelen's weapon to kill the one who took his life from him." His voice is stern, hard.

That's what he would want me to do. To fight for him, for everyone that lost their lives by that piece of shit's hands.

I tighten my grip around the dagger's hilt, holding it firmly. A burst of power rips from the blade, sending pulses of white light through my veins, knocking the air from me. I crouch forward, the dagger falling from my hands onto the cold, stone floor. Sharp sounds of metal against stone cut through the air, ears ringing painfully.

The blade pulses more strongly now, it's like I can feel it calling for me. A force greater than myself pulls me towards it, moving my legs as I follow reluctantly. The room is cast in a white glow, radiating from the blade. Lucien stands in front of the small table, stunned by it all. His eyes are wide, breath vanished. I pick the blade up again, power exploding through the hallway, blinding light swallowing the room.

"What is happening?" Lucien shouts, hands covering his eyes. The air hums loudly with vibrations, ears screaming for help.

"Please, make it stop!" I beg whoever is listening. Paintings shatter as they hit the stone floor, glass spreading across the ground.

Lucien ducks, shielding his head, dust raining over him from the stone ceiling. Sprinting footsteps thunder through the hall, Rowan racing towards us. I fall to my knees, hands clamping down over my ears as streaks of red slither down my neck. Rowan drops to the floor, his hands on my shoulders.

"Cor," his dark voice makes the vibrations even stronger.

"Cor, what's happening?"

I look at him, panicked, words refusing to leave my mouth. I shake my head profusely; *I don't know!*

Power surges, blanketing the hall in pitch black, swallowing every particle of light, before releasing us back into the faint orange glow of the evening sun. The air quiets, no deafening vibrations or shouts. Warily, I glance over at Lucien, the mage still shielding his eyes.

Looking around us, Rowan checks for intruding spirits, anything that could have been the reason, but nothing. Shaking, I lower my hands from my ears, a sharp ringing still echoing through them, and turn the blade facing us. The hilt feels hot, but not painful. The blade itself pulses in dark purple shadows, looking almost… alive.

"I guess that's what happens when a star breathes," I huff, voice cracking in panic. The runes etched onto the hilt glow a faint blue, showing the delicate carving of elven words:

*"For Corvyn; were you ever to choose the stars, this blade will never let you fall."*

I look over at Rowan, his eyes wide as dinner plates.

"I guess I chose the stars."

# *PART TWO*

# Chapter 22

## Tharion

My ears ring as my face smacks against the training mat, again. Groaning loudly, I stagger to my feet. The room is slowly spinning, my eyes trying to figure out which of the five Luciens standing before me is the real one. Grabbing onto the dark brick wall, I close my eyes. With sore lungs, I drag in air, filling them with sweet oxygen.

"I keep telling you, you need to keep your guard up! Your face will be permanently stuck like that if you don't, and trust me – you don't want that," Lucien grins widely, his wicked laughter ringing through the yard.

We've been up before dawn every day, like we promised, to train. Two weeks of this, and I still fall flat on my ass. Yes, I've become a lot better, and my blade skills are impressively good for a beginner, but I need to be able to fight hand-to-hand if I want to have a chance against Vorathiel.

I shake my body loose, vision slowly straightening, shooting Lucien a playful scowl. We go at it for a few more rounds; I knock him on his face a couple times, and he whacks me on mine a few more, and only when the fresh orange hue bathes us in new sunlight do we know our session is over.

I grab my rag, dragging it across my forehead and behind my neck, soaking up sweat. Lucien walks over, handing me his flask and I take a big glug of fresh, cold water. The liquid chills me down and refreshes my senses, invigorating me from the inside out.

"You're getting a lot better. Keep practicing that guard and you'll be unstoppable."

His calloused hand slaps me on my shoulder, the sweaty fabric letting off a sloshy sound.

"Same time tomorrow?" I ask, already knowing the answer. Lucien dips his chin confirmatively, like he does every day.

"Will you join us for breakfast? It's pancake day," he nudges my ribs, a sore groan vibrating from an exhausted chest. The mage laughs mockingly before hauling his satchel over his shoulder and walks towards the barracks.

"See you there!" I shout after him, and a wave is all I get in return. Gathering my things, I rush to my rooms for a quick bath before breakfast. My body feels strong, refreshed… and really sore – but I shrug it off as "the good kind of pain" as the brave warriors keep telling me during our afternoon weapons training.

I've got a pretty good hang of my rune blade now, and I've learned how to throw smaller blades – hitting targets even while running. The thought has pride blooming within me, warm and bubbly.

Drying off, I put on a fresh set of training gear. My leather vest and cotton trousers are starting to wear, but I enjoy seeing the black leather fade with every blow and strike, meaning I'm getting stronger and more ready for the battle to come.

In the last two weeks we've had three attacks on the castle and nearby villages, all by Nochtras and Ravoch. More are seeping through the Veil, and every day we fear will be the day Vorathiel finally gets out. His name fogs my brain, casting it in shadows.

King Vaelrick is getting the army ready for battle, blessing us with his fifty thousand soldiers. People of Stormbrook have sent their best flyers, keeping eyes on the realm from above, and healers from

Meadowrest arrive each day, also here to help us should we need medical care. So far, none from Sylvarn have come, not that we expected them to.

Sylvarn is a forest village, and while the people are strong as bears from building and farming, we seldom fight with anything larger or stronger than a rabbit. A sting of longing rips through me, thoughts of Axel, how he's doing and what he's up to. I miss him dearly.

*He knows the outcome of this, Father has shown him. He knows you will be okay.*

I remind myself of all the reasons why Axel would choose not to come here, but still, there is a sense of disappointment in me. If he could see me now, the changes to my body and mind, would he be proud?

A soft knock on my door takes me out of the daze, my focus back in place. Grabbing the handle, I pull the door open just as Eleanora pushes through, slamming straight into my chest.

"Ow! Damn, Tharion. You almost broke my nose!" her nasal voice seeps through her hand, a look of utter betrayal on her face.

I laugh, "*I* broke your nose? *You* walked into *me*!"

Her posture relaxes, a pained chuckle pushing past her lips. *Her perfect, now pouty lips.*

My eyes fall, settling on them, bumps scattering across my neck. Raging heat courses through me, cheeks almost blistering.

Eleanora raises a brow, cocking her head to the side, "are you okay?"

I avert my gaze, molten lava running through my veins as I try to calm myself down. A shiver runs through me, making me visibly quake. I look around the room, focusing on things around me.

*The table, two chairs, my desk, my bed, her bed, her under me in her bed, me inside her under me in her bed. Fuck.*

"Kyrris to Tharion. Where are you headed?" she waves her hand in front of my face, teeth peeking out from her smile. The delicious sound of her laugh melts my brain even further.

As I watch her cackle, my heart clenches painfully tight.

"I could listen to you laugh forever."

The words escape me before I have the chance to stop them. Eleanora's eyes widen, the smile fading slowly.

I clear my throat. "We should get breakfast, the guys are waiting for us in the mess hall."

A faint nod is all I see before turning on my heel and storming off down the endless hallway.


I arrive first, Eleanora following just behind. We walk to mess as the last few people clear out, the hall almost completely empty. Lucien and Falck sit by their usual table, the mage ogling a steaming stack of fresh pancakes slathered in sticky syrup and freshly churned butter melting shamelessly on top.

Picking up our own plates, Eleanora loads up on some fresh berries and apple slices along with her stack while I go down the same disgustingly sweet road as Lucien. We slump down on our seats, Lucien – the picture of comfort, studying us carefully, gaze lingering on my deep red cheeks.

"I see. That's why you were late," he shrugs playfully, "I don't judge. Would do the same if I had a feisty witch like you under me too," he winks at Eleanora, that cheeky smirk back in its place. Eleanora's cheeks go violently red, I can practically see the steam coming off her.

Clearing my throat, I cut him a look: *back off.*

Lifting his arms, a silent surrender is offered. I chuckle, stabbing my stack with my fork. The fluffy cakes melt on my tongue, sickly-sweet syrup coating my mouth in a barrier of sugar.

"Goddess, these are good," Eleanora chomps, berry juice dripping down her mouth, "we never had anything like this at – "

A loud bell rings through the castle's thick walls, alarms going off in everyone's eyes. I look over at Lucien, his face hard, dead serious. His eyes meet mine, and I instantly know: *an attack.*

We jump up, scanning the area around us. A male dressed in army colours runs in, headed towards Falck.

"Sir! We have a breach, a horde of flesh eaters have gotten beyond the front gates!" his voice is clear, loud, panicked.

"Secure the King, get every soldier out there. Now!"

The male jerks his chin swiftly before turning on his heel and sprinting back out into the hallway. The thundering sound of heavy boots hitting the cold stone floor bounces off the walls.

I look at Eleanora, but she's already headed out, her raven locks fluttering in the air behind her as she sprints towards the upcoming battle. I run after her, several of the King's soldiers following us as we speed through the barracks.

Rowan falls into line with us as we pass the solar foyer, Corvyn right behind. In his hand is his weapon, The Bow of Eternal Hunt. While running, he reaches out his hand, Eleanora's Orbs of Stella safely stored in a leather pouch. She grips it, holding it securely in her hand. I have my rune blade strapped to me, the same for Corvyn, and soon we burst through the main doors out into the courtyard – where the overpowering stench of death and rot hits us like a wall.

Dozens, no, hundreds of rotting, half-dead corpses moan and cry as we surround them, rotting flesh falling off in chunks as they move. Their dead eyes glow a faint yellow, evil seeping through their pores. The blinding sunlight casts dark shadows around them, painting the courtyard in black.

Movement to my left snaps my head, a demon launching itself my way. Reaching for one of the smaller blades strapped to my leg, I pelt towards the ugly creature, locking my target on its neck. The sharp steel releases from my hand, slicing through the stench before lodging itself deeply in the demon's rotting throat. A wail erupts, air cracking like glass.

Dark clouds blanket the sky, suffocating the once bright sunlight. Deep thunder roars across the heavens before cold rain pours down on us. The demon lunges after me, arms flailing as thick, black tar seeps from its neck. While running, I drop to my knees, sliding across the muddy ground, stopping just behind it before springing back and planting my hands on either side of its throat, ripping its head off from behind.

Ash rains over me, covering my vest in dark grey dust. I look over my shoulder as scorching heat brushes against me, singeing the tips of my eyebrows, closely followed by the smell of burnt flesh. I hold my breath, the vile smell making my entire body churn. White flames engulf the spirits, their decomposing bodies burning to a crisp in a matter of seconds. Eleanora moves gracefully through the horde, incinerating them as she goes.

I hit the ground with a wet thwack as a demon runs straight into me, head bouncing off the stone on impact. White pain shoots to the back of my eyes, blurring my vision.

The noise from the battle slowly fades, replaced by a high-pitched ringing. Long claws bury themselves in my chest, pain sweltering through me. I scream in agony as the monster lowers itself to merely an inch off my face, snapping its half-hinged jaws.

My hand searches for the hilt of my blade, only to find it missing. Panicked, I try to push the demon off me, but my hands keep dropping into its body, flesh so rotten it gives way instantly. I pull my hands back, now covered in a thick black liquid smelling like death itself, and try rolling us to the side.

The half-dead corpse keeps on, its claws still deep in my chest. I feel my flesh separating as the sharp nails push deeper into my torso, blood pooling around its fingertips. It lifts one hand, getting ready to slash me, just as the tip of an arrow shoots through its skull, splattering me in cold, black slime.

The creature cries out, covering its eye when two large hands plant themselves on either side of its neck and decapitates it, turning it into thick grey mud. Rowan stands behind where the demon just stood, panting and bloody. He reaches out his hand, and I grab it, getting me up from the ground. My head goes light as I stand up, blood gushing from my chest. Knees buckle, sending me tumbling towards him.

"Healer! I need a healer!" Rowan calls out, still holding on to me. I stumble, feeling dizzy and weak. My vision fades into pulsating black, consciousness clinging on to whatever it can, but ultimately loses as I feel myself falling into cold, dark nothingness.

# Chapter 23
## Eleanora

I duck as a demon tries to strike me, coming up behind it. I shove my foot at its back, sending it tumbling forward, slipping on wet stone. Magic hums under my skin, thick vines bursting through the ground, circling around the demon's neck so tightly it pops right off, leaving a muddy trail of ash behind.

The piercing sounds of blades hitting bone, flesh ripping and blood hitting the ground ricochet around me, laced in the smell of decomposing flesh. I'm covered in tar-like blood, the substance reeking of rot. In the distance I hear Rowan calling for help, and as I look over my shoulder, I see Tharion on the ground, lifeless, with Rowan's large hands pressed down on his chest.

Stopping in my tracks, my heart sinks into my stomach. *No. Not Tharion.*

Not here, not like this. Ice floods my veins, heart raging away, desperately trying to escape. I look to Corvyn, his blade slashing and cutting away at a handful of demons, all hungry for the raven.

I push my hand into my leather pouch and cop one of my orbs, the green glass dancing with white flames, ready to burst free. Aiming the orb at the horde of demons gathering in the middle of the yard, I throw it as hard as I can. The sound of glass shattering is all the warning we get before a wall of blazing heat hits us, knocking the air from our bodies. I throw myself to the ground, covering my head as the stench of rotting corpses blankets the air.

The yard quiets. There's no sound of weapons defending their soldiers, no sloshing of blood and no ripping of flesh. It's dead quiet, only the gentle sound of rain bouncing off the stone.

Carefully, I raise my head. Lucien is standing next to Corvyn, holding his palm firmly over a slash on the raven's arm. Rowan and Tharion are gone, and soldiers are spread across the cold ground, wounded, bleeding. Healers pour from the castle gates as wing-shifters stoop from the skies, all trying to help the wounded warriors.

Panting, I look around, frantically searching for Tharion. A large man covered in grey dust and dark stains runs towards me, his boots hitting the ground with heavy thuds. I instinctively reach for my blade as Falck reaches me, crouching to my level.

"Eleanora, are you okay?" his eyes search my face, looking for injuries.

"Tharion," I mumble, exhaustion taking over, "where is he? Where's Tharion?"

"They took him to the infirmary. A demon got to him, he's in bad shape." Deep frowns form between his brows, his voice drenched in worry.

I push myself off the ground, steadying myself for a second before steadily planting one foot in front of the other, picking up speed, running to the infirmary. The halls feel excessively long and narrow, like I'm never going to reach him in time. I make turn after turn, whisking down spiral stairs and through dark hallways underneath the castle grounds, before finally reaching the door leading to the healer's bay. Busting through the door, Rowan's arms catch me, holding me back.

"Eleanora! Eleanora, please. He's okay," Rowan wraps his arms around me as I desperately try to get out of his hold, "listen, he's okay."

I stop, looking up at him with teary eyes. The panic in my body rings in my ears, hands sweating profusely. A sob breaks from my soul, convulsing as tears fall freely from my eyes, burying my face in Rowan's dirty shirt.

He puts his hand under my chin, lifting my face to meet him. His eyes are calm, kind. There is no worry etched in his brows, no frowns to be seen. My racing heart slows down its pace, and I can finally hear properly.

"H-he's okay?" my voice cracks, fear still lodged in my throat.

Rowan nods, eyes smiling gently at me.

"A demon got to him, he lost a lot of blood, but the healer got to him in time to patch him back without much effort."

I let out the breath I've been holding, lungs screaming for oxygen.

"Can I see him?"

Releasing me from his embrace, Rowan tugs me along to the bay where Tharion is resting. His body is relaxed, chest slowly rising and falling with each breath. My teary gaze drags across his body, at the white bandages covering his upper torso, chest tightening at the sight. I hate seeing him in pain.

"We'll come back tomorrow, let him rest now."

I nod, unable to speak, and we turn to leave the room. Giving him a last glance, I close the door to the infirmary and walk the long way back to Lucien and Corvyn.

As I emerge from the long hallways, Corvyn has a soldier's arm around his neck, helping them onto a chair nearby. The soldier's arm is bleeding heavily, a deep gash stretching from the female's shoulder down to her wrist. Moans of pain hang in the dusty air, deafening, snapping me out of my haze.

Corvyn, Rowan and I help as many as we can, and luckily, we didn't lose a single soldier during the battle. As the yard empties, the wounded safely taken to the infirmary, the three of us slump down on the stone edge surrounding a massive fountain in the middle of the now destroyed yard.

"You did well, friends. We thank you for your help," Lucien's deep voice vibrates through my chest, a genuine gratitude linked to the words. Looking up at him, his face is dusty, and his brow has a minor cut, but other than that he's unharmed. I give him an exhausted smile, body aching for some rest. Suddenly, a twinge cuts through my stomach as I remember Vaelrick. Is he okay? Is he unharmed?

"The king. Is he safe?"

Lucien's eyes harden, his mouth pressed into a thin line. With a sharp nod, my shoulders fall.

"He's unharmed, thanks to everyone's fast reaction. We got him out and locked in before the battle broke out."

The three of us let out deep sighs, relieved by the information.

"Now, I could seriously use a hot bath before dinner. And I suggest you do the same." The mage winks at us before turning back towards the barracks, leaving us.

I get up, stretching my arms above my head, a deep yawn carrying into the air.

"I second that. Great job today, guys. See you at dinner?"

Nodding, they smile at me before I turn and make for my rooms, exhausted and pumped to the brim with adrenalin. We've dealt with smaller battles during our stay here, but nothing as big as this. Things are getting worse, more spirits are escaping the cracks and soon Vorathiel will be here to greet us. By then, we will be ready.


Closing the door behind me, I let out the sobs that have been lodged in my throat. Seeing Tharion hurt, lifeless…

My thoughts wander through scenarios of the upcoming battle, how likely I will have to see him wounded again, perhaps even worse than he was today.

Hot tears release from closed eyes, slowly falling down my cheeks, coating the corners of my mouth. Scenarios play out in my mind, where Tharion, Rowan and Corvyn all suffer, they all fall to swords and spirits, they all… die.

Sorrow rips through me, refusing my lungs the air they so desperately need. I heave, tears and snot mixing in my mouth as silent cries slip from my lips. Falling to my knees, my head hangs heavy on my chest.

*I cannot let them die.*

I lift my head, inhaling a deep breath.

*I will not let them die.*

Dragging the back of my hand up my nose, coating it in snot, I wipe my eyes.

*They will not die.*

I will not let them fall to swords or to spirits, not if I can help it.

# *Chapter 24*

## *Tharion*

*It's black, everything around me is black. I look down at myself, but there is nothing.*

*"Hello?" the reflections of my voice ricochet through the air, carrying it far into the void beyond me.*

*I try to move, but find only the echo of movement. No feet, no weight, only thought. I can hear, I can smell and breathe, I must be alive, right?*

*"Hello? Is anyone there?" I call out again, this time a faint white light breaks the darkness far ahead of me. The weak light grows in strength, illuminating where I am, as wooden walls and a ceiling surround me. Footsteps break the silence, snapping my focus behind me.*

*A figure dressed in a dark brown cloak approaches me, their hood dragged down over their face. The faint smell of wet grass and old wood surrounds me, a warming familiarity. I stand still as panic refuses to move my body, heart pounding in my ears.*

*The dark figure stands in front of me, still masked by their hood. They raise their hands, slowly pulling off the heavy fabric, revealing long auburn hair. I notice their pointed ears, and I've seen that exact birthmark before – a small fern on the side of their neck. Realization hits, knees weak under my trembling body.*

*"Father?" I whisper, voice cracking. The figure lifts their head, my father's deep emerald eyes staring back at me.*

*Shocked, my mouth falls open, taking in all his features. Is he really here? My eyes fill with water, pressure building in my throat. I leap into his arms, finally able to hold my father once more. Tears stream down my cheeks, dripping from my chin.*

*"Father, I missed you so much. I..." my words mix in my mouth, relief washing over me like a waterfall of hope and love, "I missed you so much," I repeat, still not fully realizing he's standing here, holding me.*

*Sobs echo through the room. As my shoulders shake, Father releases me, cupping my cheeks. He looks me deep into the eyes, an adoring smile across his young face.*

*"Hello, son." His voice is exactly as I remember, warm and loving. I bury my face in his cloak, dragging in the scent that is him, but there is none. Confused, I lift my head off his chest and look up at him.*

*"Where are you, Father?"*
*His face softens, the warm smile fading slightly.*

*"I'm right here, my dear boy. I have always been right here."*
*"Are you here to relay a message for me?"*

*Father nods softly, his eyes sparkling in the faint light of the small room.*

*"The day is almost here, my son. The day we knew would come. I have watched you from afar, seen how you have grown both in strength and as a person. I am so proud of you and who you have become, Tharion."*

*The words wrap around my heart, almost painfully tight. I swallow, trying to loosen the knot in my throat.*

*A loud crash sounds behind my father, shadows swirling, blanketing us in black. The air fills with the overbearing smell of ash and choked flames. I reach out for him, trying to find him in the darkness, but he's not there.*

*Veins freezing, I cry out for him, but there is no answer. Instead, a tall figure with long black hair and silver tattoos snaking up their torso and neck, strides towards me. The figure has deep blue eyes and majestic horns stretching from the top of their head, spiralling beautifully before ending at a sharp point.*

*I look around me, the small room transforming into a dark black void. There is no door, no walls, no ceiling. Just black. The man walks towards me, a sly smile on his face as malicious laughter fills the small space.*

*"How nauseatingly sweet, I might actually throw up. Hello, Tharion. I have heard so much about you." His voice is deep, low, evil.*

*"Who are you?" I cry out, body trembling under his gaze.*

*The stranger tuts his tongue, shaking his head in disappointment.*

*"Tharion. Surely you know who I am? We are destined to meet, very soon," smiling viciously, sickening.*

*Chills race down my spine, a light going off in my mind. Vorathiel.*

*Heat explodes through my veins, jaw so tight I can hear teeth cracking. Without thinking, I sprint towards him, ready for our battle to begin. He darts my strike with ease, laughing villainously.*

*"My dear boy. This is not the time nor the place. We will meet, and we will battle, but not this night," a sly smile still plastered on his smug face. I lunge forward again, but instead of darting, he conjures a long sword and pierces it through my stomach, plunging me into darkness once more.*


Heaving, I wake, sitting upright in bed. My heart is hammering in my chest, sweat trickles down my temples, body trembling like a leaf. In a panic, I feel my torso, trying to locate the stab wound from just moments before. I can still feel the sensation of the sharp weapon slicing through my flesh, cold steel separating layers of skin in one swift move.

Thankfully, there is no wound here in the waking realm. Looking around, I slowly recognize my surroundings. I am in bed, in my rooms, in Catariel. I shudder.

*What a horrible nightmare.*

Vorathiel spoke to me, taunted me. He believes I don't have what it takes. *I'll show him.*

My head spins, hands clammy and cold. I think back to the dream, how my father's embrace felt warm and safe. Thinking about seeing his smile and hearing his voice. The lump in my throat returns and for a moment, I forget how to breathe. *I need air. Now.*

Throwing off my covers, I get up and stab my feet into my slippers. My legs are stiff, exhausted from being on bedrest after the battle at the castle gates, aching as I take the first steps in days across my bedroom floor. Heading out into the dark hallway, I take in the silence, dragging in the cold night air. There are no footsteps, no voices, no sounds from aides pitter pattering around the halls.

I find my way to the kitchen and grab myself a cup of water. The cold liquid runs down my throat, cooling my overworking heart. Finally, I feel like I can breathe. Looking out the floor length windows, moon bright on the night sky, casting a white curtain of light over Kyrris. All the villages are dark, people safely sleeping in their homes.

Safe, for now.

Glancing up at the sky, I see the faint white shimmer of the Veil. It glitters in the moonlight, but I know it's not as it seems. Along the borders are cracks, letting those awful flesh-eating monsters out into the realm of the living. Chills run through me at the thought. I need to warn the others. The battle is happening soon, and we need to be prepared.

· · — · ✳ · — · ·

"What do you mean, Vorathiel came to see you?"

Corvyn's brows almost vanish into his hairline, eyes wide while I share the contents of my dream with the others.

"It means that Vorathiel found a way into his mind while Tharion was dreaming, that *sneaky fuck*," the words almost spat out in anger, Eleanora's voice hard as steel.

"But how did he get into your dream?" the raven asks, still puzzled.

I look down, visions of my father's embrace punching me in the gut.

"He used my father."

"He did *what?*" her voice is now five times louder than before, body vibrating next to me.

Rowan puts his hand gently on Eleanora's forearm, eyes stern, but soft as Eleanora lets out a deep breath.

"I thought your father died years ago?" Corvyn's face scrunches, apology written in his eyes. The lump trying to choke me only gets bigger as I desperately try to swallow it down.

"He did. My father was a Seer… He…" I close my eyes.

"He knew he would die, and he knew I would be the one to save us. He told me in a dream before all this happened."

A sharp breath escapes Corvyn's lips, his brows have returned to just above his eyes, now forming a deep frown, wrinkling his skin.

"Tharion… I'm so sorry. I…" closing his eyes, he lets out a sigh, "I didn't know."

A tug to the corners of my mouth is all I can muster, but it seems to be enough for now.

"We need to be ready for him. We don't have time to sit around anymore. It's time to save Kyrris."


The following days go to intense training, mastering my magic and getting better at handling my rune blade. Magic almost feels like an extension of me now, energy flowing effortlessly from my hands. I still lose battles to Lucien, but I also win some – and that proves I have what it takes, for the most part.

Eleanora is spectacular in her battles with the mage, handing Lucien's ass to him on a daily basis. Pride beams from her every time he calls for a time out, every time he walks away in shame.

Rowan is mastering his archery skills too, the arrows flying like smoke from his hands, even on horseback. Corvyn has his blade, the blade we all need to end this – to put light into the darkness that is Vorathiel. The only weapon that can truly kill him. Day in and day out we prepare, but still, there is no sign of the demon.

Days turn into nights, nights into weeks, and nothing. There have been no more attacks on the villages or the castle.

*Something is wrong.*

I can feel it deep in my gut. He must be scheming, planning his return to the living. The thoughts give has my stomach turning, goosebumps racing across my scalp. We need to stop him before he emerges, before he gets too strong for us to conquer.

"We need to take the battle to him."
Three pairs of plate-wide eyes stare at me, mouths gaping.

"We need to get to him before he's too strong. Before our chance to win fades away."

Silence. They just stare at me for what feels like years, no one moving a muscle. Rowan closes his mouth, eyes sliding from mine.

"He is right. We should go to the place where the living meets the dead, where Alaric and Camille found Amariel – to Veil's Eclipse."

Eleanora swings her head to him, shocked beyond words.

Corvyn nods softly, his eyes falling to the blade fastened on my thigh.

I grab the hilt, feeling the metal humming under my skin. Looking at my friends, we all silently agree: *we need to leave.*

"Tomorrow will be our last night in this castle. Tomorrow, we plan our next move, we train harder than ever before. We're taking this demon down before he even sees us coming."

The gang nods, hard looks plastered on their faces. Eleanora stands up, her hand curled into a tight fist.

"That piece of shit will not hurt anyone else. He dies. Now."

# *Chapter 25*

## *Eleanora*

*That was too close.* The air splits as a ball of light tumbles through the training yard. My knees hit the ground, dirt stinging my eyes. *Let's see how good your aim is when you can't breathe, mage.*

Spotting Lucien, I smirk, arms lifting in front of me. With a curl of the wrists, he falls to the ground clawing at his throat. I watch as his dark eyes widen with panic, mouth gaping like a fish out of water. I flick my wrist back, the mage heaving for air.

"That is dirty play!" he croaks, throat completely dry.

"There is no dirty play in war, little wizard," my sinister laugh fills the space around us, bouncing off the stone walls. Giving me a sour scowl, Lucien stumbles to his feet, gently massaging his chest.

I've wanted to bend the other elements, like air, for a long time but have only been practicing on candles. Images of a dancing flame flickering before suddenly dying, lack of air suffocating it in an instant, flash before me.

"You are one dangerous female."

"You have no idea," I wink.

I gloat as I walk over to him, handing him my flask. Big gulps of water soothe his dry oesophagus, colour returning to his cheeks.

The cold drops slide down his chin, dripping onto the ground.

"How long have you been working on that trick?"

I laugh, shrugging nonchalantly. "Since I got here"

He looks at me, a blank expression on his face.

"You learned to steal the air from my lungs in such a short amount of time?" A short burst of air escapes his mouth, "Vorathiel should count his days." Lucien hands me back my flask and stands up, rubbing his chest softly.

I chuckle, a warm feeling spreading through my body. If he thinks Vorathiel should fear me, I'm not as scared anymore.

We end our training session with that. I throw my bag over my shoulder before starting back to my rooms. Seeing as this is our last night here before we head out to cause trouble, I need to pack.


Walking, I think back to our time here. Nights buried in Tharion's arms, waking up next to him. Thinking back to my training sessions with Lucien, how empowered it has made me feel.

During our short stay, I've learned how to fight, to wield a weapon and call on my magic to perform incredible things. I've watched Tharion go from an anxious, quiet male to a man with confidence, strength and bravery. Rowan has found a special kind of happiness in Corvyn, and the same for my raven friend. I know they feel the connection, I know Rowan knows what it means.

He has waited his whole lifetime for his mate, and the Gods gave him to him right before we all might die. Such pricks. I'm not sure if Corvyn has acknowledged the bond, if they have admitted it to each other, but we all know it's there.

Reaching my door, I drag my feet through the bedroom and into the giant washroom. I turn on the faucet and use my magic to start the small fire underneath. Looking in the mirror, my hair is dishevelled, filled with dirt. My face has splotches of mud and ash from our training battle, and my clothes are torn, too. Steam fills the room, the now familiar scent of lavender soap rising off the hot, misty water.

Throwing my clothes in a pile, I step into the tub, tension exiting my body immediately. As I sink down, the water sloshes over the edge, dripping to the floor. I cross my arms over the tub's edge, resting my chin on them. Tired eyes gaze out over our realm, our kingdom. Kyrris.

I reflect on how things have changed in such a short time, how things are about to change even more. My eyes fall to Sylvarn, imagining smoke rising from chimneys, lights flickering in people's windows as they go about their lives. I think back to how Tharion and I met, that night in the forest all those years ago. Heat blooms in my chest, relishing in the happiness of the memories playing out in my mind.

I sink further, submerging myself completely in the water. The steady beats of my heart pound in my ears, long raven-black hair floating around me, the comfortable heat of the water embracing my body. Clamping my eyes shut, the black feels welcoming, calm.

The black nothingness changes, a tall, auburn-haired character coming into view. Tharion. I watch as he smiles, laughs, studying me with hunger and affection. My body aches for him, impatient for his touch.

He walks my way, soon standing directly in front of me, his hands stretched out as if he was holding mine. I watch as he leans closer to me, his face mere inches from mine, eyes closing carefully. Just as his lips are about to claim mine, his face blurs, barely visible as my lungs cry for air.

I burst through the surface, gasping as my lungs drink down oxygen. My heart hammers in my chest as water crashes to the tile floor below me. What just happened? Did I just… fantasize about Tharion?

I stumble out of the bath, almost slipping on wet tiles. The steamy air is filled with warm lavender soap, helping my racing heart calm down. I drag in the floral scent, taking steadying breaths.

Wrapping a towel around me, I dry off and put on a fresh set of clothes. I'm supposed to meet the others for a meeting, to plan our upcoming journey to Veil's Eclipse, all of us wanting to be as prepared as possible. There is no room for failure, for surprise.

The door closes behind me, and I make my way to the dining hall, where we first met with Vaelrick. As I cross the threshold, I find my friends deep in conversation, heatedly discussing if potatoes are better roasted or mashed.

"A roasted spud gives you crunch, softness, saltiness and has an array of things to flavour it with!" Corvyn's arms flail, his voice desperate to be heard. Tharion shakes his head, refusing to listen.

"Mashed potatoes are creamy, fluffy and buttery. You can serve it next to anything!"

The raven lets out a defeated breath, shoulders slumping.

"I guess we will have to agree to disagree."

"I can agree that you both are idiots," I shoot in, both males turning my way. Tharion clutches his heart in a theatrical expression of shock, Corvyn's reluctant chortle bouncing off the stone walls.

I sit down next to Rowan, my familiar beaming as his eyes focus on Corvyn.

Rolling out a large piece of parchment, a map of Kyrris, Rowan places it on the table between us.

"The fastest route to Veil's Eclipse is through Meadowrest. It will take us two days to get there." He draws a line from Catariel to Meadowrest, mapping out places to camp and rest. We nod as Rowan describes the route, how we need to ride through mountain valleys and thick forests.

"Healers reside in Meadowrest. We should try our luck finding a healer that can go with us to Veil's Eclipse in case we get badly injured."

Nodding intently, we follow Rowan's instructions, making notes of what to look for, where to camp, the dangers that may find us on the short, but daring journey.

We discuss for about two hours, all of us feeling confident and ready to leave the capital. I feel apprehension build in my body. All the training and battling over the last few weeks have made us stronger, faster, better prepared. No, we're not masters of the craft – obviously, we've only trained for a few weeks, but we have a better chance than we did before we arrived here.

A soft knock on the doorframe ends our meeting, Vaelrick leaning inside the large room.

"I would like to host a feast tonight, for all of you. To say goodbye."

My chest tightens at the thought. He has been so much happier over the last few weeks – perhaps it was the company. The thought of leaving him to himself again breaks my heart.

"It would be an honour, my liege," Rowan bows his head, the rest of us following suit. Vaelrick gives us a soft nod, mouth grinning wide before heading back out.

I look at my friends. "I don't like having to leave him alone again. Did you see that smile?"

Rowan puts his hand on mine, squeezing it gently.

"We will be back. He will see us again, Ela."

A moment of silence goes by, only broken by the sharp clap of Tharion rubbing his hands over his trouser legs, signalling that it's time to get up. We escape back into our own rooms, I start packing up my old clothes and new training gear that the King so thoughtfully gifted us and place my orbs safely in the middle.

Walking over to the bed, I lift the small wooden doll that has been my protector during these chilly nights, holding it firmly in my hand.

Memories of us as stupid teens play out in my mind, a smile creeping over my face as I think back to all the things Tharion, Rowan and I would get up to in order to escape our painful realities at home. Rowan might not have been a teenager when we met, but he would always have fun doing whatever we did. Climbing trees, sneaking out during the night, going swimming in nearby lakes. He never felt like he was centuries old at the time, he still doesn't.

My core feels warm, heat spreading throughout my limbs as gratefulness blankets me. I would never be where I am without them, and now we're set to save the realm together. Carefully placing the doll in my bag, I pull the drawstrings tight, closing it.

I turn as a hard knock comes from my door, two aides walking in with a beautiful gown, a pair of shoes and a box of jewellery, just like the first night we had here. I chuckle at the memory, the confusion and overwhelming feeling I had as they tied my hair up and forced my feet into heels.

"Good evening, lady Eleanora. Would you like to take a bath before dinner?"

I had one only hours ago, but this might just be the last one I'll ever take. I nod, giving them a thankful smile before they rush into the washroom to start my bath, luscious lavender once again seeping through the air into my bedroom.

Walking into the washroom, I watch as the aides pour the bubble mixture into the hot water, white peaks forming in seconds. The aides close the door behind them, leaving me to myself. I undress, clothes getting neatly folded and placed on the marble countertop and sink into the perfectly tempered water. My head leans back on a folded towel, letting me rest.

Shutting out the upcoming battle, all my thoughts surrounding it, my shoulders sink and I slowly drift off.

The bubbles have vanished; it's time to get out. Stretching, I feel my muscles let go of the tension I've built.

*Don't worry, you will build it back up over the next few days.*

Slowly, I emerge, stepping out onto the warm tiles. After a quick dry, my body feels calm and relaxed. I wrap my hair in the towel and step out to put my new gown on.

Holding it up, I gasp softly at its beauty. The heavy fabric flows in a deep burgundy red, perfectly mirroring my eyes. Dark green ivy leaves stretch across the mesh bodice, making it look like vines snaking around me.

I slip it on, and to no surprise – it fits like it was made for me. The deep heart neckline perfectly complements my fair decolletage, short sleeves delicately falling off my shoulders. The dark colour grants the illusion of blood pooling at my feet, by the hands of my elemental magic. Chills run down my spine. I love it.

As I let my damp hair down, the aides from before enter the room, ready to tackle the crow's nest. Violent brush strokes scratch my head as heavy jewellery is placed around my neck. My hair is carefully twirled and braided into a crown, small ivy leaf clips placed in it to tie the look together. The rest of my raven curls hang delicately down behind me, with two small braids weaved in for protection, leaving a few face framing curls falling from my forehead.

Appreciation sweeps over me as I watch them bring my witch heritage into the hairdo, feeling seen. Finished, I step out into the hallway and begin walking to the dining hall. The castle is glowing under the late-night sun, orange and yellow hues painting everything in a golden sheen.

The dining hall has been decorated in deep green trees and plants, table set with meadow flowers resting peacefully on a forest-green runner, with small candles spread across making the room feel warm and intimate. Ivy garlands hang from the ceiling, mimicking a forest clearing.

I look around me in awe, chest blooming with warmth, vision blurring behind adoring tears. Vaelrick stands at the end of the table, hands folded in front of him, grinning from ear to ear.

"Lady Eleanora, you look beautiful. How did you find the gown?"

I give him a twirl, my skirt flowing in the air like blood in water, mesmerizing.

"I adore it, your Grace. Thank you so much," I curtsy, bowing my head deeply in respect.

"Come on now, Eleanora. We're long past that," his white smile radiates off him, forcing out my own. The room smells of wet forest, just like home, the familiarity striking me to my core. Looking behind Vaelrick I see the wall covered in wildflowers, the different colours dancing under dim candlelight.

"It is to remind you of what you are fighting to save, to show you what you are risking your lives for," his husky voice comes out brimming with pride. I look at him, studying his features closely. His eyes are soft, forehead relaxed. The smile on his face actually reaches his eyes for a change, making me warm inside.

"You really think we can take this guy?"

With only a sharp dip of his chin, Vaelrick gives me all the hope I need. *Bring it, demon fuck.*

# *Chapter 26*

## *Tharion*

Fluffing out my high-collared shirt, I pull on my jacket. Our last dinner with the King here in his castle. The time has come. I stretch out my arms, the final touch being a dark burgundy pocket square in the finest silk I have ever touched. The burgundy fabric reminds me of the deep pools in Eleanora's eyes, and they go perfectly with my dark forest green attire.

Walking down the hallways, the blooming smell of roasted lamb makes my mouth water. Behind me, deep voices ring closer, Falck and Lucien in deep conversation. Lucien waves at me, a wide smile lighting up his face.

"Ready for the meal of a lifetime, lad?" Falck's heavy accent sings every word like a melody. My stomach rumbles, like on cue, the males breaking into laughter.

A delicious smell of food wafts closer as we walk down the hallway, but every sense I have combusts as Eleanora turns to greet me. Her gown is breathtaking. *She* is breathtaking.

The fist-sized muscle in my chest stops beating, lungs refusing to draw air. I study her from top to toe, drinking in the sight of her as she practically beams in the entryway. Her eyes finally meet mine, the intensity behind them dark and sultry. Every fibre in my body wants to rush to her, fingers twitch and skin burns as I keep myself in place.

"Well, don't you look dashing." Her shy smile hides the purr of her voice, the melody like a siren's song to my soul.

"Little witch," Lucien smirks from beside me, "you clean up nicely. I prefer the training gear though, to be frank." With a wink, he trots down the steps to where King Vaelrick awaits. Falck gives me a slap on the back, knocking even more air from my system, following his fellow soldier.

I take a step towards her, my knees weak and wobbly.

"Ela… You…" a heavy *phew* slips past my lips.

"You look incredible."

Watching a dark pink blush paint her fair skin, eyes darkening with every shaky inhale.

A heavy thump restarts my heart, now racing into overdrive as I swallow dryly, scratching my throat. She walks up to me, taking her sweet time, eyelids heavy over two enchanted rubies.

"Are you hungry, Ari?" the words come out a low, deep whisper. My body enkindles in her presence, sweat beading on my forehead. It takes everything I have not to push her against the nearest wall, to feast on her, devour her.

A teasing chuckle falls from her lips, and my mind is fucking lost. I rev my throat violently, desperately trying to cling to a sliver of sanity.

Hips swaying, Eleanora steps away, her gaze locked with mine before turning and walking down the stairs to our waiting friends below. Letting out a deep exhale, I wipe my forehead with the back of my hand.

"You feeling okay there, friend?"

I turn, meeting Corvyn's violet eyes, his brows softly scrunched.

Words elude me, the brain in my skull just a bubbly cauldron of mush. I nod, taking a deep breath before following him down to the rest just as Rowan joins us.

"Welcome friends, my family, our heroes."
King Vaelrick captures our attention effortlessly.

"Tonight, we dine for the last time, before our brave brothers –
and sister," he winks at Eleanora, "set out to save our realm from
darkness. I ask that you eat, drink, and love with your hearts tonight. This
may very well be the last time we are all gathered. It has been an honour
having you stay at my castle, and I hope it is not the last time I am graced
by your presence. Now, let's feast!"

He claps his hands, echo bouncing off the walls as a flock of
servers rush the dining hall carrying plates covered by silver cloches. The
servers delicately flow over the floor into lines behind us, setting the
plates down in one swift move, perfectly in sync. As the domes ascend,
the smell of decadently roasted meat fills the room.

I look down to find a big cut of perfectly roasted lamb resting
delicately over a bed of soft mashed potatoes. Sprigs of rosemary and
thyme are neatly stacked on top, giving the meat a delicious herby taste.

The potatoes are fluffy, soft, butter oozing from under the slab of
meat, making my mouth flood. Beside it all are roasted garden peas,
honey-glazed carrots and caramelized onions. I have never seen such
beauty on a plate before, it makes it hard to believe I will actually be
eating it.

A loud moan rings through the air, my eyes drifting to find Falck
with his fork still in his mouth, eyes closed and leaned back in his chair.
The table laughs and digs into their own plates, soft whimpers of delight
slipping occasionally from us all. The mood is comfortable, easy.
Conversation carries effortlessly, like we're one big family. I look at my
new friends, gratitude filling my every pore.

The tight sensation in my chest makes a comeback, although a
tad softer than normal, as the thought of never seeing them brushes
against me. It would really suck if I never got to meet them again, to
never have my ass handed to me in training battles, never have Falck's
ridiculous accent make stupid jokes, never see the look of happiness on
Vaelrick's face during our evening meals.

My vision blurs faintly as tears line my eyes, a lump in my throat
pushing a sob. Strangling it, I look down, blinking away the blurred
lines.

"I want you to know," the chatter stops as six sets of eyes land on me, "the last few weeks have been the best of my life. All stakes considered, I have made friends and memories that I hope I never lose."

Corvyn's face softens, dark eyebrows lifting slightly as a smile creeps over his face.

"I agree. These last weeks have taught me many things, shown me many more. I will be eternally grateful for it all."
Corvyn puts his hand over Rowan's, my stomach fluttering at the sight.

"All I saw was darkness before you showed up. After Rowenna…" Vaelrick's words fade as he strains his throat, "I found friendship and laughter again, and for that I thank you."

He raises his glass high in a toast, the rest of us following. Our glasses float in the air as we search each other's eyes, a silent poem of gratitude hanging as we drink to each other.


The evening drags out while we feast, laugh, sing and drink sparkling wine. The bubbles staining our lips and slowing our brains warm my chest as one by one, our group retires for the night.

Vaelrick is slurring his words, singing and mumbling into his cup before slumping into his chair, fast asleep. I laugh as two aides rush to help our drunken King to bed. Rowan, Corvyn, Eleanora and I also get up to leave, Corvyn stumbling over his feet on the way up the stairs.

"Whoa there, princess. Let me help you to bed," Rowan chuckles as he picks up the raven warrior, carrying him like a maiden in his arms. Corvyn wraps around Rowan's neck, whispering something into his ears.

I watch as the tips turn a dark red, eyes darting back at us as if to check that we didn't accidentally hear anything. I laugh, giving him a cheeky wink, watching as they disappear into Rowan's rooms for the night, the door softly closing behind them. Again, Eleanora and I find ourselves alone in the foyer outside our rooms, the orange tiles reflecting around us, casting the room in a deep glow.

I look over at her, cheeks splotched with pink as her eyes glisten from the wine-haze beyond them. She dips her head, shyly fiddling her fingers as she sways carefully before her door.

*This is it. It is now, or never.*

Heat blooms in my chest as my heart's voice finally reaches the surface. Tenderly, my hand glides over her dipped cheeks, lifting them to meet my eyes.

"Eleanora, you are the most beautiful being I have ever laid my eyes on." Words slip through my lips before I have the chance to stop them. The breath in her chest hitches, a soft gasp escaping her lips.

"You make my heart skip a beat, my lungs forget how to draw air. I cannot hold these feelings inside anymore."
My heart hammers in my chest as the confession glides off my tongue.

Eleanora's eyes glimmer in the low light, dark burgundy roaring with orange streaks. Slowly, Eleanora interlaces our fingers and starts walking, gently pulling me along with her. I follow, bewitched by her touch. A soft click is heard before the door opens quietly, Eleanora crossing the threshold, still facing me.

My heart is pounding ridiculously hard, drumming away in my chest. Our stares lock, boring deep into each other. Her eyelids are heavy, seduction radiating from the deep sultry pools. In the middle of the room, she stops, letting go of my hand, the absence of her touch cold and empty.

"Once, you asked me if I felt this pull between us. This pull that our friendship couldn't quite describe," her voice is low, enchanting. She slips off her shoes, one by one, falling to her regular, perfect height.

"Truth is, Tharion, I have always felt it. I felt it from the day you gave me that silly wooden doll, but I have rejected it out of fear."
I listen to her, stunned by the way her mouth moves while she talks, trapping me in a spell. Her hands reach behind her, followed by the soft sound of silk laces untying. The gown loosens around her body, barely hanging on. I keep my eyes trained on her, chest feeling tight and electric at the same time.

My skin is humming, a low vibration coursing under it.

"I will not reject it any longer, Ari," her hand reaches the corset's neckline, pushing it to the floor with a heavy thump. The sweet scent of lavender soap clings to her skin, dizzying me more than any wine.

Eleanora stands before me, only covered by her bottom undergarments. Heat rushes through my body, eyes taking in every inch of her. Her breasts bounce slightly, sending bolts of electricity down my spine. They are perfect, pouches filled with my deepest desires. I forget how to breathe.

"I am yours, Tharion."

That's all I need as I rush to her, pushing my hand into her hair, closing the distance between us. A soft yelp rips from her, the sudden movement taking her by surprise.

"I have waited years for those delicious words to come from your mouth. Say them again, my sweet Eleanora." My words come out demanding, desperate. Her chest rises and falls quickly, warm breath bouncing off my skin. Our eyes lock as her tongue darts out across her bottom lip. The glisten of her mouth makes me feral, the need to taste them overwhelming.

"I am yours, Tharion. I am –"

It's all I allow before my mouth crashes down on hers. The kiss is desperate, starving. I open my mouth slightly, inviting her in, and when she returns the gesture, I taste her tongue on mine, wine and desire lacing it. Heavy breaths are shared between us as we clash tongue and teeth, the kiss filling my entire being with hunger and need.

With a swipe of my arm, I lift her up, her legs straddling me as we make our way back to the door. A moan escapes her mouth, forcing a deep growl from my chest. The soft thud of pushing her bare back against the wooden door sends pulses of heat through me, famished.

She hisses, the cold door surprising her, and I let out a breathy laugh. Our lips meet again, violently, needing. Nails rake over my body, resting in my hair, holding it tightly in a desperate grip. A guttural sound leaves my chest, meddling with our impatient breaths, Eleanora smiling into our kiss.

"I need you, Ari. Please," her breathy begs have me wild. With her legs still wrapped around my waist, we sail across the floor. I stand in front of the enormous bed, placing her down gently. Her soft body bounces slightly as she lands on the springy mattress, entrancing me.

Shaking my head in pure disbelief, I rip off my shirt, buttons bouncing off the floor. Boots and trousers heedlessly shed, falling to the stone tiles, leaving me bare. As I stand before her, naked as the day I was born, I take her in.

"How I have dreamt of this, my sweet Eleanora."

Soft whimpers slip past deep mauve lips, cheeks flushed pink and her breath shallow. I set one knee between her legs before leaning in close. The warmth of her skin wraps around me, seeping into my soul.

Desperate hands envelop her head, eyes dark and filled with lust. I kiss her again, beyond famished, starving for her taste. My hand carefully caresses her curves, feeling her skin pucker in goosebumps as I follow the soft dips of her waist, then round hips and finally slide my hand under her, cupping her perfect ass.

As our kiss deepens, her breaths become more impatient, hungrier, starving. Our bodies heat, the feelings we have drenching our souls as my heart seeps deep into hers. Her hand flicks, guttering the candles around us, plunging the room into darkness. The world narrows to her breath against my lips, her heartbeat echoing with mine. And then, nothing exists but us.

# Chapter 27

## Eleanora

I wake as Tharion's warm body moves away from me, cold air filling the void of his absence. My body shivers slightly, craving his touch to return. Laying on my back, my eyes glide across the golden mural on my ceiling for the last time. The intricate details glitter in the early morning sunlight.

My mouth feels dry and my head has a slight thumping, but I don't care. I drift back to last night's magical ending. Our bodies swirled around each other, breaths mixed, hearts beating as one. My soul feels whole, seen, heard. I feel *chosen*, safe.

A tingling warmth spreads from my toes, up my thighs, pooling in my stomach. The wide grin spreading across my face hurts my cheeks, but I don't stop it.

Tharion's sleepy grunts tear me from my lustrous daydreaming as his hand snakes across my waist, pulling me flush against him. His strong body curves perfectly around mine, swathing my body with his, protecting me as we lay in my bed, bare and sore. I dip my head, dragging in his sleepy scent. It feels different, like it has another dimension added to it – deeper, layered.

"Good morning." His raspy morning voice sends jolts of electricity through my bones. I turn in his arms, facing him. Planting a kiss on his lips, a soft whimper glides from his lips to mine. The arms around me tighten, holding me fast as we fall into each other once more.

"We need to go to breakfast," I say, breaking the kiss begrudgingly.

His breathy chuckle sings to me, "I'll have my favourite breakfast in bed today."

In one swift motion, my back lands softly on the sheets, Tharion looking down at me. The mural on the ceiling crowns him in gold, sunlight casting his features in a veil of soft passion. His eyes burn with emerald fire as his bottom lip catches between his teeth.

My core melts, aching, wanting, his touch like a drug I never want to quit. Calloused fingers drag over my skin, mapping out the journey from neck to hip as a growl vibrates from within his chest. He leans down, hovering above my ear, his breaths deep, sultry.

"Let me devour you, my goddess. Let me fuel my body with your soul."

I combust. Hands entwine in auburn locks, a deep moan tearing from my throat. His teeth drag across my sensitive skin, shivers racing through me as I pull his face to mine. Our lips crash, tongues mingling, urgency lacing every breath.

Tharion breaks the kiss, planting delicate pecks down my neck. His body lowers, mouth exploring my curves. Sharp stings shoot through me as his teeth gently graze my nipples, the pooling heat in my core now an inferno of desperation.

I whimper. "Tharion, please." It's too much.
His mischievous laugh brushes over my stomach, goosebumps racing down my thighs.

"Impatient little thing, you. Where do you want me?"

My mind is blank. *Everywhere.* I want him everywhere, anywhere.
The bed rustles as his knees plant beside my shoulder, his towering frame casting me in shadow.

"It seems your need for taste overwhelms you. Let me ease that need, my sweet Ela."

My lips part as a soft gasp slips past. A strong hand reaches for my hair as Tharion feeds himself into my mouth, cheeks stretching as the taste of him crashes over my tastebuds. My mouth waters, feasting on him like I'll never eat again, swallowing down every drop.

Soft moans coat the air as Tharion leans forward, his hand steadying him on the wall above me. The clutch on my hair releases, his rough fingertips tracing the curves of my body, massaging that aching spot in my core with delicate precision.

"Gods, the sight of you around me. You will be the end of me, Eleanora," his words pierce through gritted teeth, pushed out between growling moans. I tense up, legs shaking with his accelerating rhythm, delicious release brushing against me as I feel the edge coming closer.

With a *pop,* he pulls out. The mattress moves as Tharion's hungry body lowers from my shoulders, his knees now planted between my legs, soft kisses tracing the side of my neck.

He stops, taking in the sight with flushed cheeks and glossy eyes. As his mouth finds mine, his body thrusts, filling me to the brim. I cry out, his name dancing off my lips in prayer. The edge is closer, clawing for me to throw myself over it. His pace is slow, deep, panting, all-consuming. Throwing my head back, Tharion pushes me over the intoxicating edge, following me into the depths of our release.

Walking into the mess hall for the last time, soldiers inhale their morning meals with laughter and clinks of glasses filled with fresh milk.

Standing before the food station, my eyes glide over the feast waiting for us to dig into it, filling my plate with bread, cheese and jams and a bowl of rice porridge topped with fresh berries. I place it down on the table and as I turn to grab a cup of Dawnflower tea, a steaming mug is placed directly in front of me. Looking up, Rowan's warm eyes smile at mine, his large body filling the chair beside me.

"How was your night?"

I look at him, cheeks burning, unable to keep eye contact. A soft giggle slips from him, no need for explanation. Corvyn slumps down across from us, dark circles heavy under his eyes.

"I slept better than him, by the looks of it," I gesture towards the raven with my spoon. His hair is quite literally a bird's nest, the black strands of hair standing in every direction.

He drops his head into his hands, letting out a shaky breath.

"I am never having sparkling wine ever again."

Laughter bursts from my chest, defeat written all over Corvyn's face.

"Lucky for you, it will be a while before we have that privilege again. Eat up, we have a long ride before us today."

With shaky hands, Cor lifts his spoon of steaming rice porridge to his mouth, giving it a moment to cool before it vanishes into the pits of his stomach. Rowan slides a mug of Dawnflower tea across the table, our raven friend gratefully accepting the mug with both hands.

Lucien joins our table, then Falck, and lastly Tharion. I look over at him and my cheeks reignite, warmth spreading like a wave through my entire body. I feel my hair dampen from sweat, feet nervously bouncing off the ground. He sits down, flashing a warm grin my way, eyes still blaring with last night's emotion.

Rowan looks between us, a sly smirk plastered on his face. I stab him in the ribs with my elbow, erasing the smile instantly as a burst of air leaves his lungs.

We eat, taking in the last impressions of the castle, saying our goodbyes to Falck and Lucien and the rest of the soldiers before grabbing our bags and heading to the stables, where Vaelrick awaits us.

"The time has come, friends. It is time for us to part ways," his voice is soft but reluctant, "I hope our paths cross again, preferably under different circumstances." The smile on his face doesn't quite reach his eyes, understandably.

Loading up the horses, we strap on our saddles and mount our brave steeds. With a sharp wave, Vaelrick whistles for the gates to open. The heavy wooden doors creak, slowly unveiling the path beyond. Casting a last glance at the King, we head off into the misty autumn air.

Already on alert, my eyes sweep the landscape before us. Rowan, in his fox form, glides over the forest floor, in one with the nature around us. Corvyn soars above the treetops as Tharion and I ride horseback.

The crisp autumn air is damp and cold, stinging the tops of my cheeks as our horses run through the forest. Our goal is to reach the mountain canyons by nightfall, getting us halfway to Meadowrest.

As we gallop past the red-leaved trees, the sun above us casts everything in a deep orange glow, reminding me of the solar foyer outside our rooms back at the castle. I will miss that, the luxury of a bed, a bath, the safety it provided.

The smell of damp soil and pine trees cloak my senses, giving me a brief taste of home. The forests of Sylvarn are mostly made up of pine trees, the familiar scent hitting me in the chest. I look over at Tharion, watching him breathe in deeply, relishing in the familiarity of home, even so far away. Ironically, we're travelling to the opposite end of the realm, as far from home as we can possibly get.

The scenery changes before our eyes, deep green pines fading into an open, rocky landscape of steep mountains crowning the pebbled path we're riding on. Tall peaks are covered in snow, towering hundreds of feet above us. The air feels lighter, clearer, out here, and the cold is much sharper. The tip of my nose dyes a deep red, fingers feeling numb as cold penetrates the thin skin.

Riding further into the canyon, less of the sun shines down on us, the temperature dropping severely. I pull my heavy cloak around me, trying to block some of the cold from seeping in, but I fail.

Rowan chirps, the temperature a comfortable cold for his thick fur, he runs further before us, wind cutting through the orange and white fur. I keep my eyes trained on him, watching him jump and speed through the rocky terrain surrounding us.

Without warning, a boulder beside him explodes, debris scattering through the air. Tharion and I stop our horses as Rowan is picked up and flung through the canyon, hitting the ground with a heavy thud. An ear-piercing screech cleaves the air, forcing us to the ground as more stone crashes down around us. I rush over to Rowan, a deep slash carved across his chest, red blood pouring onto the stone floor.

"Corvyn!" I cry into the air, but he's already heading towards us, the black raven diving through the skies at alarming speed. He lands beside us, sprinting our way. Another painful screech slices through our eardrums, making them ring in a high-pitched note.

"What happened?"

Corvyn opens his satchel, pulling out bandages and ointment with one hand as the other presses down on the oozing wound. Rowan pants in short breaths, eyes clamped shut.

"I don't know! One second he… I don't –" my words stick to my tongue, brain unable to focus. Blood keeps gushing from the slash on Rowan's body, I can sense him weakening in our bond.

"Eleanora!" Corvyn's voice forces my attention away from the bleeding mess of my familiar, "you need to tell me what happened so I can help him."

"I don't… He was, we were watching him, and then he flew through the air and the stone exploded, I don't –" tears streak my face, dripping down on my cloak. Frantically, I look around me to find Tharion on guard, his rune blade firmly held next to his head, watching our surroundings.

In the distance, parts of the mountainside break off, tumbling down on the path in front of us, partially blocking it. Behind us, another avalanche rumbles through the air, blocking us from both sides. The canyon is dark, sun dipped past the peaks, setting slowly. My ears rip apart as another screech carries in the wind around us.

In a second of clear mindedness, I remember a protection spell I learned in school years ago.

"Tharion! Get behind me!"

I grab my knife, slicing open my palm. As the thick crimson drops hit the earth, I call on my magic, holding my palms to the ground.

> *"Light around me, strong and near,*
> *No dark spirit may come here."*

I chant the spell repeatedly as white light bursts from the rocky pathway, enclosing us in a protective dome of magic. The dome stretches around us, keeping us all safe – for now.

I strengthen the wards with a few extra chants, one eye fixated on Rowan and Corvyn as I watch the raven prod, cover and wrap my familiar. Finishing my chants, I run over to them. Rowan is unconscious, his breathing still shallow.

"Will he be okay?"
I feel the lump in my throat getting heavier by the second, the thought of losing him suffocating.

Corvyn fastens the last bandage with a tight knot, a deep frown etched between his brows as droplets of sweat trickle down the side of his face.

"We almost lost him." The words come out just louder than a whisper, his eyes deep with fear as they meet mine.

"What did this? How did we not see it?"

He looks around us, scanning the area before stopping – his eyes widening as his brows shoot up into his hairline. With a shaky hand, he points to the place Rowan was injured. I follow his hand, and as they land, blood freezes in my veins. A pair of bright red eyes stare back at me from just outside my protective ward.

"Wh… Cor, what –"

"How strong are your wards, Ela?" his eyes still fixed on the red orbs of malice.

"Strong enough… I hope."

"Let's pray they are."

The red horrors vanish in the blink of an eye, leaving us in complete darkness, and bone-chilling terror.

· · — · ✳ · — · ·

I watch as grey smoke rises from our campfire, drifting out through the white ward, into the cold night air. The bowl of oatmeal in my lap has gone cold, my appetite shredded by that *thing*.

"We've met that thing before."
Cor stops eating. "What do you mean?"

"In Sylvarn. Rowan and I met it back home before we came to Stormbrook." Shivers course through me at the memory.

He puts down his bowl, turning towards me.
"It's called a Nochtra. According to stories, they only show their eyes as

a form of terrorizing their victims. It is said that the last thing people hear before being attacked is a scream so terrible it makes your ears bleed."

The memory of that awful screech has me clamping my eyes shut with force, stars and shadows swirling behind my eyelids.

I look over to Rowan, still in his fox form, curled up under a woollen blanket. His shifter magic will heal him faster as a fox, this way his wound will be manageable by morning. I lean my head on Corvyn's shoulder, exhaustion setting in my bones.

"He'll be okay," his warm hand lands gently on my knee.

"I know." I give his hand a squeeze as we watch the orange and white flame dance before us.

With a rustle, Tharion emerges from our tent, ready to take the first watch of the night. I get up, stretching my arms above my head with a yawn.

"Are you coming to bed?"
Cor's gaze is locked on Rowan. He shakes his head.

"I think I want to stay here for a while, just in case something happens."

Tharion turns to me. "I will watch him, Ela. Get some sleep."

Casting a glance at Rowan, I give my friends a nod before walking into our tent and climbing under the blankets. There's no use in all three of us being exhausted, so I might as well try to sleep.

Crawling under my blanket, I stare at the tent's dark green walls. I try to imagine them to be the tall treetops of Sylvarn, trying so hard to distract myself, but my thoughts only fall back to Rowan. I toss and turn, sleep avoiding me as I desperately try to find some peace, to no avail.

The glowing red discs of terror haunt my mind every time I close my eyes, racing with all types of crazy scenarios. Is the ward strong enough? Will Rowan recover? Will we meet that thing again? How many of them are there out there? My thoughts are deafening, voices shouting over one another, the first louder than the next as time races by. Pale moonlight is replaced by the white gloom of autumn overcast, heart thundering in my chest, stomach twists and turns.

Ripping off the blanket, I grab a fresh set of clothes from my satchel, pulling on a woollen undershirt with a cotton tunic and matching trousers. My boots are lined in wool, so my feet are nice and warm during the day, and my cloak protects me from the biting winds that surf through the rocky canyon.

As my shoelace does one last loop, rustling from outside catches my attention. I quickly tighten the loop and stand up, dull white light blinding me as I walk out into the small camp, fire still going while Tharion stirs a pot of oatmeal.

"How is he?"

Rowan is still sleeping soundly, only now his breath is even, steady, deep. Relief washes over me at the sight, his deep gash now but a dark pink scar, his flesh knitted itself together during the night. Corvyn places a hand on my shoulder, a tired smile on his face.

"Better."

As if he knows, Rowan chitters something unintelligible before slowly opening his eyes, his skin heavy underneath, the usually bright auburn colour dull and lifeless. I kneel beside him, trousers soaking up the damp ground. Tears shoot to my eyes, gratitude flooding my system.

"Ro. Ro, it's me…" I gently cradle his furry cheek, "Ela. It's me, Ro. I'm right here."

My heart is jackhammering in my chest, so hard I can hear it in my ears. His cold nose gently nudges my hand, waves of relief radiating up my arm. I lean closer, dragging in his familiar scent. The tears building in my eyes fall over the edge, rolling down my cheeks. I bury my face in the orange and white strands, his heartbeat drumming steadily under thick skin.

"He will be okay. I know he will, I can feel it." Corvyn sits down beside me, his arms pulling me into a warm embrace. As silent sobs slide through my lips, I feel his hands rubbing soothing circles on my back.

"I need him to be okay. I feel his pain, Cor… I felt him fade," my eyes snap shut, lungs gasping for air, the horrible memory stabbing me in the chest.

A soft kiss to my head calms me, the gentle rubs persist.

"He will be okay. Our bond says so."

# Chapter 28

*Rowan*

Pain rips through my body in waves, consciousness flickering like a flame in the wind. It's nauseating, deafening, excruciating. I feel the broken layers of flesh weaving themselves together, blood coagulating to shut the wound from the inside. That fucking Nochtra. I should have sensed it – the air smelled rancid as we rode into the canyon. Fuck. I should have picked up on it.

Another wave of pain tumbles through me, pulse picking up its pace as I clamp my eyes shut. Warm hands cradle my face, hands I know better than my own. Eleanora. I can feel the embers of our bond radiate between my bones, pushing the pain aside. It feels stronger, more desperate, than ever before.

Her aura encapsulates me, lifting me out of the dark cave surrounding me, out into bright sunshine and warm winds. Stretching my face to the sun, I bathe in its hot rays, fuelling my broken body. My eyes open, blinded by the sunlight.

To my surprise, the aura I felt is not the deep red I know to be Eleanora's. Instead, thick waves of violet snake around me, holding me high in the sky. I feel her hands around my face, her crying eyes buried in my fur, but it is not her aura, not our bond, carrying me out of the darkness.

As my weightless body floats through the air, the ripping pain left down in that dark cave, my body fills with light. The violet mixes beautifully with my auburn, swirling around each other, fading into one.

*My fox. Please, I need you to come back.*

The voice sings to my soul as it dances in my mind, filling me completely.

*Come back, Ro. I need you. Just please, come back to me.*

I burst, ripping at the seams as violet smoke smothers me, boiling me from the inside out. The bittersweet pain sends me soaring, gasping for air.

Pushing back, I try to find where the smoke resides, but a part of me already knows. A part of me always knew.

*Korax.*

The bond explodes, fireworks of burnt orange and rich violet envelop me, tight and warm. I feel safe, whole.

*Korax. Korax, are you there?*

The echoes of my voice carry through the dimension of my consciousness, drifting off far beyond my vision. Calling on my magic, I pour the powers into my wound, closing it completely, my fox clawing to wake me up.

The corners of my consciousness darken, closing in on me with rapid speed as I tumble down towards a grass meadow stretching below me. Before I hit the ground, my vision blacks out – plunging me into complete darkness.

My eyes shoot open, the grey skies of the canyon casting a bright light, forcing me to squint painfully. I bury my face in my fur, curling into a ball as Eleanora's puffy eyes meet mine.

"Ro!" The corners of her mouth shoot to the sky, those familiar burgundy eyes glittering in tears.

Chirping, I lift my head to meet her gaze, hand scratching the underside of my furry chin.

"I'm so happy you're okay. I was so scared. I thought…" the words fade from her lips, but I know what weight they carry.

Her hands are warm as I nuzzle them, comforting her as she comforts me. My familiar. My family.

Strong hands drag across my fur, shivers racing under my skin. Lifting my gaze, I watch as Corvyn's tired smile stretches all the way to his eyes. Pulling my energy to my limbs, I lift my body off the ground.

"Careful, Ro," Eleanora's voice is laced in fear, exiting her mouth with deep trembles.

My exhausted legs lift my body off the ground, wobbling slightly under me. As I take my first step, my front elbow buckles, sending me crashing nose-first to the gravel pathway.

My familiar's arms wrap beneath me, holding me close to her, but I push out of her grasp – determined to shift back to my human form. I try to walk, but every time I take a step, I fall.

Whimpering, my body refuses to stand once more. Corvyn kneels beside me, the frown back between his brows, as his hands glide over my ears, giving them a comforting scratch.

"I know you want to. I know you think you need to be strong. But right now, you need to heal."

His eyes are soft, but his words are stern, serious. I give him a gentle nod, accepting defeat. He's right. I do need to rest, to heal.


I glide in and out of sleep as we ride through the morning and early afternoon. Cradled in front of Eleanora, her arms keeping me safe as I lay, toasty, under a woollen blanket. The rocky terrain of the canyon has long since been replaced by beautiful red forests once again, leaves riding the winds as they woosh beside us, falling feather-light to the ground.

The sound of hooves crunching on dry leaves have always been a sound I enjoyed, so I take them in with comfort. Eleanora steadily hands me a flask of water, demanding I drink every now and then. I feel stronger, healthier, thanks to her and her care. Her comforting emotions are shot as a constant stream down our bond, filling me with warmth as we ride towards the meadow villages on the far west of Kyrris.

Sometime during the early day, we stop beside a small lake to cook up a meal. Corvyn has hunted down a large rabbit for us to roast over the fire, and Tharion picked up some berries on our way here. The lake is calm, mirroring the tall treetops surrounding us.

As the campfire crackles, air filling with smoke and the smell of roasted meat, I drift in and out of sleep, storing as much energy as I can before we resume our journey. My sleeping mind is filled with warmth, with love and passion. Images of Eleanora laughing, of Corvyn looking at me as we sit close, Tharion telling stupid jokes and making us all feel like a family. I like it there.

Corvyn sits down beside me, two plates in his hands. He sets one down in front of me, rabbit, berries and steamy oatmeal, making my stomach growl impatiently.

A light chuckle slips from his mouth.

"I take that as a sign that you're feeling better."
I meet his gaze, those beautiful violet moons casting me in their enchanting shadows. A calloused hand drags across my fur, shivers racing under my skin. Low rumbles vibrate in my chest, his touch calming me. I burrow my face in his side, the cold fabric scratching against my whiskers.

"Think you will be able to change back soon?"
I nod. My body feels stronger, healthy, ready.

I sit up to eat, the meat falling apart on my tongue, juices running down my throat. Proteins rush to my muscles, building blocks stacking tall as they grow stronger. Licking my plate, I stand on all fours.

A quick shake bursts through me, running from my face all the way down to my tail, fur floating in the air. Taking a step, my leg wobbles slightly before finally holding my weight. The next step is easier, and before I know it, I zoom around Corvyn, his laugh ringing in my ears as I rush around our campsite. Eleanora watches with water-lined eyes, happiness radiating from her.

As we pack up our camp, Eleanora jumps up on her horse, waiting for me to join. I shake my head, wanting to walk beside them, checking my strength.

We set off, leaving the lake behind as beautiful blues, oranges and lilacs stretch in front of us, meadows as far as our eyes can see. The citrusy-sweet scent of flowers forces itself into my senses, warmth spreading alongside it.

We walk through tall grass until a village unfolds, small wooden houses with grassy roofs and enormous flower beds scattering the village. The air is light, easy, like there is nothing but peace out here. Music hums in the wind, the gentle strokes of instruments harmonizing in beautiful song.

Bards and healers reside here, living in peace for millennia. For having lived as long as I have, I have never been here. I take in the sights and sensory input as we walk through the grass, onto a stone pathway.

We watch as people bustle from place to place, healers cooking up potions and grinding herbs, bards tuning their instruments and practicing their sword abilities. The village is the definition of serenity.

Walking between the small houses, Corvyn lands behind us. His body is tense, on guard. His arms hug his body, and I can feel his heart picking up speed. Is he scared? Why would he be?

Grabbing my satchel in my teeth, I scurry into a bush nearby, gathering my magic to change back. My bones crack and reshape as my fur is replaced by deep brown skin, face transforming back to my human self. I feel my vision dulling, the colours brightening and senses fade as my emotions heighten.

Pain radiates through me, though much lesser than before. As I stand there on two legs, naked and weak, I stretch my limbs. Rummaging in my clothes, I drag on underwear and a pair of cotton trousers in a light sand colour, and push my woollen-socked feet into my boots. Looking down on my torso, I follow the long pink scar that stretches from my lower abdomen to just above my heart.

*That fucking thing tried to take my heart.*

I shudder at the thought. Grabbing a shirt, I drag it quickly over my head before walking out. I fall in line beside Cor, pecking him lightly on his shoulder. Turning, his brows shoot up his anxious face before throwing his arms around me.

"Ro!" his face buries in the nook of my shoulder, "you're back. I'm so glad to see your smile again."

The vibrating sensation returns to my chest, his closeness centering me. I wrap my arms around his strong body, fisting the back of his head, dragging in his scent. *Mine.* My eyes shoot open, studying his face. Both hands cup his jaw, staring into his breathtaking eyes.

"I'm here. I will always be here, *korax*."

Corvyn's pupils dilate, taking me in wholly. Does he know I felt his aura, our bond, while I was out? Does he know what we are?

A knot forms in my stomach, the thought that he might not know is upsetting and uncomfortable. Shaking my head, I focus on why I shifted back.

"Why are you afraid?"

His eyes avert mine, shoulders back under his earlobes, shaky breaths slip through his mouth.

"This is where Serenya lived," he swallows hard, "where Kaelen met her all those years ago."

Of course. She was a healer, an elf. I pull him back into my arms, holding him close as quiet sobs dampen my shirt. How did I not realize that before we left?

"Would you like to find her parents?"

Sniffles sound from my dear raven's nose, his sorrow deep, palpable – but he nods. I dip my chin, determined to help him get some peace.

"Let's find a place to stay, then we will go out and search for them. Would you like to share a room with me during our stay?"

I watch as his eyes glow, the sorrow fading with his tears, apprehension taking its place. The corners of my mouth tug into a smile, a breathy chuckle vibrating from my chest. I give him a gentle kiss to the top of his head before we turn and meet up with the others, their horses slowly plodding up the cobblestone street.

We walk around, taking in the beautiful architecture of the houses, the warm scent of flowers and the light air filling our bodies to the brim.

Coming into the village centrum, music bounces off the walls, people gathering around a male singing loudly. His voice carries far across the dense crowd while people dance, laugh and sing along.

The male is tall, taller than most, with long white hair - a daedal braid resting over his shoulder. His eyes are ice blue, almost unnaturally so, the tips of his ears meeting in delicate points.

The bard is wearing a nice tunic in the colours of meadows, different shades of green and orange, with dark trousers underneath. His song tales of ancient battles and fallen warriors, of our Gods and their honour, telling the story from our past with grace and vulnerability. His voice is beautiful, pure, his notes enchanting the crowd.

*"...Yet the crone, she laughed, with a voice of stone:*
*"Child of ash, you are not alone.*
*The dark you wield is a borrowed flame,*
*And I have walked long before your name."*

*They battled till dawn, till the sky grew black,*
*With the words they said, the earth would crack.*
*And though no mortal recalls who won,*
*The stars still whisper what was done.*

*That wisdom is sharper than demon's fire,*
*That age can bind what youth desires.*
*So heed, O folk, when the night grows long—*
*A crone's frail voice may be stronger than song..."*

People sing along, singing about the Crone of White Flame, about the very demon we were here to kill.

*How fucking ironic.*

The crowd goes wild as the bard finishes his song and jumps down, flowers raining over him. As he gathers the fallen blossoms, I walk up to him.

"Do you know the truths of the tales you sing?"

His eyes lift from the ground, scanning me with a smirk.

"Why? Are you willing to teach me?"

Scoffing, I cross my arms over my body, creating a barrier between us.

"The demon you sing about. My companions and I have travelled far just to kill him. Again."

He laughs, throwing his head back as his shoulders shake vigorously.

"Sure, and I have a dragon chained in my garden," he pats my shoulder in passing, not bothering to look back. I watch as his long white hair sways behind him, blending into the crowd while they continue singing about the crone, oblivious to the weight the stories carry.

· · — · ✷ · — · ·

Walking up the street, an Inn stands behind large green hedges with yellow flowers neatly scattered across. A big wooden sign hangs on metal chains, "The Lark & Lyre" carved in beautiful lettering.

Walking inside, calming lavender hits me like a wall. I scrunch my nose, my fox's senses still working their way out of my human form.

"Hello, dear travellers! Welcome to the Lark and Lyre, a safe resting place for bards, travellers and knowledge-seekers. What can I help you with, my kind sir?"

The innkeeper is a large male with dark green eyes and bright orange hair. His smile is crooked, tinted with the yellow hue of too much Dawnflower Tea, but still radiates warmth and kindness.

"Good evening, my lord. My three friends and I seek a place to sleep for the next few days as we've travelled from the capital. Would you have any rooms vacant?"

The male smiles widely, brightening up the cozy hall.

"Well, of course! How many rooms do you need?"

Heat washes over my face, cheeks darkening as I think about our sleeping arrangements.

*Corvyn is sleeping with me. Together. Us. In the same bed.*

The steady pulse in my neck picks up the pace, now a raging river of waves. The innkeeper tilts his head, still waiting for an answer. I snap back to reality, clearing my throat with a hard drag.

"Uh… Two, we will need two rooms."

With a sharp nod, the kind man hands me two sets of keys.

"We serve breakfast at the tavern across the street. They have some mouth-watering croquettes made of roasted chicken and meadow flowers. Just talking about them makes me hungry."

His laugh is deep, genuine. It thunders through the small room, vibrating into my very core. I thank the male and walk outside, waving the keys in my hand.

"I have our rooms. Now," I look at Corvyn, "let's go search for Serenya's parents."

# *Chapter 29*
## *Corvyn*

Meadowrest is beautiful. Kaelen would tell stories of the village whenever he came home from visiting, how peaceful it was, the kindness of the people, how he could see himself living there with Serenya when they grew old. I couldn't agree more. Whenever we pass someone, they greet us with grins and waves, wishing us welcome. Someone even made a flower crown and placed it on my head.

The bright flowers contrast violently with my pitch-black hair, but I refuse to take it off. Rowan laughed when the female placed it, eyes glistening with sweet affection.

"Kaelen?" a female voice breaks through the laughter. I turn, searching the busy street.

"Kaelen, is it really you?" the voice is trembling, hopeful. As I meet the sparkling blue eyes of the person behind this palpable hope, disappointment slaps her across the face.

"I apologize. I thought you were someone else," her voice fades, body turning away, but I put my hand gently on her arm.

"Kaelen was my brother. I am Corvyn, I knew Serenya well." The female's eyes clamp shut, tears threatening to fall as she throws her arms around me in a tight hug, pushing air from my lungs.

"You look so much like him, our dear Kaelen," she looks up at me, deep cerulean eyes like pools of flowing water under the tears. We stand there, holding each other tight for a long time until her arms fall from me. Stepping back, her eyes scan my face, taking in my raven features with a smile.

"It's nice to meet you, Corvyn. My name is Mirenya, I am Serenya's mother."

Mirenya takes us to her cottage, the front garden filled with colourful flowers splayed delicately over green beds, bees and ladybirds happily indulging on the sweet treats.

She steeps a pot of Sunflower Tea, the earthy scent filling the small home with warmth. Filling our cups with steaming, yellow liquid, she then pushes them gently over the table. On a wooden platter lies an array of fresh pastries, each formed to look like the many different flowers one would find on their beds outside.
Taking a sip of the tea, I work up the courage to talk.

"Miss Mirenya, I was wondering –"

Mirenya waves her kitchen towel, a light laughter flowing past her lips.

"No need for formalities here, Corvyn. We are family. Call me Mir." I smile into my tea, the knot in my throat still making it challenging to speak. I swallow hard, setting the cup down on the table.

"I was wondering if it might be possible to maybe… to maybe –" I take a deep breath, calming my racing heart.

"Could we go see Serenya's resting place? I would like to say goodbye to her, too."

Mir goes quiet, eyes glossing over again as she sucks in a deep breath. Resting her small hand over mine, she smiles at me.

"Of course we can, my sweet boy. I will fetch Galathil, and we can all go, okay?" her voice radiates care, the words embracing me like a warm hug. I nod, unable to speak, my heart lodging itself in my throat. I look over at Rowan to find him already watching me, his face soft and safe.

We finish our cakes and our tea, heading out to Nimlothiel, where Kaelen buried Serenya. Her father, Galathil, greets us with a firm handshake and a warm hug, the same kindness radiating off him as with Mir. The love and adoration they had for both Serenya and Kaelen is palpable, a force I can touch with my bare hands.

We walk up a hillside, stepping over stones and weaving through tall grass before emerging to a breathtaking lake. I stop in my tracks, taking in the sight. Surrounding the lake are large trees with vines hanging low, teasing the water's surface as they sway in the wind.

The vines are decorated in large white flowers, the pure colour almost blinding. Along the water's edge are lily pads with glittering white lotus flowers, the lake almost looking like it's covered in snow. On its surface, the water is bright blue, glittering under the autumn sun. Leaves sail over small ripples, butterflies in whites and blues dancing through the winds.

I exhale the breath stuck in my chest, lungs yearning for air. Rowan's warm hand folds over mine, interlacing our fingers. I look over to Mir and Galathil, watching them stare out across the water, Galathil's arm gently folding around Mir's shoulders in a loving embrace.

Soft whimpers escape Mir as she rests her head on Galathil's broad shoulder, tears streaking her face. Dragging my feet, I walk up to her, taking her hand in mine.

"This place is beautiful. A burial worthy of a queen. In many ways, that is what she was to the people around her." Mir squeezes my hand, straightening her posture.

"Go to the lake, talk to her. She has been waiting just as long, son."
Looking at the lake, I walk up to its edge with careful steps, dropping to my knees. As they hit the earth, my trousers soak in the damp soil. I lower my head and close my eyes, stifling the tears threatening to fall.

"Serenya, my sister. I miss you. I think about the things we did together, the talks we had and the memories we shared, how I miss seeing your bright face. I think about the time we should have had, the memories we didn't get to make." My voice falters, cracking with choked tears.

"I hope you are with Kaelen, living your lives in the Afterlife as you wished you could in the living. I hope you have built a home, that you can love each other every day, not ever being apart. I hope you have found the peace you helped me find while you were still here. We will meet again one day, but until then - I hope you are happy. Goodbye, my sister."

A faint ripple races across the water's surface, the familiar scent of Silverleaf hugging me, a gentle greeting from the Afterlife. I smile, sending a kiss out into the air, the closure I wanted finally letting me close a chapter I have skipped for too long.

Turning, I'm met by Rowan's safe arms. He holds me tight as I rest my head on his shoulder, weight slowly lifting off mine. I take in a deep breath, the heaviness in my chest gradually fading. Mirenya and Galathil both wrap their arms around us, a sandwich of love and loss. We share the emotions, share the grief, finally able to move on and eventually - let ourselves be happy. Mir buries her face in my raven locks.

"I am proud to be your family, Corvyn. And so was she." The warm whispers of her voice travel across my skin, rooting themselves in the pits of my thundering heart.

As we walk back to the village, saying goodbye to Mir and Galathil, Rowan and I slowly make our way to the Inn. His hand brushes mine, sending rays of lightning up my arm and into my soul.

The Inn smells of freshly brewed tea and lavender, calming my hyperactive emotions. I take it in, filling my lungs with the delightful scent before we walk up the stairs. Midway, I stop, reaching for Ro's hand. His golden pools of molten metal gleam in the late-night candlelight, eyes resting on mine.

"Thank you for going with me today. I don't think I could have done it without you."

His hand caresses my cheek, warmth washing over me, cheeks burning in with a deep magenta.

"I would go to the ends of the realm with you if you asked, *korax*. There is no place I would not want to be by your side."

His eyes burn with deep golden flames, trapping me.

*Korax.*

The voice echoes in my head, catching me off-guard. I look at Rowan, his mouth closed in a warm smile.

*Korax. It is me, your fox. Your soul is bound to mine as mine is to yours. You were made for me, and I have waited centuries to find you.*

I close my eyes as the voice of my fox sings to me, chest combusting with the heat of a distant star. His finger hooks under my chin, lifting my face to meet his fiery gaze.

"I will never let you walk this earth without me, and I will destroy the one that makes me walk it without you. My mate."

His mouth crashes down on mine, lips soft as they caress mine, devouring my mouth as if it is the air he breathes. Our tongues wrap around each other, the taste of him coating my soul as I pull him closer.

My back hits the wall behind me, picture frames crashing to the ground around us. A breathy laugh mixes with our needy moans, Rowan deepening the kiss, body crumbling under his touch. My hand shoots up his back, grasping his hair in a firm grip, forcing a guttural growl from him.

*My fox. My mate.*

As we make our way up the stairs, stumbling into our shared room, I kick the door shut.

"Tell me you feel this too," Rowan's breaths are warm on my neck as tender kisses devour it. I nod, unable to speak. His face lifts from my throat, and I instantly feel cold withdrawals.

"Tell me, *korax*. I need to hear you say it," his eyes are pleading, desperate.

"I feel it. I have always felt it. My mate."
I have barely said the word before his mouth is back on mine, sealing our fate. A surge in power rushes through us, our bond finally locking into place. I feel his golden aura wrapping around mine, mixing to one while his arms hold me close.

*I will never let you go. Not ever, in this realm or the next, my korax.*

His voice carries through the deepest parts of my brain, shattering all the walls I built when Kaelen died. Now all I see, all I crave, is the male in front of me.

We move in a messy dance, hands exploring as our bodies collide on the mattress under me. His earthy, foxy scent fills me with need, wanting to submerge myself in everything that is Rowan. His hands race over me, waves of lightning exploding under my skin with every brush. I relish under his warm touch, like a moth to a flame I crave it.

The pale moonlight shines in through the window, casting his rich brown skin in a metallic sheen, making him glow. I drink in the sight of him, *he is perfect.* With gentle fingers, I drag them over his long scar, the emotions coming back just as fast. Slamming my eyes shut, I try to block them out.

*Look at me. I am here. I will always be here.*

His hands cradle my face, our eyes locking for a moment. Then, lowering his head, he places a tender kiss on my lips.

*Mark me. Please, be my mate in truth, my fox.*

Desperate pleas explode from me, needing him to be mine in every way possible. His eyes darken, now roaring in the silver moonlight. Rowan leans down, sitting back on his heels. Slowly, he opens my shirt, one slow button at a time. With every button open, a tender kiss is placed on the skin underneath. I shiver with anticipation, an overload of emotions and sensations.

As he kisses his way down my torso, I gulp down mouthfuls of air while my hands hold his short locks between my fingers.

Lifting his head, Rowan stares at me. He takes me in, all of me, as I lie bare chested beneath him.

"You are breathtaking." The raspy voice sends me spiralling, craving him. Rowan's face lowers, hovering gently over the crook of my neck, hot breath sending goosebumps down my spine.

*Ready?*

I let out a desperate moan, Rowan answering with a laugh before delicious pain shoots from my shoulder. His fangs sink deep into my skin, our magic mixing in our bond as we mate in truth. I cry out, Rowan filling me with his fox as I push my raven to him.

With a warm tongue, he laps the two puncture wounds, sealing it.

*My mate.*

I watch him as his tongue licks my blood from his lips, panting, studying me. His face contorts into a wide grin, laughter erupting from us both as we let ourselves feel our bond.

Grabbing his head, I pull him down in a desperate kiss.
As the stars dance for us above the Inn, my heart dances in my chest, and in this moment, it is only us.

# Chapter 30

## Tharion

Yawning, I munch down on my delicious stack of fluffy pancakes. The spongy discs of pure happiness fill my stomach to a perfect fullness, sweet rose syrup delightfully coating the inside.

My teeth are stained a light blue from the fresh forest blueberries, but I wash it away with a good swig of my Dawnflower Tea. The warm liquid spreads through my body, waking it up. Glancing over at Eleanora, her fork pushes the eggs around on her plate, eyelids falling heavy above the plum-coloured moons.

Turning in one swift move, she lifts her fork up, face scrunched into a frown.

"They kept it going *all night!* How were we supposed to sleep?!" Letting out a frustrated breath, she shoves a piece of bread in her mouth. I chuckle, shaking my head.

"Do you think they got much sleep the first night we finally took the same step?" I wink at her. The memory sends pulses of heat through me, heart fluttering at the images racing through my mind. Eleanora's cheeks turn a delicious shade of red, turning her face away as I gloat.

Heavy footsteps echo through the small tavern as Rowan's large frame comes into view. His skin is radiant, the rich dark brown all but glowing in the sunlight. His hair is damp, strawberry blonde locks perfectly placed as he walks towards us, the grin on his face nauseatingly wide. I scoff.

"Good morning, my dearest friends." Putting his arms on each of our shoulders, he pulls us into a group hug.

"What a lovely day it is, is it not?" the light rumble of a laugh erupts from him, dancing through the air as he plops down across from us.

"I'm guessing you slept well last night?" Eleanora's annoyed tone makes me laugh too. His glowing golden eyes drag upwards, the smile beneath infecting his whole face.

A stack of pancakes land in front of him, Rowan inhaling the sweet scent of vanilla and cardamom, exhaling in an exaggerated *aaah*. Rolling her eyes, Eleanora downs her tea in big gulps.

Rowan's gaze widens, the smile returning. Corvyn stands in the doorway to the cozy tavern, smiling fondly at the fox. He jumps up and rushes over to him, holding the raven in a tender embrace as their lips lock.

Looking over at Eleanora, I raise one brow, jerking my chin in a quick move: *want to head upstairs?* Eleanora giggles, her hand covering her face as she nods enthusiastically. We inhale the rest of our food before darting past our newly mated friends, not an ounce of attention given to us, and make our way across the street, back to bed where the early morning sun shines on our bare bodies for the next few hours.

· · — · ✳ · — · ·

The street is just as busy today as we make our way down to the village bakery, the scent of freshly baked goods wafting down the cobblestone pathway. A familiar face meets my gaze as we walk, the blinding white hair of the bard from before coming into view. He waves as we meet, his tunic a bright orange today.

"Good afternoon travellers!" the sing-song voice dances in the air between us. Rowan crosses his arms, standing partially in front of Corvyn. Is he… territorial? I chuckle. *They're mated, all right.*

Reaching out my hand, the bard's rough palm falls in mine, a firm grip returning the shake.

"Good afternoon. We heard you play yesterday. You have a wonderful voice."

He chuckles. "Why thank you, kind sir. The name is Elandir, it's a pleasure to meet you." The instrument hanging on his back is beautifully carved, delicate flowers of all varieties scattered over the light wooden surface.

"My name is Tharion. This is Eleanora, that is Rowan and his mate, Corvyn," looking back to find Corvyn's genuine smile painted on his face as I introduce him as Rowan's mate makes me feel all fuzzy inside.

"We arrived from Catariel just yesterday, we're staying a few nights in hope to find someone willing to help us on our mission." Elandir looks at our faces, eyes narrowing before his gaze lands on Rowan.

"You really weren't kidding, huh."
I turn, Rowan's eyes firmly trained on the bard, a stern look on his face.

"You're here to kill the demon in my songs, according to your fox."
My brows vanish in my auburn hairline, how does he know Rowan is a fox? Eleanora steps forward.

"We are. We need to find a healer."
The corners of Elandir's thin lips curve into a smirk, his body relaxed.

"Join me for some sweet treats and then I'll take you to one. I know everyone in this village."

Eleanora looks at me, wary. I avert my gaze to Rowan, a quick nod signalling we should take his offer. Together, we walk to the bakery, people buzzing in and out with baskets filled with pastries in all shapes and sizes, flaky crusts and dusted sugar, the sight making my mouth swim.

Finding a table inside, five mugs of mulled wine are placed before us, the spicy mist of herbs and fruits filling the air. I take a sip, the warm liquid easing some lingering tension in my chest immediately.

"So, tell me. Who is this demon and why do you need to kill him again? I thought the whole deal with dying was that you only did it once."

Eleanora snorts into her cup, unable to hold her mask up. I shoot her a sharp glance, her posture straightening instantly. Tipping my mug, I take another sip, clearing my throat before telling Elandir of our journey so far.

I watch as his eyes widen, brows lift high onto his forehead, mouth hanging open as I go on about the things that have happened to us in the short amount of time since we left Sylvarn. His face reacts as one should to a story like ours, but there is also a spark in his eyes that makes me uncomfortable, a strange sensation building in my core. As he *oohs* and *aahs* at the tale, his eyes glitter in the darkness.

"And that's why we need a healer, to come with us to Veil's Eclipse," I finish. A loud clap of his hands has me jerking back, taken by surprise, as he lifts his cup to his mouth.

"Will you let me be your bard for the journey? It would be my honour to tell the tales of your bravery in every village of the realm."

*It wouldn't hurt having an extra set of hands in case something goes rogue, right?*
I look over at the others, trying to read their faces. Rowan gently shakes his head, not convinced as Eleanora shrugs indifferently. Corvyn has his eyes locked on Elandir, a scowl painted on his face.

Hesitating, I puff my chest. "I don't think a bard is necessary, but I thank you for your kind offer."

"I must insist. Not to brag of my own skills, but I am exemplary with a sword and with my Elven magic, I can call on the spirits of the earth itself for help." His cerulean irises darken as a smug grin makes another appearance.

*Has this male lost his wits? Who insists on joining battle? Does he _want_ to die?*

Sitting back in my chair, I study the male. There doesn't seem to be a way to avoid this, might as well take the offer and have an extra pair of hands.

"Fine. You can come. But you must help us find a healer in the village before we leave."

Rowan's shoulders tense, brows scrunching so hard I can see them trembling.

Elandir laughs, "ah! This will be the adventure of a lifetime, and the start of a great friendship. I know a healer we can ask, meet me at the village square this evening and we will go together."

I dip my chin, keeping my eye on him as he stands up with a smile, and heads out the door.

Rowan turns to me. "Tharion, I do not trust him. He smells… off." I look over at the fox as he follows Elandir's every move until he is safely out of sight.

"It's probably just his kind, us elemental people do have a herby smell." I try to lighten the mood but remain the only one laughing. Eleanora's fingers fiddle with the handle of her tea mug, twisting it around in her hands.

I clear my throat. "Well, we just have to give him a chance. Like you heard, his skills with a sword are supposed to be good. We could use extra power during our battle."

"We do not even know if he will battle with us or against us. Like I said, his smell is off. It doesn't smell like elf nor human. I would know, I have smelled *you* most of your life," his snarky comment has me jerking back in my chair. Why is he attacking me now?

Corvyn places a hand over his mate's arm, Rowan's posture softening at the touch. He leans over and places a tender kiss to his temples, dragging in his scent.

My fingers twitch, wanting to copy the gesture with Eleanora, but I keep myself seated. Side-eyeing her, I watch her reposition herself in her seat.

I stand up, turning towards the door.

"I need some air. Maybe I'll run into someone who will help us. I'll see you for dinner," I say, leaving my friends behind as I step out into the cold autumn air.

·  ·  —  ·✶·  —  ·  ·

Walking through the streets, I watch the people bustling about, going from place to place, talking and laughing. The wind hauls sweet smells of meadow flowers around, dousing everything in calmness.

Trees sway gently as wind wraps around their branches, leaves flowing effortlessly in the air. The deep reds and oranges remind me of the glowing light of the solar foyer back at the castle. Of our rooms and of the memories made there. I feel warm and fuzzy inside, but just for a second.

A wave of anxiety hits the shore of my mind as thoughts of the upcoming battle replace the peacefulness of Catariel's dreams. I shudder. The click-clack of hooves on stone echoes around me, carriages transporting people between establishments and market stalls.

I round a corner beside a stall selling fine silk scarves just as a glimpse of white hair disappears into an alleyway. *Elandir?* Carefully, I walk towards the alley, treading lightly to not make myself caught. Dark brick walls stretch into the distance, the air clammy in my lungs. There's no one here, not a single person wandering the pathway.

*What is he doing here?*

Faint voices follow the narrow walls, the smell of potions and herbs heavy. As I make it closer, the tall frame of our new friend comes into view. His hair blows around him, the colourful tunic dancing in the wind, but his eyes are different. The icy blue is dark, almost black.

A faint blue glow grabs my attention, my eyes lowering to a rune etched on his neck. Studying it, I imprint it on my mind so I can ask Eleanora about it later. *What is it for?*

I lean closer, but my shoes slip on a rock, catching Elandir's attention. His eyes meet mine for a split second before turning around, darting into the dark alleyway. I bolt from my hiding spot, trying to catch him, heading further into darkness.

As I round the corner, something hard strikes my head, white hot pain shooting to the back of my eyes before the world turns on its axis, and then - everything turns black.

# Chapter 31

*Eleanora*

My head hits the pillow, dust puffing into the air, body thumping down on the hard mattress. It's cold without Tharion's warm body next to me. I think back to our encounter at the bakery, how Rowan's body had stiffened, Corvyn looked ready to peck Elandir's eyes out and the sticky, sly smile on the elf - goosebumps race over my scalp at the image showing in my thoughts.

*How come Tharion left us like that? He never just walks out.*

Desperately trying to make sense of the situation, my mind fogs. I mean, the bard *was* strange, his behaviour was a bit out of touch, but I don't think it's a reason for those reactions. Twisting my body to the side, my eyes rest on the indent in Tharion's pillow. The soft waft of his herby scent lingers in the bed we share, the scent calming and safe.

A pang hits me, body aching to be around him.

*You are so attached, it's embarrassing.* I scoff at myself, at how fast my walls have shattered around him, how fast I let him in. But just as those thoughts rush through me, shame lurking beneath the surface, the pleasant warmth of his affection, of the way he makes me feel, how he adores me for the person I am, ebbs the searing sting into a delightful pulse.

I sit up, looking out the window. The sun is almost setting, it's time to meet Elandir at the square like he asked. But where's Tharion?

Walking over to Rowan's room, I knock on the door. Rustling sounds come from inside, the faint giggles and hushing from the males tugging on my lips before the door opens softly. Rowan's short locks are ruffled, cheeks a rosy pink and his eyes like hot pools of liquid gold, fire burning bright behind them.

He straightens. "Eleanora. Are you okay?"
I chuckle. "Not as good as you, by the looks of it," a cheeky wink sends a wash of rose over his glowing face.

"Have you seen Tharion? It's time to go, but he's not here."
The fires go out, his smile fading.

"Have you checked the tavern? He might have gone there for a drink, or maybe even to find a healer by himself."

He *did* go out to find Corvyn by himself after he fainted back in Stormbrook, so the theory isn't too ill-fitting. I nod, turning on my heels and head to the tavern as Rowan closes his door and the rustling continues.

Rushing down the stairs, I give the kind Innkeeper a quick wave and head out into the chilly night air, the sun low on the distant horizon. I hug myself, biting cold numbing my bones as I cross the street, stepping into the busy tavern.

The strong smell of spiced wine assaults me, stopping me in my tracks as loud chants and bellowing laughter bounce off the timber walls. Looking around, the place is packed with people of all kinds. Elves and humans mingle, dance and cheer while drinks flow and large planks of bread and cheese get passed from table to table.

My eyes scan the area, but I can't find my friend. *Shit.* Turning, I head outside again. Someone should meet this male if Tharion won't be there. Perhaps he's already waiting at the square.

Walking down the now quiet streets, I find the stage. The market stalls have long since been closed for the night, only empty shells remaining. The stage where we first laid eyes on Elandir is empty, all the flowers now gone. Walking up to it, I wait. Tharion isn't here.

The heavy sound of boots hitting stone echo behind me, but as I turn to face them, the only eyes I meet are the dark pits of Elandir. In the fading evening sun, his bright oceanic eyes now look black and empty.

"Eleanora! Are your friends hiding, or did you just want some time alone with me?" the words fall from his lips like venom, making me take a step back. I cross my arms, tightening my posture.

"You said you knew of a healer. Take me to them," I shoot my chin to the air, forcing my tone steady. His smile falters, but only for a second, before it returns as if it was always there.

"I'm terribly sorry. My friend, the healer, was busy tonight. An emergency that needed their attention immediately."
My frown deepens, the heavy thumps of my heart now a steady race. Something feels wrong.

"But I will take you to him first thing tomorrow! I figured I would come here to give Tharion the message. Would be rude to have him wait for me at this hour. Speaking of, where is our friend?" He looks around us, scanning for Tharion.

"He was busy too," I retort, the words coming out sharper than I wanted. His face flinches, but the facade remains. Laughing, he takes a step towards me, dragging the tip of his finger down my cheek. Chills race down my spine, stomach turning violently.

*Rowan. Rowan, something feels off.*

The bond between us hums below my chest as my burgundy shadow pushes the message to him. Auburn rays race towards my soul, his aura already in motion.

*Where are you? I'm coming. Stay where you are.*

*The village square. Tharion is missing, something feels wrong.*

"What's the matter? You cold?"

His eyes narrow on my mouth, "I have something that will warm you right up." Bile rises in my throat, his disgusting aroma of sweat and dying weeds assaulting my nose.

My legs are frozen in place as he steps closer to me, now only inches from my face, dragging his nose across my cheek and down the side of my neck. With a deep inhale, he fills his lungs with me before letting it out slowly, a low growl sounding from his chest. I clamp my eyes shut while my fingers twitch, breath coming out in stutters. I can't move.

A cold hand drags from my shoulder, down my arm, landing firmly on my waist with a small squeeze. I jump. My heart hammers in my chest. I feel colder than ever as the male lets out a ragged breath.

Inside me, something breaks, whimpers escape my lips. That deceitful smile returns to his face.

"You like that, do you? You like it when I play a little rough?" a malicious chuckle sounds from behind his teeth, my mind now shutting everything out while the male pushes me against the edge of the stage. I try to resist, but my body won't listen.

Shaking, tears fill my eyes, vision blurring, the male but a silhouette behind them. I feel my pulse rampaging in my chest, dizzying me while his hands follow the curves of my body. His dark eyes find mine, taking me in as if I were a meal, licking those repulsing lips. I try calling on my magic, but it refuses to show. Glancing at Elandir, a faint blue rune glows on his neck, cold and thrumming. My magic thins and slips away.

Adjusting my head, I try to get a better look, but the collar of his coat covers it too much to make out the spell. With a burst, I yank my knee, colliding with his groin with blinding force. Elandir folds in two, holding his sorry excuse for a dick with his hands, crying out in pain.

"You bitch!" His voice cracks, pride racing through my veins. I slash across his neck, nails filling with flesh, severing the rune.

Magic explodes under my skin, filling me to the brim. I call on it, vines ripping through the earth, shards of stone soaring in the air as the vines entwine around the bard, holding him high. Walking up to him, I watch him scramble helplessly.

"What's the matter? You don't like playing a little rough?" I mock him with an exaggerated innocent voice, "here I thought that was exactly what you wanted."

His face contorts, a deep scowl of rage and hate meeting my eyes. I laugh as a snarl splits the air, Rowan ripping him from the thorny vines. Dirt and rocks fly as the bard's body crashes to the earth. Agonizing cries rip from his rotten core, Rowan slashing open his chest, the metallic tang of blood coating my nostrils.

His upper torso is ripped open, deep crimson blood sloshing as it hits the ground, the nauseating taste of warm metal sticking to my tongue. My knees buckle under me, sending me towards the ground once more. I land, but the ground is soft and hairy – warm and breathing. Rowan.

Setting me down, he looks over at Elandir, the male barely able to sit up as blood gushes from his right pectoral. His breathing is ragged, strained, blood coating his teeth in a malicious smile.

A bright flash of blue light blinds us momentarily, Elandir vanishing before our eyes, leaving only the reddish-brown stain on the ground where he laid.

I let out a sob, my magic finally coursing freely through my body. Reaching for it, warm vibrations healing me from inside. Healing what Elandir broke as he tried to take my body from me. Releasing the tears, I let out a scream so loud they must have heard it in Sylvarn, tearing my soul to shreds.

Warm hands snake around me, Rowan holding me close to him.

"Eleanora. I am so sorry."

He kisses my hair, stroking gentle circles on my back, my breath shaking,

"I am so sorry. He will never hurt you again."

I lean into his cold shirt, tears staining it as they fall. Reaching inside me, I desperately try to find a bond between Tharion and me, searching my soul for him. Why did he not come? Why did he not save me?

My body falls weightless as Rowan lifts me into his arms, cradling me against his warm body. He holds me all the way to the Inn, up the stairs and into his room. Corvyn's mouth hangs open as he sees us walking in, immediately leaping out of bed. Rowan places me gently down on his bed, his mate covering me with a blanket.

My body shifts as Rowan lies down behind me, his body flush against mine, holding me safe. Shielding me from the evils of Elandir. As I lay there, trembling, Rowan keeps me tight.

"He will never hurt you again. I will see to it," anger radiating through his words. I close my eyes as hot tears fall across my nose, down my cheek, dampening the mattress under us. My shoulders shake, breath hitching in my throat, silent screams tearing through me.

Turning, I cocoon myself in Rowan's safe embrace, burying my face in the nook of his neck. His hands gently run along my hair - comforting and warm. Next time my eyes rest on Elandir's sickening face, it will be the last breath he ever takes. *I* will see to it.

· · — · ✱ · — · ·

I scream, sitting up in bed, sweat pouring down my scalp. My heart races as I struggle to orientate myself.

"Eleanora," familiar hands envelop me, pulling me close,

"Eleanora, you're safe. I am here with you. You are safe. You are safe." Rowan repeats the words, weaving them into my brain with gentle rocking motions. I hold him tight, images of Elandir's rotten smile cursing my memory even as I sleep. Shaking my head, I try to rid myself of him.

"It was a nightmare. He is gone. Come here, I will keep you safe, *vulpin*." His nickname grounds me, the image going up in dust as the familiar scent of Rowan fills my chest. Dragging my lungs full of air, I exhale deeply and lay back down in his arms.

"Is Tharion back?" My voice is hoarse from crying. I feel him shaking his head, defeat washing over me as a lump forms in my throat.

"Corvyn is staying in your room, he promised to let me know if Tharion returned. He has yet to give word."

"I don't understand, Ro. He never leaves like this. He wouldn't."

"A lot is at stake now, remind yourself. Give him time, he will return."

But it doesn't feel right. Something is wrong. An aching stab in my chest tells me that something bad has happened. I know him better than anyone - even myself. I know this isn't him.

I toss and turn through the remainder of the night, watching as the morning sun erupts behind the eastern mountains, clouds closing in on each side.

My head is thundering, limbs heavy as anvils. I let out an exhausted breath, looking over at my familiar. Rowan is fast asleep, his breathing even and deep. Gently removing his arm from my waist, I carefully make my way out of bed. Brushing my teeth and washing my face, I change my clothes and make my way to the door.

"Where are you going?"

I stop in my tracks, hunching as the voice reaches me. I turn, a fake smile plastered on my face. "Breakfast. I'm starving."

Rowan lifts the blanket off, sitting up in bed.

"You should not be alone right now. Let me accompany you."

I wave my hands in front of me, "no, no! I'm good as gold. You stay in bed, I'll grab some food and a hot mug of Dawnflower at the tavern. No need to worry."

His eyes narrow, scanning my posture. I straighten, retouching the smile.

"Be right back!"

Even *I* don't buy the cheery sing-song voice, but it's the best I can muster. I turn before he can retort, closing the door behind me with a sharp bang.

Leaning against the door, my chest tightens. I know he only wishes to help, to protect, but I need to find out where Tharion is. Taking a moment to breathe, I say a silent apology. I run down the stairs, out into the busy street. Walking straight past the tavern, I set out to find my best friend.

# Chapter 32

## Rowan

The door slams shut, Eleanora barging outside. I know she's hurting, scared, her mind is wrapping around itself in a mess of thoughts. I can feel it.

*That fucking elf. You should never have let her go by herself.*

My thoughts race, images of my familiar on that stage, that greasy *creature* preying, hunting her, taking her. My fingers twitch, heat pooling in my stomach. I throw the covers off, getting out of bed. Corvyn is in Eleanora's room, waiting for Tharion to return. Where is he? She's right, it's not like him to just leave, to vanish.

I pace around the room, clenching my jaw so hard my teeth hurt. Inside my chest, my heart goes amok. Heavy beats, each a reminder of fleeting time, of the dangers to come, of the lives I cannot save. Each beat, one beat closer to possibly losing the people I care most for in this gods-forgotten realm.

I think back to my time before all of this, before I met Eleanora, before my life had purpose. I think back to my pack, to the people that raised me. My mother and father, my brothers, my friends.

*And because you were obsessed with fate, you missed their burials.*

I clamp my eyes shut, pushing the voice away. For as long as I can remember, my soul has felt empty. The void left by the Fates slowly consumed me, devouring me from the inside. I have always felt lonely, so incredibly lonely, and the search for my mate completely took over my life.

Then, Eleanora was there. A stubborn teenager drenched in involuntary solitude, anger and palpable sorrow. I knew, the first time our eyes met, I knew. She was my familiar. Not my mate, but something else connected to my soul, instantly easing the suffocating emptiness I'd been feeling for centuries.

*"Hello?" her voice calls out, brushing against me as I watch her from the shadows. This female, a young girl, she's crying. She does that a lot. Day after day, she cries, tears soaking into the earth below her body.*

*Something in me is telling me she's important. That I need to talk to her. Is she my mate?*

*"I can see you, you know," she sniffles, wiping a tear off the red, swollen cheek, "your eyes are literally glowing."*

*I step out from the place I've been hiding, walking to her in long strides. Her eyes widen more with each step, my giant statue towering over her.*

*"What do you want with me? I know you've watched me for the last few days." Her voice has a slight tremble, but I can hear her working hard to keep it steady.*

*"I'm Rowan. I'm sorry you're having a hard time. Mind if I sit?" The female shrugs, moving slightly from her spot on the damp grass. I sit down beside her, turning my head. As our eyes meet, lightning shoots down my arm. My heart skips a beat, the fox below my skin clawing to get out. My soul heats as foreign shadows of deep burgundy stretch around my golden aura.*

*She's not your mate. She's your familiar.*
*The girl stares at me, mouth hanging open.*

*"What just happened? What was that? Why do I feel like this?"*
*A smile stretches across my face, cheeks heating.*
*"Let me rephrase that. I'm Rowan, your familiar."*


The memory plays out like a dream in my mind, emotions crashing like waves against my chest. The thought of losing her, of losing *them,* it's too much.

My fist crashes against the wall, cracking the wooden panels. Pain shoots from my hand, white and hot, pulsating below my knuckles as blood seeps from small rifts.

*How could you let her get hurt? How could you bring her into this?*

The inside of my brain is like a symphony of noise, every voice desperately begging to be heard, to be understood. But I refuse. I will not lose her. I will not lose my mate. I will not lose my family.

My knees hit the ground, one hand cradling my chest, the other holding me up. Tears gloss my vision, everything around me but a blur, a nightmare. The door opens, Corvyn crashing to the ground beside me.

"My fox, what is happening? Are you okay?"
Tears tip over the edge, falling down my face. I can't do this, I cannot protect everyone.

Corvyn's gentle touch breaks the spiral, lifting my face towards him. His violet eyes search mine, raven brows scrunched in a deep frown.

"I can't… I-I can't lose you," I croak, the words no louder than a whisper. Warm hands wrap around my shoulders, pulling me closer to him.

"My love. Stop these thoughts. I am not going anywhere, not leaving your side. You will not lose me. We will make it through, okay?"

We rock, gently, tenderly, from side to side, his heartbeat drumming against my temple. My mate's scent swirls around me, a cloak of safety, a promise of eternity. The suffocating feeling in my chest lifts, only a little, lungs finally able to draw air.

Releasing me, Corvyn cups my jaw in his hands, violet moons casting their ever-glowing light on the embers beyond mine.

"You do not have to be strong for everyone, my fox. Even you, are doomed to break, to fill, with fear and the suffocation of impending sorrow," he plants a kiss to my forehead, "but do not let it cloud the world you live in right now. Do not let the fear of tomorrow take from the joy of today. Let me rephrase something a wise male once told me."

Corvyn drags me to my feet, standing so close to me that I can feel his breath brush against my ear.

"Denying yourself love is denying yourself, me, us. Let us love today, forget about what we cannot change right now. Let yourself feel, let yourself crack. I am here to pick up the pieces and put you back together."

I bury myself in my Corvyn's arms, breathing, cracking. I let myself feel, and I let my mate carry the pieces broken from my soul. Just for today.

# Chapter 33

## Tharion

The smell of mold and slime infuses the air, making my stomach turn. A headache splits my head, spreading to my bottom jaw. Clamping my eyes harder, I breathe through the ache, trying to regain focus. Slowly, light slips through my eyelids, but only faint. As I try to rub my eyes, my arms resist me. I'm bound.

My eyes snap open, panic tightening around the heart thundering in my chest. My feet are bound to the chair I'm sitting on, wooden legs creaking with every move. Looking around me, a few candles light up the small stone cell. Somewhere, water drips, the steady *drip, drip, drip* maddening. Where am I?

The dull ache in my head intensifies, sending high-pitched ringing through my eardrums. My jaw clenches, pain ripping through me.

"Hello?" I call out, but only silence answers.

"Is anyone out there? Hello?"

I try calling on my magic, but it's like it's sleeping under my skin. I try again, but nothing. Not even a hum. Turning my head to the side, a sharp sting burns my neck, heat washing over me. *A blocking rune.* I curse under my breath. That means I have to figure this out on my own.

Calming my breath, I look around me. To my right is a heavy metal door with large hinges and a small latch in the middle. To my left is a small table with a burning candle, a bucket placed on the floor next to it.

Footsteps echo behind the door, the clanging of keys rattling loudly before the heavy metal door swings open, hinges screeching. A dark figure casually walks inside, swinging the keys around by the chain.

The figure is covered by a cloak, black fabric heavy with silver details. I follow his body all the way to the tip of his hair, hanging just below his waist. *His white hair.* My eyes snap to his. *Elandir.* His face is bloody and dirty, his breath laboured.

"Your witch knows how to fight, I'll give you that."
He walks over to the small table, setting down a small blade and a carafe of water.

"… and she tastes delectable."
His eyes find mine, a devious smile creeping up his face. My body goes cold, vision fading to red.

Throwing my bound self around, I try to get out of the bonds. Elandir laughs, watching me struggle.

"There is no need for that. Unfortunately, her fox friend managed to overthrow me. Next time, she will not be as lucky. Feisty little thing."

"You will not lay a hand on her! You hear me?"

"Or what, little fae? What are you going to do, bound to that chair of yours? Stare me to death?" His laugh makes me sick.

"What do you want? I thought you wanted to travel with us?" Elandir scoffs. "Do you really think I cared about your silly quest? You were solely my guide to Vorathiel - you still are," he crouches before me, "or else I will take your little witch in more ways than one."

Reaching out for my magic, it fails me again. Nothing. Elandir's sickening laugh rings through the small room, my body scorching hot in his presence.

"You, and only you, will take me to Veil's Eclipse. I will give your friends a message from you, saying that you headed off without them, that the thought of putting them in harm's way was too much for you to bear," his voice is melancholic, mocking and cold.

"Why are you doing this?"
He cackles, chills racing across my scalp.

"To free Vorathiel, of course. That damn crone should never have put him behind that veil." He stands up, putting his hands on each of the chair's arms. His breath brushes against my lips, gags locked in my throat.

"When he sees what I went through to free him, I will be named his right hand. I will serve directly under him, serve him as I always have."

Elandir's hair transforms, thin grey strands replacing the luscious whites, face morphing before my eyes. The golden skin fades, a dull beige surfacing from underneath. The deafening cracks of bones breaking and reshaping hurt my ears as the tall statue turns into a crooked, short demon. His cerulean eyes are replaced by fiery red ones, boring into me. The smell of rotten flesh assaults my senses, bile rising in my throat.

"I have waited centuries for him to return. I will not let you, a cowardice fae, stop me from freeing my one true saviour."
Spit flies from his mouth as he snarls, landing on my face in slimy droplets.

"I will never help you. I will never let you destroy our realm!"
I shout, voice echoing through the hallway. Shrugging, Elandir turns back to the small table, grabbing the blade. He twists it in his hands, candlelight reflecting in the metal. Tutting his lips, he tilts his head to the side.

"That's a shame. For you. But I came prepared." A flash of metal is all the warning I get before a scream rips from my body, the blade's hilt the only visible thing standing out of my thigh. Excruciating pain shoots up my body, a high-pitched, sonic noise ringing in my ears. I look down, watching as warm blood pools around the blade before dripping to the dirty floor below me.

Snaking his bony fingers around the hilt, he turns the blade. My vision blurs, the scent of my blood filling the room. With a snap, he yanks the blade free, blood gushing from the wound. The scarlet drops hit the stone floor beneath me.

White flashes of light catch my attention, Elandir balancing a ball of crackling electricity in his hands. With a swift move, he shoots the ball into my chest, frying me from the inside out. My voice breaks as lightning explodes through me, the pain overbearing. As heat escapes my body, Elandir retracts his hand, my head falling forward in exhaustion. Breath evades me. I heave repeatedly as I try to regain control. The faint smell of urine permeates the air.

"Pathetic," Elandir spits at my feet. My head hangs heavy above my chest, consciousness threatening to leave me as the sharp sound of metal against metal clangs through the room - Elandir closing the door behind him as he leaves. The lights flicker out, blanketing me in darkness. Only the steady *drip, drip, drip,* counting down the seconds until I break.

# *Chapter 34*

*Eleanora*

The wind bites my cheeks as I wander the streets of Meadowrest. Towering trees surrounding the small village are a beautiful shade of red, mimicking the setting sun in the west. The street is busy, people walking in and out of market stalls, deeply engaged in conversation.

My mind drifts to the rune on Elandir's neck. How did he make a rune that blocks magic? I search my memory for a spell he could have used, but to no avail.

*This village is filled with healers, someone must know a spell.* I stop, looking around me. My eyes fall to a sign above a small stall, purple smoke rising from a brass cauldron. *"Root & Remedy"* is carved in deep lettering above the stall, calling me to it.

Walking up, a small female with deep brown hair stirs her cauldron. I make my way up to her as a customer turns away.

"Welcome, friend. What remedy can I conjure for you today?" Her smile is warm, inviting. Her eyes are a deep chocolate brown, like pools of hot cocoa. I clear my throat, straightening my spine.

"Yes, hello. I was wondering if you knew how to make a rune to block someone's powers?" Her stirring stops, letting the cauldron go, her brown eyes widening.

"What on earth would you want that for?" she crosses her arms, one eyebrow lifting.

My cheeks flush. "I don't need it. It was used on me, and I need to find out how to block it from being used again."

Her mouth opens, hanging wordless as her brows scrunch between her eyes.

"My poor girl. I am so sorry, but I don't have an antidote for runes of that kind."

My shoulders slump, defeat washing over me.

"Have you seen a male, a bard, with white hair and blue eyes, around here lately?"

She lowers her face as she thinks, tapping a finger on her chin.

"There was one a few days ago, he asked to borrow one of my spellbooks. Elandir, was it?"

His name tastes like vomit in my mouth, shivers ripping through me. I nod, words evading me.

"He wanted to make a healing potion, said he was going out on a dangerous adventure."

*A few days ago? We arrived here two days ago. Could he have followed us from Catariel? Surely, we would have spotted him?*

My mind races as the new information sinks in.

"By any chance, would you have one more of those spellbooks?"

She dips under her table, rummaging through a box before dragging out an old leather book. Wiping off the dust, the deep maroon cover pops with gold lettering.

"As a matter of fact, this was my mother's copy. I kept it for sentimental reasons, but I knew it would come in handy one day! You can look through it if you want, just bring it back to me by the end of the day."

I thank her, noting the location of her stall as I tuck the book under my arm and rush back to the Inn, hoping to find Rowan. Hoping to find a spell that will help us find Elandir, and Tharion.

My fist pounds on Rowan's door, the wood creaking underneath.

"Rowan!" I slam at the door, "Rowan, let me in!" My breath is shallow and fast from running, hair stuck to my forehead as sweat drips down my temples.

The door swings open, Rowan looking about ready to fight someone.

"What the fuck is happening?" he shouts above my head before his eyes land on me.

He exhales. "Eleanora. What are you doing? You scared the life out of me!" He pulls me in, throwing his arms around me. I drag in his scent, the familiar foxy smell now mixed with the earthy scent of Corvyn.

Planting my palms on his chest, I push away.

"I found a spellbook that might help us find Tharion. It's the same one Elandir has." Rowan flinches as I mention his name. I push the door open and walk in beside him, slamming the book down on a small table.

Flipping through the pages, runes of all kinds are drawn. Runes to make crops grow faster, runes to make limbs grow back, and finally - a rune to block someone's magic.

I look at it, my body freezing as images of the night before race through my mind. The intricate drawing looks exactly like the one glowing on Elandir's skin.

"This is it. I broke it by scratching him, breaking the lines. It didn't work on me after that."

"And Tharion? How do we find him?"
I flip further, the pages falling delicately as my fingers brush across them.

"There are all kinds of spells here, there must be one to locate someone," I huff as the pages left thin out increasingly. As the last pages emerge, I stop.


*"Heart's Compass"*


I stare at the page, the words calling to me like a siren's song.

*"Use your heart's compass to locate one lost. As love leads the way, this*

*spell cannot find strangers to one's heart. To reveal the direction of one whose heart is bound to yours, the elements must move freely. "*

I study the spell, chest constricting as the absence of Tharion crashes over me. I need to find him. The rune looks simple enough, I know I can make it. Looking up at Rowan, I watch as he reads the spell repeatedly, a deep frown carved between his brows.

"We need to try, Ro. We need to find him."
A soft knock on the door distracts us. Corvyn zips to the door, opening it widely.

"Good evening, travellers!" the kind Innkeeper smiles at us,

"I received a letter addressed to you, Miss Eleanora. The messenger said it was urgent." He hands me the letter, the parchment old and worn with splotches of dirt. I unfold it, taking in the words as I read them out loud:

*"My dear friends,*

*I have decided to leave, alone. The weight on my shoulders is heavy enough without having to put your lives at risk, so I will be fighting this battle alone. Do not come for me, do not look for me, but do remember me.*

*Your friend,*

*Tharion "*

Rowan and Corvyn stare at me, their mouths hanging open. Reading the words again, I throw the letter away from me, body trembling with rage.

"How dumb does he think we are?" I pace around the room, breath coming out in short bursts.

"Does he not think we know Tharion? Does he really think we would believe this letter was from him?" I scoff.

"I don't understand," Corvyn says, his tone careful.
Turning, I lift the letter so it's facing him. Pointing at the words, "this is not Tharion's handwriting. He would never leave. I keep telling you that something bad has happened, can you *please* listen?!" My voice is loud,

frantic, as the room closes in on me. Rowan steps towards me, face laced in worry.

"Ela. I apologize. Will you please tell us your theories?"

I let out a breath, fingertips prickling in anger.

"Tharion would never leave like this, and he sure as *fuck* would never send a measly letter to deliver bad news. This reeks of Elandir - that disgusting elf."

Rowan's eyes harden. "What do you need from us?"

My gaze flicks between the males, both panting with anticipation.

"I need you to help me find our friend."

· · — · ✱ · — · ·

I map out the rune on the stone ground at the square. A spiral forms in the middle, the symbol of longing. From there I draw four lines emerging from the spiral, the four winds. At last, I draw an arc above it all, the listening ear. The moon is high in the sky and stars light up the late night. I flick my hand, candles coming to life around us.

"Are you ready?" I look to my friends standing outside the ring of salt around the rune - kept there for protection. I sit back on my heels, hands flat on my lap. Placing my hand above my heart, I start chanting:

*"Tharion. Tharion. Tharion."*

Each whisper is softer than the last. A soft hum fills the air around me, vibrating deep inside. Taking in a steady breath, I reach into the pocket of my cloak.

The small wooden doll lies in my hand, smiling up at me. Bringing it to my lips, I press them gently to the carved wood, closing my eyes. Placing the doll in the middle of the rune, I reach for my knife. The cold metal slices through my flesh, cutting the inside of my hand - blood seeping out before falling to the ground. A soft glow pulses from the doll as magic courses within it.

*"By bond unspoken, and thread unbroken,*
*Heart to heart, show me the way."*

I close my eyes, listening. At first, the air is silent. Then, the faint light from the doll enhances, turning into a bright beacon. The light spreads in a single line, stretching far beyond my field of vision. I look at Rowan, his eyes trained on me.

"Can you see that?" I shout through the deafening vibrations. Rowan shakes his head. I look at the glowing thread, a wide grin stretching across my face. Warily, I pick up the doll, hoping the thread remains. It does. Running over to my friends, I drag them with me.

"Come on! Let's find Tharion."

# Chapter 35

## Tharion

Cold water rains over my head, jolting me awake. I gasp as the water coats my tongue, forcing itself into my lungs, chest burning.

"Wake up, princess," Elandir's voice cuts against my eardrums. Water seeps into the wound on my leg, setting it on fire from within. I cry out, hissing and cursing as the burning subsides. His sickening laugh fills the room.

"Have you had a chance to think about my proposal? Or do you need some more… convincing?"
I wince. My leg throbs, a painful reminder of said proposal.

His shape is no longer the grey demon from before. The annoyingly handsome and witty elf, Elandir, stands in front of me, flicking a knife between his fingers, eyes scanning my broken body.

"I delivered your note. I'm sure Eleanora is devastated right now, crying that you left her. I'm sure she will need a shoulder to cry on pretty soon, and I will happily oblige."

"Eleanora will rip your shoulder from your body before crying on it," I spit at him, hands clenching to fists behind my back. My head is whipped to the side as Elandir's fist collides with it, teeth cracking in my jaw on impact. Hot metal fills my mouth, and I spit it at his feet. His hand clamps around my jaw, fingers digging into my cheeks as his face leans closer to mine.

"I will rip *your* shoulders from *your* body just for speaking to me like that." He tosses my head from him, my neck straining to hold it steady.

"But first, let's see how well you wield your blade without a hand to hold it in."

He turns, storming out of the cell, thundering down the hallway. My heart pounds so hard I can hear it in my ears, hands cold and numb. I need to get out, right now.

*Okay, focus now, Tharion. How can you get out?*

I look around me, searching for something, anything, to get me out of this rotten cell. The knife he used to stab me is gone, nothing left but the candle and bucket. I can't use those.

The chair beneath me squeaks as I turn, an idea forming. I lean left before throwing myself right, rocking the chair sideways, repeating the process until the two left legs lift completely, sending me tumbling to the ground. A loud crash bounces off the walls as the fragile chair crushes under my weight, splinters flying. I wiggle myself upright before sliding my arms under my feet, to where I can untie the knot.

The echo of footsteps sound from down the hallway, my heart beating faster and harder. I manage to untie my feet, jumping upright as the footsteps close in on my cell. My hands are still tied together, but I can still use my bodyweight to knock him over as he walks through the door.

The footsteps are now right outside, and as the metal hinges scream, Elandir walks in. Holding an axe in his hand, he scrambles to find me. With force, I jump out from behind the door, throwing my bound hands around his neck, strangling him from behind. The axe falls to the ground, arms flailing to the gurgling sound of sweet suffocation.

Trying to push me off, he wriggles under me, but my arms are strong and I hold on. His breaths are squeaky and short, fair skin turning a light shade of blue as he thrusts his elbow into my ribs. Breath escapes me and I fold in two, heaving for air.

The sound of metal scraping against stone snaps my head to him just as he throws the axe through the air, aiming at my head. I lift my hands, metal slicing through the rope, freeing me. A loud roar erupts from his throat as he continues to throw the axe around him, snarling like a wild animal.

I try calling on my magic, but it is still gone. Then, I remember the rune on my neck. Using my index fingernail, I cut my skin, and thus the connecting lines of the rune. The faint blue glow of the intricate lines fades to a pale beige. My mind explodes as magic rushes to every crevice of my body and soul, fire burning in my palms.

"Finally," I breathe, "we even the fight."
My hands clench to fists, pumping blood to numb fingers. Elandir's eyes are wild, unhinged, the demon crying out. He runs towards me, axe held high above his head, as I summon my magic.

Bursts of pale green energy shoot from my palms, but the demon evades them, closing in on me. I try again but his body crashes into mine, throwing us to the ground. The smell of sweat and mold hits my nostrils, turning my stomach in the process.

With brute force, the axe comes down, just missing my shoulder while I struggle to hold him off me. He swings again, this time nicking the side of my neck. The tangy smell of metal mixes with the moldy scent of the demon, coating my tongue as we fight. I try rolling him to the side, but he's too big, and ends up straddling me.

My legs are trapped beneath him, unable to move. Bursts of energy eject from my palms, but they bounce off him like raindrops. His sickening smile peaks from his cut lips, coated in dried blood and dirt as the axe lifts over his head again.

"My master will be so pleased when he learns that I was the one that killed you, the one foretold to save the realm. Oh, he will treat me to my heart's desire," his laugh is maniacal, twisted.

Tilting the axe as far as he can reach it, I close my eyes. Images of Eleanora flood my mind, warmth spreading to the deepest pits of my soul as I envision everything we've ever done. The regrets I have for keeping my feelings hidden, the joy I felt the night we finally admitted it all. I think back to Rowan, and Corvyn, and all the people we have met during our travels. Everything that has led me to this point.

Time stands still as I await my fate. The axe falls with a clang to the ground, Elandir crashing beside me with a dull thump. Flinching, I roll to the side instinctively.

As I open my eyes, I watch a deep red pool form under him, blood oozing from the demon. Searching the dimly lit room, the scent of lavender soap fills my nostrils. I look around, Eleanora's eyes meeting mine as Corvyn lets out a heavy breath, his dagger coated in blood.

Eleanora throws herself around my neck, tears streaming down her face. My body screams in pain, but the sensation of her body against mine dulls the sound to a hush. Releasing me, she cradles my face in her warm hands, scanning me.

"You found me," I whisper.

"My heart found you. I am so sorry, Tharion." Her eyes fill with water as I pull her in for a kiss, my bleeding lips crashing against hers. I take her in, the taste, the feel, the scent of her.

"I never thought I would see you again. If you hadn't come when you did…" I fold, my stomach emptying itself on the stone floor as adrenaline exits my body.

"How did you find me?" I ask between heaves of air, my stomach determined to empty every last drop.

"Like I said - my heart found you. I put a location spell on the doll you gave me. Our souls are bonded to one another, Ari."
The thought fills me with hot pulses, delicious and exciting. Wiping my mouth with the back of my hand, I straighten.

"I knew we were. From the moment I saw you, my soul belonged to you and no one else."
Eleanora's cheeks deepen, the rosy pink I have come to adore returning to her face.

Rustling steals my attention as I look at Elandir's bleeding body, now convulsing as if regenerating itself.

*Fuck, his head!*

"Quick! We need to remove his head, he's a demon!"
My strength is diminishing as I rush around the room, searching for a blade to cut the demon's head off. Eleanora steps forward, holding up her hands, and I halt.

"If anyone is to kill that piece of shit once and for all, it will be me." I watch with my mouth hanging wide as she crouches beside Elandir, his body twisting and turning as he helplessly gulps down air.

Grabbing the knife from the leather sheath on his hip, Eleanora slides it tantalizingly slow across his neck, splitting skin and flesh. Planting her hands on each side of his head, she smirks.

"You should have known – I don't need magic to end you."

… and rips his head clean off.

Ash rains over us as Elandir's body ceases to exist, nothing but the memory left of him. Eleanora pants as the ash settles around her feet, staring at the pile.

"You did it, Eleanora. You killed him. He can never hurt you again." Rowan walks up to her, placing his hand softly on her shoulder.

*Again? That demon shit hurt her?*

I feel scalding rage build in me, my pulse quickening as my body runs hot. The world fades to red as I lunge across the room, pulling Eleanora into my arms.

"I am so sorry I couldn't protect you, Ela. You are a warrior." Her face buries into the dirty fabric of the half-ripped shirt on my torso, holding me tight. We stand like this for a moment, listening as the world quiets around us.


Rowan assists me as we find our way out of the murky cell, up into fresh air. I gulp down mouthfuls, savouring the sweet scent of meadow flowers and grass. With one arm across Rowan- and Corvyn's shoulders, we make our way through the main street of Meadowrest. A faint call rings through the night, a female stopping us in our tracks.

"My dearest me, what has happened here?"
Bending down, she gets a better look at my face and gasps.

"My boy, let's get you fixed up." I look at her, hesitant.

*What if she is another shapeshifting demon, just like Elandir?*
My stomach drops at the thought. Shaking my head, words escape me, fatigue stealing the last of my strength. With wide eyes, the strange female studies us.

"What happened to you?"

"A demon attacked him, a demon disguised as a bard,"
Eleanora's voice is hard, cold. Gasping, the female steps back, hand
placed over her mouth.

"A demon? In Meadowrest? Impossible!" But we know it isn't.
We know too well that it is very possible.

Dragging my feet, we start walking again, the female fading in
my field of view. Soon, the sound of boots catches up to us, a hand
grabbing the top of my arm.

"Please. At least take this, it will help with your healing. We call
it Silverleaf Salve." My heart stops as the words leave her lips, her hand
stretched out to me. *Silverleaf Salve.*

"Did you learn it from Serenya?" Corvyn asks, curious.
Her face softens, the corners of her lips dragging upwards into a warm
smile.

"As a matter of fact, I did. Did you know her?"
Corvyn takes the small pot from her, a grateful nod as he shoves it into
his pocket. The violet in his eyes glistens, glossing over with tears.
Rowan shoots the raven a soft look before turning back to the female.

"My mate was her mate's brother. We know of her, she sounded
like a beautiful person."
With a dip to her chin, the female turns and walks away, leaving us both
puzzled and thankful for the coincidental rescue.

The street narrows as the Inn comes into view. Walking inside,
Rowan tips me into his arms and carries me up the stairs, his breath
heavy as he sets me down on shaky legs.

"Take a shower, I will bring you some food before you go to
sleep."
He turns, returning down the stairs, rushing across the street and into the
busy tavern. I look over at Eleanora, her eyes already watching me.

"What now?" her words come out through deep trembles.

I swallow hard.

"Now, we find this demon, and we end this - once and for all."

# Chapter 36

### Eleanora

I watch Tharion inhale his supper, piling his plate with bread, jam and cheese.

"You need to slow down, or you will end up being sick," Rowan scrunches his face as he watches our friend make a mess of himself. Tharion answers something about not eating for days, or maybe it was that he could eat a fae, but his mouth is so full that neither of us understand him.

I clear my throat. "We need to come up with a plan. If we storm the Veil now, we'll get our rears handed to us tenfold. Vorathiel may be impatient, but he is not stupid."

My gaze drops to the table, images of Elandir flooding my mind again. The smell of his rotting body, his disgusting smile and the sight of him bleeding out on the cold stone floor makes my body shiver.

Outside, the moon is still high in the sky, dawn still hours away. The smell of fresh bread makes my mouth salivate, a low rumble in my stomach answering. Snatching a piece off Tharion's plate, I stuff the fluffy vessel topped with jam into my mouth.

"I say we stay the night, have a good meal and then when the day fades into night - we ride to the Veil." Rowan looks between us, searching for acceptance in our eyes. I nod, mouth filled with food.

"I like that," Tharion rubs his chin, "take them by surprise at night." Nodding enthusiastically, Rowan cracks a faint smile.

"Now, let's get to sleep. We need all the rest we can get, there will be no more after this one."

My stomach drops.

*Tomorrow, we will be fighting Vorathiel. Everything we have trained for will actually happen.* Goosebumps race across my arms and neck, hands feeling clammy and cold. I swallow hard and dry, scratching the inside of my oesophagus as nerves build in my body. This is it.

Finishing his meal, Tharion and I make our way up to our room. The space feels cold, empty, impossibly small as I take it in in its entirety. It settles in my body that this might be our last night here, our last night together at all, and my eyes fill with water.

The thought of losing any of my companions is too much, too agonizing to think about. I could never live without Rowan, without Tharion or Corvyn. They are my family, *we* are a family of our own. A silent tear trickles down my cheek, warm hands snaking around my waist, pulling me closer.

"My sweet Eleanora. This is not the end. It is a new beginning, a new life for us. When this is over, we can be whoever we want to be, live wherever we want to live. Our choices are limitless."
The raspy voice makes my stomach all fluttery, the butterflies laced in flames as they swirl in my belly. Turning, I take in the mossy green eyes staring at me, heat increasing inside me.

Tharion puts his hands on my face, cupping my cheeks as he leans in to plant a kiss on my forehead. I come apart, tears now streaming without stop. I weep, agonizing sobs tearing from my throat. Stammering, my words hitch in my mouth. Tharion's head lowers, meeting me at my height.

"Breathe, Ela. A deep breath in," he inhales deeply and I mimic, "and out." He lets out the breath through his mouth, the gentle breeze caressing my shoulders. I repeat it until I can talk without falling apart, gathering words in my throat.

"I don't know what I would do if I lost you, Ari," the lump builds once more, fingers dripping with sweat. He places another kiss to my forehead, leaning his against mine as he stares into the deepest pits of my soul.

"Not even death will separate us, Eleanora. Even from behind the Veil, I will always be yours." The gentleness of his voice has hardened, truth evident in every word.

"The feeling between us that our friendship cannot describe… is love. Raw, naked, honest love. You have seen every part of me, every weak moment, every failure I have ever achieved. And you still stayed."

My stomach rolls, his words enveloping me. I crave them, need them, never wanting them to end.

"We chose each other before we even knew we did. And I will spend my life choosing you. Because believe it or not, Eleanora Luna - I love you." The drum in my chest stops for a moment, I forget how to breathe. Swinging my arms around his neck, I bury myself in his shoulder. The world stops spinning as the realm quiets around us. It's only me and him, just us. Releasing the deathly tight grip on him, I wipe my tears.

"I love you, too, Tharion Ashveil."
I watch as his shoulders drop, relaxed, elated. His mouth stretches into a beautiful, beaming grin, the mossy pits of his eyes gleaming down at me.

Lifting me up, he swings us around in the room, holding me tightly at the waist. Our laughs mingle, bouncing off the walls in our tiny room. Stopping, he disintegrates the pining distance between us as our lips meet, this time with need and lust - and love.

My body fills to the brim with heat, tickling my chest as my heart tries to escape through my mouth. The delicious vibrations humming at my skin when he laughs has me in tatters, clambering to the sound with claws and nails. He holds my hands, interlacing our fingers as he kisses my knuckles one by one.

"I love you," he kisses one, "I love you," he kisses the next, "I love you," he keeps going until the last kiss finds my mouth. A rush of heat courses through me, needing him close. With a light push, his body bounces heavily on the mattress.

Slowly, I unbutton my shirt, watching his eyes widen, mouth slowly unlatching. The shirt falls open, barely covering my naked chest. I push down my trousers, kicking them to the side as I stand before him, all my curves and attributes on display. Tharion swallows hard, his eyes scanning my every inch.

Reaching for me, his hands explore my soft curves, making me shiver. The room goes dark as I close my eyes, savouring his delicate touch on my hyper-sensitive skin.

"Tharion…" I whisper, a soft moan exiting my mouth. His teasing chuckle has me spinning, and I push him flat on the mattress.

"If this is our last night together in peace, I want you to make love to me as if tomorrow will be our last day in this realm."
Sitting up on his elbows, a moment goes by before he finally opens his mouth.

"I will make love to you as if my soul is to crack and no trace of me will exist. For only that would ever stop me from finding you."

· · — · ✳ · — · ·

Scattering of birds wake me from a deep slumber, my heart stammering as my eyes shoot open. The room is silent, only broken by Tharion's deep breaths where he lies next to me, far off into the realm of the Dreaming.

Studying him, his face is completely relaxed. Freckles scatter across his face like paint splotches, the deep auburn brows like brushes crafting the masterpiece that is him. His mouth is slightly curved, smiling even in his dreams after we got him back to us.

Shivers run through me as thoughts of the last two days replay in my mind. The constant anxiety while we searched for him, the looming dread that some awful fate had fallen upon him. The thought of losing him. But he's here, back with us, with me.

I watch him sleep, peace cocooning me as memories of our past flood my mind.

*"See that one up there?" Tharion points to a cloud shaped somewhat like a flower, "one day we will have a garden filled with*

*flowers, in all the colours of the rainbow." I watch as the cloud drifts across the sky, feeling the grass itch slightly under my head. Pointing to another one, this one is shaped like a bear's head.*

*"Do you think we will ever fight a bear in our lifetime?"*
*I shudder, the thought of meeting something as large and dangerous as a bear fills me with dread.*

*"I hope not. We would never survive. My magic is nowhere near strong enough to take on something that large." His face turns from me to the sky, a distant look in his eyes.*

*"Do you think I will ever master my magic, Ela?" Leaning on my elbows, I watch self-doubt flare under his skin.*

*"Of course you will, Ari. You're so much stronger than you think. It's only a matter of time." We sit like that for a while, surrounded by silence, watching each other. No tension, no awkward silence - just us.*

The memory makes my chest warm, gentle heat encompassed in compassion and loyalty. Back then, all those years ago, we could never have imagined a life where we had to save the realm. We never wanted a reality like that bestowed upon us. We lived in the belief that we would grow up to be farmers and scholars, not heroes or warriors.

My thoughts drift to Sylvarn, to my parents and Axel. Do they miss us? Have my parents even noticed my absence? Turning, my eyes find the small cracks in our wooden ceiling, following the lines as they dip into the wood.

*If I die in this battle, I will be proud to have lived my life as I have. You might be born into a family, but the family you choose yourself is the one that really matters.*

Images of Corvyn, Rowan, Camille and Alaric float like moving pictures inside my brain, filling me with happiness. I hope I get to see our friends in Stormbrook again, bringing them Amariel - completing their broken family.

Shooting up in bed - I suddenly remember I haven't figured out how to break her spell. I glance over at the table next to our bed, the spellbook I borrowed is still there. Careful, as not to wake Tharion, I sneak out of bed.

Slipping on a pair of woollen socks, I make my way over to the small table. I open my hand, forming a small ball of light in my palm - just enough to read the pages without waking Tharion.

Flicking through the old spell book, I search for a spell to break someone out of a curse. *A spell about healing wounds. No. One about necromancy. Fuck no. Another one about conjuring fresh water. Might put that in my notebook.* I stop as I reach just past the middle point.

*Breaking darkness' hold.*

That's it! Snapping my notebook and a pencil from my satchel, I draw the rune at the very beginning and write down the chant. Taking some time to note other useful spells, the chitter of birds breaks my attention. It's morning.

Tharion turns in bed, his deep slumber coming to an end. With a stretch followed by a whining exhale, his eyes fall to mine.

"Good morning, my love." Shivers dance through my body, his morning voice once again putting me under a spell.

Making my way over to him, my robe falls to the ground as I climb under the warm covers, inhaling his sleepy scent. It's the best smell, the innocent scent of dreams and peace - nothing can compare. Planting a kiss to his lips, he pulls me closer.

"Good morning."
Heat gathers in my cheeks as I look down at him. He is perfect. Snaking his arms around me, I find myself briefly in the air before crashing down on the mattress under him. Peeking out the window, one of his brows lifts menacingly.

"It's only dawn. I say we spend a little more time in bed, don't you agree?"
I chuckle as his lips crash down on mine once more, our bodies melting together as one. Our hands wander, taking in every nook and cranny of each other's bodies, forcing everything to memory as if we won't make it to tomorrow.

I drag my teeth over his neck, tasting his salty skin, inhaling the sweet scent of Tharion. A deep moan escapes his lips as my nails slice across his back. I can feel his need, his lust for me, heat pooling in my core as a result.

Tracing his strong abdomen, I wrap my hand around his arousal, feeling as it pulsates and hardens in my grip.

"I need you. Now," he pants. My head bobs in agreement as his hand finds its way to my core, gently massaging that aching spot. I throw my head back, a rough moan piercing past my lips.

Tharion leans down, kissing my neck, travelling further south, lapping my breasts, my sensitive ribs and hips, before his hot tongue splits my core, devouring me with insatiable hunger.

"*Tharion,*" his name tastes like pure honey in my mouth, coating my soul in delicious decadence. The vibrations of his smirk make my legs tremble under me as I feel the peak of my arousal approaching.

As if he senses the short distance left, he crawls back up to me, leaving me panting and wanting - so excruciatingly wanting. His lips meet mine in a hungry kiss as he thrusts inside me, gulping down my moans as if they gave him life.

"I love you," he breathes into me as I feel my fingers tingle and my legs clench around him.

"I love you. To the very end of my life, I will always love you," he thrusts harder, faster, with desperate need. Our mouths clash, teeth and tongues mixing as we leap over the edge together, crashing to the shores of our desires as one. With heavy pants, his pace ebbs to a halt, eyes searching mine.

"I love you," I answer and his body palpably trembles. I drag the back of my hand across the side of his face, watching as the redness fades and his eyes soften.

Tharion lies down beside me, radiating heat and safety as our bodies interlace, wanting to be as close as possible. His hand gently drags across my hair, lulling me, my eyelids falling heavy on my cheeks, the world fading away around me as sleep pushes me under.

# Chapter 37

## Rowan

The low rumbling of Corvyn's gentle snores wakes me as the sun lightly kisses my cheeks. The sunlight feels almost cruel, a golden lie over a world that will soon burn. Rubbing the sleep out of my eyes, I look over at my mate. *My mate.* The word rolls in my mind like music, warmth enveloping my body.

His raven hair falls like silk over his pillow, long black locks reminding me of shadows in the night. Heavy breaths raise and lower his chest as he still roams the realm of the Dreaming, perfectly content.

With a gentle touch, my hand slides over the left side of his face, pulling a faint smile from him. How lucky I am to have found him, even if the timing could be better. My fingers twitch, aching to touch him all over, to wake him from sleep so I can gaze into his deep violet eyes as his hands explore me - but I won't. He needs the rest, as do we all, before we leave Meadowrest.

Purple haze finds my stare as he slowly opens his eyes, my heart racing already.

"Good morning, *korax*." His sleepy eyes have put me under a spell so deep I could never escape - so I just stare. Corvyn's hand finds mine, interlacing our fingers, leaning closer to me.

"Good morning, my fox." Heat blooms in my chest, my arms snaking around him before I even notice, pulling him close to me.

"Today is the day, huh," his voice scratches every itch in my body in euphoric relief. I nod, fingers stroking circles on his shoulder as he lays on my chest.

He tilts his head. "Are you afraid?"
I swallow. Am I?

"I have lived for centuries, seen what this realm has to offer in every way, and the fox I once was would have said no. Then you came, and my life suddenly had purpose. I live to be with you, and there is nothing that scares me more than the thought of not having that."
A silent breath hitches in his throat, those violet eyes falling to my lips.

"My fox. I will divide this realm myself if it tries to take you from me. Not even Death herself could hide you. I will always find you, in every life, in every realm."

He sits up, scanning my face, as if memorizing every freckle. Leaning in, our lips meet in a delicate, soft kiss. In this moment, my mind overflows with everything that is Corvyn; his laugh, his smile, the way the left side of his face scrunches when he says particular words as if his mouth can't keep up, the bounce in his step whenever he walks in front of me, showing off those perfect, onyx wings.

I put my arm around his neck, pulling him closer to me. My soul aches to eliminate every molecule of distance between us, to keep him as a part of myself, because that is what we are - one. A soft whimper slips through his lips, my heart bursting as tears fall down my face.

"My fox," he pulls away slightly, "what is happening?"

I sniffle, feeling sobs build in my chest as it constricts. It's too much.

"I can't…" my lungs refuse to draw breath, "I can't lose you. The thought eats my heart. Korax, I –" Corvyn raises his hand, placing it over my heart.

"I know, my fox. I know."
I let out the sobs trapped under my ribs, pulling him so close to me that I

think he might explode. His strained breaths pull me out of my dark spiral, snapping me back to reality. He sits up, crossing his legs as he pulls me with him. Taking my hands in his, he looks me in the eyes.

"My fox. We will make it through this. You will go through life with me by your side, sharing every day together. Do not let your heart break already, I am still here. Love me today, kiss me today. Be with me in this moment, today. Now."
I throw myself around his neck, dragging in his scent like it's my life's force. His avian aura snakes around mine, violet mixing with my gold as our bond strengthens.

*You will always have me, my fox. The world can break, but not before we face it together.  I love you.*


*I love you, too.*


· · — · ✶ · — · ·


Walking down to the tavern, the sun now high in the sky, autumn wind kisses my cheeks as the smell of damp soil and sleeping flowers brush against me. Inside, Tharion and Eleanora are already eating, deep in conversation as they stuff their faces with fresh bread, meat and eggs. My stomach rumbles, eyes falling to their plates.

"Good morning, friend! What can I interest you with this fine morning?" Thinking, my body needs a sustainable meal to keep me going for possibly a whole day.

"I would like some meat, potatoes and eggs. And a large mug of Dawnflower Tea. This will be my last meal for a while. Thank you." The kind Innkeeper's smile fades as his brows furrow between his eyes. With a jerk to his chin, he turns on his heel and walks into the tavern kitchen.

Turning, I lean against the counter, taking in the cozy venue. The candles flicker as the door goes open and shut, bards and elves coming in for a meal or a drink. The heavy lavender smell is grounding, centering.

The kitchen door swings open, the Innkeeper carrying a large plate stacked with food making my teeth swim in saliva. He places it in front of me, flipping a mug right-side up before filling it with steaming tea. Giving him my thanks, I pick up my meal and head over to my friends.

Eleanora has a glow to her, her cheeks are a bright pink and her eyes glisten in the low candlelight. If I didn't know better, you'd think she was… happy. Tapping the chair beside her, I sit down. After a moment, Corvyn joins us, too. We eat, joke and laugh, like nothing evil awaits us. But that is a lie. The uncertainty of it all is chipping away at me, a knot rooting itself in my stomach.

"So… today we ride." Eleanora's voice is careful, but stern. We nod, the colour of her face slowly fading. Tharion stands up, his fists planted on the table.

"Today we will fight, and we will win. Vorathiel will not defeat us, he will not destroy this realm. There is too much to lose," he looks at Eleanora, "for all of us." No one dares to utter a word, Tharion's chest rising and falling in heavy pants.

"I found a few spells that can help us. A healing spell, a spell to conjure water and a spell that should break the curse on Amariel."

*Amariel.* I had forgotten about the poor daughter of Alaric and Camille. We promised to get her home. Now, the battle is even more important. We cannot lose.

For the remainder of our breakfast, Eleanora tells us about the spells and how they work.

"I will need to carve or paint a rune on Amariel's skin, either by knocking her unconscious or by holding her down. Only when the rune is placed can I chant the spell to break the curse." We listen intently, noting every word, mapping out our plan to save her – and our realm.

"The moment Vorathiel gets out, we will know. And by then, we will be ready."

· · — ·✳· — · ·

As we ride through the forest, the air feels electric, like the moments before a storm. The sun is low on the horizon, casting the realm in a deep orange glow. My eyes scan from left to right, looking for spirits that might be lurking in the shadows.

This time, we all ride horseback, not taking any chances. The looming smell of decay is heavy in my nostrils, my fox sensing the evil watching us from afar. Hooves on stone ring between tall trees, echoing far beyond us.

Rattling in the bushes grabs my attention, head swivelling to the side as a grey silhouette charges towards us.

"Get down!" I shout, jumping down from our horse. Drawing my bow, I aim at the being, waiting for it to reveal itself. Glowing green eyes emerge from under a shadowy hood, its brown teeth stretched into a wicked smile as an air-splitting screech pierces our bodies.

I fold, clamping down on my ears. Through gritted teeth, I catch a glimpse of the being. Snaking a hand over my shoulder, I reach for an arrow, stretching the bow string taut before my fingers release, the arrow soaring silently through the air before hitting the being in the middle of its chest.

Crying out, it falls to the ground, letting out a deafening scream. I charge, sprinting towards it, unsheathing my knife. The being catches a glimpse of me, jumping up on its feet. Just a foot's distance before him, I sling the knife into its neck, black tar-like blood trickling down its shadowy cloak.

I drop to my knees, sliding around it, using my claws to sever its Achilles. With a wail it falls to the ground, unable to stand. I grab hold of its head and yank, a sickening squelch before its head releases from the body, going up in ash.

"We're getting close!" I call out, sweat beading on my forehead. The air changes as the words escape my mouth, ground trembling with thousands of feet sprinting through the forest from afar. In the distance, screeching and growling can be heard, chills racing over my body as we get ready for battle.

"Forget that, get ready to fight!" I haul myself onto the horse, digging my heels into its side. We set off, galloping through the forest at blinding speed. The forest around us transforms as the luscious red tree tops fade into naked branches, the life stripped from them completely.

The faint glow of white tells me that the Veil is not far, my heart combusting in my chest as realization hits me: *it ends now.*

# *Chapter 38*

## *Tharion*

The sky fades, dark clouds closing in on us, as does the sense of hope embedded in our souls. Chills race across my scalp, heavy stomps of spirits ring through the air, sprinting closer as we reach a clearing, just before the Veil's Eclipse.

The white glow is strong, casting the grey clouds in a haunting shimmer. Our horses come to an abrupt halt, sending us tumbling off. I hit the mud with force, wet soil seeping into my clothes as I slide across the ground. Stumbling to my feet, I snatch the hilt of my blade. Eleanora readies herself, Corvyn's grip on his dagger makes his knuckles white, and Rowan pulls his bow string. We're ready.

The stomping sounds close in on us, a horde of grey crashing through the bushes, green eyes glowing under their hoods, long limbs dragging along the ground. Screeches and menacing laughs echo into the heavy air. My heart is hammering in my chest, dizzying me.

A warm hand grabs mine. Eleanora watches me with a firm gaze, giving me a sharp nod before firmly securing her satchel of orbs. We watch as the horde closes in on us, every footstep one step closer to a horrible demise.

Rowan looks back at us. "On my signal, we spread out. Corvyn with me. Eleanora and Tharion, you have each other's backs. It's time."

Eleanora throws her arms around her familiar, not to say goodbye, but as a token of strength. He nods to us before setting his eyes on the grey mass of evil. Regripping the hilt, I raise my blade to my face. Eleanora readies her stance, satchel in one hand and her small blade in the other.

*"NOW!"*

The signal sets us off, Eleanora and I running to the west as our friends head east, a wall of darkness crashing in on us. I swing my blade, severing heads as demons rush beside us. The air fills with grey dust, blanketing the dead ground. Blood spatters around us, covering our clothes in splotches of black and scarlet. I duck as long limbs fly above my head, cutting them off with my blade.

Calling on my magic, I fire blasts of energy from my palms, engulfing the demons in pure white energy. Eleanora's grunts and sharp breaths sound behind me as vines burst through the ground, ripping the spirits apart.

Limbs, heads and blood permeate the air, covering every tree, bush and boulder surrounding us, smothering us in the smell of decay.

Looking over my shoulder, Rowan and Corvyn have changed into their animals, ripping and clawing at the demons. I feel my arms burning from wielding my blade, my palm bubbling from my magic burning my skin, and as we fire off shots of energy, we watch the unfathomable number of demons fade around us.

I sprint towards another group of evil, sliding across the ground on my knees. My blade cuts through the demons' bones as if it were butter, falling around us like flies. With a surge of power, I send a wall of flame over them, turning them to ash with their heads still intact. White light pierces the air as scorching heat engulfs me.

The ground below the demons is black in char, Eleanora's orbs disintegrating everything within its reach. Watching her fight, her moves are swift but hard, dancing through hordes of demons with elegance. Hair sticks to her face as sweat trickles, spraying around us. She grits her teeth, growling loudly as her small blade cuts through flesh.

The world turns on its axis as I hit the ground with breathtaking force, my vision blurring. Long nails soar through the air just in time for me to react, magic shooting from my palm, dismembering the limb, watching it fall to the ground beside me.

The demon wails, the other limb finishing the job as it lodges in my shoulder. I cry out, the pain paralyzing. Lifting my blade, I drive it straight through the demon's stomach, pushing it off my body. It falls to the ground with a thud – its face contorted in a disgusting smile.

Retracting my rune blade, I swing it, decapitating the demon before a cloud of ash shoots into the air.

Panting, a sinister laugh rings through the sky, filling the entire clearing. I look up, but only dark skies are there. Searching my surroundings, spinning on my heel, a dark figure emerges from the shadows. A black cloak made entirely of shadows float above the ground, umber skin with silver tattoos peeking through it. Shadows bend around him, as if drawn by their creator. My gaze follows the tattoos, the figure's face showing. The face from my nightmare looks me straight in the eyes. Dark cerulean eyes, black beard and two towering horns on the top of his head tell me who it is: *Vorathiel.*

"So, you are the one chosen to defeat me?" His laugh is dark, malicious, sickening. My stomach turns as he throws his head back, shoulders bouncing with loud cackles.

"The Fates have failed. I will not let a *child* defeat me," he spits.

"That's strange, I don't remember asking your permission."
I grasp the hilt of my blade with a firmer grip, hoisting it into position.

The smile on Vorathiel's face vanishes, a scowl replacing the laughing eyes. Charging, I sprint towards him, throwing my blade at his chest. He ducks it with ease, emerging behind me. With a kick, he sends me crashing to the earth. As I try to get up, his boot lands on my chest, pushing me further into the ground.

Vorathiel scoffs. "Pathetic. At least try. Here I thought I would at least break a sweat."
I send a burst of light to his face, his foot falling off me as he grips his face, screaming.

Rolling, I jump to my feet. His hand shoots out, shadows pouring from his palms, enveloping me in darkness. The cocoon of shadow closes in on me, ridding me of my senses as the world fades around me. My chest burns as oxygen spends in my body, lungs desperate for more. In the background of the shadows roars a creature, the hair on my neck standing up. What is that?

Swinging the blade, I try to cut through the shadows, but I'm trapped. Dark hands hold me fast, locking me to the ground, rendering me unable to defend myself. His haunting face floats through the wall of shadow, a grim smile across his face.

"You should have stayed in Sylvarn, Tharion. Your father was wrong about you, you could never be the realm's saviour. You could never be enough. Not for yourself, not for Kyrris and not for your precious Eleanora." His words puncture me, like sharp knives stabbing at my broken mind. I fold forward, clamping my eyes shut, trying to block him out. The creature roars again, shaking the ground. I search for it, the silhouette of something large blinking behind the walls of darkness.

Magic pools in my chest before blinding light explodes from my body, disintegrating the shadows around me. I send balls of white magic at Vorathiel, throwing them at him with speed and exhaustion. The orbs of light hit him time and time again, sending him crashing to the ground.

Blood seeps from the corner of his mouth, dripping to the ground as the demon struggles to breathe. Walking over to him, I pick up my blade, positioning it directly above his heart.

Vorathiel chuckles, then breaks out in laughter so evil my blood freezes.

"You really think it would be that easy? I have had millennia to prepare for this moment. My dear boy, it is far from over." I lift the blade before pushing it down, embedding it in the ground as shadows dissipate around me. Looking around, I desperately try to find Eleanora.

Her figure still dances with demons, bursts of ash raining over her head.

"Tharion! Where did he go?" Rowan pants, now back in human form. His skin is dusted in ash and black gore, reeking of rot.

The sky above us opens, a sharp clap of thunder the only warning we get before rain pours over us. The ground floods, puddles of ash and blood floating at our ankles. He shakes my shoulders, snapping me back.

"Tharion! Focus! Where did Vorathiel go?"
I shake my head, "I-I don't know. I had him pinned to the ground one second, the next he was gone." We look around us, demon dust scattered across the ground. In a split second, Corvyn races across the field.

"Kaelen!" His voice is desperate, panting. I look to the Veil, a faint silhouette hammering on the white border dividing our realms.

Corvyn crashes to the wall, ripples of energy sailing across it as he pounds his fists. Rowan bursts into a sprint, rushing to his mate. I watch as he tries to pry Corvyn from the wall, "Korax, please! He's behind the Veil. He cannot come out!"

Falling to the ground, Corvyn lets out a soul-breaking scream, shattering every beating heart around him. Squirming, he wrestles out of the fox's arms, bursting back to Kaelen.

His brother drops to his knees, tears streaming down his pale face. Corvyn keeps pounding, blinded by the need to free Kaelen, as blood smears over the haunting veil of ghostly white. He sobs until his voice gives out, a scratchy whisper now escaping his broken lungs.

As exhaustion takes over, Corvyn leans his head against the barrier, hand dragging along the translucent wall.

"Kaelen, please. I miss you so much. I need you to come back." His voice shatters, sobs ripping through him. Rowan kneels on the ground behind, arms holding his mate close.

Kaelen crouches in front of Corvyn, palms planted on the thin wall separating them.

"I am okay, brother. I am with Serenya. Please, win this battle so we can finally roam together in the realm of the living once more." His voice echoes, like an angel singing. Deep brown eyes fall to his younger brother, drowned with sorrow.

"I can't, Kaelen. I can't do this without you."

"You must, little brother. For us, for Serenya. For the kingdom we worked so hard to protect. For our brothers back home, and our parents. I know you can do this. We will be together once more, Corvyn."

Corvyn drags in a deep breath, steadying his pounding heart as he stumbles to his feet. Staring into his brother's eyes, Corvyn leans his forehead to the glimmering barrier. Kaelen's forehead meets his, one last token of affection, one last chance to save him. *One last chance.*

Corvyn closes his eyes, words coming out a bare whisper.

"I will."

He turns to Rowan. "Let's end this evil shit and put him where he belongs – in the fucking ground."

Vorathiel's evil laugh lingers in the air, electric and terrifying. His shadowy figure emerges, now only steps behind Eleanora, lifting his arms to the sky. The earth splits as spirits pour from the ground, a black flood of shadows pouring out.

I swallow, grasping my blade before we run into round two of our battle. These demons all have long wooden staffs, swinging them around like spears as they aim for our hearts, wicked laughter cutting through the air like a sharp blade.

Once again, we find ourselves ducking and stabbing, severing heads and maiming bodies, fighting our way through the wave of demons. My body heaves for air as it thickens with dust, arms burning with exhaustion.

A staff hits me in the chest, sending me flying, scraping against the ground as I land. I struggle for air, lungs giving out. I'm surrounded by black. I call on my magic, sending a wall of flame across my field of vision, the demons crying out before burning to ash.

"Tharion!" Eleanora's voice has me on my feet in seconds, searching through the sea of shadows. A burst of light followed by a wall of heat has me stumbling back a step, her orb crashing to the ground. The zip of an arrow passes right beside my ear, lodging into a demon standing behind me, ready to pounce. I nod, a silent thanks to Rowan as I dig my way over to Eleanora.

"Look!" Her arm stretches out, pointing out into the distance. A small figure stands beside Vorathiel, her light brown hair hanging in a long braid over her shoulder. As she looks at me, her face reveals itself: *Amariel.*

"Get to her, I will take Vorathiel. Whatever it takes, get that rune on her and break the spell!"

Eleanora nods, her brows scrunched between her eyes. Leaning in, I press a kiss to her lips before making my way to the demon sorcerer.

"Rowan! Corvyn! I will need some assistance!"
The males turn and run in my direction, stopping just before me.

"Eleanora will try to get Amariel alone. I need to take Vorathiel, but I can't do it by myself. Will you help me?"

"I will give my life for this realm. I will be by your side no matter what." Corvyn taps his fist over his heart, gaze trained on me. I dip my chin, lifting my eyes to Vorathiel.

Rain comes down heavier as the second wave of demons hang in the air, our bodies bashed and cut. Looking at my friends, they change into their animals. Corvyn takes to the sky as Rowan launches himself in Vorathiel's direction, and I follow. The ground splashes around us as our feet hit the earth with force. Rowan's deep orange fur is coated in grey mud, matting the hairs. My boots are filled with water, sloshing around as I move.

Glancing at Eleanora, she steadily approaches from the back as we make our way from the front. Holding my blade high above my head, a deep yell bursting from my lungs. The sky darkens even more, rain pouring over our heads. Before us, Vorathiel waves his hands above his head, a large portal opening. The roar from before splits the air as the silhouette of a creature with large wings comes into view.

Vorathiel turns to us, holding out his arms. Shadows shoot from his palms, but we split, flanking him as Corvyn dives from above. The raven drags his claws across Vorathiel's face, ripping out his left eye.

Blood gushes down his face as the demon cries out, holding the socket. Rowan leaps through the air, sinking his teeth into the sorcerer's midsection, tearing his torso apart. With a crash, his large body hits the ground, earth kicked into the air as he lands. The portal above us slams shut, shadows dissipating into thin air. I push the metal of my blade straight through his heart, Vorathiel unleashing a deafening cry as his heart stops beating. The demon lies on the ground before us, bleeding out, the earth soaking up his blood.

"It's over," I pant, looking at my companions as they gulp down air. A wave of adrenaline crashes over me, fingers twitching.

"Now, let's free Amariel."

# *Chapter 39*

## *Eleanora*

Vorathiel goes down with force, Tharion splitting the demon's heart with his blade. Blood pours from his chest, seeping into the muddy earth as rain washes away his army of abominations.

Amariel cries out, as if their souls are connected, falling to her knees. I sprint, launching myself at her, pinning her to the ground. The young female squirms, trying to break free, spit foaming in her mouth.

Her breath reeks of death and rot, bile rising in my throat. As we struggle, I manage to lay her on her chest, faced down. I hold her arm, pulling up her sleeve - exposing her pale grey skin. Dark veins of black pulsate under her skin, the shadows a part of her.

With my knife, I set it against her skin, glancing over the once mortal girl. Her eyes are still deep hazel, a mix of her parents. Her light brown hair has streaks of grey, like she's fighting off the shadows within.

The knife carves out a spiral for renewal with three crossing lines, severing the curse, topped with a circle keeping her soul intact as I pry the demonic shadows from her being. Wails erupt from her as my blade splits her skin, carving out the rune on her forearm. The lines are not perfect, but they are connected. They will work.

I lose hold of the knife when her knee crashes against my kidney, making me hunch forward. My lungs scream for air while my body rejects it, pain splitting my nerves. Heaving for air, Amariel's boot hits my ribs, sending me to my back.

I call on my magic, vines ripping through the air as the smell of mud and blood flood my senses. The vines snake around her wrists and legs, forcing her to the ground as large thorns dig into her skin. I watch, careful not to sever the rune on her arm, Amariel crying out in pain.

"Stop! Please, stop!" she screams, my heart breaking for her as she pleads for mercy. Her voice is young, innocent, she's only a child.

Amariel's eyes swipe to Vorathiel, watching his body bleed out.

"Father!" Her agony rips through me, freezing my blood.

"He is not your father, Amariel. I am here to take you to your parents. They miss you dearly." She watches me, confused and furious. I retract the vines holding her down, boring back into the wet, shattered earth. With one swift move, Amariel lunges for me, pinning me to the ground. I send hot rays of magic through her, scorching her from the inside as agonizing screams rip from her small body.

Falling to the ground beside me, I pick up an orb from my satchel.

"Amariel, please. Listen to me! You are under a curse, I am here to free you!"

"I am not cursed, I was saved. Saved from the realm condemned by the living. Vorathiel *saved* me," blood coats her teeth as her mouth stretches into a smile. Launching herself again, her body crashes with mine, sending us tumbling across the earth, mud spraying around us.

I manage to get on top of her, holding her hands down.

"I did *not* go through a gods damned nightmare for you to act like this," I mutter through gritted teeth, panting. I clench my fist, watching as the child's eyes widen, struggling to breathe. I hold it clenched, air refusing to return to her lungs.

"I am here to help, Amariel. But if you refuse, I will simply let you suffocate on your own delusion."

The blood vessels in her eyes burst, pressure building in her head, turning her eyes a deep crimson. Amariel's movements slow, eyelids heavy before I release the hold I have on her.

Desperate gasps echo into the rain as she gulps down air, filling her lungs to the brim. Bending over, she gags and coughs as fresh oxygen assaults her system.

Amariel scowls at me, her eyes crying red streaks down her face. I walk up to her, my blade firmly in hand as I drag it across my palm. The blade slices my skin open, drops of ruby falling on the earth below.

*"By mother's hand, return!"*

Amariel's body convulses, her head whipping back as a chilling screech cuts through her lips. I continue,

*"By father's voice, awake!"*

Folding in two, vomit erupts from her mouth. Black tar spills onto the earth, desperate heaves for breath cutting through her cries.

*"By love unbroken, be free!"*

I pour my magic into her, body scorching as it fills Amariel. With a scream, shadows explode from her body. The black strings of darkness shoot from her mouth and fingertips, holding her high in the air as the curse breaks.

As the last shadow escapes her, Amariel falls to the ground with a heavy thud. I sprint to her, rolling her over to her back. Her pulse is weak, and she's not responding.

For the first time in what felt like centuries, the battlefield was quiet. Too quiet. Gently, I shake her shoulders, trying to wake her up.

"Amariel. Amariel, please wake," I beg, but nothing. Giving her cheeks a clap, her eyes flinch - but only barely. Her head falls to the side, low mumbles making its way from her lips. Heat blooms in my chest, tears coating my vision in a blur.

"Wh…" her tiny voice is scratchy, raw, "where am I?"

I huff out a laugh of relief, tears racing down my face, "you're outside the Veil, Amariel. We're here to take you home."

Her eyes lock on mine, wide and confused as she lets out a sob. I sit there with her in my arms, cradling the small child, letting her settle for a moment. Glancing over at Vorathiel, her eyes widen with shock.

"No… No, you have to –" she tries to stand, but I hold her to me. Tharion starts towards us, his eyes filled with elation.

"No! No, you don't understand! He's a demon!" she cries out, desperate. Whipping my head to the side, I watch as Tharion stops in his tracks, turning around.

"You need to remove his head, if not…"

Vorathiel's body trembles, shadows forcing their way into his body as he rises from the ground. His chilling laughter fills the air, Amariel digging her face into my cloak.

"You stupid, ignorant children," he sneers, "you think you can defeat me, and to be fair - you almost did." He looks at me, digging his gaze into mine as a smirk blossoms on his face.

"So desperate to prove yourselves that you forgot the most important part, and now you will never win."

I push Amariel up, holding her hand as we sprint towards our horses. Tharion grabs his blade, charging at the demon while Rowan and Corvyn flank him. Casting a glance behind me, I watch a low chuckle slip from Vorathiel's lips, before he vanishes in a mirror of smoke.

Tharion halts, searching for the sorcerer as Rowan and Corvyn do the same. He runs towards me as we keep running to the Veil, but as we reach it, I'm yanked from Amariel, her cold hand slipping from mine.

Shadows surround me like a casket, a thrilling laugh ringing in my ears as I'm dragged through a void of endless black. Vorathiel's face bursts through the shadows, his deep blue eyes glowing with evil.

Falling, endless falling into the deepest pits of darkness, light evades me completely. Ear-piercing roars of ancient beings, shadows of lives lived and spent rush past me. Just before my back hits the ground, I crash through a border of light, so blinding I clamp my eyes shut.

Shielding my face with my arm, I slowly open my eyes - finding myself trapped behind the Veil.

# *Epilogue*

I watch as Eleanora's body vanishes in a sheet of shadows, Amariel left alone on the battlefield, her knees crashing to the ground. Dragging my legs, I sprint to her, pulling the small female close to me, eyes frantically scanning the surrounding area.

"Eleanora!" I cry out, but nothing. The heavy pattering of rain followed by a clap of thunder is the only sound bouncing off the ground.

"Eleanora!" My voice echoes across the field, carrying off into the distance. She's gone. Vorathiel took her. The pounding of my chest makes my ears rush, whole body freezing. Where is she? Rowan skids across the wet earth, panting and frantic.

"He took her. I can still feel our bond, but it's weakening. We need to find her!"
The fox paces in front of me, hands fisting his hair. The breath shooting from his lungs is shallow, hard. Before me, the faint white shimmer of the Veil pulses, a haunting reminder of the distance silently stretching us from Eleanora. A silhouette rushes forward, stopping at the barrier.

Kaelen pounds on the shield between us, desperate for our attention. Staggering to my feet, I run over to him, Amariel in tow as our hands lock.

"She's here. She's here with us. Behind the Veil," Kaelen's voice ricochets off the thin wall between us.

My blood goes cold. Eleanora is trapped in the *spirit realm*.

"How do we get her out?"

Kaelen lets out a deep breath, his eyes falling to his feet.

"The only way into the spirit realm is to leave the realm of the living."

# About the author

C. J. Saint, or Chelsie, is the definition of an indoor cat. Her nose is always deep in a book, her mind always racing with fantasy stories just waiting to be told. She prefers her own company, a nice cup of coffee and screamy music as close to her eardrums as possible. Chelsie lives with her husband and two children, balancing a full-time job with her writing!

· · — ·✶· — · ·

I want to take the opportunity to thank the people that pushed me, believed in me, when I had doubts about myself. Putting yourself out there like this is daunting, today's society being so much stricter, the strive for perfection almost impossibly tough.

To my husband, Tony; thank you for believing in me, and for being there to spar, to brainstorm and listen to me tirelessly talk about mythical beings and scary monsters. I love you.

To my kids; I couldn't have done this without you and you cheering me on. I love you, mankas.

To my dear friend, Alana; thank you for brightening my days, for spending time with me in Kyrris as my first ever outside-reader, for helping me overcome doubts and hurdles. I appreciate you more than you know.

And lastly, thank you to my fantastic reader community, my beta readers and ARC team – without your support and cheers I would've never been able to find the courage. This book is for you.

Now, on to the next chapter – Realm of Silent Screams (coming soon!)

www.ingramcontent.com/pod-product-compliance
Lightning Source LLC
LaVergne TN
LVHW040110180726
843489LV00005B/1348